V-S DAY

V-S DAY

A NOVEL OF ALTERNATE HISTORY

ALLEN STEELE

ACE BOOKS, NEW YORK

THE BERKLEY PUBLISHING GROUP
Published by the Penguin Group
Penguin Group (USA) LLC
375 Hudson Street, New York, New York 10014

USA • Canada • UK • Ireland • Australia • New Zealand • India • South Africa • China

penguin.com

A Penguin Random House Company

This book is an original publication of The Berkley Publishing Group.

Ace Books are published by The Berkley Publishing Group.
ACE and the "A" design are trademarks of Penguin Group (USA) LLC.

Library of Congress Cataloging-in-Publication Data

Steele, Allen M.
V-S day : a novel of alternate history / Allen Steele. — First Edition.
pages cm.
ISBN 978-0-425-25974-0 (hardback)
1. Space race—History—20th century—Fiction.   2. Scientists—History—20th century—Fiction.
3. World War, 1939–1945—Science—Fiction.   I. Title.
PS3569.T338425V8   2014
813'.54—dc23
2013041531

FIRST EDITION: February 2014

PRINTED IN THE UNITED STATES OF AMERICA

10 9 8 7 6 5 4 3 2 1

Cover images: New York City © Fred Stein Archive / Getty Images; rocket © iStockphoto;
paper texture © Ilolab/Shutterstock; American flag © Paul Stringer / Shutterstock.
Cover design by Diana Kolsky.
Interior text design by Kristin del Rosario.
Interior illustration of the *Silbervogel* spacecraft copyright © 2014 by Scott Lowther.
Interior illustration of the *Lucky Linda* spacecraft copyright © 2014 by Ron Miller.

For Rob Caswell

On the afternoon of October 19, 1899, I climbed a tall cherry tree at the back of [my uncle's] barn and, armed with a saw and hatchet, started to trim the dead limbs from the tree. It was one of those quiet, colorful afternoons of sheer beauty which we have in October in New England and, as I looked toward the fields to the east, I imagined how wonderful it would be to make some device which had even the *possibility* of ascending to Mars, and how it would look on a small scale if sent up from the meadow at my feet . . . I was a different boy when I descended the ladder. Life now had a purpose for me.

—ROBERT H. GODDARD

I had no illusions whatsoever as to the tremendous amount of money necessary to convert the liquid-fuel rocket from the exciting toy . . . to a serious machine that could blaze the trail for the space ship of the future . . . To me, the Army's money was the only hope for big progress toward space travel.

—WERNHER VON BRAUN

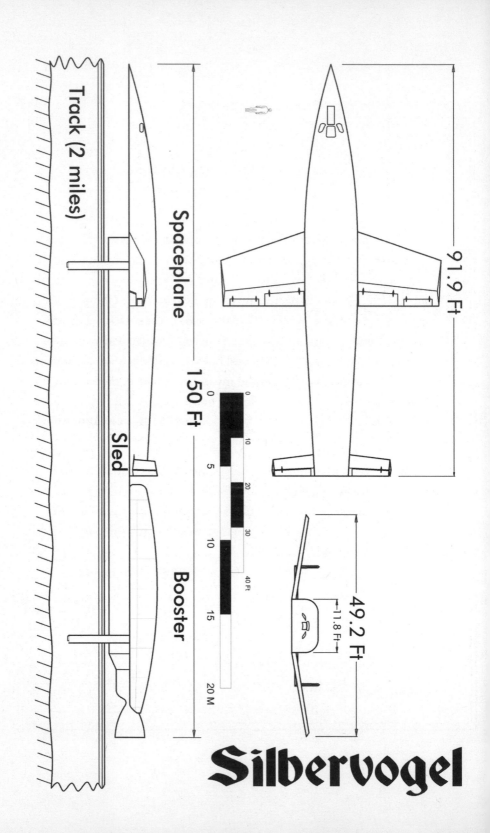

Track (2 miles)

Spaceplane

Sled

Booster

150 Ft

91.9 Ft

49.2 Ft

11.8 Ft

0   5   10   15
0   10   20   30   40 Ft
20 M

Silbervogel

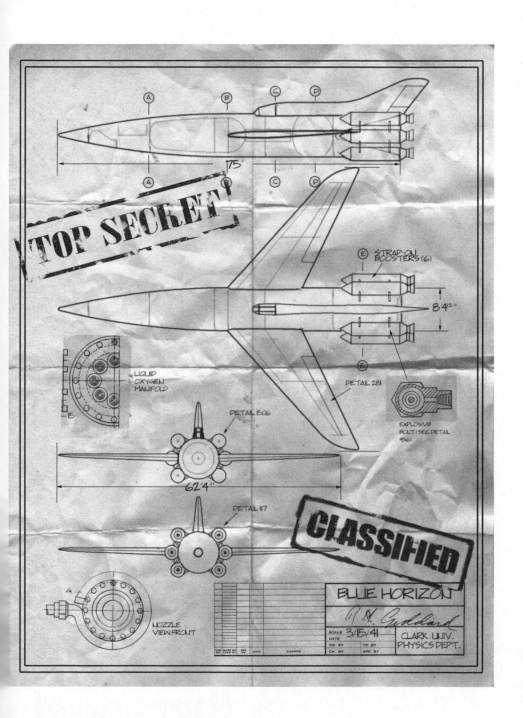

TOP SECRET

CLASSIFIED

STRAP-ON
BOOSTERS (6)

8'4"

LIQUID
OXYGEN
MANIFOLD

DETAIL 281

DETAIL 1506

EXPLOSIVE
BOLT (SEE DETAIL
456)

62'4"

DETAIL 117

NOZZLE
VIEW FRONT

BLUE HORIZON

SCALE
DATE   3/15/41
DR. BY   TR. BY
CH. BY   APP. BY

CLARK UNIV.
PHYSICS DEPT.

75'

A MORNING IN WARTIME

In the first light of morning, the B-29A Superfortress *Hollywood Babe* hovered above the Pacific a hundred miles west of the Washington coast. The sun had just risen; its golden light tinted the bomber's silver skin and reflected off the panes of its bullet-shaped cockpit. No clouds in the dark sky above the plane; the stars were still visible but were beginning to fade with the approaching day.

A little more than a half hour ago, *Hollywood Babe* had lifted off from McChord Field near Tacoma and flown due west, gradually ascending to its present altitude of thirty-one thousand feet, the bomber's maximum ceiling. Since then, the plane had flown in circles, its contrails forming an overlapping series of figure eights which would have puzzled any fishing boats that might have spotted it from below. In this way, the B-29A held its position above the ocean, allowing its crew to perform its mission: watch the skies and report anything unusual.

Inside the pressurized fuselage, a young airman first class moved forward to the cockpit, a Thermos bottle and two tin cups in his gloved hands. Passing the radio compartment and the crewman half-asleep at its panel, the corporal ducked his head to step through the forward hatch.

He ignored the civilian huddled in a rear seat as he approached the two men seated in the bomber's transparent nose.

"Here y'go, sir." The corporal handed the cups to the pilot and copilot, then opened the bottle and poured black coffee into them. "Sorry it's a little lukewarm. Hard to keep it hot at this altitude."

"That's okay," Captain Bennett replied, his voice barely audible over the drone of the B-29's four engines. "This time of morning, even cold coffee will keep me awake."

The airman grinned, then turned to head aft. Again, he deliberately ignored the passenger seated behind the captain and first officer. Although the civilian wore a fleece-lined leather flight jacket lent to him by a supply sergeant at McChord, the absence of a uniform made him conspicuous. He gazed at the airman, silently requesting coffee as well, but the crewman pretended not to notice him as he left the cockpit.

Bennett sipped his coffee, grimaced. Cold. He cradled the cup between his legs as he grasped the yoke and twisted it to the left, making the port turn that would begin another elongated figure eight. On the other side of the glass nose, the rising sun slowly traveled from right to left before disappearing behind the plane, replaced by a black sky gradually becoming dark blue.

Boring stuff, flying in circles. McChord Field was a training base for B-29 crews, and there wasn't a man aboard *Hollywood Babe* who wouldn't rather be bombing the hell out of the Japanese . . . except perhaps their passenger, a civilian scientist who looked like he should be playing with test tubes. Lloyd Kapman wasn't much older than any of the *Babe*'s crew, but for some reason the brass regarded him as a vital intelligence asset. For that reason, *Hollywood Babe* was given the assignment of providing support to him and his classified mission . . . a mission that, in the captain's opinion, was totally nuts.

Bennett completed the turn, then leaned back as far as his cramped seat would allow. "Ever read the funny pages, Bill?"

"Nope." The copilot, Bill Carlton, shook his head. "Can't say as I do, Cap."

"Well, I do. Favorite part of the paper, next to the sports pages. Alley Oop, Blondie, Dick Tracy, Terry and the Pirates . . . I love all those guys. But you know which one's my favorite?"

"I couldn't guess, sir."

"Buck Rogers . . . Buck Rogers in the 25th Century."

Kapman looked up. Bennett wasn't speaking to him, but it was clear that his words were meant for him. An annoyed expression crossed his face, but he remained quiet.

"I mean," the captain said, "here's a guy who can climb aboard a rocket ship and, boom, off he goes. The Moon, Mars, Venus . . ."

"Jupiter."

"Uh-huh, Jupiter, and it's just as easy as flying this plane. Doesn't have to worry about wasting fuel flying in circles."

Kapman slowly let out his breath. This wasn't the first time he'd heard jokes about Buck Rogers. If Bennett or Carlton heard him, though, they didn't show it. "Of course, it's the future," Bennett went on, "so anything can happen. But rocket ships?" He shrugged. "Maybe one day we'll go to the Moon, but not in my lifetime. No, sir, not in my life . . ."

"You got a point, Captain?" Kapman asked.

Hearing him, Bennett feigned surprise. "Not at all, Mr. Kapman," he said, glancing over his shoulder at him. "Just talking about the funnies, that's all."

Carlton hid his amusement by turning his gaze toward the windows on the starboard side. The last stars had vanished, but the western sky was still dark. Still, it seemed as if he could make out something high above the ocean. Bright and unblinking, leaving behind a pencil-thin vapor trail, it looked a little like a shooting star except that it was moving upward from the horizon, not downward as a meteor would.

"Then maybe you should discuss Nancy and Sluggo," Kapman said, "because I assure you . . ."

"Skipper?" Carlton stared at the thin white streak racing across the cloudless sky. "Bogey at one o'clock high." He pointed to the window. "See it? Right there."

Bennett arched his neck to stare up through the top of the nose and suddenly forgot what he was saying. Eyes wide with astonishment, he glanced back at his passenger. "Is that . . . ?"

Kapman had already risen from his seat. Leaning forward, he peered in the direction the copilot indicated. "It's not Buck Rogers," he muttered. Then he remembered what he was supposed to be doing. Turning away from the canopy, he stuck his head through the hatch.

"Call Alamogordo now!" he yelled, causing the radio operator to bolt upright in his seat. "It's coming!"

The morning sun had just touched the peaks of the Sacramento Mountains as Klaxons howled across the southern New Mexico desert. Inside a fenced-off compound near Alamogordo Army Air Field—a top secret base within a base, unknown to anyone except a very few—soldiers and technicians were running from pine barracks, some still stuffing shirttails into trousers pulled on just seconds ago. Only the soldiers who'd been on overnight sentry duty were wide-awake; they began blowing whistles, waking up anyone in the base who'd managed to sleep through the noise.

In the radio shack, the sergeant on duty at the shortwave wireless hastily typed the last words of a report. He ripped the page from the typewriter roller and shoved it into the hands of a nearby private. "Get this to Doctor G! Move!"

The private didn't bother to salute but instead sprinted through the door. As he dashed across the compound, he barely managed to dodge a small van coming the other way. The MP driving it swore at him, then hit the brake and twisted the wheel, fishtailing to a halt in front of a Quonset hut marked PRIVATE—SECURE QUARTERS. The uniformed lieutenant in the passenger seat—a tall, skinny black man in his midtwenties—leaped from the van before it came to a full stop. Another MP standing guard outside held open the door for him as he ran inside.

"Skid!" he shouted. "It's on the way!"

"Yup. Kinda figured that out." With the assistance of two technicians who shared quarters with him, Lt. Rudy "Skid" Sloman was pulling on his pressure suit, an inflatable one-piece outfit with an aluminum midsection and tubular segments for its arms and legs. "Grab my helmet, willya, Jack?" he asked, as calm as if he were doing nothing more than getting ready for a game of touch football. "I could use my gloves, too."

"Oh, for the love of . . . !" Lt. J. Jackson Jackson—sometimes known as Jack Cube—snatched the padded rubber gloves from the nearby suit locker and tossed them to one of the suit techs, then carefully removed a bubblelike glass helmet from the top shelf. "Get your ass in gear! We've got the van waiting outside!"

"Why the hurry?" There was mischief in the test pilot's dark brown eyes as he stood up to let a technician close the back of the suit. "*Linda's* not going nowhere without me."

Jack Cube was about to answer when he was cut short by a voice booming through loudspeakers outside: "*Attention all personnel! This is not a drill! Report to firing stations immediately! Repeat, this is not a drill . . . !*"

———————

Tank trucks and utility vehicles barreled across the desert, kicking up sand as they raced toward a distant structure: an enormous steel tower, shaped like an upside-down U and painted bright red, enclosing something that looked like a giant dart poised on an elevated ring above a concrete trench. Soldiers had already opened the gates of the chain-link fence surrounding the launchpad; they stood aside and watched as the vehicles rushed toward the gantry.

The trucks pulled to a halt beside the tower. Their doors banged open, disgorging a crew of technicians in white jumpsuits and hooded silver garments. Wasting no time, the fuel men hauled insulated hoses from the tanker and dragged them toward the winged craft nestled within the gantry. Within minutes, the launchpad was shrouded by a haze of fumes, cold and clammy in the desert's early-morning warmth.

Other technicians boarded an open-cage elevator that carried them to the catwalk leading to the cockpit, located midway up the vehicle's sleek white hull. Sliding open its canopy, they began preparing the spacecraft for immediate takeoff. Another team began checking the six solid-fuel rockets clustered around the spacecraft's base aft of its swept-back wings. Everyone's actions were coordinated and rehearsed; they'd spent weeks practicing for this event. Each second counted, and they knew they had just one chance to do this right.

The fuel men were still pumping liquid oxygen, nitrogen, and gasoline into the spacecraft when the van glided to a stop in front of the tower. The MP and another Army soldier jumped out and ran around back. They opened the rear door and pulled down a loading ramp, and a couple of seconds later, Skid Sloman and Jack Cube emerged from the vehicle.

Lieutenant Sloman was wearing his pressure suit, his head completely encased within the bubble helmet. Lieutenant Jackson carried the portable air conditioner that temporarily fed the suit with a low-pressure oxygen-nitrogen mix. Rudy walked slowly down the ramp. The suit made it difficult for him to move, and as he and Jack Cube stepped off the ramp and turned toward the gantry, the MP who driven them to the pad snapped to attention and gave them a rigid salute.

Rudy responded as best as he could with a half-raised hand. He was clearly amused. When they were out of earshot, he gave Jack Cube a conspiratorial wink.

"Who'da thunk it?" he said, his voice muffled by the glass helmet. "A *goy* saluting a Negro and a Jew."

Jack Cube wanted to laugh at this, but he couldn't. They stopped at the bottom of the tower to wait for the elevator to come back down. As the cage descended—slowly, much too slowly—his gaze traveled up the side of the craft standing before them. He knew every inch of its seventy-five-foot frame, from the six strap-on boosters to the radar array crammed into its pointed nose. The last sixteen months of his life had been completely devoted to the design and construction of this fuming, groaning beast; there wasn't a single rivet of its steel hide that was a stranger to him. And yet, in this moment of truth, he was scared of his own creation . . .

not just the consequences of its failure but the fact that it could kill a man he'd come to respect.

"Rudy . . ." he started to say.

"Willya look at that?" Skid wasn't paying attention to him. Instead, he leaned back to peer up at the spacecraft. Just forward of the cockpit, on the port side of the fuselage, was a hand-painted picture: a bare-breasted woman sitting astride a rocket, lusty smile across her face as she clutched a ten-gallon hat against her long, dark hair. Beneath the rocket was a scroll: *Lucky Linda.*

Despite himself, Jack Cube grinned. "Think your girlfriend would appreciate it?"

"Yeah . . . yeah, I guess she would," Skid muttered. "Oh, man . . . the things a guy's gotta do to impress a woman."

A second later, the elevator reached the bottom of the tower. As the pad tech operating it opened the door, Jack touched Rudy's arm. "C'mon. We don't have much time."

"Yep. Let's get it on the road."

———

A half mile away from the launchpad, a voice blared from a loud-speaker outside a sun-bleached concrete igloo: *"X minus fifteen minutes and counting . . . repeat, X minus fifteen and counting . . ."*

Within the blockhouse, nine men had gathered to shepherd *Lucky Linda* to her destiny. Six were seated at consoles arranged in a semicircle around the blockhouse's windowless walls. Their view of the pad came from fuzzy, flickering images displayed on cathode-tube televisions above their stations, but for the moment they ignored the screens and instead focused their attention on the dials and meters arrayed before them. Loose-leaf notebooks lay open before them; every now and then, someone picked up a slide rule and double-checked the numbers on his console. They murmured to one another, speaking an arcane dialect of technicalia only they could understand. No one knew more about the distant spacecraft than these men, and for good reason: They'd designed and built it.

An Army Air Force officer in full uniform quietly stood at the back of the room, arms folded across his chest, eyes regarding the men from beneath the bill of his cap. Colonel Omar Bliss had been Blue Horizon's project director from the very beginning; for the last year and a half, his every waking moment had been spent bringing this scenario to reality. Though normally accustomed to leadership, he knew better than to interfere with what was going on around him. Events were now beyond his control; all he could do was watch, wait, and pray.

Bliss's gaze shifted to the center of the room, where a tall, thin man with a balding head and a trim grey mustache stood before a submarine-style periscope, peering at the distant pad. Although the most senior man in the room, he had a frail vulnerability that made him seem even older than sixty-two. Bliss had a sudden urge to walk over and stand beside him, if only to offer support, but he restrained himself. Just then, the distraction would be unwelcome.

"X minus ten minutes and counting." The pad talker sat at the center console. A lean, red-haired man in his twenties, Henry Morse was the team member tasked with maintaining contact between *Lucky Linda* and men in the blockhouse—the 390 Group, the classified name for this team. Henry switched off the loudspeaker and listened for a moment to his headphones, then turned to the man at the periscope. "Just heard from Jack at the tower. Skid has entered the cockpit."

"Radio check," Dr. Robert H. Goddard said, not looking away from the eyepiece.

Harry turned to the mike again. "*Lucky Linda*, this is Desert Bravo. Radio check, over."

A few moments passed, then Skid's voice came over the blockhouse speakers: "*Wilco, Desert Bravo. Radio check one, two, three, over.*"

"We receive you loud and clear, *Lucky Linda*. Stand by for checklist."

Henry glanced at the notebook in front of him, then looked over at a Chinese-American physicist sitting nearby. "Initiate liquid oxygen and nitrogen tank pressurization," Harry Chung said, carefully watching the gauges on his console.

"Initiate liquid oxygen and nitrogen tank pressurization," Henry repeated.

Another moment passed. *"LOX and nitrogen pressurization, go,"* Skid said.

Goddard raised his eyes from the periscope and looked at the master clock on the wall above the consoles. "Clear the pad," he quietly told Morse.

———

Once again, Klaxons bellowed near the launchpad, followed by Henry's voice: *"X minus eight minutes and counting. All personnel, vacate the launchpad immediately. Repeat, X minus eight and counting . . ."*

Lucky Linda's canopy was still open. Within the cramped cockpit, Rudy Sloman lay upon an overstuffed leather acceleration couch, feet above his head. His air hose had been connected to a valve at his feet, and his hands moved across the instrument panel before him, flipping toggle switches in sequence with the checklist printed in a small spiral notebook strapped to his left thigh. Jack Cube and a technician stood on the catwalk; the technician grasped the canopy's recessed handles and started to slide it shut but stopped as Jackson reached into the cockpit and tapped his friend on the shoulder.

"Good . . ."

"Don't say it!" Skid snapped.

Jack Cube stopped himself before he spoke the words Skid considered to be ill omens. "Happy landings," he said instead.

Skid responded with a wink and a quick thumbs-up. "See you when I get back," he replied. Like he was just going out for beer and a pack of smokes.

There was nothing left to say or do, so Jackson and the technician slid the canopy into position and locked it down, sealing the pilot within his craft. The technician stooped to pick up his toolbox, then both of them left the catwalk. Once they were off the platform, the technician bent down again and swiftly turned a wheel that withdrew the catwalk from the *Lucky Linda*. That done, he and Jackson headed for the stairs; the elevator was too slow, and they needed to get off the gantry as fast as possible.

They were the last people to leave the pad. Everyone else was climbing into trucks and jeeps, and a diesel locomotive was already hooked up to the gantry. Jack Cube hopped into the back of a jeep; as it roared off, he looked back to watch the locomotive pull the gantry away from the launchpad. *Lucky Linda* stood gleaming in the morning sun, the clamps of its launch ring and the electrical umbilical leading from the nose to the adjacent launch tower its sole connections to Earth.

"Good luck, Skid," Jack Cube whispered beneath his breath.

———

"X minus three minutes and counting."

Outside the blockhouse, technicians, infantrymen, and officers watched from behind a sandbag wall. Tripods rose above the barrier, supporting movie and still-image cameras; on a wooden platform, white-coated camera operators worked the enormous television projector whose images were being seen within the blockhouse. Emergency fire and medical personnel waited beside their vehicles, engines warmed up and idling.

At the sandbag barricade, a master sergeant opened a matchbox and pulled out a pair of wax earplugs. A corporal beside him watched as he rolled them between his fingers, carefully shaping the plugs before fitting them into his ears.

"Hey, Sarge," he said, "is this thing gonna be loud when it goes up?"

"Guess so. The others were."

The corporal nodded. He'd been transferred here only a couple of weeks ago and hadn't seen any of the test rockets that were previously launched. "So they made a lot of noise, huh?"

"Yeah, they did." Sarge first plugged his left ear, then his right. "And then they blew up."

———

"Cabin pressure, check," Henry said.

"Cabin pressure 10 psi, check," Rudy replied.

The blockhouse door opened, and J. Jackson Jackson came in. Henry looked up as Jack Cube sat down beside him, then covered the microphone with his hand.

"How's he doing out there?" he quietly asked.

"Great." Jack reached for a pack of Camels on the table. "How's it going here?"

"Great." Henry hesitated, then glanced over his shoulder at Goddard. "Except for Bob," he quietly added.

Jack Cube turned to look at Robert Goddard. The team leader continued to study the launchpad through the periscope. "Looks fine to me," he murmured. "What makes you think something's wrong?"

"He hasn't said much since he got here." Henry uncovered the mike again. "Gyro check . . ."

Jack Cube shook a cigarette from the pack, lit it, and tossed the spent match in the overflowing ashtray. All the other members of the 390 Group were busy at their stations: Taylor Brickell, Harry Chung, Michael Ferris, Hamilton Ballou, Gerry Mander. Only Lloyd Kapman was missing; the team's other chemical engineer had volunteered to be stationed at Mc-Chord Field, to act as a spotter if and when the Office of Strategic Services received word that there had been a launch from somewhere in Germany.

This left just Colonel Bliss and Bob Goddard. Bliss noticed Jackson when the lieutenant looked his way; the colonel gave him a brief nod, then returned his attention to the television screens. Goddard was more tense than he'd ever seen him. The knuckles of his hands were white as they gripped the periscope handles; despite the coolness of the blockhouse, there was a thin sheen of sweat on top of his head.

"Checklist complete," Henry said. "X minus two minutes, thirty seconds and counting. *Lucky Linda*, we're about to poll the launch team. Stand by for final countdown."

"*Roger that, Desert Bravo. Standing by.*"

Morse turned to Goddard again. "Bob?"

Stepping away from the periscope, Goddard walked over to where Henry and Jack Cube were sitting. Standing behind Henry, he turned a couple of pages of the loose-leaf binder, then laid a finger at the top of a checklist.

"Range," he said.

"Range clear," Gerry Mander responded, his eyes on the radar screen. "Go."

"Fuel."

"Tanks pressurized at one hundred percent," Ham Ballou said. "Go."

"Main engines."

"Go!" Michael Ferris snapped.

"Electrical."

"Go," said Harry Chung.

"Guidance and telemetry."

"Guidance and telemetry are go," Morse replied.

"Pad safety."

"Pad secure," Jackson said.

The poll was complete, yet for a moment or two, Goddard said nothing. Noticing the silence, several team members looked over their shoulders at him. To Jack Cube, Bob Goddard suddenly seemed old and tired, as if a vast weight had settled upon shoulders that had lifted too much already. Valuable seconds ticked away as he gazed at the image of *Lucky Linda* on the nearest television monitor.

"Dr. Goddard?" Henry asked. No answer; it was as if Blue Horizon's scientific director hadn't heard him. "Bob? Confirm launch readiness?"

Goddard blinked, then looked away from the screen. "Yes," he said, his voice low as he gave Henry a slow nod. "Launch status confirmed. Proceed with final countdown."

"Thank you." Henry let out his breath, then bent to the microphone again. "*Lucky Linda*, you are cleared for launch."

"*Wilco, Desert Bravo*," Skid said. "Lucky Linda *standing by for final countdown.*"

"Final countdown commences on my mark." Picking up a stopwatch, Goddard regarded the wall clock for a couple of seconds, then snapped the watch. "Mark, sixty seconds."

Henry pushed the mike button again. "X minus sixty seconds and counting."

"Detach umbilical," Harry Chung said. "Switch to internal power."

Henry repeated the order for Rudy, and a couple of seconds later, the electrical cable extending from the launch tower to *Lucky Linda* fell away from the spacecraft.

"X minus thirty seconds and counting," Henry said.

Robert Goddard returned to the periscope. Through its lenses, he could see *Lucky Linda* clearly. Its sleek white hull was washed by the desert sun, yet its base was shrouded by ghostly fumes rising from exhaust vents, making it seem as if it were floating on top of a cloud.

"X minus twenty seconds and counting."

Goddard wiped his sweaty palms on the periscope handles. "Dear God," he whispered, his voice unheard by anyone else in the room, "please help us."

"X minus ten seconds . . . nine . . . eight . . . seven . . ."

REUNION

"Six . . . five . . . four . . . three . . . two . . . one . . . zero!"

The twelve-year-old boy pushed a toggle switch on the launch controller in the palm of his hand, and an instant later, a yellow-white jet of flame erupted from the model rocket poised fifteen feet away. A loud fizzing sound, and the rocket—eighteen inches tall, hand-built from plastic and cardboard—leaped upward from the beach.

Leaving behind a trail of brown smoke, the little rocket soared into the blue New Hampshire sky. The boy watched with anxious eyes as it arced out over a lake bordered by woodlands and summer cabins, all but oblivious to the applause of the adults gathered nearby. The only person whose opinion mattered to him was the old man standing beside him: his great-grandfather, who had encouraged him to take up model rocketry as a hobby.

"Nice launch, good trajectory." The old man's voice was low, unheard by anyone except the boy. He lifted a Panama from his white-haired head to shield his eyes against the sun. "Fifty feet . . . seventy-five . . . a hundred . . ." A quiet chuckle. "Hey, Carl, I think it might reach escape velocity."

Carl didn't smile. This was serious business. "C'mon, c'mon . . . where's the parachute?"

"Wait for it. Wait . . ."

The rocket was a tiny white speck a little more than two hundred feet above the lake when its solid-fuel engine exhausted itself. Momentum kept the rocket going for a short distance after the smoke trail ended, but then it toppled over and began falling toward the lake. An inarticulate cry of dismay rose from deep within Carl's throat.

"Oh, darn it," the old man said. "Parachute didn't deploy." The other grown-ups made remorseful noises—"what a shame" and "gee, that's terrible" and so forth—but no one had more regrets than he and his great-grandson. They said nothing to each other as the rocket plummeted into the lake about seventy yards offshore. Two men in a nearby canoe immediately began paddling toward it.

Carl gnawed his lower lip as he turned to the old man. Planting the hat back on his head, Henry Morse leaned heavily on his walking stick as he regarded Carl with sympathetic eyes. "Well . . . you had a good launch, and I think it went a bit higher this time."

"Not much. I was hoping it'd get to three hundred feet, at least. And the parachute . . ."

"Yeah, not having the chute open is a real letdown." Henry shook his head in commiseration. "I didn't see the nose cone open, did you?" Carl shook his head. "So . . . any idea what went wrong?"

Carl hesitated. He hated admitting mistakes, particularly to his great-grandfather. "I dunno . . ." he began, then stopped himself; I don't know wasn't an excuse Grandpa Henry would accept. "I guess I didn't pack the parachute right. And maybe I should have used a bigger engine, too."

"I'd say that's a good hypothesis." Henry looked out at the lake. The canoe had reached the place where the rocket went down. The man in the bow reached over the side with a fishing net, thrust it into the water, then raised it over his head and shouted something they couldn't quite hear. "Well, cheer up," Morse said, pointing toward the canoe. "Looks like your recovery team is on the job." He clapped a hand on his great-grandson's shoulder. "Well, c'mon . . . let's go back to the lodge, and I'll buy you a beer."

"Grandpa!" Unnoticed until now, a tall blond woman in her thirties had come up behind them. "He's not old enough, and you know it!"

"Ellen, it's a tradition," Henry replied.

"Not for nine more years it isn't!"

Her grandfather glared at her. "Rocketmen are exempt."

"Not in my space program." Yet she was forcing herself not to smile as she ruffled Carl's hair. "All right, enough of that. Put your stuff away, then come over here and help me set the table for lunch."

"Okay. Sure." Carl closed the controller's safety cover, then glanced at his great-grandfather. *Later,* Henry silently mouthed, giving him a conspiratorial wink. The boy grinned. It wouldn't be the first time Grandpa Henry slipped him a can of Budweiser when no one was looking.

Near the beach, tucked in among the pines and red oaks, was an old hunting lodge. Two stories tall, sturdily constructed of native oak and pine, its brick chimneys, Victorian gables, and screened-in lake-view porch hinted that it had been built about a century ago. A couple of dozen people were gathered on the shaded lawn next to the house: mainly adults in their thirties, forties, and fifties, but also a handful of children and teenagers. Ice coolers lay open, packed with cans of soda and beer, and charcoal smoke drifted up from a barbecue pit, where burgers and wieners were being cooked on the grill. Four picnic tables had been pushed together to form a long, single bench, and a volleyball net had been set up near the floating dock in expectation of afternoon games later on. An American flag, raised at sunrise that morning, hung from a tall metal pole rising from the beach.

Along the narrow dirt road leading through the woods, a Toyota Celica approached the lodge. Passing a sign—PRIVATE PROPERTY NO TRESPASSING—the car slowed down as it reached the end of the road. A dozen or more other vehicles were parked close together behind the lodge; the driver carefully slid his Toyota between an SUV and a maple tree.

A young man in his midtwenties climbed out, casually dressed in chinos and a polo shirt. He reached into his car to retrieve a canvas shoulder bag from the passenger seat, then shut the door. Hearing the children, he started to head toward the beach.

"May I help you?"

The young man stopped to look around. An old black man—hair frosted white, face heavy with age—sat alone on a bench beneath a pine tree, a half-smoked cheroot dangling between the gnarled fingers of his right hand.

"That's okay, thanks." The visitor started to walk off. "I think I can find my way."

"That's not what I asked," the old man said.

The young man turned around again. "Excuse me?"

"Should I?"

"What? I don't . . . I'm sorry, but I don't . . ."

"Excuse you." The old man puffed at his cigar, exhaling without taking any smoke into his lungs. "In case you missed seeing it, there's a sign over there that says, 'Private Property, No Trespassing.' Since this is a family gathering, so to speak, and I don't recognize you as being a family member, that means you're a trespasser. Furthermore, you've just stated you can find your way, which is a falsehood considering your status. So I'll ask again . . . may I help you?"

The two men regarded each for a moment. "I'm not trespassing," the younger man said at last. "I was invited here."

"By whom?"

"Dr. J. Jackson Jackson."

"Why?"

"I . . . I'm a writer. My name's Douglas Walker. I'm working on a book about the first American manned spaceflight."

"The *Lucky Linda* mission." A last drag from the cigar, then the old man dropped it on the ground and carefully ground it out beneath his shoe. "I assume you've already done much of your research, so you're already aware of most of the facts, hmm?"

"Well . . . I've tried to do my best, but I need to learn more."

The old man's dark eyes locked on like a missile seeking a target. "Then you've come to the right place because, if you don't recognize me, then you don't know a damn thing."

Walker's face became ashen. For several moments he was unable to speak. "Oh my God," he murmured at last. "Dr. Jackson, I'm so sorry, I . . ."

"I certainly hope so." Jackson glared at the writer. "If you do this badly with someone who's been waiting for you for the last half hour, my colleagues are going to chew you up and spit you out."

"I'm sorry I'm late. I had to stop to get directions. And I didn't recognize you at all."

Jackson smiled slightly. "I can't really fault you either way, I suppose. A bear would get lost in this neck of the woods. As for the other"—he sighed and shook his head—"well, astronauts make TV commercials while engineers get a fuzzy group photo. And since we've only been in touch with each other through e-mail . . ."

He didn't finish the thought but instead picked up an onyx-headed walking stick resting against the bench and used it to slowly push himself to his feet. Walker rushed forward to help him, but Jackson waved him off. The old man was too proud to accept any assistance, but nonetheless he smiled and shook Walker's hand.

"Well, c'mon then." Jackson began shuffling toward the lodge's back door. "Lunch will be starting soon. You're in time for this, at least. Once we've chowed down, you can have that interview you came for."

"Is the rest of the team here?" Walker fell in beside him, matching his slow pace.

"Yes . . . or what's left of us, anyway."

———

The picnic table had been set by the time Walker and Dr. Jackson got there. Covered by checkered tablecloths, it seemed as if every spare inch was taken by platters of food: not just hamburgers and hot dogs, but also fried chicken, potato salad, corn on the cob, baked beans, turnip greens, corn bread, coleslaw . . . everything one might expect at a summer holiday feast.

Sweating pitchers of homemade ice tea had been put out, with bowls of sugar cubes in easy reach if anyone cared to sweeten theirs. No one would walk away from the table hungry.

Although there was plenty of room for everyone, Walker soon discovered that it was not easy to find a seat. Little cardboard placards had been strategically set up at each place setting, identifying the person who'd be sitting there. When Walker looked closer, he noticed that beneath each name, printed in smaller letters, was another name: one of the ten men who belonged to the 390 Group. Since most of the people there were second- or third-generation descendants—children, grandchildren, and great-grandchildren, along with a few cousins or distant relatives—their surnames were often not the same as those of the team members.

Thus, when Walker finally located an unclaimed seat near the center of the table, he discovered that he was sitting across from David and Eileen Kisk; the second name on their cards was Robert H. Goddard, and once Walker began talking to them, he discovered that David Kisk was related to Goddard's wife, Esther. Which made sense: the Goddards themselves never had children. To his left were Gerry Mander's granddaughter and her fiancé, and to his right were Omar Bliss's stepson Ronald and his children, with Ron Bliss nearly the oldest person at the table.

But not quite. Surrounded by their families, J. Jackson Jackson and Henry Morse occupied the seats of honor at opposite ends of the table. Both were in their nineties, and although they appeared to be in good health for men approaching their centennial years, Walker noted that their relatives took pains to make sure that they were comfortable. Beach umbrellas had been placed beside their chairs to shade them from the midday sun, and neither of them had to reach for food; platters magically appeared at their request.

Lloyd Kapman was nowhere in sight. When Walker asked where he was, Ron Bliss told him that the elderly chemist—the team member who'd spotted Silver Bird that fateful morning seventy years ago—was confined to a wheelchair and could no longer come down to the beach. He had his own table in the lodge, with his family keeping him company.

"Don't worry," Ron said quietly, "you'll get to meet him later." He shared a knowing look with the Kisks and Melanie Mander. "When they tell the Great and Secret Story."

The others smiled, but no one explained what he meant by this remark.

As lunch went on, it became clear that everyone there knew everyone else. There was a lot of catching up, with news being traded about what they'd been doing lately. The conversation was light, with nothing being said about June 1, 1943. And yet Walker couldn't help but notice that, from the opposite ends of the long table, J. Jackson Jackson and Henry Morse often glanced in each other's direction. And when one man caught the other man's eye, an enigmatic smile passed between them. It might have simply been the shared pleasure of two old men who'd lived long enough to be feted by their families, but Walker wondered if there was something deeper, a secret no one else was allowed to share.

The meal ended informally after ice cream was served, with people getting up and leaving the table to carry their paper plates and plastic utensils to trash barrels. Walker was surprised; he'd been expecting someone to stand and deliver a speech commemorating the historic events that brought them all here. But there was nothing of the sort. A handful of women start clearing the table. A volleyball materialized from somewhere and began to be batted back and forth among the kids, who were obviously itching to divide up on either side of the nearby net. Several people strolled down to the dock to have a smoke, courteously distancing themselves from those who didn't share their habit. But no speeches, no ceremonies. Flag-waving and breast-beating had no place here.

Jackson and Morse were the last to leave the table. Escorted by their families, they slowly made their way toward the lodge. Still confused by all this, Walker approached Jackson again, just before his grandchildren helped him climb the short flight of steps leading to the back porch.

"Pardon me, Dr. Jackson?" The writer tried to be as polite as possible, but he was becoming anxious. "About the interview . . . is it possible I can speak with you and the others this afternoon before . . . ?"

"Come with me to the living room," Jackson said. "You'll get your interview there."

The back porch ran the length of the lodge's ground floor, its tall screen windows looking out over Lake Monomonac. A long oak table nearly as big as the one they'd just left stood in the middle of the porch, wooden benches on either side. Crock-Pots and empty trays showed that it had served as a way station between the kitchen and the picnic site, but at one end there was something else: the bent and waterlogged remains of a model rocket, its plastic nose cone open to reveal a small white parachute that had been removed from the casing.

Carl was seated at the table, studying an iPad. Its screen depicted a departure-angle view of the launch, footage captured by a tiny digital camera that had been aboard the rocket and downloaded into the tablet. Again and again, the beach fell away below the rocket during its brief flight, the lake becoming visible for a few seconds before the images came to an abrupt end. As Jackson and Morse walked by, Morse paused to gaze over the boy's shoulder.

"Well?" he asked. "Any conclusions?"

"I didn't fit the nose cone correctly. And the engine didn't fire long enough." Carl shrugged. "Doesn't matter. It'll never fly again."

"Then you build another one, and next time you learn from your mistakes." Morse smiled. "That's what Bob Goddard taught me, back when he and I . . ."

"Grandpa," Ellen said from his elbow, "if you're going to start in on your war stories, then take it into the living room. We need to clean up here."

"Quite right." Morse clapped a hand on his great-grandson's shoulder. "All right, sir . . . let's go see what everyone else is up to." Smiling, he bent slightly to add in a stage whisper, "We're going to tell the Great and Secret Story."

This was the second time Walker had heard this particular phrase. Everyone seemed to know what it meant except him. Yet Carl was indifferent. "I've heard it before," he murmured, looking down again at his broken model.

"You have?" Morse stared at him in shock, not knowing what to make of this. "When?"

"The last couple of times we've been out there."

Straightening up, Morse looked at his granddaughter. Ellen sadly nodded, confirming what her son just said. Morse frowned in disgust and stamped away from the table, heading for a glass-fronted door at the other end of the porch.

"Really?" He harrumphed in disgust. "Can't anyone keep a military secret anymore?"

This provoked laughter from everyone in earshot. "Look who's talking!" Jackson yelled at his friend's back. "What about Doris?"

"Now, don't you talk about my grandmother," Ellen said as she opened the door for her grandfather.

"Mom?" Carl looked over his shoulder at her. "Is Dad coming?"

"I don't think so, hon." Ellen had a hand on her grandfather's arm and was guiding him through the door. "He's still away on his business trip. Now come inside . . . please."

The living room took up most of the lodge's ground floor. Paneled with dark, well-aged oak, there was a fieldstone fireplace at one end, with the inevitable moose head peering down from above the mantel. The hardwood floor was covered with handmade rugs, and although there were plenty of couches and overstuffed armchairs, with two sturdy rockers near the fireplace, metal folding chairs had been brought in to accommodate everyone. The walls were lined with old framed photographs; as Walker passed them, he noticed that the men in the pictures were the subjects of his book, taken in this place when they were young . . . when some, in fact, were younger than he was today.

That isn't what drew his attention, though, but rather the man seated in the wheelchair parked between the two rockers. Lloyd Kapman was the oldest surviving member of the 390 Group; from his research, Walker knew that he'd turn one hundred in September. If he lasted so long; Kapman was even more frail than Morse or Jackson, and there was a plastic line leading from his nose to an oxygen tank strapped to the back of his wheelchair. Walker was surprised that he was even here. His home in Concord, Massachusetts, was only a couple of hours away, but even that distance was considerable for someone his age.

"How you doing there, Lloyd?" J. Jackson Jackson asked, as he and Henry Morse shuffled slowly to the rocking chairs. "Get enough to eat?"

Lloyd looked up at Jackson with sagging eyes and nodded. "My uncle had a good lunch," replied a rotund, middle-aged man standing beside him. "He particularly enjoyed the turnip greens . . . didn't you, Uncle Lloyd?" he added, raising his voice almost to a shout.

Kapman turned his head slightly to gaze at his nephew, and it seemed to Walker that he was quietly annoyed by the younger man's patronage. "Someone . . . get me a cheeseburger," he said softly, his voice an airless wheeze. "And a beer, too."

"Sounds good to me." Morse carefully lowered himself into a rocker. "Carl, run down to the cooler and fetch us a couple of beers. And get one for yourself, too."

"Grandpa!"

"Dr. Kapman, I'm Douglas Walker." Stepping closer, the writer offered his hand. "It's an honor to meet you, and I appreciate you taking your time to . . ."

"Speak louder!" Kapman snapped, barely touching Walker's hand.

"Oh, for God's sake, Lloyd," Jackson said. "Turn up your hearing aid."

"What?" Kapman glared at him. "What? I can't hear you."

"Wait a sec." Jackson reached to Lloyd's head, touched a tiny plastic unit behind his ear. "How's that?"

"Oh, yes . . . that's better." Kapman nodded gratefully. "Thanks, Jack."

"You're welcome, you old coot," Jackson murmured as he sat down.

"What?"

Henry Morse chuckled, and everyone else who'd witnessed this exchange politely hid their smiles behind their hands. Jackson turned to Walker. "Go on, Mr. Walker. You were saying . . . ?"

"Yes, right . . . of course." Walker found a seat in the nearest armchair and opened his shoulder bag. "As I was saying, I'd like to thank all of you for taking the time to speak with me. I realize these reunions are very special for you, and I'm grateful that you've allowed me to attend. It's the only chance I'll have to interview all three of you at once, so . . ."

"Who . . . cleared you?" Kapman asked.

"Pardon me?"

"Who . . . gave you . . . security clearance?"

Walker started to laugh, but a sidelong glance at the two other men told him that this was a serious question. In fact, none of the people in the room—several relatives had followed them from the lawn, with more still coming in—seemed to think that Lloyd Kapman's query about security clearance was strange at all.

"No one did, Dr. Kapman," he replied. "They don't have to. I mean, the *Lucky Linda* mission is a matter of public record. Nothing about it is classified anymore. Everyone knows what happened seventy years ago."

"Not true." Kapman slowly shook his head. "That's . . . not true."

"Lloyd is correct," Jackson said before Walker could object. "There are several aspects of Blue Horizon that remain secret to this day. Only the three of us"—Ellen pointedly cleared her throat—"and the people in this room who've come to our previous reunions know the full story."

"And we should keep it that way!" Kapman said angrily, then choked back a hacking cough. His nephew moved to comfort him, but the old man impatiently shook off his hand. "Cut it out, Tommy," he muttered. "I'm not . . . dying today." He took a couple of deep breaths from his oxygen tube, regained his wind, and went on. "I mean it. What . . . business do we have, breaking . . . silence?" He gestured to Walker. "If we let him . . . put it all in his book, then we could . . . compromise national security."

"Oh, bull." Henry scowled at his old friend. "It's been seventy years. What difference does it make now? Every other war secret has been revealed . . . why not this one?"

"He's got a point," Jackson said. "We've held our tongues long enough. Maybe too long. We've told this story to our families so that no one will forget, but maybe it's time to go on the record."

"But we've signed papers."

"Aw, c'mon." Henry rolled his eyes. "My great-grandson has heard this so many times, he's bored to tears with it." Remembering Carl, he glanced at the porch door. "What's keeping that beer, anyway?"

"Gentlemen, please . . ." Walker held up a hand. "I'm only trying to get the facts straight. The research I've done so far tells me that there are empty places in the historical narrative, details other writers either overlooked or have never been told. The three of you were there. You're the only ones who know."

"You're right." Jackson nodded. "We're the last of the 390 Group. Gerry, Ham, Taylor, Colonel Bliss . . ."

"Bob," Henry added quietly, sadly.

"Bob Goddard . . . they're all gone. And I don't think we've got too many years left in front of us either."

"Not even that . . . Jack Cube," Lloyd added, a sly smile on his face.

Jackson regarded him with astonishment. "You haven't called me that in years."

"Called you what?" Walker asked.

"Never mind." Jackson shook his head. "Inside joke."

Lloyd's smile faded. "Maybe you're . . . right. It's time to . . . spill the beans."

"Hear hear." Henry tapped his cane against the floor. "Besides, what are they going to do? Throw us in jail?"

Walker refrained from letting out his breath with relief. "So, now that we have that settled . . ." He reached into his bag and pulled out a small digital recorder and a notebook. "Where do you want to start? In Worcester? Or Roswell?"

"No. Not Worcester, not New Mexico, and not here either." Henry closed his eyes, as if taking himself back in time. "Long before any of us came on the scene, there was Germany . . ."

"Wernher von Braun, yes." Kapman's mouth pursed together. "Him and Dornberger . . . and Goering, and Sanger."

"Uh-huh, yeah . . . and Hitler." Henry frowned. "Goddamn Adolf Hitler."

THE WOLF'S LAIR

The Mercedes-Benz cabriolet moved through the forest, the small Nazi flags mounted above its front fender signifying its status as an official vehicle. Just ahead, two soldiers on motorcycles acted as escorts; without them, the touring car would have had to stop at every checkpoint along the road. Even so, it slowed down whenever it came upon one of the Panzers parked along the roadside, if only to let the soldiers of the elite Führer Escort Battalion render stiff-armed salutes.

In the backseat, Dr. Wernher von Braun tried to assuage his nervousness by gazing through the closed windows at the towering black conifers that darkened the forest floor. He idly wondered how many different species of birds inhabited the Masurian woods of East Prussia; owls, no doubt, but probably also eagles, falcons, and other raptors that preyed upon the rabbits and squirrels that populated this dense, remote forest. Yet every time the Mercedes-Benz passed another tank, or he caught another glimpse of an antiaircraft gun hidden beneath camouflage nets, he was reminded that the woodland's deadliest inhabitants walked on two legs.

Wolfsschanze. Wolf's Lair. An appropriate name.

"Relax, Wernher." The Army colonel seated beside him gently patted his knee. "There's nothing to worry about."

Von Braun pulled his gaze from the forest to the other man sharing the touring car's rear seat. Colonel Walter Dornberger, thin-faced and balding, had a perpetual smile that masked an intellectual intensity second only to von Braun's. A dedicated follower of National Socialism, he wore his dress uniform today with pride, eager for a meeting with the man he'd worshipped for nearly a decade.

"I'm not worried at all." Von Braun kept his voice low so as not to be heard through the glass partition separating them from the Reich Security Service officer driving the car. Catching the amused glint in Dornberger's eye, he corrected himself. "Well, perhaps a little . . . but only about the briefing."

"Let me worry about that." Dornberger pulled a handkerchief from his pocket, patted the sweat on his brow. The Mercedes-Benz's tonneau was warm with its windows rolled up, but the alternative would have been even more uncomfortable; the humid forest air was practically alive with mosquitoes, as attested to by the fact that the soldiers all had gauze nets suspended from the rims of their helmets. "I'll lead the briefing. All I want you to do is explain the technical details. Just . . ."

"Just don't get too technical. Yes, I understand. You've reminded me several times already, Walter."

Annoyed, Dornberger glared at the younger man. "Would it have killed you to wear your uniform?" he added softly.

Von Braun didn't reply. He was dressed in civilian clothing, a plain black suit with a swastika pin affixed to the right lapel. This had been a sticking point between him and Dornberger even before they'd boarded a Heinkel 111 transport at the Peenemünde airfield earlier that morning. Von Braun had joined the National Socialist Party only reluctantly, after it became apparent that he wouldn't be allowed to continue his research unless he swore allegiance to the Nazi cause. Indeed, he was the last hold-out from the old *Verein für Raumschiffahrt*, the Society for Space Travel, which was dismantled after the *Führer* became Chancellor, its leading members absorbed by the Army's ordnance division. Even so, von Braun remained a civilian until just last year, when he finally ceded to Heinrich Himmler's demand that he join the *Schutzstaffel* as well; the *Reichsführer* insisted that Peenemünde's technical director had to belong to the SS if *Wa Pruf 11*—Ordnance Test 11, the rocket program's official name—was to continue to receive funding. Yet von Braun found his own quiet means of resistance; he'd never worn his black SS uniform, and it still hung in his office closest, untouched since the day he'd received it.

Dornberger knew what von Braun's silence meant. Sighing expansively, he settled back against the seat. "And try to contain your enthusiasm," he muttered. "No one wants to hear about going to the Moon."

"Yes, Walter . . . I know." Von Braun had been swept up by the dream of space exploration as a teenager, but Dornberger didn't come along until the German Army became interested in the *VfR*'s efforts to develop a rocket capable of leaving Earth. Peenemünde's military director was only interested in developing an ultimate weapon with which Germany could crush its foes. Beneath the jovial exterior was a dedicated Nazi with little patience for thoughts of sending men to the Moon . . . unless, perhaps, it happened sometime in the distant future, when a victorious Third Reich planted its bloodred flag on another world.

The touring car slowed down. A gatehouse lay just ahead, a wooden barrier lowered across the road. The motorcycle escort veered away, allowing the Mercedes-Benz to approach the gate on its own. A soldier with a submachine gun strapped across his shoulder stepped up to the car as it came to a halt. Bending over to the driver's side window, he took a moment to examine the passengers in the backseat, then he turned to the other soldiers manning the checkpoint and raised his arm. The barrier was lifted, and the car passed through, the sentries snapping off salutes as it went by.

Now von Braun could see the sprawling compound they'd just entered. As the Mercedes-Benz slowly drove down the main road, buildings appeared from beneath the trees that hid them from reconnaissance aircraft. Here and there lay bunkerlike structures, their concrete walls with few windows or doors obviously designed to resist aerial bombing, making them even more utilitarian and ugly. Uniformed officers strode purposefully upon gravel footpaths; there were no gardens or benches, and no one paused for a casual chat. This was a place where military discipline mattered above all other considerations. Everywhere he looked, von Braun saw swastikas.

Despite the summer heat, a chill ran down his back. This was the Third Reich's nerve center, the place from which the *Führer* and his staff directed the war they'd launched against the rest of Europe. Over the past few years, von Braun had tried to distance himself as much as possible from the conflict, preferring to keep it at arm's length, but lately he'd come to realize that this was no longer possible. God help him, he was one of them.

The cabriolet turned left onto a side road, passed over a train track, then came to a stop beside a one-story building. The driver got out and opened the left-rear door, and as von Braun picked up his briefcase and eased himself from the tonneau, he saw a senior officer walking toward the car.

"Dr. von Braun! How good to see you again!" Albert Speer grinned as he offered a hand.

"General Speer. Good to see you as well." Von Braun was sincere when he said this. Tall and handsome, Speer was more than the Third Reich's chief architect. Over the last couple of years, he'd also become the rocket program's best friend in the High Command. An engineer to the core, Speer had taken an interest in the A-4 as soon as he learned of it, even going so far as to design the facilities at Peenemünde. He obviously saw himself as von Braun's colleague, another man of science intrigued by the possibility of space travel.

Which was fortunate, because it meant that the Peenemünde scientists had a champion in the *Führer*'s inner circle, someone with the clout to keep the rocket program alive. And *Wa Pruf 11* needed all the friends it could get. Plagued by technical problems every step of the way, suffering numerous setbacks for each advance it achieved, the A-4 project had gradually become a lesser military priority, losing official support to the Luftwaffe's effort to develop Cherry Stone, a jet-propelled aerial torpedo.

This visit, arranged by Speer, was the last chance for Dornberger and von Braun to make their case to the High Command. If they failed, *Wa Pruf 11* would gradually be starved to death. Already, its resources were being shifted from Army Ordnance to the Luftwaffe . . . and no one at Peenemünde wanted to have Reich Marshal Goering as their new chief.

"I trust you've had a pleasant journey," Speer said as he enthusiastically shook von Braun's hand. "I want to thank you for taking the time to come here. I know how much you hate to leave your workplace."

"It is nothing. Besides, it is we who are grateful. Were it not for you . . ."

"It's what little I can do." Speer glanced at his watch. "Almost 1700. He will be here soon. If you'll come this way, please?"

Von Braun and Dornberger followed Speer to the nearby bunker. Now that he was closer, von Braun could see that its walls were unbelievably thick: two meters of steel-reinforced concrete, with an outer masonry wall almost as an afterthought. Even Peenemünde's launch control center wasn't as solidly built. On the other side of a solid steel door was a short corridor leading to a conference room. Its walls were paneled with pine in an unsuccessful attempt to give the room a homey, rustic appearance; in its center was a long black table surrounded by wooden armchairs. A couple of windows had been opened; otherwise, the afternoon heat would have turned the bunker into an oven. A movie projector was set up at one end of the table, a portable screen positioned on the opposite side of the room.

That wasn't the first thing von Braun noticed, though. Other members of the senior staff had already arrived. Standing at an open window, hands clasped behind his back, was Field Marshal Wilhelm Keitel, the head of *Oberkommando der Wehrmacht* and the *Führer's* chief of staff. And seated at the table, hands clasped together across his ponderous stomach, was Hermann Goering.

Seeing them, Dornberger instantly snapped to attention. *"Heil Hitler!"* he proclaimed, clicking his heels together and throwing his right arm forward as if it were a javelin. Von Braun repeated the same words; the briefcase in his right hand saved him from having to make that idiotic, vaudeville-hall salute. Keitel acknowledged them with a brief salute of his own, but Goering did nothing except regard Dornberger with amused contempt.

"Gentleman, please be seated." Speer gestured to a couple of chairs on the other side of the table from Keitel and Goering. "Wernher, I understand you've brought a film you'd like for us to see?" He nodded toward a lieutenant standing beside the projector. "If you'll give it to our staff officer, he can set it up for you."

"Thank you." Opening the briefcase on the table, von Braun pulled out a box containing a 30 mm movie reel. He handed it to the lieutenant, then watched over his shoulder as he loaded the projector. Von Braun was concerned about the film's being damaged—it had been made specifically for this meeting, so there were no copies—but he also wanted to avoid Goering as much as possible. Even so, he could feel the Reich Marshal's eyes upon him; it was as if Goering were a wolf and von Braun the hare who'd unwittingly wandered by.

The lieutenant had just finished threading the film into the take-up reel when the conference room door opened again. "The *Führer*!" Speer exclaimed, and this time everyone in the room turned toward the door. All except von Braun, who'd just then been removing some notes from his briefcase. Caught by surprise, he dropped the notes and hastily turned to find Adolf Hitler standing behind him.

This wasn't von Braun's first encounter with Hitler, and his impression of him hadn't changed. For a man idolized by millions of loyal German citizens and feared by many more, he was far less intimidating in real life than he was in newsreels. He wore a grey uniform jacket with a swastika pin on the right lapel and the Reich's eagle above the left breast pocket, and his tie was knotted with military precision, but von Braun couldn't help but notice that his shirt collar was already stained with sweat. He was nearly a head shorter than von Braun, and his small body had none of the stature seen in official photographs. To von Braun, the lank, oily hair that fell across his forehead and the absurd little toothbrush mustache made him look like a peasant—a farmer or perhaps a butcher—who'd found a costume uniform somewhere and decided to wear it as a joke.

Then he gazed into Hitler's cold eyes and saw what others had seen. Determination. Willpower. Ruthlessness. And lurking beneath all that, a hint of madness.

Wernher von Braun was a baron by inherited title, the scion of a wealthy German family. He'd never admired this Austrian commoner who'd found his way into beer-hall politics. Like many others of the social gentry, though, he'd been careful to keep his opinions to himself. Some of his liberal friends had had the foresight to flee Germany when they still could, and others had elected to stay and join the ranks of silent objectors, but the few who'd spoken out against Hitler and the Nazis had disappeared, taken from their homes by the Gestapo, their estates confiscated by the government. No one had forgotten the Night of the Long Knives, and no one talked about it either.

Von Braun suddenly realized that he was the only man present who hadn't saluted the *Führer*. He had just begun to lift his right hand when Hitler stepped closer.

"Herr von Braun . . . Albert has told me much about you."

"Yes, *mein Führer*." It was all von Braun could manage. Obviously, Hitler had forgotten having already met him two years ago, when he'd visited the *Wa Pruf 11* static test facility in Kummersdorf. At a loss for what else to do, von Braun offered a handshake.

Hitler ignored the gesture. Instead, he quietly studied von Braun for several moments, not smiling, never blinking once. Then he gave a small, vaguely satisfied nod and turned away.

"Very well." He took a seat between Goering, Speer, and Keitel. "Show us what you've brought today."

———

The movie began with shots of Peenemünde while it was still under construction and continued with footage of test launches. It was silent, with von Braun delivering narration and Dornberger occasionally chiming in. Von Braun did his best to keep the information on a nontechnical level, but he was more concerned about an uncomfortable fact he and the colonel had left unspoken: the A-4 project was behind schedule, having suffered one setback after another. Indeed, the most recent launch in the film was an A-3 prototype from ten months earlier; every other rocket launched since last October had exploded over the Baltic, if not on the pad itself.

As the film unspooled, von Braun studied Hitler from the corner of his eye. The *Führer* slumped in his seat, hands folded together, watching the film with no great interest. He had been afraid this might happen. When Hitler and his entourage had witnessed a static test of the A-4 engine at Kummersdorf, there had been an impressive display of fire and smoke as the 1,000-kg engine roared to life within its vertical test stand, yet the *Führer* had remained impassive. After the test, von Braun tried to explain what they'd just seen, but Hitler listened to him for only a couple of minutes before walking away, shaking his head in bafflement.

As the film drew to a close, there was an image von Braun wished Dornberger hadn't insisted upon: an animated map of Europe and America, with a red arrow arching over the Atlantic from the United States to Germany.

"Germany isn't alone in its efforts to perfect long-range military rockets," Dornberger said, his voice fraught with menace. "America is doing so, too . . . and one day soon it may have the ability to launch an attack against the Fatherland. Clearly, the Reich must build a missile defense before other nations do so first."

Von Braun suppressed an urge to groan.

The image faded, then the screen went white, and the last few inches of leader clattered through the take-up reel. The projectionist switched on the room lights, then walked over to the windows and opened the heavy blackout curtains. Hitler winced against the sudden rush of late-afternoon sunlight and rubbed his eyes, but it was Keitel who spoke for him.

"Are you certain of this, Colonel?" he asked Dornberger. "That America is able to attack us this way?"

"At this time, Field Marshal, the answer is no. But"—Dornberger tapped a finger against a memorandum he'd laid out on the table—"as I wrote in a report two years ago, the United States undoubtedly has a technological advantage. Like us, they, too, have been aggressively pursuing high-altitude rocket research over the last ten years . . . and we have little doubt that they may already be far ahead of us."

Von Braun kept his expression neutral, but he knew that Dornberger was exaggerating to the point of telling an outright lie. No one really knew what the Americans were doing. Their rocket research was being done in secret, with no technical reports made public. Until 1930, von Braun was able to keep up with the progress being made by the sole American scientist actively pursuing space travel—a man whom von Braun secretly admired—but when he relocated his experiments from Massachusetts to rural New Mexico, he'd stopped talking to the press and refused to answer queries from anyone in Europe, including the *VfR*. Even the spies Germany had in the United States reported little recently except that he was apparently continuing to conduct rocket research.

Dornberger's assertion that the United States was ahead in rocket research was questionable, to say the least. But von Braun knew why he'd made it. If fear was the only way he could motivate the *Führer* to continue funding research and development at Peenemünde, then fear was what he'd use.

"If this is so," Keitel said, "then will it be possible for us to develop a rocket that will be able to reach America?"

"I'm not sure that's even necessary," Goering murmured. Like Hitler, he was unimpressed by the film. "America will not go to war with us. Their people are reluctant to get involved in European affairs, and their politicians know it." He glanced at Hitler. "*Mein Führer*, America poses no threat to us. We will never have to fight them."

"With respect, Reich Marshal, I disagree." Dornberger shook his head. "It's possible, yes, that America will continue its isolationist policies. Yet it's just as possible that events may conspire to force their hand. Our continued assault upon Great Britain, for instance. Perhaps even the buildup of military forces in the Pacific by our Japanese allies." Goering snorted, but Dornberger went on. "If this is the case, then we need to be prepared to counter an American rocket attack . . . or even make a preemptive strike of our own."

"Really?" Keitel raised an eyebrow. "And will your A-4 be able to reach the American continent from Europe?"

Dornberger opened his mouth to speak, but von Braun interrupted him before he could make another baseless claim. "No, sir, it will not. Once perfected"—Dornberger gave him an angry glance—"the A-4 will have a maximum range of approximately 270 kilometers. This will be sufficient to attack targets in Britain, but the United States . . . ?" He shook his head. "No, sir. I'm sorry, but that's impossible."

"However," Dornberger quickly added, "we believe it may be possible to develop a step-rocket . . . that is, a multistage vehicle . . . capable of making a transcontinental flight. The 'America Rocket,' as we call it, would essentially stack an A-9 atop an A-10 rocket . . . once both are built, of course . . . with the result being a very large vehicle . . ."

"I have another idea," Hitler said abruptly, and Dornberger immediately fell silent. "Why not fit the A-4 into one of our long-range cannons and fire it that way? This would increase its range, would it not?"

A smug smile appeared on the *Führer*'s face; apparently, he believed that he'd found an obvious solution that had eluded the Peenemünde scientists. It took all of von Braun's self-control to keep from laughing out loud. Now more than ever, he knew that Hitler had no concept of what rockets were. He clearly thought that they were no more than artillery shells, much like the ones he'd handled during the last war.

"*Mein Führer*," he said carefully, "this is . . . an interesting proposal. Unfortunately, it's not feasible. The A-4 carries its own fuel. Even if there were an artillery piece large enough for this, the discharge would instantly destroy the vehicle."

Hitler glared at him. No one in the room said anything. Von Braun noticed that even Speer had become silent. He might be a supporter of

Wa Pruf 11, but he was not going to stick his neck into a noose for the sake of the Peenemünde rocket program.

Then the *Führer* slowly nodded. "Understood, Herr von Braun. But this . . . step-rocket, as you call it . . . you believe it could reach America?"

"Yes, *mein Führer*, it might be able to do that." Remembering Dornberger's earlier admonition, von Braun took care not to mention that the A-9/A-10 was little more than a fantasy concocted by the former *VfR* members working at Peenemünde. A piloted derivative of the A-4, the A-9 had been conceived for another purpose entirely: sending a manned spacecraft into orbit, as the first step to reaching the Moon. "However, I don't want to mislead you into believing that it can be built anytime soon. It is only a hypothetical proposal, and our priority should be continuing the development of the A-4."

"A program that has run into many difficulties." Goering leaned forward in his chair to pluck through a sheaf of papers on the table before him. "Your team has been at this for . . . how long now? Six, seven years? Judging from these reports, you're had far more failures than the successes you've just shown us."

A nervous frown appeared on Dornberger's face. "This is true, yes . . . but failures must be expected in an experimental program such as this. We're building something entirely new . . ."

"Apparently not. Your little movie"—Goering nodded toward the projector—"just told us that the Americans are already ahead of us in this area. Arc you telling me that the scientists of a mongrel nation are superior to German scientists?"

Dornberger became pale. Goering had pounced, and the colonel couldn't help but notice Hitler's eyes fastened upon him. Von Braun came to the rescue. "What we're saying," he calmly explained, "is that, in order to build weapons superior to America's, we need to develop rocket technology that will be better than theirs. Already, our A-4 prototype has reached high altitude . . ."

"Altitude isn't the question, Herr von Braun," Keitel said drily. "Range is the issue. It's not enough to be able to strike Britain. Our planes can do that already. We must also have a rocket capable of striking America in the event that it becomes necessary to do so."

"And this may be inevitable," Hitler added, ignoring Goering's skepticism about the United States declaring war against Germany.

Dornberger was openly sweating by then, his perpetual smile gone. "Field Marshal, with all due respect, what you ask is . . ."

"Not impossible," von Braun quickly said, before the colonel could make a fatal blunder. "Just difficult to achieve with our current budget, not to mention our present priority rating."

"You intend to take a rocket that's only capable of traveling 270 kilometers and turn it into something that can cross the Atlantic?" Goering's expression became a cynical smirk. "How will you accomplish this, Herr von Braun?"

Von Braun suddenly realized that he'd trapped himself with his own words. He'd told these men—these very dangerous men—that *Wa Pruf 11* must build a missile better than anything the Americans might launch, but then contradicted himself by stating that the A-4 was a short-range vehicle, only able to cross the English Channel from a launch site in France. He silently cursed Dornberger for even mentioning the America Rocket. In his puppyish desire to please Hitler, he'd whetted the *Führer*'s appetite for a weapon that Peenemünde could not deliver.

"Herr von Braun?" Hitler's eyes bore into his. "Do you have an answer for the Reich Marshal?"

Knowing that he had to say something—anything, damn it!—von Braun opened his mouth to reply. Before he could speak, though, Goering turned to Hitler. "*Mein Führer*, if I may? I believe I have a solution."

Hitler looked at the Reich Marshal. "Yes, Hermann? What do you have in mind?"

"A couple of scientists at the Luftwaffe's Research Division, Eugen Sanger and Irene Bredt, have recently submitted an interesting proposal. A manned aircraft . . . or rather, a spacecraft . . . that they believe is capable of not only reaching the United States, but also delivering a sizable payload." Hitler looked blank at the unfamiliar term, and Goering substituted for it a word he'd understand. "A bomb, *mein Führer.* A very large bomb."

Von Braun closed his eyes. Sanger. He knew all about Eugen Sanger. A talented scientist, yes, perhaps even a visionary, but nonetheless an outsider to the German rocket effort, not even a former *VfR* member. Von Braun had seen Sanger and Bredt's proposal, and considered it . . . well, if not insane, then at least improbable.

"Tell me more," Hitler said.

There was a sudden gleam in Goering's eyes, and, for an instant, he glanced at von Braun. Von Braun saw the smug look on his face, and in that moment he realized that the Reich Marshal had artfully led him and Dornberger into a trap. First, allow the Peenemünde men to convince the *Führer* that America poses a threat that cannot be ignored. Next, question the Army Ordnance's ability to develop a rocket capable of responding to an American intercontinental rocket. And, finally, present Hitler with an alternative that his Luftwaffe had developed instead.

Goering had always wanted control of the German rocket effort. It appeared that he might have found a way to get it.

Helplessly, von Braun began to listen to what the Reich Marshal had to say.

SILVER AND GOLD

The first snow of winter had settled upon the Baltic coast when von Braun returned from visiting his family in Berlin. From the cockpit of his Fieseler Storch, he saw that a sparse white blanket had spread itself across Usedom Island, a knuckle-shaped peninsula projecting out into the frigid northern sea. Beneath a slate grey sky, the pine forests were frosted, and the water-front was coated with a thin skin of ice. From the air, the island looked cold and remote.

Although he knew his presence was urgently needed on the ground, *Wa Pruf 11*'s technical director took a few moments to fly over Peenemünde. The engine moaned as he banked to the right. What had once been a small fishing village on the swampy northern tip of an island best known as a summer vacation resort had become the center of the Reich's rocket program. Through the plane's ice-crusted cockpit, von Braun peered down upon assembly sheds, workshops, laboratories, a liquid-oxygen production plant, office buildings, dormitories, cabins, even a track field . . . a small town, really, resembling a college campus more than a military base. As well it should; he and Albert Speer had intended Pee-nemünde to be a model for a modern scientific research center, a place where the two thousand scientists, engineers, and researchers could live in comfort while pushing the edge of a technological frontier.

Von Braun smiled. Peenemünde was a far cry from the *Raketenflugplatz*, the abandoned factory on the outskirts of Berlin where the *VfR* had built its first crude rockets from scratch. Those were the days when the Rocket Society—Arthur Rudolph and Walter Riedel among them, now von Braun's chief assistants—had pursued Hermann Oberth's dream of sending men to the Moon. But enthusiasm, ingenuity, and a taste for the science fiction novels of Thea von Harbou and Kurd Lasswitz weren't enough. The *VfR* was always broke, even when the von Braun family kicked in a few marks, and the presence of Rudolph Nebel, an oily opportunist who'd attempted to fleece the society while pretending to advance its goals, hadn't helped either.

The *VfR* had been on the verge of bankruptcy the day a long black car pulled up in front of the Rocket Port and three men in Army uniforms climbed out. On that early-spring morning in 1932, everything changed. Nearly ten years later, von Braun's plane circled Test Stand 1, the A-4 launchpad at the northernmost tip of the island, its skeletal tower blackened by the exhaust of the rockets that had lifted off from it. How far they'd come in just a decade . . .

His smile faded. Very far, yes . . . only to have it all come to a sudden end. Never again would an A-4 roar upward from Peenemünde. After seven long years of research and development, the program had been abruptly canceled. *Wa Pruff 11* had a new mission, one so mad that von Braun had difficulty believing that it could be pulled off.

Yet failure was unacceptable. Adolf Hitler himself had given von Braun his orders. *"Der Silbervogel fliegen müssen"*—the Silver Bird must fly.

The time for sightseeing was over. Pushing the wheel forward, von Braun brought the Storch into a low, gradual descent. A few minutes later, its wheels bumped against the tarmac of the Army airfield at the northwest end of the island.

A staff car waited for him at the apron near the hangars, its driver a corporal so young that von Braun could scarcely believe that he was allowed to wear a uniform. He snapped to attention and held open the rear passenger door as von Braun strode toward him, pulling off his flying cap and gloves. The car was cold, its heater turned off in the interest of saving petrol. Von Braun pulled up the collar of his leather jacket as the car made its way from Peenemünde West through the industrial complex at Peenemünde East until it reached the administrative and development area.

The car came to a stop in front of *Haus 4*, the two-story administration building. Von Braun didn't wait for the corporal to let him out of the car but instead opened the door himself and walked up a short flight of steps to the main entrance. The building was unusually quiet, most of the administrative staff having already left for the holidays. Von Braun had decided to take his vacation early—he wanted to take advantage of the brief respite to catch up on paperwork—but he couldn't blame people if they wanted to be with their families for Christmas. God knew they wouldn't get many more breaks after this.

Nonetheless, work hadn't ceased entirely. He heard typewriters and muffled voices from behind office doors as he walked down the hall to the stairs, and more of the same when he reached the second floor. He headed for his office, stepping around two men in dirty coveralls who were sweeping and mopping the tile floors, their cart parked beside them. One of them, a small, middle-aged man wearing wire-rim spectacles, murmured *"Pardonnez moi,"* as von Braun walked by. Von Braun barely noticed him. Several hundred foreign contract workers—mainly Italians and Poles, but also some French—held jobs at Peenemünde, doing the menial tasks that needed to be done. They were as invisible as the Russian prisoners of war who handled most of the hard labor; von Braun never paid much attention to them either.

His office was small yet immaculate, its shelves filled with books, loose-leaf binders, and mementoes, the prerequisite photo of Adolf Hitler framed on the wall. Although he'd cleared his desk before leaving, memos and reports were already stacked upon the blotter. Von Braun hung up his overcoat, then pulled a cigarette out of a mahogany tobacco box and lit it with a gold desk lighter. He'd barely settled into his desk chair when there was a quiet tap at the still-open door.

"*Guten Tag, Herr Doktor.*" His secretary, Lise Muller, stood just outside. "Welcome back."

"*Danke, Fraülein Muller.*" Von Braun puffed at his cigarette as he leafed through the memos. "I assume you're leaving soon, *ja*?"

"Not until the twenty-third. I'll take the train to Frankfurt that morning." A coy smile as she gave her long dark hair a studiously casual flip. "I'm yours till then."

Von Braun noticed the innuendo but tried not to show it. He was aware of his reputation as a ladies' man, and with his classically Teutonic looks and aristocratic manner, he'd never lacked for female company. As fetching as Lise might be, though, he knew better than to take her to bed. With the *Silbervogel* project now rated Priority S, he couldn't afford to be distracted by any dalliances, particularly not with his secretary. And it was only too possible that Lise might be secretly reporting to someone else. Goering, perhaps . . . or worse, Heinrich Himmler.

"Very well, then. It's off to work we go." Picking up the top memo, he saw that it was a technical query from Johannes Boykow, the scientist in charge of developing the gyroscopic stabilizer. His group was struggling to adapt the gyros they'd developed for the A-4 to suit the new vehicle, but its different launch attitude—horizontal instead of vertical—was giving them fits.

"Lise, would you please get the *Silbervogel* study for me?" he asked. His secretary turned to the office safe, set in the wall between two bookshelves. Only she and von Braun knew its combination. Lise turned the wheel left, then right, then left again; a soft click, and she turned its handle downward and opened the door.

Inside the safe was a 175-page report within a leatherette binder. Titled "*Über einen Raketenantrieb für Fernbomber*" ("A Rocket Drive for Long-Range Bombers") Eugen Sanger and Irene Bredt's design study was one of the Reich's most highly classified documents. For the sake of security, only two complete copies had been sent to Peenemünde; Colonel Dornberger possessed one and von Braun the other. Although individual department heads had copies of individual sections pertinent to their work, if someone needed to consult another section, he had to make a specific request from either Dornberger or von Braun.

In this instance, Boykow's team was having trouble redesigning the gyro platform so that it could be smoothly integrated into *Silbervogel*'s airframe. They were considering relocating the platform from its present position in the craft's nose to its midsection, but Boykow needed to check some figures from the Sanger-Bredt report. It was a nuisance to have to work this way, but Goering was insistent. *Wa Pruf 11* was rigorously compartmentalized in order to maintain operational security, even within Peenemünde's academy-like cloisters.

"Thank you," von Braun said, as Lise placed the binder on the desk before him. "I think that will be all for now."

"You're welcome." She turned to walk toward the door, and Wernher couldn't help but steal an admiring glance at the way her rump moved beneath her wool skirt. Almost as if she'd sensed his gaze upon her, she abruptly turned around. "Oh! And one more thing . . ."

"Yes?" Von Braun felt his face burn as he hastily looked down at the report on his desk.

"Dr. Rudolph called just before you arrived. He said that he needs to see you immediately."

Von Braun looked up again. "Did he say why?"

"No. He only said that he needs to see you at his lab at once, and you're to come over there as soon as you get in." An apologetic shrug. "Sorry."

Von Braun sighed. Although Arthur Rudolph was his best friend and right-hand man, there were times when Wernher wondered if he could tie his shoes without consulting someone. His lab was located in another building in Peenemünde East. Von Braun glanced out the window behind him; to his annoyance, it had begun to snow again, and the car that had brought him from the airfield had already left. He'd have to go out into the cold once more.

"Very well." Von Braun stubbed out his cigarette in an ashtray and started to rise, then thought better of it. "Just a moment," he said, as he picked up a pen and reached into a desk drawer for a notepad. "I need you to do something for me, please."

Von Braun turned pages of the *Silbervogel* report until he found the section in which Sanger addressed the question of avionics integration within the airframe. Consulting one of the report's many diagrams, he spent a couple of minutes jotting down the numbers Boykow needed, then tore the page from the notepad, slipped it into an envelope, and handed it to his secretary.

"Please take this to Dr. Boykow," he said, standing up from his chair. "Wait to see if he thinks this answers his questions, and write down what he wants from me if it doesn't." Von Braun walked around from behind his desk, reached for his overcoat. "I'm going to see Arthur."

"Very well." Lise left the office before he did. Von Braun shook his head in wonder as he watched her stride down the hall, passing the two janitors on the way. Despite the fact that she'd have to cross Peenemünde East to reach Boykow's office, she'd declined to put on an overcoat even though it was below zero outside and spitting snow. The woman must be part snow fox, he reflected as he closed his office door and followed her to the stairs. Which was a delightful notion . . .

The two janitors paid no attention to either von Braun or his secretary as their footsteps retreated down the hallway. But as soon they were gone, and the corridor was quiet again, they raised their eyes from their work and gazed at one another. Neither of them said anything, but a silent nod was exchanged. And then they quietly approached von Braun's office.

———

The two janitors were named Yves Callon and François Latreau, but to MI-6 they were known as Silver and Gold. For the past four months, they'd been posing as custodians at Peenemünde, just another couple of foreign workers who'd been hired from a country under Nazi occupation. Even at a high-security facility such as Peenemünde, there was a need for people to do the menial labor, so that good German men could make more meaningful contributions to the war effort. Knowledge of this fact had given British intelligence the opportunity to infiltrate spies into enemy installations, with the primary objective of gathering information useful to the Allies.

Beginning a couple of years earlier, MI-6 had heard rumors of strange occurrences in northern Germany. Although Denmark was under Nazi occupation, its intelligence operations were still active, and through them, the Danes had received reports from fishermen of "flame-tailed aeroplanes" they'd seen shooting along from the western Baltic coast, usually exploding a few minutes later. Then a member of the Polish underground relayed a conversation he'd had in a Koenigsburg tavern with a drunk German soldier stationed at Peenemünde; the Nazi had bragged about his people developing a secret weapon that would win the war for Germany. Although MI-6 initially discounted these reports as fantasy— the Germans always seemed to be building one secret weapon or another— in time enough reports were received through the clandestine wireless network established between Denmark and England to convince the British that Peenemünde needed to be investigated.

To this end, MI-6 had recruited two members of the French resistance and instructed them to seek employment at Peenemünde. The British had hoped that either Callon or Latreau would be hired; as it turned out, both got jobs as janitors. Naturally, they were screened by the Gestapo, yet the resistance had already concocted "legends," or fictional backgrounds, establishing them as Nazi sympathizers loyal to the Vichy government. So far as the German secret police was concerned, the two men were nothing more than lower-class, rather stupid Frenchmen content with pushing brooms and emptying wastebaskets.

Silver and Gold arrived in Peenemünde only a few weeks after the A-4 program was officially scrapped. During the course of the first month as janitors, they saw and heard enough to confirm that the Nazis were developing some sort of long-range missile. Although this program had been mysteriously canceled on the very eve of success, it became apparent that it was being replaced by a project that was even more ambitious.

Yet they'd been unable to learn exactly what it was. All work was being done in labs and workshops the janitors were expressly forbidden to enter, and certain areas of Peenemünde West had been placed off-limits to anyone except engineers, technicians, and senior scientists.

There was one possible loophole: Wernher von Braun's office. Over the past few months, Silver and Gold noticed that von Braun had developed careless habits when it came to handling classified documents. Overworked and easily distracted, he'd become dependent upon his secretaries—particularly Lise Muller, on whom he obviously had a crush—to tidy up for him. So the spies made a point of visiting *Haus 4* on a daily basis, keeping its hallways and restrooms spotless while watching the technical director's office, waiting for a chance when both von Braun and Muller would become negligent.

That opportunity finally presented itself, and just in time. In two days, Silver was scheduled to return to Paris for the holidays, during which he was supposed to make a covert rendezvous with their MI-6 handler. It would be their first and possibly only opportunity to pass along any information. Aware that their mail was being opened by the Gestapo and analyzed by its cryptologists, the agents decided not to use the codes developed for them by MI-6. So it was now or never.

The office door was unlocked. Silver opened it quietly and peered over his glasses to make sure that the room was vacant, then he turned to Gold and held out his hand. Gold reached into their cart and pulled out the large horsehair brush they used to clean drapery. Taking it from him, Silver entered the office, his footsteps softened by the rubber roles of his work shoes. Gold stood watch outside, ready to accidentally drop his mop at the first sign of trouble.

The open door of the safe and the thick binder lying open on von Braun's desk told him all he needed to know. This was a classified document, possibly the key to understanding Peenemünde's mystery project. Carefully avoiding the windows, Silver stepped around behind the desk and, after noting the number of the page von Braun was reading before he left, closed the report. Its title confirmed his suspicions. He needed to take this to his people.

There were two concealed catches at each end of the brush's wooden handle. Beneath Silver's thumbs, they slid apart like the locks of a Chinese puzzle box, allowing him to pull the handle apart and reveal the hollow space within. Tucked inside the brush, padded by a rubber mold, was a Latvian-made Minox camera, its lozenge-shaped body only 7.5 centimeters long. Coiled beside it was a thin silver chain 45 centimeters in length, with a clip at one end and a small ring at the other.

Silver clipped one end of the chain to the camera, then slipped the ring around his left thumb. Bending over the desk, he placed his left hand next to the open report, then positioned himself so that the chain led directly up to the camera held in his right hand. In this way, the Minox was at the perfect distance for photographing documents. Peering through the miniature viewfinder, he took a couple of moments to adjust the focusing dial; when the typewritten print on the first page was sharp and clear, he went to work.

Silver had spent many hours in the resistance's Paris hideaway learning how to use the Minox. The time was well spent. Again and again he pressed the tiny stud of the camera shutter, synchronizing it with the turning of each page. He didn't read what he was photographing; every second was precious and couldn't be used trying to comprehend material that only a scientist could fully understand. Although the Minox's 9.5mm film cartridge held fifty exposures, the report had more than three times that many pages; afraid to miss any crucial information, Silver jumped ahead a few pages to snap pictures of bar graphs and tables that seemed important.

Then he came across a diagram that caused him to stop what he was doing. Staring at the cutaway drawing of a strange-looking aircraft, he suddenly realized that *Wa Pruf 11* had moved far beyond mere rocketry.

This was not a missile. This was something else entirely.

Silver snapped a picture of the diagram, then turned a couple of pages and found another that appeared interesting, a global map with a squiggly line curving up and down across the outer surface, like something hopping across Earth's atmosphere. He'd just finished photographing it when Gold's mop fell to the hallway floor.

Silver glanced up, saw the other spy through the open door. Gold pointed to his ear, then down the hall toward the stairs. Someone was coming up.

The Minox's frame counter told Silver that he had seven exposures left, but there was no time to use them. Under no circumstances could he let himself get caught in Dr. von Braun's office. Silver hastily turned the report's pages back to where the technical director had left them, then detached the measurement chain from the camera. He stuffed the chain in his pocket and slipped the Minox back into the brush handle. One last look to make sure that everything was the way he'd found it, then in four quick steps he was out of the office.

Silver had just retrieved his broom from where he'd left it against the wall when Lise Muller emerged from the stairway. Even before he saw von Braun's secretary, Silver knew that it was her; when she walked, the low heels of her patent leather shoes made a distinctive tap-tap-tap sound with which he and Gold had become familiar. He still had the horsehair brush in his hand; stepping past Gold, whose back was to the approaching woman, he reached out to put the brush back in the janitor cart.

Then its cover fell off and the Minox dropped onto the floor.

In an instant, Silver realized what had happened. In his haste to get out of the office, he'd neglected to close the two catches that locked the brush's hidden compartment. Fortunately, Gold was standing between the camera and the approaching secretary, but even as Silver squatted down to pick up the Minox, he knew that in another second she'd see . . .

"So what do you think of *Fraülein Muller*'s ass?" Gold said casually, speaking to Silver as if she weren't there. "Wouldn't you like to get your hands on that?"

Silver heard the secretary's footsteps come to an abrupt halt. Glancing up to peer between Gold's legs, he saw that Lise had half turned away, hands raised to her face to hide her embarrassment. Silver snatched up the Minox and stuffed it down the front of his coveralls. It had disappeared by the time Lise recovered enough of her dignity to face the two janitors again and clear her throat.

"Oh . . . hello, *Fraülein*." Gold was the picture of deferential servitude as he looked around, seemingly noticing her for the first time. "Nice day, isn't it?"

The secretary said nothing as she marched the rest of the way down the hall, her expression stony but her face bright red. She didn't even glance at Silver as she stormed past them; he'd already picked up his brush and, surreptitiously replacing the handle cover, returned it to the cart. Lise's shoes stamped against the bare wooden floor as she entered von Braun's office. The door slammed shut behind her, and Gold started to let out his breath in relief, but Silver quickly raised a hand. Listening intently, he heard what he'd hoped to hear: the soft, metallic clank of the wall safe's being shut.

The two men traded looks: Gold, an accusatory glare, Silver, an apologetic upward roll of his eyes. Once they were sure the hall was clear, Silver returned both the camera and the measuring chain to their hiding place. In moments, the brush was back where it belonged, and the two men returned to what they'd been doing.

Nonetheless, the blood had drained from Silver's face, and not just because of the close call. What he'd seen in the classified document on Wernher von Braun's office frightened him deeply.

The Minox film couldn't get to England fast enough.

RENDEZVOUS IN PARIS

DECEMBER 24, 1941

Sometime during the morning, a Gestapo agent had taken up a position in the doorway of a café across the street from Yves Callon's apartment. Callon spotted him almost as soon he got out of bed and looked out his kitchen window. Even from three floors up, it was impossible not to tell that the man in the charcoal overcoat, black scarf, and dark grey hat belonged to the secret police; he looked like a giant crow that had come to roost upon the sidewalk.

Callon wasn't surprised. He'd half expected to be kept under surveillance once he returned to Paris for the holidays. The Nazis weren't likely to take any chances with a French janitor who worked at one of their most secret research facilities, so it only made sense that they would dispatch a Gestapo agent to keep an eye on him. It was little comfort that he appeared to be bored and cold. Even if he wasn't alert, he could be a serious impediment to the task that lay ahead.

As Yves puttered around his small, two-room apartment—washing his face and shaving, getting dressed, having a meager breakfast of coffee and a croissant—he wondered whether it might be wise to cancel the drop. If he waited another day or two, the Gestapo might give up and leave him alone. But he'd arrived in Paris by train early yesterday evening, and he was due to catch another train back to Germany the day after tomorrow. Waiting until tomorrow to make the drop would be problematic if the Gestapo was still watching him by then; some of his actions might seem peculiar if done on Christmas Day. And if he waited until the day after Christmas and tried to make the drop before going to the rail station, his contact might be at risk if he'd been followed, and the Gestapo noticed him going to the same place at the same time three days in a row.

So Yves had no choice. He had to make the drop today, despite the danger. He simply needed to be careful, for the slightest mistake could be fatal.

Callon kept an eye on the clock above his fireplace as he washed his breakfast dishes and put them away. At ten minutes to nine, he got ready to go. He avoided looking out the window as he pulled on his dark brown overcoat, woolen muffler, and cap. The Minox film cartridge—two small black cylinders joined by a crosspiece, a little more than six centimeters long—went in his inside coat pocket, then he carefully put his identification papers on top of it. If he were stopped and searched, he hoped the folded papers would pad the cartridge enough to escape being detected by a brisk patdown. There were other places he could hide the cartridge, of course, but he had to be able to get to it as quickly and unobtrusively as possible.

Leaving the apartment, Callon made his way down the narrow stairs. He'd just reached the second-floor landing when a door opened, and one of his neighbors started to come out. A young woman whose name he could never recall, she stopped the moment she saw him. Her eyes narrowed, and a disgusted frown curled an attractive mouth; she immediately stepped back into her apartment and slammed the door. But just before she disappeared, Callon heard her mutter, *"Maudit traitre."*

Damned traitor. This was what his role as an MI-6 operative had cost him: his reputation. Almost no one knew that he belonged to the resistance, and only a couple of people in his cell were aware that he was spying for the British. So far as everyone else was concerned, Yves Callon was a Vichy collaborator, someone willing to work for the Nazis just to gain a job and luxuries like the coffee he'd just had with breakfast. He could only hope that, once the war was over and France was liberated, his true role would be revealed and he would be exonerated. Until then, he had few friends in his native city. Not even his own family would speak to him anymore.

Rue de la Huchette was a cobblestone street in the Latin Quarter, so narrow that only pedestrians and bicyclists could use it . . . not that there were many automobiles on the streets of Paris these days. Before the war, its sidewalk cafés would have been open, even on Christmas Eve, with gypsies sitting on the curb out front, playing guitars or flutes, hats turned upside down before them. But the restaurants were now closed four days a week, and the Romany had either fled or been rounded up and sent to concentration camps, so there was almost no one in sight except the Gestapo agent in the doorway, smoking a cigarette as he pretended not to notice Callon.

Yves pretended not to see him either. Closing the front door behind them, he stepped out into the street, turning right to head toward the cathedral. He didn't have to glance at the shop windows he passed to know from the footsteps behind him that the crow had left the doorway and was walking along behind him. Yet the Gestapo man was being careful not to follow so closely as to be obvious; Yves could no longer hear him by the time he reached the end of the block although he had little doubt that the secret policeman was still there.

Two blocks ahead was Rue Saint-Jacques, a wider street. Yves turned left and followed it toward the river. Notre Dame came in sight, a grand edifice of granite and stained glass towering above the Seine. Even Christmas Eve, there was little traffic on the broad avenue running alongside the river; the Nazis had claimed all the petrol for their own vehicles, leaving Parisians with nothing but horses, bicycles, and the strange-looking *velo-taxis* made from cutting a motorcar in half and hooking up the passenger end to a bicycle.

Yves dodged one of those as he crossed the Quai de Montebello to the

Petit Pont, and the Gestapo agent was only ten meters back when he strolled across the bridge to the broad plaza in front of Notre Dame. Morning services had just ended, and worshippers were emerging from beneath the ornate arches above the cathedral's massive oak doors. They tried to avoid eye contact with the German soldiers who patrolled the plaza, M-40 submachine guns dangling from straps beneath their arms.

As he crossed the plaza, Yves stole a glance at his wristwatch. His timing was perfect; it was exactly ten after nine. His steps took him toward the statue of Charlemagne, which stood to the right of the cathedral.

A white-bearded old man sat on a bench beneath the king, coat collar turned up against the cold as he tossed corn kernels to the pigeons strutting and pecking around him. He didn't look up as Yves approached the bench or show the slightest interest as he walked past, yet Yves knew the old man had spotted him. And probably the Gestapo tail as well.

If Yves hadn't been followed, the rendezvous would have been simple. He would have brought a newspaper on his way to Notre Dame, tucked the cartridge inside, and sat down on the bench beside the old man. A few minutes later, he would've stood up and walked away, leaving the newspaper behind. The paper and the hidden cartridge would have gone with the old man. That was now out of the question; the Gestapo agent would have seen through that in an instant. So Yves was forced to resort to a backup plan, albeit one that was much more complicated.

He walked the rest of the way across the plaza and entered Notre Dame. He didn't have to look back to know that the crow was still behind him. Removing his cap and shoving it in his coat pocket, he paused in the foyer to let his eyes adjust to the darkness, then took a novena candle, dropping a half franc into the offering box. A brief nod to the robed priest at the door, then he quietly walked into the sanctuary.

Notre Dame rose around him as an enormous cavern, one that seemed more like the creation of God than man. Even in midmorning, the cathedral was dark and quiet. The giant pipe organ near the altar had ceased playing the sacred music that filled every corner of the vast sanctuary, and the only light came from the candelabra on the massive stone columns and the intricate panes of the great stained-glass windows. Although the morning service was concluded, a few worshippers still lingered in the oak pews, heads bowed in meditation.

Yves walked slowly down the center aisle toward the nave. He paused within sight of the altar to cross himself and take a quick bow, then he found a seat in the third row. He sat there for a while, hands clasped together, head lowered as if in prayer, then he stood up again and quietly walked toward the small, grottolike chapels that stood in a row along the sanctuary's right wall.

Each of Notre Dame's chapels was dedicated to the memory of a particular saint; they had their own altars and pews, and some had confession booths. Above each altar was a crucifix, and on either side was a wrought-iron rack for novena candles. Yves entered the chapel nearest the nave, the one dedicated to L'Arc de Joan. No one else was there except the old man who'd been feeding pigeons outside.

Yves took the candle he'd picked up in the foyer and, lighting it from another candle, placed it in the middle row of the rack on the left side of the altar. He paused a moment to murmur a prayer—heartfelt this time even though he'd stopped practicing his faith a few years ago—in the memory of his mother and father. The old man's eyes briefly shifted in his direction as he turned to leave, but no words were spoken between them.

Nonetheless, a message had been passed.

The crow stood at the back of the sanctuary, hands in pockets, hat disrespectfully unremoved. No doubt he'd observed every move Yves made. He didn't bother to look away as Yves walked by, but Yves continued to pretend not to see him. A brief pause in the foyer to adjust his muffler and put his cap back on, then he left the cathedral, thanking the priest at the door on the way out.

The Gestapo agent was still behind him as he crossed the Petit Pont again and strolled down the Quai de Montebello until he reached the Boulevard Saint-Michel. There he turned left and began walking up the broad, tree-lined avenue, passing the Napoleonic-era fountain where the winged angel Michael, sword raised in victory, towered above a defeated and cowering Lucifer. Like the statue of Charlemagne, only its size kept the Nazis from tearing it down and carrying it away to be melted down for its iron, the fate of so many of the city's other statues. The archangel brought a sly smile to Yves's face. One day, he promised himself, the statue would symbolize triumph over evil of another kind.

However, the statue was one of the few things untouched by the Nazi presence. As with the rest of Paris, it was impossible to miss signs of the German occupation. Above the street, red swastika flags hung from the windows of offices and hotels the Germans had claimed for their own. Indeed, the Third Reich's flag was ubiquitous throughout the city; it even fluttered from the top of the Eiffel Tower, a deliberate offense to every French citizen who saw it. There weren't many people on the sidewalks, but it seemed as if there were an armed soldier on every corner. A Duesenberg limousine drove past, the first car Yves had seen this morning; two German officers were seated in the back, callous eyes regarding the beautiful city they'd raped. There were few stores or cafés open, though, so their conquest was probably tempered by scarcity.

The boulevard took him uphill, away from the Latin Quarter. Just past the Pantheon and the Sorbonne, he spotted a florist he'd visited over the years. Stepping into the small shop, he purchased a bouquet of red and yellow roses, a dozen in all. As the proprietor carefully wrapped them in paper to keep them from wilting in the cold, he casually gazed at the arrangements in the window. The crow was across the street, examining women's clothes on display in a shop window. The agent's surveillance methods were so obtuse that Yves wanted to laugh. Instead, he paid the florist and left. The Gestapo agent continued to follow him from the other side of the street.

Callon walked the rest of the way up the hill, past the sandbag barricades surrounding the Palais et Jardin du Luxembourg, the seat of the deposed French government, its fountains and gardens now off-limits to all Parisians, until he reached the Boulevard du Montparnasse. Turning right, he strolled a block down the boulevard, then turned onto Rue

Boissonade. His steps took him past a hospital until, at last, he reached his destination, the Cimetière du Montparnasse.

One of the city's oldest cemeteries, it sprawled across a hilltop overlooking the Left Bank, its grounds surrounded by a tall redbrick wall. Many of Paris's greatest authors, painters, actors, and philosophers lay here, but also some of its ordinary citizens, among them Yves Callon's parents and grandparents.

Slowing his pace, Yves sauntered through the cemetery's open gate. As expected, a German soldier stood watch just outside the gatehouse. He looked cold even though he was bundled up in a greatcoat, a cigarette dangling from a brutish-looking mouth. He stared at Yves but said nothing; the bouquet told him all he needed to know. Giving the soldier the slightest of nods, Callon began walking down the gravel path into the graveyard.

Most of the cemetery's graves were located aboveground, within concrete tombs topped by crosses, urns, testament plaques, weeping angels, and so forth. Like many family gravesites, though, the Callon tomb was located within a small mausoleum not much larger than a telephone booth. Built of concrete, with a crucifix atop its sloped tile roof, it had small glazed windows on three sides and an iron grate as its door. Stopping at the door, Yves shifted the bouquet from one hand to another as he fished in his pocket for his key ring; as he did, he searched the area from the corners of his eyes. For the first time since Notre Dame, the crow was nowhere to be seen. But there were many mausoleums all around him, and the Gestapo man could be hiding behind any one of them. In any case, Yves had to assume that he'd been followed into the cemetery and therefore continue taking precautions.

An old iron key unlocked the grate. Yves pushed it aside and stepped into the cold little room. There was just enough space in here for one person, or two if they stood very close together. The floor beneath his feet was made of concrete slabs carved with the names of his parents and grandparents. If he were to have the slabs removed, Yves would have found their coffins interred beneath the ground. He and his brother and sister would eventually be laid to rest there; Yves felt a chill when he considered that, if he wasn't careful, his residence in this place could be sooner rather than later.

Behind the slabs was a white-marble bench, waist high, with a statuette of the Virgin Mary at its center and a flower urn on either side. The urns were carved limestone, tall and wasp-waisted, heavy enough to hold bouquets without falling over. Bunches of dead flowers—daisies from the looks of them, probably left some time ago by his brother, who was cheap about such things—were still in the urns, their dry petals scattered across the bench. Yves removed the dead flowers and put them aside, then unwrapped the roses and placed them on the bench.

The windows were too high and narrow for anyone outside to peer through, and his body blocked the doorway, but, nonetheless, Yves took care not to let himself be seen doing what he was doing. As he separated six roses from the bouquet, he quickly slipped his right hand into his coat pocket. Beneath the identification papers was the film cartridge. Concealing it within his palm, he picked up the roses he'd selected and covered the cartridge with their stems. Then, raising the roses to the urn on the left side of the Madonna, he let the cartridge fall into the vase. The soft clink it made when it hit the bottom was muffled by the roses he inserted atop them.

Yves put the rest of the roses in the other urn. He carefully arranged the flowers, then took a few moments to silently stand at the bench, head bowed as if in prayer. Then he picked up the dead flowers and left the mausoleum, locking the grate behind him.

There. It was done. With any luck, the cartridge would soon be on its way to England. It would take a while, of course. The resistance would have to send it by way of special courier to Norway, where it would then be put aboard one of the fishing boats that secretly crossed the North Sea to Scotland. The French coast was effectively closed, but the underground had found ways of getting information out of occupied Europe to the

British Isles. Weeks might pass before the Minox cartridge reached its destination, yet Yves had little doubt that it would get there.

The crow was nowhere to be seen as Yves left the graveyard, dropping the dead flowers in a waste can on his way out. As he approached the front gate, though, he saw the Gestapo agent standing beside the soldier. Both were smoking, and as Yves came closer, he heard coarse laughter at some shared joke. The crow turned toward Yves as he approached the gate. The Gestapo agent made no effort to avoid being seen. It was obvious that he was waiting for him.

Stuffing his hands in his overcoat pockets and lowering his head, Yves tried not to appear nervous. The crow looked back at the soldier, and, for a moment, Yves had hope that he might be able to leave the cemetery in peace. But just as he was about to walk by, the Gestapo man raised a black-gloved hand to stop him.

"*M'seur Callon? Bonjour.*" Although his voice was heavily accented, the crow had the courtesy to address him in French. "May I have a word with you, please?"

"*Oui.*" Callon didn't bother pretending not to know who he was speaking to. Everyone in Paris had learned to recognize the Gestapo on sight.

"*Merci beaucoup.*" The crow was younger than Callon by a decade, and while he seemed pleasant enough, the hardness of his eyes betrayed his true self. "I'm wondering what brings you here today."

"Visiting my parents." There was no way he could tell the Gestapo man that it was none of his business why he'd come here. The Nazis kept the people of the countries they'd occupied on a very short leash. "They're buried here."

"Ah, yes . . . for Christmas, of course." The officer nodded. "I understand you work at one of our research facilities. The one in the Baltic."

"This is correct, *oui.*" The very name Peenemünde was considered a state secret, and Yves was careful to follow the crow's example by not speaking it in public. "I've come home for the holidays, and this is one of the things I meant to do while I'm here."

"Perfectly reasonable. I applaud your thoughtfulness. May I see your papers, please?"

Although there was no reason why the Gestapo man would want to see his identification—he already knew who he was and where he worked—Yves obediently produced them from his coat pocket. The crow unfolded the dog-eared forms and took his time examining them, while the unsmiling soldier fastened his stony gaze upon him. Yves tried to maintain an air of patient indifference, but his heart had begun to beat a little faster, and he kept his hands in his pockets to hide their tremors.

"Everything seems to be in order," the Gestapo agent said at last, almost reluctantly handing them back. As Yves put them away, the secret-police officer idly gazed around the cemetery. "Such an interesting place. I don't think I've ever been here before."

"You should come back sometime. Some very famous people are buried here."

"Along with your parents, of course." A smile abruptly appeared on the crow's face, as if he'd had a sudden thought. "Would you mind showing me their resting place? I'd love to see it."

A cold hand wrapped itself around Yves's heart, and for a moment he had an impulse to refuse. *I'm rather busy just now,* he almost said, but refusal was out of the question, and even hesitation could be suspicious. "Yes, of course," he said instead, and tried to cover his nervousness by coughing into his hand. "This way, please."

Leaving the soldier at the gate, Yves led the Gestapo agent back down the gravel path, then through the graveyard until they reached the Callon family mausoleum. "Very nice, very handsome," the crow said, looking at it so briefly that Yves was now certain that the agent had been watching him all the time from somewhere nearby. The agent grasped the door handle, gave it a quick tug, then stepped away. "Open it, please. I'd like to look inside."

It took all Yves's willpower to keep his hands from shaking as he fitted the key into the lock. He pulled open the grate, and the officer entered the mausoleum. Yves hesitated, then followed him, peering over his shoulder as the Gestapo man gazed around the tiny room.

The crow missed nothing. He stamped his feet upon the floor slabs to check their solidity and immobility, then he turned his attention to the bench. Running his gloved hands across the marble, he suddenly reached up to seize the Madonna statuette and tip it back, looking to see if there was a hollow space beneath its base. He then ran his fingers through the roses, but was unable to turn over the urn. Convinced that it couldn't be easily moved, he grunted beneath his breath, then reached for the left urn.

"Do you know why I'm doing this?" he asked, as his hand shifted through the roses, disturbing their careful arrangement.

"No, I do not," Yves managed to reply.

The Gestapo agent glanced over his shoulder at him. "Do you know someone named François Latreau?"

"*Oui* . . . of course." Yves's mouth had gone dry. "I work with him at Peene . . . in the Baltic, I mean."

"Yes. He's another janitor who was hired from this city, same time as you were." Looking away again, the Gestapo man pushed aside the roses and thrust his fingers into the urn, probing its fluted neck. "He was arrested yesterday."

"He was?" Yves had to fight to remain calm. Every nerve in his body felt as if it'd gone numb. "For . . . for what?"

"Espionage. He was caught photographing something . . . well, interesting." The Gestapo agent was trying to get his hand through the urn's narrow neck into the well. "I don't suppose you'd know anything about that, would you?"

"N-no. Nothing at all." Yves wanted to scream. He'd left François behind with the understanding that he wouldn't attempt to gather any more information on his own. They'd managed to survive this long because they worked as a team, but apparently Gold had decided not to wait until Silver returned from Paris. Maybe he'd spotted something that he couldn't resist. Or perhaps he'd just gotten cocky. Whatever the reason, he'd been caught. And the Gestapo was suspicious of Yves Callon as well.

The crow's hand withdrew from the urn. There was nothing in it. He turned around again, and Yves started to step back to let him leave the crypt. But then the Gestapo man suddenly reached forward to grab him by the lapels.

"You're sure of this?" he asked, pulling him just an inch closer, his eyes locked on Yves's. "I'm not. You're very nervous, *M'seur* Callon. I wonder why that is."

"I . . . I . . ."

Then Callon did something he himself didn't expect. He substituted anger for fear, and let it show.

"Oh, for God's sake!" he snapped, staring back at the crow. "You seriously think that, just because I clean toilets with some guy, that makes me a spy, too?" He hissed in disgust. "That's the thanks I get!"

The Gestapo agent's eyes widened in surprise. Seldom had anyone spoken to him this way. "I see," he said, letting go of Callon's coat. "You're quite adamant, aren't you?"

"Yes, I am . . . and I'll thank you not to disturb my parents' tomb!" He reached past the officer to rearrange the roses and return the Virgin Mary back to its proper place. "Is that all you want to know?"

The Gestapo man didn't reply but instead put his hands in his pockets and watched as Callon fussed over the items on the shelf. "My apologies," he said at last. "I didn't mean to give offense."

Yves sighed in exasperation as he turned to leave. He'd just stepped out of the crypt, though, when something prodded the back of his ribs. Startled, he looked down to see a Walther in the crow's hand.

"However," the crow said, "I'm afraid I'm still going to have to detain you for questioning. Just to be certain."

Callon heard tires crunch against gravel. Looking around, he saw a black Peugeot roll to a halt on the nearby road. Another soldier climbed out, submachine gun in his hands.

"Don't run," the crow quietly added. "That's what your friend did when he was caught. He was shot."

The fear came back, and this time there was no surge of anger to dispel it. Yves had no choice but to raise his hands and let the officer march him to the waiting sedan. He knew where he was going: the Gestapo headquarters at the Felgendarmerie, which many had entered but few had left.

The sedan's doors slammed shut, then the driver did a U-turn on the narrow path, nearly scraping its bumper against a couple of tombstones. The soldier standing guard at the gate raised his arm in a stiff salute as the Peugeot made its departure from the Cimetière du Montparnasse, then reached into his pocket for his cigarettes.

Lighting one, the soldier barely noticed the bearded old man who'd stood aside to make way for the sedan. The old man watched as the Peugeot drove away, then he continued through the gate, walking into the cemetery as if on a small Christmas Eve visit with the dead.

BLACK UMBRELLA

=====

A dense morning fog from the Potomac was shrouding Bolling Field when the C-60 Lodestar touched down. From their seats in the back of the U.S. Army Air Force transport, the two men who were the plane's only passengers could barely see anything through the haze. The younger of the two, wearing the blue doeskin uniform of a British Navy officer, fought back a yawn as the aircraft's wheels skipped across the tarmac and its twin engines reverse-propped. A glance at his wristwatch—7:00 A.M.—then he looked at the older man seated across the aisle from him.

"Bang on time," he murmured, a mischievous twinkle in his eyes. "You don't suppose we could drop by the nearest pub, do you, sir? I could use a drink."

"No, I don't suppose we could." His companion glared at him, not at all amused by the half-serious suggestion. "And considering why we're here and where we're going, you might want to take things a little more seriously."

"Sorry, General. Didn't mean to offend."

Major General William Donovan grunted quietly and looked away. Lieutenant Commander Ian Fleming reminded himself that the U.S.

Army's coordinator of information wasn't known for his sense of humor. They'd met only yesterday at Naval Intelligence headquarters in London, when Donovan had been introduced to him by Fleming's boss, Rear Admiral John Godfrey. Along with the attaché case that rested on the seat beside him, Godfrey had given Fleming his orders: accompany Donovan on an overnight flight to Washington, D.C., where the two of them were to deliver a high-level briefing regarding the classified material they would take with them.

Within hours, they were in the air, flying overnight across the Atlantic, with only a brief stop in Greenland to refuel. The C-60's wing lights were blacked out until the plane was well over the ocean, to prevent it from being spotted by any Messerschmitts that might be prowling the English coast; a couple of RAF Spitfires had escorted them as far as Ireland before turning back. Since then, Fleming had come to realize that Donovan considered him to be little more than a nuisance, a young bureaucrat forced on him by British intelligence. The general seldom said a word during the entire trip, preferring instead to read and reread the translated German document Fleming was carrying. Donovan was notorious for a flinty personality and demanding that things be done his way.

Right, Fleming thought. *And if it hadn't been for our people in Germany and France, you lot wouldn't have a bloody idea what the Nazis are up to.*

The plane taxied to a row of half-seen hangars and came to a halt. Its engines were still winding down as a couple of ground crewmen pushed a ladder alongside the aircraft. The flight engineer emerged from the cockpit and opened the hatch from the inside. A brief conversation with one of the ground crew, then he looked at his passengers. "All right, here you are," he said. "You've got a car waiting for you."

"Thank you." General Donovan rose from his seat. "The bracelet, Commander. Put it on, please."

Fleming had to make a conscious effort to keep from smirking. Before he and Donovan had left Hyde Park, the general insisted that Fleming secure the attaché case to his right hand with a nickel-plated bracelet. An unnecessary precaution, really, which MI-6 normally didn't take; armed military policemen on motorcycles had escorted him and Donovan to the airfield, and Fleming had little doubt that they'd get much the same reception in America. It seemed to make Donovan feel better, though, so he slipped the handcufflike bracelet around his wrist and snapped it shut before picking up the attaché case and following Donovan off the plane.

A dark brown Ford sedan awaited them on the apron. As Fleming expected, a pair of motorcycles were parked nearby, each mounted by an Army MP. As the driver held open the rear door, Fleming saw that the Ford already had a passenger, a thin, middle-aged man who regarded them from behind wire-frame spectacles.

"General Donovan, Commander Fleming," he said as they took seats beside him. "Welcome to the U.S. I'm Dr. Vannevar Bush. I hope you had a pleasant flight."

"It was tolerable." Donovan didn't bother to offer a handshake. "Let's go, driver." The lieutenant who'd been sent to pick them up slammed the door shut, then climbed behind the wheel. "I take it we're going straight there."

"Of course," Dr. Bush said. "He's waiting for us." The Ford pulled away from the plane, following the two motorcycles. "I certainly hope this is as important as you've made it out to be, General. He's not someone who appreciates having his time wasted."

"I wouldn't have requested this meeting unless I thought it was." Donovan gazed straight ahead, hands resting on his knees. "MI-6 considers the document Commander Fleming is carrying to be of the highest importance, and so do I."

"I didn't think otherwise. It's just that . . ."

"Pardon me, Dr. Bush." In deference to the general, Fleming had remained quiet, but his curiosity finally prompted him to speak up. "Exactly whom are we going to see? Someone in the War Department, I assume."

"You'll eventually be attending a meeting at the Pentagon, yes. Probably more than one. But that's not our first destination." The slightest of smiles touched Bush's lips. "The next stop is the White House. The president would like to hear what you have to tell him."

Ian Fleming said nothing, but he suddenly wished that he'd been a bit more insistent on that drink. Just then, he could have used a pint. Or better, a vodka martini.

———

The briefing was held in the Cabinet Room, just down the hall from the Oval Office. Two men were already there by the time Bush, Donovan, and Fleming arrived: Cordell Hull, the Secretary of State, and Harry Stimson, the Secretary of War. Everyone had just finished introducing themselves to one another when a door at one end of the room opened and President Franklin D. Roosevelt came in.

Like most people, Fleming was aware that Roosevelt was a polio survivor. Nonetheless he was stunned to see the president seated in a wheelchair being pushed by a Negro butler; the press scrupulously avoided taking photos of Roosevelt that would show him to be a cripple, so few members of the public had seen him this way. And the president looked much older than his pictures suggested: his face had become gaunt, his eyes shadowed, his physique frail. Fleming reminded himself that the president was in his third term and had already shepherded his country through the worst economic depression in its history; no wonder he looked so worn down. Nonetheless, he almost wished that Roosevelt had let his senior cabinet members handle this meeting; the commander in chief should have stayed in bed an hour or two longer.

Yet when the president spoke, his voice was surprisingly strong. "Good morning, gentlemen. I understand you'd like to see me." He let the butler push his chair to a vacant space midway down the oak conference table that dominated the room. "Thank you, that will be all for now." The butler nodded and disappeared through the door, closing it behind him, and Roosevelt took a moment to scan the faces of the men who'd just taken seats across the table from him. "I've met everyone here before," he said, then his gaze settled upon Fleming. "Except you. May I ask who you are, sir?"

"Fleming, Mr. President . . . Lieutenant Commander Ian Fleming. I'm from His Majesty's Naval Intelligence, on temporary assignment with Section Six." At a loss for what else to do, Fleming leaned across the brightly polished table to offer a handshake. Donovan pointedly cleared his throat, and too late Fleming realized that this might have been a *faux pas*, but the president smiled and reached forward to return the handshake. Roosevelt's hand was like papyrus, his grasp almost weightless, and Fleming's impressions were confirmed: the president of the United States was seriously ill.

"Pleased to meet you, Commander Fleming." Roosevelt's gaze shifted to the thick document resting on the table between them, the one that had been in the attaché case recently manacled to Fleming's wrist. "So Bill," he said to General Donovan, "is this what brings you all the way from England?"

"Yes, sir, Mr. President," General Donovan said, "and it's the damnedest thing I've ever seen. But perhaps I should let Commander Fleming explain how we came by it. After all, it's MI-6 who should be thanked for finding it and getting it out of Germany."

Everyone looked at Fleming, and he reflexively sat up a little straighter. At least Donovan had given credit where credit was due, but no one had told him he'd be leading the briefing. Trying to hide his nervousness, he pulled the document toward him. "Yes, well . . . Mr. President, this is a translation of part of a larger report that was discovered last month by two French operatives working under deep cover at a Nazi research facility near the Baltic."

The copy was bound by brass fasteners and sealed with a paper strip that read TOP SECRET—EYES ONLY. The cover sheet bore the report's Section Six code name: BLACK UMBRELLA. Fleming tore off the strip and opened the document to the first page. "We're uncertain of exactly how the operatives came by this report since both were apparently arrested by the Gestapo shortly after it was passed to the resistance movement in Paris. We've verified its authenticity, though, and furthermore believe that it came from the office of a German scientist working at the highest levels of the German Army's weapons development program."

"Dr. Wernher von Braun," General Donovan said. "He's their leading expert in the field of rocketry. Before the war, he was involved with a civilian effort to build a manned rocket ship . . ."

"A rocket ship." Roosevelt's voice was icily skeptical. "I see."

". . . until he was conscripted by Nazis to do military research. Very little had been heard from him since then until he emerged as technical director of what my people and Section Six believe to be an effort to build long-range ballistic missiles. Acting on reports that the Germans were apparently conducting rocket research near Peenemünde, on an island off the Baltic coast, MI-6 recruited two French resistance operatives, code-named Silver and Gold, to penetrate the facility and search for information." A glance at Fleming. "Commander, please continue."

Fleming picked up the thread. "Until recently, Silver and Gold had given us little to believe that the Nazis were making much headway. According to them, their rockets tended either to blow up, sometimes even before they left the ground, or veer wildly off course and crash in the Baltic. So there wasn't much to worry about, really. However, beginning late last year, it appeared that the Nazis had taken a new tack and were apparently shifting their focus to develop something other than missiles. It wasn't until we received this report and translated it"—he tapped a finger against the top page—"that we knew what this was."

"And that is . . . ?" Harry Stimson asked.

Fleming hesitated, but Donovan didn't. "Mr. Secretary, the Germans intend to build a manned rocket vehicle capable of attacking the United States."

No one said anything for a moment. The room was so quiet, Fleming heard an automobile horn blare on Pennsylvania Avenue. "Pardon me?" President Roosevelt said at last. "They mean to build a *what*?"

"Preposterous," Cordell Hull muttered, his Tennessee accent drawing out each syllable as an indictment of its own.

"I know it seems far-fetched," Donovan said, "but my science lads have studied the report, and they assure me that it isn't as absurd as it sounds." Sliding the report away from Fleming, he turned a couple of pages to a brief preface and pointed to an initial "S" that had been signed to it. "They think this stands for Eugen Sanger, an Austrian physicist who is believed to be working for the Luftwaffe. If that's so, then this alone gives the report credibility. About ten years ago, Sanger conducted research at the University of Vienna and made major advances in rocket-fuel mixtures. He also published a monograph on space travel in which he proposed a rocket plane much like the one described here. If he's working for the Nazis, then they have an expert capable of producing a weapon that could pose a major threat to us . . . and by that, I mean the United States itself."

"I find that hard to believe." Roosevelt was openly skeptical. "America's distance from Europe is a sufficient deterrent against attack, I would think."

"Mr. President," Fleming replied, "with all due respect, that distance is an illusion."

The president's eyes widened at the young British commander's audacity. Cordell Hull scowled, and from the corner of his eye, Fleming could see Donovan regarding him with irritation. But Fleming had noticed the antiaircraft guns on the roof of the White House and knew how pitiful they would be against the weapon described in the Black Umbrella report.

"Sir, your country has been in this war for only six weeks," Fleming said. "My country has been under attack from Germany for the last eighteen months. We once thought the Channel would protect us, but it doesn't anymore. If the Nazis can assault us on a daily basis from the air, then you may rest assured that, if they can find a way to conquer the Atlantic, they will. And if they do, last month's attack on your naval base in Hawaii will seem like only a preamble."

While Fleming was speaking, Vannevar Bush quietly pulled the Black Umbrella report over to his side of the table. Hunched over the report, he closely studied it, absorbing details as fast as he could turn the pages. "Commander Fleming is correct, Mr. President," Donovan said. "I would not be wasting your time if I thought this was anything that shouldn't be considered with the utmost gravity."

Roosevelt was quiet for a moment. The skepticism had disappeared from his eyes, replaced with guarded interest. "Very well, then, General. Tell me why you're so concerned about this . . . rocket plane."

Donovan knit his hands together on the table. "In brief, what Sanger has proposed . . . and what the Nazis appear to have undertaken . . . is a rocket-propelled vehicle, nearly the size of our largest bombers, that would be launched from somewhere in Germany and ascend to an altitude well above Earth's atmosphere. It would then proceed to circle the planet in a series of shallow dives, descending and ascending again and again, so that it would skip across the top of the atmosphere like a flat stone tossed across the top of a millpond. It would continue this way, traveling eastward across Europe, Asia, and the Pacific Ocean, until it reached the North American continent. It would then make a terminal dive that would bring it within range of the East Coast, whereupon it would release its weapons . . ."

"Three incendiary bombs, each one weighing a little more than one ton," Fleming said. "The target will be Manhattan Island, in the heart of . . ."

"I know where New York is located," the president said coldly. "I was once the state governor. How do you know this is the target?"

"A targeting diagram is on the last page." Donovan pointed to the report, and Bush flipped to the end. "Unfortunately, we don't have the complete study. Apparently, our operatives were unable to photograph the entire thing. But they got enough to let us know the trajectory it would take and the means by which they can accomplish it."

Bush turned the report around to let Roosevelt see a map of the greater New York City area, with a series of concentric circles radiating outward from Midtown. "And this is the vehicle, Mr. President," he added before flipping back a couple of pages to reveal a cutaway diagram of a futuristic vehicle: stub-winged, flat-hulled, with two vertical stabilizers but lacking the familiar propellers of a conventional airplane. "Looks rather like a torpedo."

"A torpedo, yes, but much larger . . . and piloted." Donovan indicated the small figure seated inside a cockpit within the craft's sharp prow. "Putting a man aboard means that they wouldn't have to rely on an automatic guidance system. What we're talking about, really, is a long-range bomber, just one that uses rockets instead of propellers." He glanced at the Secretary of State. "Not all that improbable, once you really think about it."

Hull didn't respond, but his expression told Fleming that he was still unconvinced. "Perhaps not," Stimson said, "but I don't understand why they'd choose to fly all the way around the world to reach New York. Why not simply fly straight across the Atlantic?"

"My scientists have analyzed this," Donovan said, "and they believe that, if the craft . . . they call it *Silbervogel*, or 'Silver Bird' . . . is launched from west to east, it can take advantage of Earth's rotation to give it an additional boost during the ascent phase, thereby reducing the fuel necessary to reach outer space and increasing the payload capacity. As explained in the report itself, skipping Silver Bird along the top of the atmosphere would also allow it to achieve the necessary velocity to reach its target while further conserving fuel."

"The takeoff itself would be done on an elevated horizontal track . . ." Fleming began.

"The vehicle would be mounted on a mobile sled with another rocket engine at its rear," Bush said. Fleming was impressed; in just a few minutes of quick study, the science advisor had already gleaned the report's important details. "The rocket sled will accelerate to five hundred meters per second, and at the end of the track, the craft will be catapulted into the sky. The rest of the ascent phase will be under its own power."

"All right then." Stimson shrugged. "So we wait until we see the damn thing coming toward us, then we send interceptors to shoot it down."

"I think not, Mr. Secretary." Donovan shook his head. "By the time it reaches New York, its altitude will be seventy kilometers . . . that's about 43.5 miles, far above the range of our planes." Again, he nodded to the report. "That's the whole purpose of this operation . . . to provide the Germans with a weapon that can't be defeated."

"Not by conventional means, at any rate," Fleming added.

Bush glanced up from the document. "You have something in mind, Commander?"

He'd only been thinking out loud, yet Fleming suddenly discovered that every eye had turned toward him. President Roosevelt was looking straight across the table at him; both Stimson and Hull were waiting for

whatever he had to say, and he didn't have to look around to know that
Donovan had locked onto him as well. Perhaps he should have kept his
mouth shut, but it was too late.

"I've just been thinking"—he coughed in his hand to clear his
throat—"pardon me, I've just been thinking that, if the Germans are developing an intercontinental rocket as an offensive weapon, perhaps the
proper response should be to develop one of our own as a deterrent."

Hull made an unpleasant sputtering sound with his lips. "The proper
response should be to bomb the hell out of Peenemünde."

"Unfortunately, sir, the Germans still have air superiority over most
of Europe." Fleming shook his head. "Their radar is more effective than
we believed, and they're capable of putting interceptors in the air whenever
we launch an air raid. Only lately have we been able to send our Mosquitoes over the German borders, and even then they haven't been very effective. We've suffered major losses when we've tried daytime raids, and
high-altitude bombing runs at nighttime have missed the target more
often than not. The RAF fully intends to bomb Peenemünde . . . but not
until we're confident it won't be a suicide mission."

"I'm afraid he's right, Mr. President," Stimson said. "We're a long way
from successfully mounting air raids deep within German territory." He
nodded to Fleming. "Go on, Commander. I'm interested in what you have
to say about building a rocket deterrent of our own."

The last thing Fleming wanted to admit was that he barely had an
inkling of what he himself had just suggested. All he could do was wing
it. "I'm just thinking that . . . well, if aircraft can't intercept Silver Bird,
and it's beyond range of ground artillery, maybe the solution should be
to tackle the problem by much the same means . . . we construct a rocket
of our own to shoot it down."

Again, no one spoke for several moments. "All this sounds rather far-
fetched, Mr. President," Hull said at last, still not persuaded.

"Cordell, I couldn't agree more, but . . ." Roosevelt sighed, shook his
head. "We can't afford to take that chance. We've already had one sneak
attack. We can't have another, particularly not on the American mainland."

"I agree, Mr. President," Bush said. "The public is still reeling from what happened at Pearl Harbor. If the Nazis dropped a bomb on New York . . ." He let out his breath. "I'm not sure which would be worse, the actual damage and loss of life or what it would do to home-front morale."

"You have a point there." Roosevelt nodded. "Having the Nazis be able to launch an attack on American soil is unacceptable." He paused reflectively, staring at the document as if it were a rattlesnake. "So what do you think? Can we build a rocket capable of shooting down this thing?"

Bush absentmindedly drummed his fingers on the table. "If this report is correct, the Nazis have a long head start on us. If we decide to get into this, it will have to be crash program . . ."

"Like the one we have already? The Manhattan District project, I mean." Catching a curious look from Donovan, Roosevelt gave him a dismissive wave of the hand. "Nothing to be concerned about, General. Just a military construction program we've lately undertaken."

Somehow, Fleming had a sense that it was far more than that. He didn't say anything, though, as Bush went on. "Yes, sir . . . although, in this case, we have even more to go on. After all, the Manhattan project is based on little more than conjecture and a recommendation from . . . ah, a couple of physicists." He laid a hand on the Black Umbrella report. "Here, we have tangible evidence."

"Sounds to me like you're suggesting that we shift our resources from one program to another."

"If it comes to that, yes, sir. In fact, if this is where the Nazis are putting their resources, I'd recommend that we discontinue that program entirely. After all, we're pursuing that line of research mainly because, up until now, we've believed that's what they're doing. If they're not . . ."

"Understood." The president nodded.

"Which brings us back to your original question. Can we build a rocket of our own?" Bush shrugged. "The truth of the matter, Mr. President, is that because we don't have a rocket-development program, we'll have to create one from scratch. And fast."

"I see." Roosevelt pondered this for a moment. "So . . . the Germans have von Braun and Sanger. Do we have anyone who knows just as much about this sort of thing as they do?"

"Yes, sir, we do, but . . ." Bush hesitated.

"Who is he?"

"Goddard, sir . . . Dr. Robert H. Goddard." A wan smile. "And even if we can find him, I'm not sure he'll work for us. I'm afraid he has . . . um, a bit of a history when it comes to dealing with our military."

"I don't care," Roosevelt said. "Find him, Van, and tell him that he's now the most important scientist in America."

Hiding a smile behind a raised hand, Ian Fleming felt a surge of satisfaction. During the long overnight flight across the Atlantic, he'd been kept awake by the thought that the Americans wouldn't take Black Umbrella seriously. He'd been afraid that Yankee conservatism would win out over the willingness to imagine what had once been unthinkable. Yet once again, President Roosevelt had turned out to be a visionary leader. He was willing to do whatever it took to protect his country even if it meant stepping into the unknown.

Fleming had no idea how this would all turn out. *But when you stop to think of it,* he mused, *it would make a really smashing novel.*

NELL'S FATHER

"Company's coming," Esther Goddard said.

Henry Morse looked up from the counter where he was peeling potatoes. Through the open kitchen window, he spotted a dusty fantail rising from the dirt road leading across the New Mexico grasslands to Mescalero Ranch. Esther's voice came from the front porch, where she'd been taking a break from preparing lunch to have a cigarette and read the morning paper.

"They're early, I think." Henry dropped the potatoes in a bowl and wiped his hands on a terry-cloth towel. The car was still a mile away, but they already knew who was in it and where they were coming from. "Must have followed the directions I gave them and turned right at the second cow instead of the first."

Esther laughed. The fifteen-acre ranch was notoriously hard to find by anyone who wasn't a local, which was just the way the Goddards and everyone else who lived out there liked it. Henry heard the rustle of newspaper as she put aside the *Roswell Morning Dispatch*. "Think I should get Bob, or . . . ?"

"No, not yet." Henry carried the potatoes over to the stove, where

Esther would fry them. "Let's talk to these guys first. If they're not serious, then we can always tell 'em that Bob's gone fishing or . . ."

"Fishing?" Another laugh. Esther had a point; *gone fishing* was a weak excuse when you're living at the edge of the desert.

"Or something, I dunno." Henry shoved his shirttails into his trousers. He briefly considered going to his bedroom to grab a necktie but decided against it. No one out here put on a tie unless he was going into town for dinner and a movie. If their visitors didn't like the informality of Mescalero Ranch, they could go back to Washington. "We'll tell 'em we needed milk, and he went in search of the nearest cow." *Or rattlesnake,* he silently added. *If these guys are from the Pentagon, they might actually believe that.*

Esther still hadn't gotten up from her seat when Henry swung the screen door open and stepped out onto the porch. After the coolness of the ranch house's adobe walls, the dry warmth of a Southwestern winter day was almost enough to make him start sweating. As they watched the car rattle across the cattle guard at the front gate, Esther crossed her legs beneath her short summer skirt and tipped her straw sun hat forward a bit to shade her eyes. When she made no effort to rise, Henry knew it was his job to greet their guests and shoo them away if necessary.

The car was a four-door Pontiac sedan, khaki brown with a serial number stenciled across the driver-side door. Probably from the motor pool at Albuquerque Army Air Base, where their visitors had flown in earlier this morning. The Army was currently building another airfield in Alamogordo, much closer to Roswell, but its runways hadn't been finished yet. The Pontiac came to a stop beneath the cottonwood out front, and Henry waited until the two men inside climbed out before he ambled down the steps to meet them.

"Can I help you, gentlemen?" he asked.

Both men wore Army uniforms. Although they'd had the good sense to take off their jackets and loosen their ties, Henry wondered why anyone wanting to keep a low profile would wear uniforms in a place where dressing up meant putting on a clean shirt. The corporal driving the car didn't look old enough to buy a beer in the enlisted men's club, but his companion—the silver eagles pinned to his collar told Henry that he was a colonel—was almost Bob's age, with a small pot at his belly and dark brown hair turning grey at the temples.

"Yes, sir . . . I mean, I hope you can." The corporal squinted at him, his stammer betraying uncertainty about his location. "We're looking for . . . um . . ."

"We're trying to find someone who lives around here," the colonel said. "Professor Robert H. Goddard, from Clark University in Massachusetts." His gaze flitted to the renovated adobe house. "Is he present?"

"And who might you be?" Henry absently scuffed a toe of his work boots against the driveway sand.

The colonel's mouth pursed slightly. He obviously wasn't accustomed to being questioned. He looked past Henry to the woman casually seated in a rocking chair on the front porch. "Mrs. Goddard, I presume?"

"Perhaps." Esther coolly studied him from behind her rimless spectacles, not giving him an inch. Henry suppressed a smile. Esther was a woman who knew Charles Lindbergh as "Slim" and called one of the richest men in the country "Harry"; she was not easily impressed by a bird colonel. "You still haven't told us who you are."

"Colonel Omar Bliss, of the U.S. Army command in Washington, D.C. This is my aide, Corporal Max Hillman."

"Hello, ma'am." Hillman gave her a polite nod. Henry noted that his eyes were traveling up and down Esther, taking her in, probably believing that she was ten years younger than her actual age. She affected every guy that way when they met her for the first time; even at forty, she'd managed to hold on to her looks, elegant and sublimely sensual. *If you think her legs are swell,* Henry thought, *just wait till you get to her brains.*

"Hello to you, too," Esther replied, favoring the kid with a smile that probably stopped his heart for a moment. "Yes, this is Dr. Goddard's place," she continued, standing up from her chair and sauntering down the steps. "And yes, we've been expecting you. Thanks for calling in advance. We're not crazy about having people show up unannounced."

"You're welcome, ma'am." Bliss was still being patient, but only barely.

Esther didn't faze him in the slightest. "Now, if I could see your hus-band . . . ?"

"Dr. Goddard is busy at the moment. He's gone fishing." Esther didn't care about the absurdity of her lie. "If you could tell me why you're here, I . . ."

"Sorry, ma'am, but that's official business. I'm not at liberty to discuss it with anyone but him."

"Really? Oh, well, then . . ." Esther nodded toward the gate. "Quickest way back is to head down Mescalero Road until you get to town. Turn right at Route 285, then . . ."

"Esther?" A voice came from the screen door. It creaked open, slammed shut. "Who's here?"

Everyone looked toward Robert Goddard as he stepped out onto the porch. Even for Mescalero Ranch, his appearance was sloppy: baggy trousers with loose suspenders, dirty undershirt, worn-out loafers with no socks. Oil stains on his hands showed that he'd just come from the workshop; Henry guessed that he'd come in through the back door. His question was most likely a ruse; he'd probably been standing just inside the house for a little while, eavesdropping on the conversation.

"These men have come to see you, Doctor G," Esther said, using her favorite nickname for him. "Colonel Bliss says it's about something so important that he can't discuss it with anyone but you."

"Oh, really?" Tucking his hands in his pockets, Goddard ambled down the porch steps. "Well, now . . . did the Army finally change its mind about that shoulder-fired rocket I offered them?"

Henry grinned. Everyone who worked with Bob was familiar with the story. During the last war, Goddard had developed a prototype for a portable solid-fuel artillery rocket that an individual soldier could carry onto the battlefield for use as a tactical weapon. The rocket had worked well during field demonstrations, yet the Army had given it a pass. With the "war to end all wars" coming to an end, many in the War Department believed that the coming armistice would make new weapons unnecessary.

In the end, several years of research and development had been wasted, and Bob had come away empty-handed. He'd been skeptical about working for the military ever since. Not that he needed War Department funds anymore. Clark University and the Smithsonian had underwritten his research during the twenties, and for the last twelve years he'd been the beneficiary of a sizable private grant from the Guggenheim family. So he didn't need to go fishing; in fact, he could tell Colonel Bliss to go jump in a lake.

"No, sir, this is something different." Bliss looked him straight in the eye. "I've been sent here to consult with you about a project of the highest priority . . . one which we believe you are uniquely qualified to handle."

"Oh?" Goddard raised an eyebrow. "And who is 'we'? Besides yourself, I mean."

Bliss didn't immediately respond. Instead, he reached into a pocket and pulled out an envelope. Without a word, he handed it to Goddard. Curious, Henry glanced over Bob's shoulder. The envelope itself was blank, but when Goddard pulled out the typewritten letter inside and unfolded it, Henry caught a glimpse of the letterhead. It was from the White House.

Stepping aside, Goddard read the letter. For a few seconds, he said nothing, until at last he slowly let out his breath and looked up at the colonel again. "I see," he said softly as he handed the letter to Esther. "This changes everything."

"I thought you might say that." Bliss turned to Hillman. "Corporal, would you please get the report? Dr. Goddard, it may be easier if you simply read what we've brought you. It'll explain things a bit better than I could."

As he spoke, Henry walked over to Esther. "Is that from who I think it's from?" he whispered. She silently nodded but folded the letter before he could read it.

Hillman returned to the car, came back with an attaché case. Using a key to open it, he pulled out a thick manila folder. As the corporal handed it to Goddard, Bliss said, "I'd prefer it if you'd read this by yourself and not discuss it with anyone."

"I'll read it alone," Goddard said, "but I won't make any promises about the second condition." He nodded toward Esther and Henry. "My wife and Mr. Morse here are two of my closest assistants, as are the two other men who are my employees. Anything I may agree to do for you, I'll need their help. Keeping this a secret from them is out of the question."

Bliss hesitated. "All right, have it your way. But we'll need to have them sign security agreements . . . and the FBI will probably want to check their backgrounds, too."

"Uh-oh," Esther said, giving Henry a sly wink. "You're in trouble now."

Bliss looked at her sharply. "Why? Is there something we should know about?"

"Henry has suspicious political affiliations."

The colonel's eyes narrowed as he turned to Henry. "You're a Communist?"

"Worse than that . . . he's a Republican." Goddard had already opened the folder and was peering at the document inside. "I wouldn't worry about my associates, Colonel. They've all signed confidentiality agreements with me. Esther, please take our guests inside and give them some lunch. Henry, ask Lloyd and Taylor if they'll come in, too. I'll be in my office."

"Okay, Doctor G," she said, but he'd already turned away and begun walking back up the stairs, tripping slightly on the first riser. "Colonel, Corporal . . ."

The two Army men nodded and followed her. Henry watched them go, then headed for the assembly shed behind the main house. He still hadn't any idea what this was about, but if the president's signature was on the letter Bliss had presented Bob, then it was a good bet this couldn't be about shoulder-fired missiles.

———

Lunch was enchiladas with fried potatoes, served at the battered pinewood table that took up most of the dining room. Taylor Brickell and Lloyd Kapman were there as well, both of them just as oil-stained and filthy as Bob. The rocket men cleaned themselves up before coming to the table, but Colonel Bliss wrinkled his nose a bit when he saw them. Henry couldn't blame him; except for Esther, everyone at Mescalero Ranch looked like an automobile mechanic.

Bob didn't join them for lunch. From his office at the back of the house, they could hear Bach playing on the old windup Victrola he and Esther had brought with them from Worcester. At one point, Henry got up to visit the bathroom. On the way there, he passed Bob's office. The door was half-open, and through it he saw Goddard leaning back in his armchair with his feet propped up on the desk, intently studying the report while smoking one of his foul black cigars. Bob didn't look up even though Henry's footsteps caused the floorboards to creak, and Henry knew that his former professor was completely riveted by what he was reading.

Conversation at the lunch table was light. Inevitably, the subject turned to why the Goddards had moved from Worcester, Massachusetts, to this remote corner of New Mexico almost twelve years ago even though Bob continued to serve as the chairman of Clark University's physics department. The most obvious reason, of course, was Bob's health. The New England climate had never been kind to the tuberculosis Goddard had suffered since childhood. Indeed, it had very nearly killed him when he was a teenager; at one point, his doctors had given him only a couple of weeks to live ("He got better," Esther said, an understatement if there ever was one). The dry Southwestern air allowed him to breathe freely for the first time in his life; nonetheless, he still smoked, a habit that he'd picked up from his father.

The main reason, though, was the nature of his research. The first rockets Robert Goddard built—including the world's first liquid-fuel rocket, launched on March 16, 1926—were sent up from his Aunt Effie's hilltop farm in Auburn, Massachusetts, just south of Worcester. Goddard kept them secret for quite a long time because he wanted to protect his designs from imitators—particularly Hermann Oberth, the German scientist whom Bob knew was pursuing the same line of research—yet public discovery was inevitable once he was awarded patents and published his work as a Smithsonian Institution monograph.

"When that happened, the newspapers were all over him," Esther said.

"Before he knew it, every reporter in America wanted to do an interview with him. And they all wanted to know when he was going to build that rocket to the Moon."

"A moon rocket?" Hillman still hadn't been able to take his eyes off Esther. Henry couldn't blame him. With her sun hat gone and her soft blond hair cascading down around her shoulders, she was as lovely as a desert rose. "Why would they think he's building something like that?"

"At the end of the paper, Bob speculated that it might be possible to fire a rocket to the Moon with an explosive charge aboard, to blow up when it crashes there so that astronomers could see it and know that it had arrived." Esther reached for the lemonade pitcher. "Of course, it was just idle speculation on his part . . ."

"Aw, c'mon, Esther . . . you know that's not entirely true." Lloyd polished off the last of his enchilada and wiped his mouth with a napkin. A small, gnomish man with curly black hair, he peered at her over the top of his glasses. "Bob's intent all along has been to build something that will take him into outer space. And not just to the Moon, either. He wants to go to Mars."

"Mars?" Bliss was incredulous.

Henry winced. Lloyd might just well have said that Mescalero Ranch was in the business of weaving magic carpets. "It's Bob's dream to construct a vehicle that one day"—he carefully emphasized this—"might be capable of transporting people to another planet. He's had this ambition his entire life, ever since he read *The War of the Worlds* as a kid. But that's not what we're doing here, Colonel. We're just taking the first steps."

"Anyway, if the press wasn't bad enough, there was also . . . well, the accidents." Ice chuckled in Esther's glass as she poured herself some more lemonade. "The big one in particular. One of those rockets went off course and crashed, starting a small fire that the Auburn fire department had to put out. When the local papers heard about it, they claimed that it was a giant moon rocket and that it had blown up."

"Yeah, that was a good one." A bit on the chubby side, Taylor Brickell had a round and pleasant face that made him look more like a stock clerk than an aeronautical engineer. "I liked that almost as much as the *New York Times* saying that Bob's a crackpot because everyone knows rockets wouldn't be able to work in space because . . ."

"There's no air for them to push against." Bliss smiled. "I know . . . I read that story in his intelligence file."

Esther shot him a surprised glance. "Army intelligence has a file on Bob?"

"You didn't think we'd completely forgotten about him, do you?" The colonel shook his head. "Granted, we sort of lost track of him after he stopped using Camp Devens as a test area . . . why did he do that, anyway? It's a perfectly good place to launch rockets."

"Are you kidding?" Henry almost laughed out loud. "Sorry, Colonel. I know the Army was trying to be generous, letting him use that place . . . but it was a marsh, for God's sake. Mud, mosquitoes, briar patches . . ."

"The Army meant well," Esther said, cutting him off, "but it was unsuitable for our purposes. Besides, with Bob's now spending so much time outdoors, we felt we needed to leave Massachusetts. Auburn passed ordinances prohibiting rocket launches in town limits, and Clark University wasn't keen on his working with explosive materials on campus, so we started looking elsewhere."

"And that's how we landed here." Lloyd leaned back in his chair, cradling his head in his hands behind his neck. "Thanks to Harry Guggenheim. He bought the land we're on and writes the checks."

"Yes, I understand that's where your funds have been coming from," Bliss said. "Him and Charles Lindbergh."

"My . . . you have been keeping tabs on us, haven't you?" Esther's eyes were as sharp as tacks.

"As I said, we've been keeping an eye on him . . . somewhat." Bliss hesitated. "Matter of fact, Mrs. Goddard, I'm a big fan of your husband's work. I studied his work when I was an engineering student at MIT."

"You're an MIT grad?" Taylor asked, obviously surprised to find a fellow alumnus at the table.

Bliss smiled and raised his left hand to show off his class ring, turned around on his finger so that the beaver etched upon its face has its paddle-like tail pointed toward the person looking at it: *kiss my tail*, as the in-joke went. "That's why the Army sent me," he said. "If Dr. Goddard agrees to help us . . ."

"Then I'd be working for you, is that it?"

Unnoticed until just then, Goddard had quietly walked into the dining room, the thick folder cradled under his arm. Everyone looked around as he came to the table. "Is there any lunch left, dear," he asked his wife, "or did you eat everything?"

"No, there's some enchiladas left." Esther reached for the pan that Taylor had been eying hungrily. "Sit down and . . ."

"That's all right. I'm not sure I have an appetite left." Goddard took the vacant seat at the end of the table, carefully placing the folder between him and Bliss. He let out his breath as a long sigh as he turned to the colonel. "This is . . . one hell of a thing you've brought me. One hell of a thing."

"Isn't it, though?" Bliss solemnly nodded. "It startled me, too, when I read it."

Henry started to pick up the report, but Hillman reached forward to stop him. "I'm sorry, sir, but it's . . ."

"Go ahead and let him see it, Corporal." Bliss shook his head. "I'll trust them to abide by their agreement with Dr. Goddard. Besides, if he agrees to work for us, he'll probably want to pick his own men, and Mr. Morse here will undoubtedly be one of them." He glanced at Goddard. "Isn't that right, sir?"

Goddard didn't reply but instead opened the folder and ruffled the report's pages. Henry caught a glimpse of single-spaced type, equations, diagrams. "I'd love to know how you came about getting your hands on this, but I imagine that's a long story."

"It is. For now, let's just say that a couple of men probably gave up their lives in order for us to see this, and be grateful for their sacrifice." A quiet gasp from Esther, and the colonel looked in her direction. "Yes, ma'am, it's that important."

"What is it, Bob?" Lloyd asked. "Are the Germans building rockets, too?"

"Worse than that. They're working on something that goes beyond anything we've done here." Goddard absently ran a hand across the hairless top of his head, almost as if he'd come down with a sudden fever. "I've known that they've been doing rocket research for quite some time, ever since their man Oberth wrote to me and requested that I send him the technical details of my own work . . ."

"You didn't, did you?" Bliss stared at him in horror.

"Oh, of course not. Besides the fact that I have my patents to protect, I had little doubt that they hadn't overlooked the military implications. And when Hitler took over . . ." He shook his head. "No, whatever progress they've made, they've achieved it without my assistance. But I'd never suspected that they'd moved so fast, so quickly. Oberth . . ."

"We don't think Hermann Oberth is directly involved with this. The Nazis have found other people instead . . . a fellow by name of Wernher von Braun, and another chap named Eugen Sanger. Heard of either of them?"

"Von Braun, yes . . . he's Oberth's protégé. A very talented young man. Sanger, though, I don't know." Goddard tapped a finger against the report. "And you say this is his proposal?"

"It's Sanger's work, yes, but von Braun appears to be the man the Nazis put in charge of actually implementing it." Bliss paused. "Do you think it's possible, sir? I mean, it's not just some pipe dream but something the Nazis could actually pull off?"

Goddard drummed his fingers against the table for a few moments as he regarded the report Henry still hadn't picked up. "If they have enough money and people to throw at it," he said at last, "yes, I think they could. There's nothing there that isn't possible."

"I see." Bliss hesitated. "And do you think you could find a way to defeat it . . . that is, if you had enough money and people of your own?"

As an answer, Goddard pushed back his chair. "Come with me, Colonel," he said, standing up. "I'd like to show you something."

Colonel Bliss rose from the table to follow Goddard. Everyone else fell in behind them as they walked through the house to the back door.

––––––

The shed located out back wasn't much to look at, a T-shaped wood-frame workshop about sixty feet in length, with windows running along its sides. Goddard led everyone through one of the two doors set side by side at the short end of the shed; past a row of offices and storerooms was a large laboratory with a bare wooden floor, the ceiling's rafters supported by slender beams. The lab was filled with machine tools of all kinds—metal lathes, drills, acetylene torches—and its walls were lined with shelves and workbenches, with canvas aprons hanging from hooks near the door.

In the middle of the room, lying atop a long assembly table, was a rocket. About thirty feet long, it looked like an enormous silver pencil made of duralumin. Panels had been removed from its sides to expose its interior: three cylindrical fuel tanks, with insulated pipes and compact fuel pumps leading from one another, everything feeding into the combustion chamber at the aft end. The nose cone had been closed—it would eventually be reopened so that the rocket's recording instruments and parachute could be fitted into it—and the four guidance fins were stacked against the wall, waiting to be attached.

"This is Nell," Goddard said, fondly laying a hand upon the rocket's side.

"Nell 21, to be exact," Henry added. "They've all had the same name."

Bliss gave him a questioning look, and Esther laughed. "We started naming the rockets Nell after the crash at Aunt Effie's farm. There were so many mistakes in the newspaper that it reminded us of a line from a Broadway musical: 'They ain't done right by our Nell.'"

"Cute," Hillman murmured, then turned red as he caught an angry glance from Esther. "No offense, ma'am, but . . . sorry, I never would've thought of giving a rocket a girl's name."

Esther said nothing, but Henry knew that the corporal had touched a sore spot. The Goddards never had children, nor would they ever. Bob's doctors didn't want Esther to even kiss her husband, for fear that she might contract tuberculosis; raising a family was out of the question. Esther was nineteen years younger than Bob, and surely the thought of having children with him had crossed her mind, but so far as Henry could tell, their relationship had always been more cerebral than physical. Theirs was a love affair of the mind, and Nell was their spiritual daughter.

"Yes, well . . ." Goddard made an uncomfortable grunt. "As Henry says, this is the twenty-first rocket we've built since we've been in New Mexico, and so far we've had a pretty good success rate. Three years ago, one of Nell's sisters set the altitude record for an unmanned aircraft . . . 6,565 feet at sea level, although from here the actual altitude was 3,294 from ground level." He paused, then added, "Of course, the Germans may well have exceeded this, but we'll never know."

Bliss strolled down the length of the table, bending down now and then to closely inspect features of the half-finished rocket. "Very impressive . . . and you've had how many people working on this?"

"Just the five of us," Taylor said, arms folded proudly across his chest.

"And how much does Mr. Guggenheim give you each year for your research?"

"Our annual budget is $10,000," Esther replied.

"I see." Bliss looked up from the rocket. "Dr. Goddard, your Uncle Sam is willing to write you a blank check and give you as many men as you need to complete your research, provided that you deliver us a rocket capable of shooting down whatever the Nazis put up. But I don't think I have to tell you what the challenges are. You've reached an altitude of almost seven thousand feet . . ."

"I know." Goddard's expression was stoical. "And you need something that can reach forty-three miles, at least."

"What?" Henry couldn't believe what he'd just heard. He stared at the colonel. "Are you kidding?"

"I wish I was, but I'm not." Bliss calmly gazed back at him. "And we need to do this as soon as possible, or else . . ."

"A lot of people will die," Goddard finished, "and it's possible that

Germany will win the war. You'll see what he's talking about when you read the report." He looked at Bliss again. "All right, Colonel, you've got me. Consider me your man."

"Glad to hear it, sir." Bliss smiled and nodded. "So . . . what's the first thing you need to get started?"

"People. I need people . . . the right people."

GODDARD'S PEOPLE

=======

"That's where we come in," Jack Cube said.

By then, everyone in the living room had settled in for a long story. Douglas Walker was surprised that so many people had gathered here; surely, they'd heard the tale so often that they could probably recite it themselves. Perhaps they were only being polite to the three old men sitting near the fireplace, or maybe it was a ritual part of these get-togethers, yet he suspected it was something different. This was something they never got tired of hearing; it had become the folklore of their extended family, a story retold again and again because it brought meaning to the reunions.

In any case, even the children had become quiet as J. Jackson Jackson, Henry Morse, and Lloyd Kapman took turns recounting the events leading up to this historic day seventy years ago. Through the door leading to the adjacent kitchen could be heard the sounds of wives and mothers cleaning up from the picnic. Otherwise, everyone's attention was focused on the surviving members of the 390 Group.

"See, here's a part most people don't know." Henry took a sip from the beer he'd been nursing. "Even when they've heard of Operation Blue

Horizon, they think the guys who worked on it just materialized from nowhere. Bob snapped his fingers and, abracadabra, there we were. What they don't realize is that it's almost a miracle that we were able to come together on such short notice."

"Bob knew some . . . of us already," Lloyd said, speaking haltingly in between breaths. He had a beer as well, although he'd barely touched it. "Henry and I . . . and Taylor, too . . . were already at the ranch when . . . Bliss showed up. We had been working with . . . Bob and Esther . . . since after they'd moved from Worcester. Bob recruited us . . . to help him build the rockets he made . . . once he left Massachusetts."

"The ones he built after the Clark University rockets that he launched from his aunt's farm," Walker said.

"Right," said Henry, "so we were already on tap. Bob had found Taylor, Lloyd, and me after reading papers we'd published in various technical journals, but he knew that, for something like this, he'd need more than just the three of us and Esther. He had to find more guys with practical knowledge of liquid-fuel rockets, and in 1942 there were damn few people who had that kind of know-how." He chuckled. "In America, anyway. We knew several more, but they were all in Germany."

"Couldn't really . . . ask them," Lloyd wheezed, and several people laughed.

Jack Cube stretched out his legs. "The fortunate thing is, because there were so few people like that, most of us already either knew each other, or at least knew about each other," he said. "The main organization for this sort of thing was the American Rocket Society, which started off as sort of an amateur club but had begun doing research of its own before the war. They'd asked Bob if he wanted to join as sort of a senior advisor, but he declined because he didn't want to share any proprietary information . . ."

"Bob was very protective of his patents," Henry added. "People thought he was shy, and he was, but the main reason why he was so reclusive was because he didn't want to share the details of his research before he found a way to make money from it."

"Yes, right, of course." Jack Cube waved an impatient hand. "But even though he wasn't involved with the ARS, he knew a lot of people who were, and he knew which ones were serious engineers and not just science fiction fans . . ."

"Don't knock science fiction fans," Henry said, interrupting him again. "That's how we found Mike Ferris. He used to write letters to *Astounding Science Fiction*, which both Taylor and I read . . ."

"Weren't you . . . trying to get stuff published in . . . that magazine at the time?" Lloyd asked.

"You remember that?" Henry grinned. "Yeah, I had a typewriter set up in my room at the ranch, and whenever I had spare time, I'd bang out a story or two. So did Bob, as a matter of fact, but for him it was just a hobby. He never seriously tried to get anything published." He shrugs. "I eventually sold a few stories, but that wasn't until after the war, and no one remembers them anymore. Anyway, that's how Taylor and I found Mike, who was studying aeronautical engineering at Caltech at the time."

"Mike Ferris and Harry Chung were the only guys we recruited from Caltech," Jack Cube said. "It had the Guggenheim Aeronautical Laboratory, but Bob didn't trust GALCIT even though Harry Guggenheim was funding them as well. The whole patent-protection thing. Mike only got in because he knew a lot about solid-fuel propulsion, and . . . well, we didn't want the other guy they had."

"John Whiteside Parsons." Henry scowled. "Brilliant, but . . . ah, rather unstable."

"Creepy," Lloyd agreed, shaking his head.

"When the FBI did a background check on him," Henry continued, "they discovered that he had an unhealthy interest in the occult. He was pen pals with Aleister Crowley and belonged to the California branch of the Church of Satan, and . . . anyway, when the feds found that out, they considered him to be too much of a security risk. Which was too bad, because we could've used him. But Mike had worked with Parsons, so he knew almost as much as he did, so . . ."

"The FBI also gave us some trouble with Hamilton Ballou," Jack said.

"Taylor knew him from MIT and recommended him as a liquid-fuel chemist, but when the feds looked into him, they discovered that Ham had once belonged to the Communist Party. Of course, Ham had been a commie just the same way a lot of other kids were in the thirties . . . sort of a liberal fad, before most people learned that Russia wasn't the workers' paradise it was cracked up to be. He'd dropped out long before Taylor met him, but he'd signed the petitions that put him on the FBI watch list, and it took a lot of smooth talking by both Bob and Colonel Bliss to get him cleared."

"The feds weren't happy with . . . Harry Chung either," Lloyd said.

"Yeah, Harry was also at GALCIT when the war broke out. A few weeks after Pearl Harbor, though, he and his wife were rounded up and sent to an internment camp." Jack gave a disgusted snort. "Didn't matter that he was third-generation Chinese-American or that he'd been born and raised in San Francisco. Anyone with yellow skin was considered suspicious, and the feds really didn't want a guy like him working on a top secret military project. But Bob knew his work as an aeronautical engineer, so he twisted the FBI's arm until they surrendered."

"They weren't wild about a guy with black skin either, as I recall," Henry said quietly.

"The FBI didn't think I was a security risk," Jack replied, a crooked smile on his face. "They just couldn't believe a black man would know enough about rockets to make him worth military deferral. And to tell the truth, I wanted to be in the service. After I got out of Tuskegee University with a degree in mechanical engineering, the first thing I did was join the Army Air Corps, so I was in flight school when I got the call. Again, it was a matter of connections. Mike Ferris knew about me because we were both ARS members and had been trading letters back and forth, and we both knew about Gerry Mander because . . ."

"Gerry was the wild card," Lloyd said.

"Yeah, he was the deuce, all right." Henry smiled at the thought. "The rest of us were college boys, but Gerry's formal education stopped at high school. He was a farm boy from Alabama, and his family didn't have enough money to send him to college. That didn't stop him, though, once the space bug bit him. He built his own rocket from bits and pieces of scrap metal, going by what he'd read in magazines and library books about Bob's first rockets. Pretty remarkable, when you stop to think about it."

"But he didn't know anything about gyroscopes," Jack said, "so when he launched it from a cow pasture on his family's property, it spun out and crashed through the roof of a neighbor's barn. The kerosene he was using for fuel blew up and set the place on fire, and it burned to the ground before the fire department got there."

"Had to . . . spring him from jail," Lloyd said. "Gerry was . . . working on a road crew . . . when Colonel Bliss showed up to . . . offer him a job with us. He said, 'Sounds like a . . . nice idea. Let me . . . think about it.'"

"I never heard that," Walker said, laughing along with everyone else in the room. "How did Bob know about him?"

"He didn't," Jack said. "Mike and I had both read about Gerry's experiment in the ARS newsletter, and we thought that any kid with that much gumption belonged on our team. Bob agreed, so we recruited him."

"Gerry was the last guy to join the team," Henry said. "He was also the youngest . . . I think he was only nineteen when he showed up . . . but not by much. Most of us were in our early twenties, although Taylor was about thirty, if I remember correctly."

"I was . . . almost in my thirties, too," Lloyd added.

"I stand corrected." Henry shook his head, smiling at the fond memory. "We were all kids, really, kind of a band of misfits. Too smart for our own good, socially awkward, not really fitting in well with anyone around us. I think there's a name for guys like us . . ." He looked over at his great-grandson. "What's the word I'm looking for, Carl?"

"Geeks," Carl said.

"Thank you . . . yeah, that's what we were. Depression-era rocket geeks." Henry shrugged. "Probably just as well that Bob got to us before the Army did. Of course, Jack here is probably the only guy a draft board wouldn't have rejected as 4F . . . but even if they hadn't, I don't think any of us would've lasted a day in North Africa or Sicily."

"Not that New England was much better." Jack looked around the room. "You wouldn't believe how cold this place gets in the middle of winter. There was one time . . ."

"That brings me to the next thing I'd like to know," Walker said quickly, not wanting anyone to get ahead of himself and thus lose the chronological thread of the story. "Once the team was selected, why did you go to Worcester? That's where Blue Horizon got started, of course . . ."

"The R&D work, yes," Henry said. "Everything else stayed in New Mexico."

"Right . . . at Alamogordo Army Air Field, once the project was relocated from Mescalero Ranch."

"Uh-huh, that's correct. The ranch wasn't big enough for the job. Besides, everyone in Roswell knew that Bob was building rockets out there, and Colonel Bliss didn't want anything being done in a place where just about anyone could drive up and see what was going on. So the decision was made to move everything to Alamogordo . . ."

"But not the rocket team. You were sent to Massachusetts. Why?"

"For a couple of reasons," Jack said. "The first was that the people in the War Department wanted their brain trust as close to them as possible, so they could easily keep tabs on what we were doing. They'd put Omar Bliss in charge of the project, but even he was something of a . . . y'know, a wild card, to use that term again . . ."

"We didn't know it then, but Omar was something of a geek, too." Henry grinned. "The only person who didn't think he was as weird as a three-dollar bill was Vannevar Bush, who'd met him at some Pentagon conference. That's why Bush put Omar in charge . . . he was the one person in the War Department who didn't think space travel was something straight out of the funny pages."

"Anyway," Jack continued, "some of the big brass weren't sure they could depend on the colonel to lead something as important as this. As for the rest of us . . ."

"They trusted us . . . even less," Lloyd said.

"Right," Henry said. "Worcester was close enough to Washington that the big shots in the Pentagon felt like they had us under control, but far enough away that we'd be out of sight of any German spies who might be lurking around D.C." His smile faded. "They were wrong, of course, but . . ."

"The other reason was Bob himself," Jack said. "Bliss was bothered by Bob's hands-on engineering approach. When the colonel heard that he and the other guys would fuel the Nell rockets themselves and even go out to the launch tower to make last-minute adjustments . . ."

"Like we had a choice," Henry said. "It was just the five of us. We didn't have a ground crew."

"Anyway, Bliss didn't want to risk having Bob or the rest of us getting blown to kingdom come, so he decided to move us across the country. And again, the logical place to put us was in Worcester."

"Bob wasn't happy about that at all," Henry said. "He and Esther had been living in Roswell for quite a while. They put down roots in the community, and I think they would've been happy to stay there for the rest of their lives. Officially, he was still on the Clark faculty and was still drawing a salary as its physics department chairman, but he didn't go back very often. So moving back to Massachusetts . . ."

"He . . . didn't want to," Lloyd rasped. "He fought like crazy to . . . stay in Roswell."

"Yeah, well . . . he did fight, all right, but this is the U.S. Army we're talking about, and during wartime . . ." Henry shook his head. "I thought they were wrong, too. I told Bliss he was making a mistake. But the colonel had his orders, and they came straight from the top. Blue Horizon . . . that was the code name the Army had given the project by then . . . was to be relocated to Worcester, and that was final."

"And that's . . . when we all got . . . to meet each other," Lloyd said.

LAST TRAIN TO WORCESTER

FEBRUARY 9, 1942

J. Jackson Jackson awoke to the screech of railcar brakes, the swaying vibration of the train slowing down. Opening his eyes, he looked out the frost-rimmed window beside him to see the lights of a small city coming into view. The night was overcast, the moon hidden by dark clouds, but in the glow of streetlamps he caught a glimpse of narrow streets blanketed by fresh snow.

"Worcester!" The conductor walked down the aisle, calling out the place where the train was making its next stop. "Worcester, Massachusetts!" He pronounced the name in a nasal Yankee brogue that silenced the "ch" and dragged out the "er." *Woostah*, not *Wore-chester*, the way Jackson had been pronouncing it all along; he made a mental note of this.

Jackson's fellow passengers stirred from the uncomfortable naps they'd been taking since the previous stop in Hartford. Everyone here was black, including the conductor. Their car was just behind the locomotive, with the baggage car separating it from the rest of the coaches; it was an antique, the seats' upholstery old and faded, the windows grimed with engine smoke. Since Washington, D.C., where Jackson had transferred from the train that carried him from Alabama, the aisles had steadily collected discarded sandwich wrappers and pop bottles, the refuse of the only meals they'd been able to eat en route; the dining car was off-limits to coloreds. At least the baby girl making the trip in her mother's arms had finally stopped crying although a lingering fecal stench told him the reason why: With no washrooms in this car, her mother had had to change the child's diapers in public.

The train lurched again, and Jackson returned his gaze to the window. Union Station was just ahead, its twin towers looming above a Gothic edifice of white limestone. As the train clattered the rest of the way into the station, Jackson reached beneath his seat to pull out the battered cardboard suitcase that held all his clothes. It appeared that nearly everyone in the colored car was traveling on to Boston because only a couple of other people stood up.

The train finally came to a halt, and Jackson joined the disembarking passengers as they shuffled down the aisle to the door. The night was cold, a stiff wind from the northeast spitting fat snowflakes into his face as he stepped out onto the platform. This was the first time J. Jackson Jackson had been anywhere above the Mason-Dixon Line; in that frigid moment of first contact with New England, he imagined that he was somewhere just south of the Arctic Circle. He paused to put down his suitcase, pull up the lapels of his wool overcoat and clamp his fedora more firmly to his head, then he picked up the suitcase again and followed the signs to the station entrance. Someone was supposed to be meeting him there . . .

"Lieutenant Jackson?"

A young white man stood just inside the door, a snapshot photo in his gloved hands. Jackson nodded and the other man put away the picture. "Hillman . . . Corporal Max Hillman," he said quietly. "Glad to see you made it, sir. How was the trip?"

"All right, I suppose." Jackson wasn't surprised to see that Hillman wasn't in uniform or that he hadn't saluted him. Apparently he'd received the same orders to dress and behave as a civilian; Jackson had left his uniform in Alabama and instead worn his best suit on the train. He looked around at the handful of other passengers. "Am I the only person you're picking up?"

"Uh-huh . . . I mean, yes, sir. You're the last guy in. Everyone else is already here. This way, Lieutenant . . . the car's out front."

They walked down a circular staircase to the ticket foyer and passed through another pair of doors leading to the station's main hall. The Washington train must have been the last one in for the evening; the wooden benches were nearly vacant, the luncheonette and newsstand closed. Jackson took a few moments to find the COLOREDS ONLY restroom; Hillman was waiting for him in the lobby when he came out. Just outside the front door, a Plymouth sedan was parked at the curb. Jackson tossed his suitcase in the backseat while Hillman slid in behind the wheel. The corporal cranked up the cold engine and turned on the windshield wiper, and the Plymouth rumbled away from the station, its tires crunching through the slush in the street.

"We've got you staying with the rest of the group, sir," Hillman said as he switched on the heater. "You'll be sharing a boardinghouse just a few blocks from the Clark campus." A quick smile. "I'll be there, too. My job is to act as your military liaison . . . sort of a go-between for you and . . ."

"I know what a liaison is." Even on a dark winter night, Jackson could tell that Worcester wasn't much larger than Memphis, his hometown. The tallest buildings were the clock tower of what he assumed to be City Hall and a couple of church steeples; all the others were low redbrick buildings no more than six stories tall, sparsely illuminated by cast-iron streetlamps. Not a pretty city. "Where's the colonel?"

"Colonel Bliss? We'll see him only every so often. He'll be dividing his time between here and Alamogordo, with occasional visits down to Washington to report in." A wry chuckle. "If I were him, I'd stay in New Mexico as much as I could. A little warmer down there."

Jackson nodded, preferring to say as little as he could get away with. If it were up to him, he wouldn't have been here either, and not just because of the climate. He had been just a few weeks away from earning his wings and joining the 332nd Fighter Group when Colonel Bliss had come to see him at the Tuskegee Army Air Field, along with a nameless FBI agent who'd spoken little but had regarded him with the skeptical eyes of a man who couldn't believe that a Negro would be interviewed by a member of the War Department's command staff. Bliss wanted to know about Jackson's engineering degree and the interest he'd shown in rocket research; he'd said little concerning what this was about except that it involved a classified project being undertaken by Robert H. Goddard. The subsequent offer to join the project wasn't entirely voluntary; although the colonel didn't come right out and say so, he had given the young lieutenant the distinct impression that, if he didn't agree to go on detached duty, he'd spend the rest of the war sweeping hangar floors, not in the cockpit of a P-51 Warhawk.

Working on a military project with Dr. Goddard intrigued Jackson. All things considered, though, he'd rather be flying.

Hillman drove past the town commons, then turned left at City Hall onto Main Street. The stores were all closed; only a few restaurants and bars were open. Almost no traffic except for a trolley making its way up the street, its bars sparking as they touched the electric lines overhead. Leaving the town center, they entered a leafy urban neighborhood of apartment buildings and small houses, until they came upon a collection of ivy-decked buildings clustered along the right-hand side of the street.

"Here's the Clark campus," Hillman said, as if it could be anything else. Turning right onto Maywood Street, he slowed down as they came upon a four-story redbrick building close to the sidewalk. "That's the Science Building, where you'll be working."

Jackson noticed that its windows were dark. "I take it we're not going there right away."

"No, sir. We're going straight to the boardinghouse. That's where everyone else is . . . except Dr. Goddard, of course. I think he and his wife are staying home tonight to unpack." Hillman gave him a sidelong glance. "Have you ever met either of them? Dr. and Mrs. Goddard, I mean."

"I haven't met anyone except the colonel," Jackson said.

"That so? Well, you'll meet them soon. Incidentally, you'll be the only people staying there. We've rented the whole place for your group, just to make sure that you're left alone."

The Plymouth continued up Maywood, leaving the Clark University campus and entering a residential neighborhood of narrow streets shaded by oak and maple trees. The snow had lessened by then, yet the streets hadn't been plowed; Hillman drove slowly to avoid skidding out. A left turn onto Birch Street, then, three blocks down, he pulled up to the sidewalk across from a wood-frame apartment house, three stories tall with a small front porch, indistinguishable from any other New England three-decker they'd already passed.

"Here we are, sir." Shutting off the motor, Hillman climbed out. "C'mon in . . . I'll introduce you to the rest of the boys."

Jackson darted a look at him, but there was no trace of condescension on Hillman's face; apparently, the kid didn't know what "boy" meant to a black man. Jackson decided to let it slide as he retrieved his suitcase from the backseat and followed Hillman across the street and up the front steps. The corporal didn't knock or ring the doorbell but instead walked straight in, holding the door open for Jackson.

They found themselves in a darkened foyer with a row of metal mailboxes on the wall across from a stairway. Straight ahead was a hallway; light gleamed from a half-open door at the end. "Hey, there!" Hillman called out as he stamped his feet on the doormat, shaking off the snow. "Anyone home?"

"Back here," a voice from the door responded. "C'mon back."

Still carrying his suitcase, Jackson let Hillman lead him down the hall. "Hey, guys," the corporal said as he pushed open the door. "Here's the last member of your group . . . Lieutenant J. Jackson Jackson, U.S. Army Air Corps."

Jackson walked into a small but cozy parlor. Six men were seated in armchairs, with two sharing a couch near a window; most were reading books or magazines, but a couple were hunched over a checkerboard. A radio in the corner quietly played dance-hall jazz; the room was filled with cigarette and pipe smoke. Through a door on the other side of the room, Jackson spotted the kitchen. Two more men were in there, washing dishes; Jackson guessed that they were cleaning up from dinner.

Everyone stared at him. Jackson knew that look; he'd been getting it his entire life, from high school to college to the Army. *What the hell is a Negro doing here?* Even the Asian fellow—Chinese, he guessed; couldn't be a Jap, not on a classified military project—seemed incredulous. The only sound in the room was the Benny Goodman Orchestra.

"Good evening, gentlemen." Jackson put down the suitcase, took off his hat. "Pleasure to meet you." He gave them a measured smile, friendly but not ingratiating.

The silence lasted for another second or two, then a tall, slender man pushed himself to his feet. "Glad to meet you, too, Lieutenant. Name's Morse . . . Henry Morse."

"Hello, Henry." Jackson offered his hand. When Morse shook it without hesitation, he knew he had at least one guy on his side. "And don't bother with the rank . . . my friends call me Jack."

"Jack?" Another guy, a wiry little fellow with glasses and a mustache, lowered the *Life* he was reading. "Did I hear Max correctly when he said your last name was Jackson?"

"Yes, you did."

"And your middle name is . . . ?"

"That's Jackson, too."

"Jackson Two?" A wide grin as the others chuckled. "Then I take it your first initial stands for . . ."

Jackson felt his face growing warm. He hated this part of introducing himself to anyone, especially white folks. "I think that's obvious."

"Jackson Jackson Jackson?" This from an overweight, balding man who appeared to be the oldest person in the room. "No wonder you want to be called Jack."

"No, no, no . . . you don't get it." The little guy shook his head. "If his middle and last names makes him Jackson Two, then the first name makes him Jackson Three. That's Jackson Cube . . . Jack Cube!"

That broke everyone up, and for an instant Jackson felt anger surge within. Then he realized that this was a joke only well-educated men would appreciate, a mathematical pun that would've gone right over the head of a cracker back home. These men weren't laughing at him, really; they were laughing at a joke spawned years ago when his parents decided to give their baby boy the most unforgettable name possible.

"Yeah, well . . . that's cool," he replied, managing to keep a straight face. His remark was greeted by a long and heartfelt groan: a pun answered by another pun.

All of a sudden, the room was just a few degrees warmer. One by one, the men got up and came over to introduce themselves. Names accompanied handshakes; the wiry guy was Lloyd Kapman, the plump one was Taylor Brickell, and the Chinese-American fellow was Harry Chung. They were followed by Hamilton "just call me Ham" Ballou, who looked like a stand-in for Clark Gable except for the postadolescent acne that covered his face. Michael "I'm Mike" Ferris was the only person with whom Jackson had had any previous contact, from letters exchanged through addresses gleaned from the American Rocket Society newsletter. Mike obviously hadn't been aware that his pen pal was black, because Jackson hadn't believed it necessary to tell him, but he didn't say anything about it. For Jack's part, he was surprised that Ferris was apparently his own age; he'd always assumed that Mike was a bit older.

Indeed, everyone was unexpectedly young. Harry, Lloyd, and Taylor were the oldest members of the group, and none of them had yet reached his thirties. Jackson had pegged everyone as being in his twenties when the two men who'd been in the kitchen came in, and he discovered that this estimate was wrong. Gerry Mander—yes, that was his real name, he'd later learn—wasn't even old enough to drink or vote; a skinny, awkward-looking kid with a bad haircut, he was also the one who appeared most surprised to discover that J. Jackson Jackson was black.

"Where're you from?" Gerry looked Jack up and down, not immediately accepting Jack's offered handshake. His Southern accent was unmistakable, a drawl that could only have come from somewhere deep in the heart of Dixie.

"Memphis," Jack said. "You?"

"Muscle Shoals." Gerry hesitated. "I hear we're gonna be roommates."

The room fell quiet again. From the corner of his eye, Jack could see that everyone was nervously watching this exchange. "I suppose we are . . ."

The other man from the kitchen coughed in his hand, interrupting him. In his midthirties, he was taller and more muscular than anyone else, but what set him apart wasn't his size but the Smith & Wesson .45 tucked into the shoulder holster he wore over a starched Arrow shirt. Jack instantly recognized him for what he was: a federal agent, probably a G-man.

"We weren't aware of any . . . uh, personal differences . . . when we made the room assignments," he said, his gaze shifting between Gerry and Jack. "Is there going to be a problem here?"

"Not as far as I'm concerned." Jack looked Gerry straight in the eye. "Do you have a problem?"

Again, Gerry Mander hesitated. Then a grin slowly spread across his face, exposing a pair of crooked front teeth. "Well, hell, why not? Half the guys in the workhouse were colored." He stuck out his hand. "Put it there, boy!"

Jackson bit his lip as he shook Gerry's hand. For now, he'd have to settle for acceptance and work on respect later. "And you are . . . ?" he asked the G-man.

"Frank O'Connor, Federal Bureau of Investigation." His handshake was firm enough to crack walnuts. "I've been assigned to be your security detail while you're here. Where you go, I go."

"Don't let him fool you," Lloyd said. "He's really our valet. Cooks a mean roast chicken."

The others laughed again, and Agent O'Connor managed a shrug. "Got some leftovers in the icebox if you're hungry."

"Man, I'm not hungry . . . I'm starving." Even as he said this, Jack Cube felt his stomach rumbling. The last time he'd had anything to eat was the egg-salad sandwich in Washington between trains. "Take me to it."

He started to head for the kitchen, but O'Connor raised a hand. "Don't worry about a thing, Lieutenant. I'll set you a place at the table. Just make yourself comfortable and get to know everyone."

He returned to the kitchen, and Jackson looked around to see Gerry staring at him in astonishment. "Lieutenant?" Gerry asked; apparently he hadn't overheard Corporal Hillman's initial introduction. "You're a lieutenant?"

"Army Air Force, 332nd Fighter Group." Jackson ignored his expression as he turned to the others. "Anyone got a smoke? I used up my last cigarette somewhere around Philadelphia." Henry produced a pack of Camels and shook one out. "Thanks. So what's the story here? When do we see Dr. Goddard?"

"First meeting is tomorrow morning, at the college." Henry struck a match, held it out to him. The rest of the men were already going back to what they'd been doing when he arrived. "That's when you'll get the details."

Something in the way he said this got Jack's attention. "You know what's going on?" he asked, letting Henry light his cigarette.

"Uh-huh . . . but I think it'd be better if Bob explains it himself." Henry's face was solemn. "Believe me when I tell you," he quietly added, "we've got our work cut out for us."

Esther Goddard was unpacking yet another carton of books—it seemed as if books accounted for half the stuff shipped back from Roswell—when there was a knock at the front door. "I'll get it," she called out to Robert as she made her way through the cardboard boxes that had transformed the living room into a maze. The knock was repeated by the time she reached the front door; its impatience gave her a clue as to who their late visitor was even before she opened the door.

"Hello, Wallace," she said, managing a smile that she didn't feel. "Nice to see you again."

"Good evening, Esther." Wallace Atwood, the president of Clark University, stood on the front porch, hat pulled low and overcoat lapels turned up against the snow that was still falling. "Is Robert in?"

"Of course. Please come in." She stepped aside and waited for Atwood to stamp the snow from his rubber overshoes. It had been many years since she'd last seen him, and as he walked into the house and took off his hat, she noted that time hadn't treated him well. Now that he was in his seventies, time seemed to have caught up with him; a big man in past years, his shoulders had become stooped and his frame a little less ursine, and his hair had gone white and had almost completely receded from his forehead. It was remarkable that President Atwood hadn't retired, and perhaps he would soon, but not before he confronted his old nemesis one more time.

"I'm sorry that I can't offer you any coffee," Esther said as she took his hat and coat, "but I haven't unpacked the percolator yet." A lie; it was one of the first things she'd pulled out of a box when the moving van showed up a couple of days ago. But coffee was tightly rationed and not to be splurged; besides, she didn't want dear old Wallace to stay any longer than necessary.

"That's quite all right. It's only a quick visit." Atwood gave the stacked boxes a disdainful glance. "Still getting settled in? I would've thought . . ."

"We've been gone almost twelve years, and we stopped renting out the house after the last tenant made a mess of the place. It takes a while to move back in, you know."

Wallace gave her a stiff-necked nod, still not looking at her. This was the house where Bob had been born and raised; it had been in his family for two generations, perched atop Maple Hill in one of Worcester's more pleasant neighborhoods. Even after he and Esther moved to New Mexico, he decided to keep the place, for reasons both sentimental and practical. Had he put the house on the market, it would have signaled that he never intended to return to Massachusetts . . . and Wallace Atwood would have taken advantage of that.

"Yes, well . . ." Atwood noisily cleared his throat, and Esther tried not to laugh. No one could harrumph as well as Clark University's president. "If you could tell your husband that I'm here . . ."

"And so you are!" Bob exclaimed as he strode into the living room, arms open as if to give their caller a hearty embrace. "Good evening, Wallace! How wonderful to see you again!"

Esther couldn't keep from grinning. In baggy old pants and a wool shirt filthy with dust brought all the way from New Mexico, the smoldering butt of a cigar clenched between his teeth, Bob looked like a desert rat magically transported to Massachusetts. Atwood was dressed in the same tweed suit he'd probably worn to church for the last twenty years, and he recoiled from Bob as if afraid he might be carrying a virus.

"Ah . . . um . . . pleased to see you, too." Atwood nervously extended a hand and visibly winced as Bob clasped it with both of his own. "Your lovely wife was just telling me . . ."

"We're still unpacking, yes, yes. May take us a while to get squared away." Bob took the cigar from his mouth and waved it at the living room furniture, some of which was still covered by canvas sheets. "If you're dropping by to give us a hand, that would be terrific. We could use all the help we can get. You can start in here by . . ."

"Well, no, if you don't mind, I'd rather not. Actually, the reason why I've stopped by is to discuss the nature of your return. That is, I'd like to know why you've . . ."

"Come back after so many years?" Noticing that his cigar had gone out, Bob searched for a place to dispose of it. "Why, to teach, of course. And to pursue a research project, as you've no doubt heard already."

"That's exactly what I want to talk to you about. You haven't . . ."

Atwood was interrupted by footsteps clumping across the upstairs hallway. He glanced upward, surprised to find that there was someone else in the house. "You have a guest?"

"Oh, yes." Bob dropped the cigar butt in the small ceramic candy dish he'd been using until Esther could dig out a proper ashtray. "In fact, I believe you've already met." He turned to the stairs and raised his voice. "Colonel? President Atwood is here."

Colonel Bliss descended the staircase, the evening edition of the *Worcester Telegraph* in hand. Although his tie was missing and his sleeves were rolled up, he might just as well have been wearing a full dress uniform; Bliss had the sort of military bearing that didn't disappear even when he was in civilian clothes. "Good evening, Dr. Atwood," he said. "I thought I'd heard you come in."

"Hello, Colonel." Once again, Atwood was startled. "I wasn't expecting to find you here."

"Omar is visiting for a few days while Bob gets his project started." Esther picked up a rag to dust off her hands. "I imagine you'll see him from time to time."

"Probably not very often. Just when I need to make sure that everything is going well with Dr. Goddard's work." The colonel reached the bottom of the steps but didn't offer a handshake. "Pardon me for eavesdropping, but I couldn't help but overhear you from the guest room . . . you have a question about his schedule?"

"Yes, well . . ." Atwood shifted from one foot to another as he turned to Bob again. "I've been told that you've requested that you teach only one class, a seminar in advanced physics. Furthermore, you're reserving approval over any students who sign up for this."

"That's right," Bob said. "Physics 390 will be the one course I'll teach this semester, and the only students who take it will be the ones whom I personally approve. And I've already picked my students."

"Not even the Introduction to Physics or Introductory Calculus classes you've normally taught?" Atwood asked, and Bob shook his head. "I'm afraid that's not satisfactory."

"As chairman of the physics and math departments, it's my privilege to teach as few classes as I choose, and every professor at Clark has the option of selecting the students he wants for his graduate-level courses."

"And that's not satisfactory either," Atwood said.

Bob shrugged. "Well, I'm sorry, Wallace, but you'll just have to be satisfied."

And there it was, the source of the long-standing feud between the two men. Atwood became the university president in 1920; three years later, he promoted Goddard to the chairmanship of the physics department following the suicide of his predecessor. They had gotten along well at first, with Atwood securing the university grants that Goddard used to jump-start his rocket research, and Goddard in turn becoming one of the university's crown jewels. It wasn't long, though, before Goddard began to outgrow Clark University; once he acquired new funding sources, first from the Carnegie Institute and the Smithsonian, and later from Charles Lindbergh and the Guggenheim family, he no longer needed the university's meager financial support. When this happened, Goddard committed less effort to his job at the college, preferring to spend more time with his rocket experiments.

Yet Atwood couldn't afford to fire him. By then, Dr. Robert H. Goddard was one of the most famous scientists in America, while Clark University remained in the shadows of Harvard and Boston College to the east and Amherst, Smith, and Mount Holyoke to the west. Clark needed Goddard more than Goddard needed Clark, and Atwood knew it.

Bob's marriage to Esther hadn't helped either. Esther Kisk had been a recent high-school graduate working as a typist in Atwood's office when she met Doctor G, and the puritanical and churchgoing university president had disapproved of the romance between the teenage girl and the middle-aged professor. To make matters worse, Esther had taken charge of Bob's personal affairs once they were married; she'd become a formidable defender of her husband's private life, and Atwood soon discovered that he couldn't easily intimidate her.

The final break had occurred when the Goddards moved to Roswell. Bob had told the university that it would only be a short sabbatical, yet as time went on, and his visits to Worcester became increasingly infrequent, it became apparent that he was gone for good. Yet he'd refused to relin-

quish his chairmanship of the physics and math departments, even after
Atwood had eliminated most of the graduate programs, and when the
president requested that Goddard give up his chair and take a pay cut,
Goddard had retaliated by tendering his resignation. Atwood had
no choice but to let Goddard retain his chairmanship and salary even
though he was an invisible man on campus. Like it or not, losing Goddard
would have been a major blow to the university's prestige.

All this must have been in the back of Wallace Atwood's mind because
his face reddened and his eyes narrowed. "Just who do you think you are?"
he snapped, glaring at Goddard as if he were a freshman caught soaping
Atwood's office windows. "You're gone twelve years, then you come back
thinking you can just waltz in and . . ."

"Dr. Atwood, may I remind you that the War Department has specifically requested Dr. Goddard's reinstatement?" Leaning against the
banister, Colonel Bliss remained calm in the face of the president's bluster.
"We've already discussed our arrangements. The reasons why he's here
are none of your concern, nor are the conditions he's requested. You're to
give him everything he wants and leave him alone, and that's all you need
to know."

Atwood's angry gaze swung toward Bliss. "And if I don't?"

"You tell me . . . how much federal aid does your school receive each
year? And while you're at it, you might also wonder how many of your
teachers and students have requested and received draft deferrals." A cun-
ning smile. "Uncle Sam can be very generous in his support of higher
education, Dr. Atwood, but his generosity has its limits."

Before Esther's very eyes, it seemed as if Wallace Atwood actually
shrank a few inches. His haughty demeanor vanished like snowflakes on
a hot frying pan as he gaped at the colonel, his mouth opening as if to
object, then closing without another word. Bob said nothing, but when
Atwood turned to Esther, she simply held out his hat and coat.

"Always a pleasure to see you, Wallace," she murmured. "Do come
again, will you?"

"Perhaps we could have lunch some afternoon," Bob added.

Atwood silently took his hat and coat, then walked out the door. Esther caught it before it slammed shut and watched as he stormed down the front walk, the snow muffling his footsteps as he headed for the car parked at the front curb. Its headlights had barely vanished when Bob let out a sigh.

"Well," he murmured, "that was . . . unpleasant."

"Really?" Esther smiled. "I don't think so. Remind me to bake him some cookies, will you?"

And then she went back to unpacking books, humming a happy song as she ignored the stares from both her husband and their houseguest.

PHYSICS 390

"I cannot stress too strongly the need for absolute secrecy," Colonel Bliss said. "No one, but no one, outside this room can know what we're doing. Not your families, not your friends, not your colleagues . . . no one. This is why some of you have received phony draft notices, while others like Dr. Chung have received job offers in other parts of the country."

"You hear me complaining?" Gerry Mander asked. "Coupla weeks ago, I was breaking rocks on an Alabama road crew."

"In your case," Robert Goddard replied, "I'd say you're moving up in the world."

Everyone laughed except the colonel, who remained stoical. The nine members of the research team were seated on wooden stools around the long, unfinished pine table that ran down the center of the second room of the physics lab. The laboratory was comprised of two adjacent rooms in the basement ground floor of the Science Building. Separated by only a square arch, they had whitewashed-brick walls, oak-plank floors, and high wooden ceilings. A coal furnace stood in one corner between shelves containing a variety of tools, flasks, and pieces of scrap metal. An enormous vacuum pump was located in the middle of the first room, just in front of the sturdy double doors, which had been closed for the meet-ing. Frank O'Connor, the FBI agent, leaned against the door, arms folded across his chest.

"If secrecy is so important," Henry Morse asked, "shouldn't we do something about that?" He pointed to the row of tall windows on one side of the two rooms; halfway up the wall, they looked out upon a small courtyard, where an elderly custodian was shoveling snow from the walk-way between classroom buildings. "Anyone can peep in here and see what we're doing."

"We've ordered blinds. Until they arrive, we'll make sure that this"—Bliss tapped a knuckle against the blackboard behind him—"is covered or erased after each meeting. Furthermore, all notes are to be kept in those file cabinets over there, which will be locked when not being used. I'll also ask that you not remove any notes from these rooms or take anything back to the boardinghouse."

Several of the men groaned and shook their heads. "Fat chance of that," Lloyd muttered under his breath. Telling a scientist to keep his re-search confined to the workplace was like ordering a restaurant chef not to take home any leftovers.

Bliss ignored the protests. "Agent O'Connor will be in charge of se-curity. He will escort you to and from the boardinghouse where you'll be staying, while Corporal Hillman will do the same for Dr. Goddard. So far as anyone is concerned, you're graduate students enrolled in an advanced-studies program, Physics 390, with Dr. Goddard as your instruc-tor and Dr. Chung as his teaching assistant. The boardinghouse will be your primary residence, and we'd prefer that you keep your social ac-tivities to a minimum."

"So joining a fraternity is out of the question, I take it," Ham Ballou said.

The others laughed again, but Bliss was not amused. "You take it cor-rectly. In fact, I'd appreciate it if you shaved off your mustache. It makes you look older."

Ham chuckled, then he caught the expression on the colonel's face, and his smile faded. "You're serious, aren't you?"

"I've never been more serious about anything." Bliss looked at the rest of the team. "Believe me when I say this . . . the outcome of the war, and the future of the United States, may very well depend on what goes on in here. From this point on, you're no longer private citizens but military scientists working on a project at the highest levels of national security. Very few people . . . the president, the Secretary of State, and the White House science advisor, select members of the War Department and the intelligence community . . . are aware that this program even exists. So it goes without saying that you must keep what you know to yourselves." Bliss paused, letting his gaze travel around the room. "Have I made myself understood?"

No one spoke. An uncomfortable silence fell upon the lab as they all glanced at one another. Then Goddard coughed into his hand. "Thank you, Colonel," he said. "I think these men realize the gravity of the situation."

"Would you like to continue the briefing, Dr. Goddard?"

"No," Goddard said, "I'd rather get to work." The others quietly laughed or hid smiles behind their hands as he stood up and strolled to the blackboard. "If I may . . . ?"

Bliss moved aside, giving Goddard the floor. "Thank you," Goddard said as the colonel took a seat at the table, then he looked at the team. "If I haven't personally met anyone here already . . . well then, welcome to warm and sunny Worcester, the Paris of New England."

Once again, everyone laughed. After Colonel Bliss's no-nonsense approach, Bob Goddard's deadpan humor was a relief. "This is the first time my wife and I have been back in quite a while," he continued, "so a little housewarming party is in order. Esther and I would like to have you all over to the house next Saturday for a chicken dinner . . ."

"Dr. Goddard!" Bliss snapped.

"Oh, you're invited, too, Colonel, if you're still in town by then . . ."

"I'm sorry, but we can't permit that. The team can't be seen with you outside the classroom."

Goddard stared at him. "Oh, good heavens . . . why not? Students have always come to my house."

"The colonel's right, sir." O'Connor spoke up from his place near the door. "Security considerations . . . when you're not here on campus, it would be unwise to have you seen with anyone who might be identified by German intelligence operatives as being another rocket scientist."

"Oh, come on . . . German spies, really . . ."

"Always a possibility," Bliss said.

"Damn," Henry murmured to Jack Cube. "There goes a free dinner."

Goddard glared at O'Connor and Bliss. When neither of them appeared willing to compromise or back down, he shrugged. "Well, then . . . perhaps another time. Maybe we should devote ourselves to the task at hand."

Turning to the blackboard, he flipped its panel upside down, revealing what had been hidden on its other side: a chalk sketch of the Silver Bird on its horizontal launch track, with several rows of figures beneath it. "As you've already been informed, allied military intelligence recently learned that the German Army and the Luftwaffe are planning to build a manned spacecraft . . . what they call an antipodal bomber . . . which will be launched by means of a rocket-propelled sled moving along a horizontal track. This *Silbervogel*, as they call it, or Silver Bird, will have an approximate length of ninety-two feet and a wingspan of forty-eight feet, with a dry weight of approximately one hundred tons . . ."

As he spoke, Ham Ballou leaned over to Lloyd Kapman. "Man, I don't like this," he whispered. "Are we going to have G-men chaperoning us the whole time?"

"I hear you," Lloyd replied, his voice subdued as well. "Can't even visit the john without Frankie tailing us."

"Yeah, well, look . . . I spotted a nice little bar downtown, right across the street from City Hall. Maybe we can shake the babysitter later and . . ."

"Gentlemen? You have something to add?"

Ham and Lloyd looked to see that Goddard had interrupted himself to look at them. So was everyone else in the room. "Umm . . . just discussing fuel options, Bob," Lloyd said. "Alcohol-derived versus oxygen-hydrogen mix."

A few knowing chuckles; some of the others caught the joke. The only people who didn't laugh were Goddard, Bliss, and O'Connor. "Sounds interesting," Goddard said, not smiling. "Perhaps you can discuss this later, though. For now, I'd like to have your attention."

"Sure thing, Bob . . . sorry," Lloyd said, and Ham nodded. As Goddard turned back to the blackboard, though, Henry glanced back at them. He gave them a quick smile and wink, and Jack Cube did the same.

Later, indeed.

———

As it turned out, getting away from O'Connor was almost ridiculously easy. A fire escape ran up the back side of the Birch Street boardinghouse; after dinner, each of the team members said good night to the others and casually went upstairs to his room, closing the doors behind him. After waiting a few minutes, they quietly left their rooms and tiptoed to the window at the end of the hall where the ladder was located. It was a childish stunt, but so far as the FBI agent was concerned, the scientists were tucked away for the night. By a quarter to nine, they'd walked down to Park Avenue and caught a streetcar that would take them downtown.

The big clock on top of Worcester City Hall had just struck nine when they got off the trolley. By then, the streets were nearly empty, the Worcester Commons quilted by heavy white snow that glistened in the streetlights. As the streetcar trundled away, the eight men stood huddled on the corner of Main and Front, hats pulled down against the wind and hands shoved in their coat pockets.

"Think we lost him?" Mike glanced nervously over his shoulder.

"Of course we lost him." Gerry grinned. "Serves Frankie right for not watching the back of the house."

"And even if he figures out we're missing," Ham asked, "how is he going to find us?"

"Oh, yeah, that's right." Mike rolled his eyes. "This is only the FBI we're talking about." Looking away, he spotted a neon BAR sign on the other side of the Commons. "Is that the place, Lloyd?"

"That's it. C'mon, gents . . . first round's on me."

The eight men trudged across the Commons, trying not to slip on the icy concrete path. Crossing Franklin Street behind City Hall, they headed for the warm lights of what appeared to be a hotel taproom, passing a sidewalk newsstand along the way. Incredibly, the stand was still open, its elderly proprietor huddled against the cold. Seeing this, Morse figured that he must either be desperate for business or just didn't have anything else better to do.

"Think they're gonna let me in?" Gerry murmured, eying the bar warily. "I mean . . . guys, I'm just nineteen."

"Sure they will. You look twenty-one to me." Walking beneath the entrance awning, Henry grabbed the brass door handle and was about to open it when he looked back. "Hey, what's going on? Aren't you coming in?"

Everyone was about to follow him inside except Jack Cube. He'd stopped on the sidewalk, gazing at something displayed in the front window. "Umm . . . 'fraid not," he said quietly. "I'm going to have some trouble with this place."

Wondering what was going on, Henry let go of the door and walked out from beneath the awning to see what had stopped Jack. In the window was a handwritten sign: NO COLOREDS.

"Oh, hell," Lloyd muttered. "Jack, I'm sorry. I didn't see . . ."

Everyone stopped except Gerry, who'd taken hold of the door handle. He was about to walk in even though the older men had suddenly become reluctant. Jack Cube was embarrassed; the sign was a reminder that racial barriers existed even outside the South.

"That's okay," he said quietly. "You fellows go on in. Maybe I can find a coffee shop somewhere."

He started to walk back up the sidewalk, heading toward Main Street. Henry hesitated, then raised a hand. "Hey, wait up!" he called. "I think I'll join you for that coffee!"

Harry Chung glared at the window sign. "Y'know, I bet they won't let me in either," he murmured, then turned to follow Henry and Jack.

"They probably don't like Jews," Lloyd said, as he fell in behind the other three.

Ham shook his head. "I wouldn't be surprised if they've got something against second-generation French-Canadians." Then he walked away from the bar.

"Coffee works for me." Taylor joined the exodus.

"Place looks like a dump anyway," Mike added. Stepping away from the door, he looked back at Gerry. "What about you, kid? Still want to try your luck?"

Seeing that it was hopeless, Gerry let his hand fall from the door handle and hurried to catch up with the others. "They would've just thrown me out," he said with an indifferent shrug.

Henry clapped him on the shoulder, then something caught his eye that made him stop. Within the glow of the bare lightbulb dangling from the newsstand's ceiling were the magazines on its racks. *Argosy, Life, Collier's, Detective, The Shadow, The New Yorker, Doc Savage, Western Romance*, and so forth . . . and in their midst, the current issue of *Astounding Science Fiction*.

On impulse, Henry dug a quarter out of his pocket, dropped it on the counter, and picked up the pulp. The old man grunted as he scooped up the quarter with a gloved hand. "Never miss an issue," he said, as the others watched with amusement. "Who knows? Maybe it'll give us some ideas."

———

They didn't find a coffee shop, but neither did they have to settle for one. A couple of blocks down Main was another bar. It was considerably less fancy than the one on the Commons, with a flickering Pabst Blue Ribbon sign in the window and a stale beer stench in the air, but at least the bartender didn't seem to care who came in so long as they paid cash. The group pushed together a couple of tables in the back of the room, and

Lloyd made good on his promise by ordering three pitchers of beer. The waitress brought them a couple of bowls of peanuts as well, then went back to the newspaper she'd been reading when they came in.

"Nice place." Taylor examined the dimly lit barroom with a critical eye. It was nearly empty, the inevitable wino slumped over the bar the only other patron. "When do you think the city health inspector last set foot in here?"

"Look at the bright side . . . O'Connor probably won't find us either." Mike poured a glass of beer for himself, then passed the pitcher to Henry. "Put down the magazine and have a drink. You can read it later."

Henry closed the issue of *Astounding* he'd just bought and placed it on the table. Curious, Harry reached over to pull it a little closer. On its cover was an illustration of a sleek silver craft descending through a grove of tall sequoias. "Beyond This Horizon" by Anson MacDonald was the featured story.

"You know," Harry murmured as he studied the magazine, "there may be something to this."

"A spaceship?" Ham gave him a disbelieving smirk. "You can't be serious."

"Well, maybe not *this* spaceship, but still . . ."

"This isn't a science fiction story. We've got to come up with something real."

"Why not?" Henry passed the pitcher to Taylor. "You heard what Bob said this morning. Even if we manage to build a missile capable of reaching Silver Bird's altitude, making a direct hit would be a crapshoot . . . unlikely at best. The only way we're going to get something accurate enough to bring that thing down is to put a pilot aboard. And that means building a manned spacecraft of our own."

"But putting something into orbit . . ." Ham began.

"It could be done," Lloyd said. "Henry will tell you . . . down in New Mexico, we've built rockets that have broken altitude records."

"Besides, who's talking about reaching orbit?" Henry asked. "All we need, really, is a craft capable of making a suborbital jaunt. Launch from

New Mexico, intercept over North America, land somewhere on the East Coast. If it can reach an apogee of just forty to fifty miles, then we've got it licked."

"But the thrust we'd need . . ." Ham shook his head. "Besides, we'd have to build a step-rocket for something like this. Two stages, at least."

"No . . . no step-rockets." Jack Cube tapped a finger against the table. "A two-stage rocket means we'd have to design, build, and test two different engines. I don't think we have time for that."

"You've got a point there." Harry absently leafed through Henry's magazine. "But I think Ham's right, too. I doubt a single-stage rocket would do the trick. Besides, I'm not sure I'm comfortable with relying on just one engine. If it cuts out during launch . . ."

"What about solid-fuel rockets?" Gerry asked. "For boosters, I mean."

Everyone stopped to look at the end of the table where the teenager was seated. "Come again?" Henry asked.

"Umm . . ." Gerry appeared nervous by the attention he'd suddenly drawn. "What I mean is, you build a single-stage rocket with a liquid-fuel engine, then strap on some solid rockets as boosters during launch. When they burn out, you just throw 'em away." He hesitated. "Oh, maybe that's a dopey idea."

"No . . . no, it isn't." Taylor looked at the others. "Really, he might have something there." He glanced down at Gerry. "Nice thinking there, kid," he added, and Gerry grinned.

"Yeah, Harry and I were working with solid-fuel rockets at Caltech." Mike played with his beer glass, absently sliding it back and forth across the battered tabletop. "You don't have much control over them once they've ignited . . . you can't throttle them up or down, or even shut them off . . . but they're simple to make, and you can get a high impulse-per-second thrust ratio from them."

"What sort of propellant?" Jack asked.

"Ammonium nitrate would be my guess."

Harry nodded. "Yeah, we've had good results with the ammonium nitrate–black powder compound we tested for our jet-assisted takeoff project. Of course, we'd have to make something a lot bigger than that, but it could work."

"Which leaves us with the liquid-fuel main engine." Taylor shook his head. "I don't even want to think about what a monster that would be."

"You're going to have to if we're going to get anywhere with this." Henry pulled out a pack of Camels and shook one loose. "Besides, that's not all that hard to figure. We've done pretty well with the turbopump system we've developed at Mescalero. All we'd need to do, really, is build much the same thing on a larger scale."

"Are you listening to what you're saying?" Ham was incredulous. "You're talking as if getting something forty or fifty miles into space is simple as"—he pointed to the magazine Harry was still skimming—"as this stupid stuff."

"Science fiction isn't stupid." Henry glared at him, a lit match halfway to his mouth.

"You don't hear Bob talking about it, do you?"

Henry lit his cigarette, leaned back in his chair, and blew a smoke ring at the ceiling. "Ever read Buck Rogers?"

"Sure. Who doesn't?"

"Ever notice that Dr. Huer . . . y'know, Buck's pal, the inventor who builds all those rocket ships . . . looks a lot like Bob?" Henry grinned. "It's not a coincidence. Dr. Huer is based on Bob." Ham snorted in disbelief. "You think I'm joking," Henry went on, "but I'm not. You should see Bob's notebooks sometime. He's got things in there that make everything in Buck Rogers look like kid stuff. Rockets that use atomic engines and ion-propulsion systems, plans for spaceships that could land like airplanes . . . he was thinking this stuff up years ago."

"Think he'd let us look at them?" Jack asked. "They might give us a head start on what we need to do."

"So long as you're careful how you ask." Lloyd frowned as he reached for the beer pitcher. "He's kept this stuff hidden for years. He's been afraid that, if the wrong people saw it, they'd just call him a crackpot. He caught a lot of flak when he wrote that Smithsonian monograph. As if the newspaper stories weren't bad enough, he also had other university profs coming up to him to ask when he was going to build a moon rocket."

"Another reason why he moved to New Mexico," Henry added. "He got tired of taking crap from idiots. He . . . hey, Harry, what are you doing?"

Unnoticed until then, Harry Chung had pulled out a pencil and begun sketching something on a cocktail napkin. Looking up from his work, he gave Henry a shy smile. "Just an idea."

"Okay if I see?" Henry asked, and when Harry nodded, he reached across the table to turn the napkin around. On it was a crude drawing of a slender ellipsoid, sharp at one end and blunt at the other, with three smaller cylinders positioned around its blunt end.

"Just an idea," Harry said with an offhand shrug.

"Umm . . . yeah, okay, but there's something missing." Taking the pencil from Harry, Taylor slid the napkin away from Henry and added a pair of long, swept-back wings to either side of the fuselage. "Something like this, for its launch and descent phase."

"A rocket plane." Mike leaned over to study the drawing. "Sort of like what the Germans are building."

"Guys, maybe we shouldn't be talking about this." Jack Cube dropped his voice as he glanced over his shoulder at the bartender and waitress. "Not here, at least. You heard what you-know-who said about secrecy."

"You kidding? They don't care what we're saying." Henry started to reach for the nearest pitcher, then saw that it was empty. They'd gone through the beer pretty quick. "I'll get the next round." He twisted around in his chair to raise a hand to the waitress. "Hey, miss? Another . . . oh, hell."

The door had just opened and someone else had come in: Frank O'Connor. The FBI agent spotted them at once. Not bothering to take off his hat and coat, he walked across the barroom. No one said anything as he stopped at the end of the tables and glared at them, his mood as black as the night outside.

"It figures," he murmured. "Third bar I check . . ."

"Hello, Frank," Henry said. "Pull up a chair. I was just about to order another round."

"Don't bother. It's last call so far as you're concerned." Pulling out his wallet, he produced a couple of dollars. When the waitress came over, he handed the money to her. "This will cover the tab, I presume." She nodded and walked away, and he turned to the scientists again. "Get your coats . . ."

"Aw, c'mon, Frankie," Lloyd said, "you can't be serious. All we did is . . ."

"If you'd let me know that you just wanted to step out for a drink, I wouldn't be so upset. I might have even joined you. But this whole business of creeping out of the house . . ." He shook his head in dismay. "Max dropped in, started wondering why you guys were so quiet. That's why we went upstairs to see what you were doing. When we found your beds were empty . . ."

Gerry couldn't help it. He sniggered under his breath. He tried to cover it with his hand, but the infection began to spread. Jack Cube choked on a mouthful of beer, and Lloyd was turning blue trying not to laugh; when everyone else saw their faces, the breakdown was inevitable. Within seconds, the group was roaring, tears leaking from their eyes as they slapped the tables with their hands.

"Out!" Agent O'Connor was furious. "Get your butts outta those chairs now!" He grabbed the back of Gerry's chair, yanked it out beneath him. "You're not even supposed to be here!" he yelled at the kid as he spilled out onto the floor. "You're not old enough to drink!"

"What did you say?" Hearing this, the bartender shot up from his stool. "What are you clowns tryin' to do, make me lose my liquor license?" He jabbed a finger at the door. "Get out!"

"Hey, hey . . ." Mike raised his hands. "Take it easy . . ."

"Out!" The bartender wasn't about to be placated. He grabbed a baseball bat from beneath the counter and started to come around the bar. It only made the scene more hysterical. They were out of their chairs, still laughing despite themselves. A pitcher fell over and splashed beer across Henry's magazine, and Gerry slammed his head against the bottom of the table as he scrambled to his feet.

"And don't come back!" the bartender roared, as the eight men tumbled through the door and out onto the sidewalk, still pulling on their hats and coats.

Two cars were at the curb, headlights on, fumes drifting from their exhaust pipes. Half the group reluctantly piled into the one where Max Hillman was waiting, the other half joining O'Connor for the ride back to the boardinghouse. The FBI agent put the Plymouth in gear and pulled out into the just-plowed street.

No one said anything for a couple of minutes, then Taylor coughed. "Sorry, Frank," he said quietly, no longer laughing. "We didn't know this would piss you off so much."

"Yeah, what he said." Mike was just as apologetic. "We weren't trying to be smart-alecks. Just wanted to get a drink, that's all."

"Yeah, well . . ." By then, Frank had calmed down a little. "The colonel doesn't have to know about this, I don't reckon. He wants you guys to stay focused on the job."

Beneath the wan glow of the passing streetlights, Harry Chung gazed at the rumpled napkin he'd managed to snatch up from the table. "Believe me," he murmured, a wry smile on his face, "we've thought of nothing else."

X-1

"This is impressive," Colonel Bliss said, "but do you really think it's possible?"

Standing at the workbench in the Physics 390 lab, he studied the blueprints spread out before him. Seven pages of preliminary designs for a manned rocket ship, detailing every major feature from the radar array in the nose to the engine bell aft of the twenty-eight-foot wings and the horizontal stabilizer. The craft looked like nothing in the sky. It didn't even look like anything on the cover of a science fiction magazine; it was more sophisticated than that.

"We've been working on this for the last five weeks." Robert Goddard stood beside him, fondling an unlit cigar. The team had made him promise not to smoke in the lab; his cheroots reeked, and security precautions prohibited them from opening the windows. "There's still a lot of work to be done, of course, but it'll give you an idea of where we're at just now."

"To answer your question . . . yes, sir, we think it's possible." Henry Morse stood on the other side of the bench with the rest of the 390 Group, as the Pentagon had recently started calling Goddard's rocket team. "We wouldn't have wasted our time if we didn't believe that."

Bliss didn't respond. He continued to leaf through the blueprints, examining each one for a minute or two before turning to the next one. He hadn't visited Worcester very often lately; most of the last five weeks had been spent shuttling between Washington, D.C., and New Mexico, along with a brief trip to London for a meeting with the MI-6 office tasked with keeping track of Silver Bird. During his occasional visits, he'd learned from Goddard that the 390 Group was working on a rocket that would be a radical departure from his previous efforts, but this was the first time he'd seen anything in detail.

He finished looking over the blueprints, then returned to the first one, an overview of the as-yet-unnamed craft. "And you think a piloted vehicle is definitely the answer?"

"It's the only answer," Goddard said. "You'll remember that one of the very first things we discussed was the manned option. The more we've studied it, the more we're convinced that a surface-to-air missile won't do the trick."

"Making a killing shot that precise from the ground is almost impossible." Michael Ferris used his unlit briar pipe to point to the calculations written in chalk on the blackboard behind him. "Based on what we've learned from the Sanger-Bredt study, Silver Bird's velocity will probably be about thirteen thousand feet per second by the time it reaches New York. Not to mention a possible altitude of more than forty miles. Even if we surrounded Manhattan with missile batteries and fired them all at once, our chances of hitting it would be about the same as a hunter trying to take down a deer while blindfolded."

"Which one's wearing the blindfold?" Gerry Mander asked. "The hunter or the deer?"

Everyone chuckled except the colonel, who scowled at the group's youngest member. Gerry just grinned back at him, his impudence irritating Bliss even more. Wisecracks had become common, even during the most serious discussions; it was a way of letting off steam that Goddard condoned and even encouraged but Bliss never understood.

"I understand," the colonel said, ignoring Gerry and returning his attention to Bob, "but putting people in this thing adds a whole new level of complexity."

"That's why we make the rest of the vehicle as simple as possible . . . relatively simple, at least." Goddard opened the blueprints to the second page, a cutaway diagram of the ship. "Look, we're going to use liquid oxygen, nitrogen, and kerosene for the main-engine fuel mixture even though we'd probably get a better ips ratio from liquid oxygen and liquid hydrogen. Manufacturing and storing liquid hydrogen is difficult, especially if you're talking about a vehicle that'll need to be fueled on a minute's notice. Since that means we'll have less thrust for escape velocity, the payload mass will have to be stripped down to the essentials."

"Uh-huh." Bliss bent closer to the table. "That's why you're planning to put only one person aboard. I would've thought you'd want a pilot and copilot, maybe even a gunner."

"No. Just one person, the pilot. He'll have his work cut out for him, but it will reduce the payload requirement and make life support a lot easier. So . . ."

"I don't see any armaments. Where are the guns?"

Goddard didn't respond at once. They all looked at one another. "We're still working on that, sir," Jack Cube said at last.

"'Still working on it'?" Bliss stared at the junior officer. Even out of uniform, neither man forgot his respective rank in the Army. "Lieutenant, I'd think arming this bird would be your first consideration, not the last."

Jackson looked away, embarrassed. Goddard came to the rescue. "What Jack Cu . . . Lieutenant Jackson means is that we're studying alternatives to wing guns. This is one area where this craft won't resemble a normal fighter because firing guns beyond the atmosphere would cause a recoil effect that could alter the craft's trajectory. We need to come up with something else."

"Rockets?"

"Yes, sir, that's a possibility." Jack Cube had recovered his poise and was once again speaking for himself. "But again, there's the problem of accuracy. Since Silver Bird and the X-1 . . ."

"That's what we're calling the ship for the time being," Goddard interjected, and Bliss nodded.

". . . will be traveling at different velocities, hitting the target is going to be very difficult, even if our pilot gets close enough to open fire. That's why we're still working on a solution . . . sir."

"I see." Bliss seemed to regard Jackson with a little more respect. "Lieutenant, you've received flight training, haven't you?"

"Yes, sir, I have. But I didn't get my wings before I was reassigned to . . ."

"Have you . . . and by that I mean your team as a whole . . . had any thoughts about what we'll need to look for when we search for a pilot?"

A wary smile ticked the corners of Jack's mouth. "Well, sir, I'd volunteer myself were it not for one thing . . . I'm too tall." He pointed to the cockpit, located about halfway down the fuselage. "Whoever we find is going to need to be five-ten or less if he's going to fit into the cockpit."

"Well, that's a start." Bliss paused, as if sizing up the young black officer. "Lieutenant, I'd like to speak to you later. I think I have a special job for you."

Jack Cube nodded, and once again Bliss turned to Goddard. "So this is it? This is definitely what you want to build . . . not a missile, but a manned vehicle?"

"Like Henry said . . . we wouldn't be wasting time with this if we didn't think it wasn't a viable solution." Goddard looked him straight in the eye. "The Germans are building a spacecraft. Why can't we?"

"Since you've brought that up . . ." Bliss reached down to pick up the briefcase he'd brought with him. He started to open it, then paused to look at the men gathered around him. "What I'm about to show you is classified top secret. You're not to discuss it outside this room. Understood?"

Everyone nodded, and the colonel pulled out a manila folder holding three photographs. "Although the Allies are still reluctant about mounting an air raid on Peenemünde, they've begun sending high-altitude reconnaissance planes over the Baltic coast in an effort to gain intelligence. These pictures were brought back last week by one of those recon missions . . .

at great risk, I might add, since the P-38 barely escaped the Luftwaffe fighters dispatched to shoot it down." He spread the photos out across the table. "Bob, I'd particularly like to get your opinion on what we're seeing here."

Adjusting his glasses, Goddard bent forward to study the pictures; the rest of the team crowded in to get a closer look as well. The images were distant but sharp; although they'd been taken from a great altitude, the camera had used a zoom lens to increase the magnification, making objects appear much closer than they'd actually been. It wasn't difficult to tell what they were looking at: a large collection of buildings of all sizes, separated by paved roads running between them, with a long beach running nearby.

"Looks like a college campus." Goddard pointed to a small oval on the left side of one of the photos. "There's even an athletic field. See the running track?"

"That's not what interests us." Pushing another photo closer to him, Bliss tapped a finger against an object in the center of the frame. "MI-6 has some ideas of what this is, but we'd like to get your take on it."

The object was near the beach and appeared to be some sort of tower. One end rose straight up, while a long, horizontal structure jutted out from the other end, making the whole thing look a little like a half-finished suspension bridge. The tower was surrounded by a broad white border, apparently a concrete apron. The nearest building was some distance away, but there appeared to be large trucks on the road leading to the tower.

Goddard examined the photo carefully. "I'll have you know, Colonel, that I despise air travel. I've only been up in a plane once, and it scared the devil out of me. So this is an unusual perspective." He stood erect, took off his glasses, and cleaned them on the sleeve of his lab coat. "However, I'd say that we're looking at the test stand for a rocket engine, and quite a large one at that."

"I agree." Henry laid a finger on the horizontal structure. "I bet that's a bridge crane for unloading rockets from trucks, and the tall thing over here is the gantry tower."

"Besides, look at all this concrete." Mike ran a finger around it. "They wouldn't lay down this much for any reason except to provide a blast radius. And putting it next to the beach . . ."

"Uh-huh." Gerry was leaning across the table, trying to get a good look. "If they launch a rocket, and it goes out of control, it'll go out over the water, where it won't hit anything."

"Like a barn, you mean," Jack Cube murmured. The others chuckled, and Gerry scowled at his roommate for a moment before managing a sheepish grin. The two had been getting along better lately, once they'd learned to put racial differences aside.

"That's what MI-6 thinks, too." Bliss appeared satisfied. "Thanks for confirming our suspicions. However, what's just as important about these pictures is what we don't see. There isn't any sign of a launch track being built."

No one said anything for a few moments. Everyone knew what the colonel was getting at. Silver Bird's launch rail was supposed to be two miles long; something that big would be obvious from the air. If it wasn't on Peenemünde . . .

Goddard cleared his throat. "This could mean one of three things. First, they haven't yet begun to build any launch facilities for Silver Bird. This is probably a static test stand converted from their old missile program. Second, the facilities, including the track, are under construction, but they've been camouflaged to prevent their being spotted from the air. Third, the launch site is somewhere else."

"I agree with all that, and those explanations have occurred to our intelligence people, too." Bliss hesitated. "However, we can't ignore the fourth possibility . . . Silver Bird is an elaborate hoax, something intended to distract us from . . . well, whatever else the Nazis may actually have in the works."

Goddard stared at him. "You can't seriously believe that."

"I'm just telling you what other people have said. Lord Cherwell, the British Defence Ministry's so-called rocket expert, thinks the whole thing is nothing more than a red herring."

"Then Lord Cherwell is an idiot. Negligent at best." Goddard jabbed a finger at the photos. "Look at these facilities, Colonel. Look at that test stand . . . you can even see blast marks around it. That took time to build, not to mention a lot of money and manpower. No one makes an effort like this simply to stage a hoax . . . particularly not a country at war like Germany, where they need every available resource to keep their military machine going."

"But the Nazis might . . ."

"The Nazis aren't stupid!"

Everyone stared at Goddard, stunned by the outburst. Most of the time, he was genial, soft-spoken, able to make or take a joke; for some, he was like a favorite uncle, even a father figure. No one except those who'd worked with him for a long time—Henry, Lloyd, and Taylor—even suspected that he had a temper to lose.

Bliss was probably the most startled of all. He regarded the professor as if he were a viper who'd just lunged at him. "Bob . . ."

"Omar . . ." Goddard took a deep breath, closed his eyes, waited ten seconds, then opened his eyes and let out his breath. "Sorry. Please forgive me. It's just that I have a low tolerance for fools, and one of my definitions of a fool is that he's someone who ignores the obvious."

"I don't believe anyone is ignoring anything," Bliss said quietly.

Henry spoke up. "Colonel, with all due respect, I disagree. What Lord Whatshisname . . . or anyone else who thinks this is a hoax . . . is overlooking is the Sanger-Bredt report itself. Every person on this team has gone through it over and over again. Everything in it checks out. I mean, we're actually kind of impressed. No one would go to this much effort just to pull a gag. It makes no sense."

"Silver Bird is real, sir," Jack Cube said. "And we'd be making a serious mistake if we came to believe otherwise."

Bliss slowly nodded. "I think it is, too. There are people in Washington who are unconvinced, too, but I think they'll listen to me if I tell them that you believe that the threat is real." He absently stroked his mustache as he contemplated the blueprints. "In the meantime, we need to get to work building this thing . . . the X-1, as you call it."

"My feelings exactly." Goddard smiled; he was relaxed again, back to his usual self. "Once we finalize the main-engine specs, we'll start assembling a scale model for testing . . ."

"I'm sorry, but that's out of the question." Bliss shook his head. "One of the reasons why we've separated Blue Horizon's design and test operations is to prevent accidents that would put your group at risk. Fabrication and assembly facilities are already under way in Alamogordo. All you need to do is supply the final blueprints, and our engineering team will . . ."

"No." Goddard's tone was adamant.

Bliss met his determined gaze without flinching. "Bob, this has already been settled, and may I remind you that you agreed to it. Your job is to design the rocket. It'll be someone else's job to build it."

"Doctor G agreed to this," Ham said, using Esther's nickname for her husband that the others had lately adopted as well. "The rest of us haven't."

"You weren't asked," Bliss shot back, "but you're expected to abide by his agreement."

"You're asking rocket men not to get their hands dirty," Henry said. "It doesn't work that way, Colonel. We built and fired twenty-one Nell rockets in Roswell, and never once did we put ourselves in serious danger." He was stretching the truth; there had been a few close shaves, such as when Goddard had once walked out to the launch tower to see why a rocket hadn't lifted off, only to have it blow up before he was halfway there. Bliss didn't need to know that, though. "You can't isolate us like that and expect this project to be a success."

Bliss was quiet for a moment. "All right . . . a compromise. Once we've assembled the test rocket, we'll let some of your people come in to supervise the launch."

"So long as it isn't me." Goddard forced a grin. "As I said, I detest airplanes."

"Okay then . . . that leaves us with one more thing." Bliss laid a hand on the reconnaissance photos. "Army intelligence and MI-6 want to try to locate their launch site . . . that is, if Silver Bird is not going to launch from Peenemünde. This is crucial even if it's beyond our bombers' current operating theater. Once Silver Bird takes off, it'll take only a little more than an hour and a half for it to circle the globe and reach New York. So it's imperative that the Allies try to put someone nearby who can watch the area and send word if it appears that a launch is imminent."

"So what do you want from us?" Taylor asked.

"You people know Silver Bird's capabilities better than anyone else. That said, you probably have the best shot at figuring out possible launch sites in Germany."

"We might be able to do that." Goddard looked over at Henry. "I think we can spare you for a day or two. Want to take a crack at this?"

"Sure, why not?" Henry grinned. "At least it'll get me out of the lab for a while."

He avoided looking at Frank O'Connor, but everyone knew what he meant. Ever since the night they'd been caught sneaking out to a bar, their FBI escort hadn't let the 390 Group out of his sight. The men went from their boardinghouse straight to the physics lab and back again. During the weekends, they were allowed to go out for dinner and a movie, but only under supervision and with any public discussion of Blue Horizon strictly prohibited. So the men eagerly took any opportunity to slip the leash, if only for an hour or two.

"Very well. I think that takes care of everything." Bliss stepped away from the table. "Meeting adjourned. Lieutenant Jackson, may I speak with you a moment?"

Henry watched as Bliss and Jack Cube walked over to a corner of the room. They kept their voices low and their backs turned to everyone else, so he couldn't hear what they were saying.

Lloyd slid up beside him. "What do you think that's all about?" he murmured.

"Haven't got a clue, and it's probably none of our business anyway." Henry walked over to the coat hooks and pulled down his overcoat and hat. "Well, it's off to the campus library for me," he said breezily, relishing Lloyd's envious glare. "Can I bring you anything? A good book, maybe?"

"Screw the book. Bring me a coed."

"If I meet any nice Jewish girls, you'll be the first to know." Putting on his hat, Henry headed for the door. "See you at dinner, Frank," he said to the FBI agent, and got a cold stare in return.

———

The university library was located a short distance from the Science Building, about halfway across the Clark campus. Henry took his time getting there; spring was just a week away, and the last of the winter snow was melting beneath the red oaks and sugar maples of the commons. He opened his overcoat and whistled just under his breath, enjoying a rare moment when he was going somewhere without another team member or Agent O'Connor tagging along.

The library's reference room was located on the ground floor. Students were hunched over books and notepads spread open upon long oak tables, intent on preparing for the upcoming midterms; the only sounds were the faint scratch of pencils on paper, the click of slide rules, and the occasional whispered conversation. Henry knew what he was looking for, so instead of approaching the reference desk, he went straight to the atlas collection and pulled out the largest one he could find.

Its maps were arranged by geographic area and were detailed enough for him to locate specific cities and towns. Unfortunately, what he needed was something else entirely: a map of Germany that would reveal topographical features as well, and also a global map that would show him precise lines of latitude and longitude between Europe and North America. He checked the other atlases, but they were no better than the one he already had. Clearly, he ought to find something better.

A young woman was seated at the reference desk. She had shoulder-length chestnut hair and a pretty face, and the mannish fisherman's sweater she wore wasn't baggy enough to hide some nice curves beneath it. She was reading a detective novel—*Farewell, My Lovely* by Raymond Chandler—when Henry approached her, but she didn't look up until he pointedly cleared his throat. Then she peered over her tortoiseshell glasses, and Henry found himself being regarded by a pair of startling green eyes.

"Yes?" she said, her voice low and slightly annoyed at being interrupted from her reading. "May I help you?"

It took Henry a second or two to find his tongue. What came out of his mouth was a quiet croak. "Umm . . . ahh . . . well, yes, I'm . . . ah . . ."

"Not interested. Thanks anyway." She returned her attention to her book.

Henry blinked. "Pardon me? I don't understand . . ."

"Yes, you do." She turned a page. "You were about to ask me if I'd like to have a drink with you, or maybe go out for dinner, or something like that, and I've given you my answer. No thanks, not interested." Her fingers made a shooing motion. "Now go away."

It was Henry's turn to become annoyed. "If you want to catch up on your reading, then why are you sitting at the reference librarian's desk?" He gazed past her; there was no one else behind the counter. "Where is she, anyway? I could use some help."

The young woman looked up at him again. "I'm the librarian," she said, a bit less dismissive. "May I help you?"

"Now that you ask, yes, you could. I need a good global map, with enough detail to show me major geographic features as well as cities and borders, and also exact lines of latitude and longitude."

"Mercator or Lambert projection?"

"Umm . . ." To him, a map was a map; he was unaware of any differences. "I don't know," he admitted, and was surprised when she smiled at him. "I guess I'm looking for something I can use to figure out . . . ah, air travel routes between here and Germany."

"Oh, really?" The green eyes became curious. "Then you'd need an Azimuthal projection." Putting down the book, she gazed up at the ceiling for a moment, her lips pursing together and twitching back and forth in a pensive but very becoming way. "I believe we have one in the cartography collection. Follow me."

She stood up and walked out from behind the desk, and, as she strolled across the room, Henry noticed two things. First, every guy in the room watched her go by. Second, she didn't walk; she seemed instead to float across the floor, her low-heeled shoes barely touching the checkerboard tiles. No wonder she'd become accustomed to college boys' trying to ask her out. She was an angel in glasses.

She led him to a large map case at the back of the room, and in the second drawer down she found what he was looking for: a world map that not only displayed political borders, major cities, and geographical features such as mountain ranges and rivers, but was also laid out so that the latitude and longitude lines were straightened, therefore showing how many miles lay between one point and another. The map was larger than normal, big enough that it had to be unfolded and spread out across the nearest table. There was a freshman sitting where they needed to be, but he grabbed his books and scurried out of the way before the librarian even had to ask him to move. One does not argue with angels.

"Yes . . . yes, I think this will do nicely," Henry said once the map was laid out. "Thank you." The librarian nodded and started to glide away. On impulse, he blurted out, "Oh . . . um, one more thing. Do you have a ruler I could borrow? Maybe even a yardstick?"

"A ruler. Or a yardstick." She stopped and turned back to him; again, the curious gaze, this time with one eyebrow raised ever so slightly. He nodded, and she smiled. "Yes, I may have one. I'll look." And then she went away, once again drawing every male eye in the room.

Henry had taken off his overcoat and pulled out his pencil and pocket notepad by the time she returned. "Ruler and yardstick," she said, laying them on the table beside the map, then her eyes widened in horror as he picked up the yardstick, laid it across the map, and bent toward it with pencil in hand. "Oh, no you don't!" she hissed, reaching forward to snatch the pencil from him. "You are not going to draw on . . . !"

"Relax. I'm not going to do anything of the kind. Just plotting points, that's all." Henry removed the pencil from her hand, and she watched closely as he moved the yardstick until one end rested on Germany's northwestern Baltic coast, and the other end extended across eastern Europe. Being careful not to touch the pencil tip to the map, he used it to

carefully align the yardstick with Peenemünde, then he opened his notebook and jotted down the exact latitude and longitude.

As he continued to work, steadily moving the yardstick due east in a
straight line until he reached the map's right border, then picking up again
from the left side and moving it across the Pacific until it reached the
North American continent, Henry became conscious of the librarian
peering over his shoulder. "If you're trying to figure out an air route between here and Germany," she whispered at last, "wouldn't you want to
plot it to the west, not the east?"

"It's a little more complicated than that."

"I'm sure it is." She continued to watch as he jotted down some more
figures. "You're not a student, are you?"

"Actually, I'm a grad student in the physics department."

"Ah, of course . . . physics. That explains why you're interested in plotting a flight around the world."

There was a trace of amusement in her voice, but also a little too much
interest in what he was doing for his comfort. "I'm studying with Dr.
Goddard, in his Physics 390 program. We're trying to . . ." Henry stopped,
at a loss for words. There was no easy way to explain what he was doing
that didn't involve telling her a lie. "It's complicated," he finished.

"You said that already." She pulled back a chair and sat down, resting
her chin on her right hand as she continued to watch him work. "Sorry I
was so rude a few minutes ago. It's just that . . . y'know, I get a lot of kids
trying to . . ."

"Say no more. I think I understand." From the corner of his eye, he
saw that she was no longer studying the map but him instead. "I'm
Henry . . . Henry Morse."

"Pleased to meet you, Henry. My name is Doris Gilbert." She extended
her hand; when he shook it, he found that her touch was soft and warm.
"Yes," she added.

"I'm sorry . . . come again?"

"Yes, I'd like to go out and have a drink with you. So long as it's coffee because I don't drink." She paused. "That's what you were thinking, weren't you?"

"Actually, it wasn't, but . . . sure, that would be swell." Then he remembered Frank O'Connor, and how difficult it would be to get out from under him. "But I'm going to have to do that some other time. Dr. Goddard keeps me pretty busy."

"Certainly. I understand completely." Doris stood up. "You know where to find me, Henry. Come back anytime." And then she returned to her desk, her hips moving gracefully beneath her long woolen skirt.

If you think her brains are great, Henry thought as he watched her go, *just wait till you get to her legs.*

A VISIT FROM THE *REICHSFÜHRER*

With a muffled roar, the wind tunnel's high-velocity fans came to life, their vibration shaking the thick double panes of the observation window. Red smoke poured across the stainless-steel model fixed to a slender pylon in the middle of the tunnel, a miniature jet stream to be studied by the men on the other side of the window. A clear space gradually formed beneath the model's flat underbelly, stretching from its sharp nose to the twin stabilizers at its rear. The half-meter-long replica trembled slightly in the artificial windstorm but otherwise remained stable.

"As you see, *Silbervogel* is remarkably aerodynamic," Wernher von Braun said, pointing through the window. He had to raise his voice to be heard over the noise. "We've been working to improve upon the ogival shape of the bow so as to give it greater lift during the ascent phases, thereby reducing the amount of fuel the engines will need to . . ."

"How many bombs will it carry?" Heinrich Himmler asked, almost shouting.

The *Reichsführer*'s question was characteristically blunt, conveying an impatience with technical details. The engineers conducting the test carefully kept their attention focused on the model; only Arthur Rudolph glanced at Himmler, and just for a moment. Along with everyone else, he was only too happy to let Peenemünde's technical director handle their visitor.

"*Silbervogel* is designed to carry a 3.75-metric-ton payload." Von Braun moved a little closer to Himmler, cupping his hands to his mouth so that he could be heard. "This can be one single bomb, of course, but we believe the best option would be three 1.25-ton incendiary devices. This would allow for a greater dispersal over the target area once the craft reaches . . ."

"Less than four tons?" Himmler's eyes flared behind his round glasses. "*Nein!* Unacceptable! This machine must carry fifty tons at least!"

Von Braun fought to keep his expression impassive; the laughter he wanted to let loose would have been fatal. "*Reichsführer*, with all due respect, a fifty-ton payload is out of the question. In order to achieve escape velocity and complete its circumnavigation of the Earth, *Silbervogel* can carry only the bare minimum. Even its pilot cannot be more than 1.8 meters in height or weigh more than eighty-two kilograms."

"But only three one-ton bombs . . . *pfft!*" Himmler made a dismissive gesture. "A Heinkel bomber can carry more than that!"

No, it couldn't, von Braun thought, *nor would it have the range.* But challenging the *Reichsführer*'s understanding of the facts was a risky proposition, so he was careful with his response. "Our studies conclude that three incendiary devices dropped in the New York metropolitan area will bring about destruction surpassing their weight. Dropped from an altitude of seventy kilometers, terminal velocity alone will cause significant damage, and the firestorm that follows the initial blast would doubtless spread across the entire city. Even if only one bomb hits Manhattan, with the other two landing in the surrounding neighborhoods, the city will be devastated. More bombs are unnecessary."

Himmler said nothing but instead continued to watch the test. Was it von Braun's imagination, or was Arthur keeping it going longer than necessary? From the corner of his eye, he caught a glimpse of him standing at the control board. He'd stopped writing down figures on his clipboard and was now doing nothing more than watching the model get buffeted by the fans. Perhaps he was hoping that the noise would drive Himmler away.

If that was the idea, it succeeded. Himmler suddenly turned and marched toward the door, trailing an entourage of junior officers. To von Braun's quiet disgust, Colonel Dornberger had joined them, if only temporarily. Although *Wa Pruf 11*'s military director was just as terrified of the *Reichsführer* as anyone else, he wasn't above using his visit to Peenemünde to curry favor with a member of Hitler's inner circle.

As much as von Braun was dismayed by Dornberger's behavior, though, he was also disappointed with his own. For the first time, he'd put on the black SS uniform that until then had only hung in his closet. It was necessary; wearing civilian clothes when the SS leader came to visit would have been disrespectful, perhaps even making Himmler suspect him of disloyalty. That was something no one could afford to let happen. It was whispered that Himmler's enemies tended to land in concentration camps or die with a piano wire wrapped around their necks.

Von Braun couldn't wait for the *Reichsführer* to leave so that he could take off this damned outfit. *At least I look better than he does,* he thought. Despite the knee boots, jodhpurs, and death's-head insignia on his jacket lapels, Himmler looked like what he'd been before he joined the Nazi party: a chicken farmer, a mediocre little man with a fuzzy mustache and a weak chin. Heinrich Himmler would have been contemptible if he hadn't been so powerful or so thoroughly evil.

"So . . ." Himmler wheeled around as soon as they'd left the windowless concrete shed. "When do you think we'll be able to launch your spaceship, Dr. von Braun?"

Von Braun had heard this question before: from Goering, from Goebbels, from Speer, from everyone else in the High Command who'd suddenly taken an interest in Peenemünde after Hitler had given the order to proceed with *Silbervogel*. "We're hoping to be ready to fly by next summer," he replied, a truthful yet evasive answer that he and Dornberger had devised a while ago. "There are still many technical obstacles in our way, but we're working to overcome them."

Dornberger stepped in. "We'll soon be ready for static tests of the new rocket engine, *Herr Reichsführer*. It will run on a revolutionary new mixture of liquid oxygen and a hydrocarbon suspension of aluminum particulate that promises to produce a higher thrust than the fuel we used for the A-4 prototype. The turbopump assembly for the main combustion chamber is nearly complete, once we finish testing the main coolant loop for . . ."

"Yes, yes, of course." Himmler was impatient with details, and von Braun doubted that he understood them anyway. He continued walking toward the large, warehouselike shed that Dornberger had indicated would be the next stop on their tour. "I know your scientists are technically competent. What concerns me is whether you'll be able to produce a weapon of this sort before the Americans do."

"I'm positive we shall," von Braun said. "We're already far ahead of their own rocket program."

Dornberger shot him a look. What von Braun had just said came dangerously close to contradicting the colonel's contention that Germany was in a race against America to produce an intercontinental rocket. And they had another concern as well. Himmler was Goering's rival. He'd already taken the Gestapo away from him, transforming it into an arm of the SS, and it was whispered that he wanted control of the Luftwaffe as well.

It was bad enough that Dornberger and von Braun had to answer to Goering. It would be worse if Himmler became their new boss. There was nothing either of them could do about that except prepare for the worst and expect that Himmler would win the power contest. If that happened, the *Reichsführer-SS* needed to be convinced that the *Silbervogel Projekt* was proceeding according to plan. Otherwise, the two of them might receive a visit from men in black trench coats, followed by an automobile ride to parts unknown.

"Hmm . . ." Himmler abruptly stopped and turned to gaze around the area. "Where will the launch site be located? I see nothing that indicates that the track is under construction."

"We've been considering a new location, *Herr Reichsführer*," Dornberger said. "The original plan was to build it here on the island, but lately we've come to believe that this might not be a good idea."

"About a month ago, the RAF began making reconnaissance flights above us." Von Braun nodded toward the overcast sky; Himmler instinctively looked up, as if expecting to see a British P-38 or Mosquito. "The Luftwaffe commander has sent up Messerschmidts to intercept them, of course, but they managed to get away. I have little doubt that they've taken high-altitude photographs of our facilities, and even if British intelligence hasn't figured out what they are, an elevated rail three kilometers long will certainly draw their attention. If the British and American air forces decide to make an air raid . . ."

"It will not succeed." Himmler's tone was flat, decisive. "No bombs will drop on the Fatherland, I assure you."

"Nonetheless, may I respectfully submit that the rail be built elsewhere, for the sake of security?" Von Braun knew that he was perilously close to contradicting Himmler, so he decided to change tactics. "Besides, the closer to the equator the launch site is located, the more we'll be able to take advantage of the Earth's rotation during takeoff."

"Yes . . . yes, I see your point." Again, Himmler became contemplative. "Perhaps it could be built in an occupied country near the Mediterranean. Southern France, or perhaps Egypt . . ."

"Those are the optimal locations, yes, but then we'd have a new problem . . . moving *Silbervogel* there once it's assembled. The vehicle will be twenty-eight meters in length and have an empty weight of ten metric tons. Transportation out of the country will be very difficult, and should the craft be damaged in any way during transit . . ."

"There's also the necessity of having a large workforce," Dornberger said. "Several thousand people work here, including the war prisoners we've assigned to hard labor. Moving this operation elsewhere will mean that we'll have to find a new source of labor. This will be difficult if the project is relocated to France or North Africa."

"I understand." A dry smile appeared on Himmler's pinched face.

"Let me look into this. I may be able to find an alternative within our borders."

Von Braun inwardly groaned. Without intending to do so, he'd given Himmler another reason to give Hitler why the Luftwaffe in general, and *Silbervogel* in particular, should be turned over to him. Himmler's first priority was his own ambitions. Anything he could use to further them was fair game.

"That would be helpful, *Herr Reichsführer*," he said. *"Danke."*

"Still, this matter about the American rocket program bothers me. How can you be so certain that we're ahead of them? We've had little recent intelligence about what they're presently doing."

Von Braun found himself at a loss for words. Himmler was correct; they really didn't know where the Americans stood in terms of rocket development. Neither he nor Dornberger could afford to admit this, though, because it would have undermined the myth upon which the *Silbervogel Projekt* was built: America was far ahead of Germany in the field of rocketry, and Silver Bird was the Third Reich's best chance of catching up.

"It might be possible that their program is being done in secret, just as ours is." Von Braun had no idea if this was true; he just hoped that it didn't sound like he was making it up on the spot. "It would make sense that their foremost scientist, Robert Goddard, would be involved in any sort of long-range project that the Americans might have undertaken . . ."

"Has doubtless undertaken," Dornberger quickly added. "Yes, I agree. The project is being kept hidden, naturally, and Goddard is probably in charge. This is probably why our intelligence operatives have yet to determine its purpose or whereabouts."

Von Braun nodded, even as he and Dornberger shared a conspiratorial look. Both of them knew this was an utter fabrication. What little they knew about Goddard's recent activity was that he was somewhere out in the American desert, tinkering with rockets that probably couldn't reach the next state, let alone Europe. Himmler wouldn't be aware of this, though. If he could be led to believe that the Americans had their own Peenemünde, with Robert Goddard as its mastermind, then the *Reichsführer-SS* and the rest of the High Command wouldn't suspect that they'd undertaken a massive and enormously expensive research-and-development program in response to a threat that simply didn't exist.

Perhaps we'll be lucky, and the war will be over before this thing is ready to fly, von Braun thought. Like Eugen Sanger and Irene Bredt—who were involved in the project only as Luftwaffe Institute advisors, with no direct role, at least as yet—he'd come to view *Silbervogel* as a space vehicle rather than a military weapon. Perhaps one day it could be used for more peaceful purposes, like carrying the components of a Mars expeditionary fleet into orbit for assembly. Until then, though, he'd have to focus on carrying out an attack on America, a goal he'd come to like less and less as time went on.

"Yes . . . yes, that would make sense, wouldn't it?" Himmler slowly nodded. "You're quite right. Dr. Goddard should be investigated. I'll have to request that the *Abwehr* look into this. Perhaps their operatives may learn something new."

"It would be prudent," von Braun said carefully. *Let them take their time,* he silently added. *The longer it takes for them to find him, the safer we'll be.*

"*Reichsführer,* if we may . . . ?" Dornberger stretched out his hand, beckoning them to return to the tour.

"Of course." Himmler strode forward, his retinue in tow. Von Braun walked alongside Dornberger as he led them toward the nearby assembly shed. The guards snapped to attention, arms raised in rigid salutes. The *Reichsführer* ignored them as he allowed Dornberger to open the door. Von Braun stepped aside and let everyone enter the shed before him.

The shed held one of Peenemünde's most closely guarded secrets. Ever since last Christmas, when a French spy had been caught lurking outside with a Minox camera, no one was allowed to enter without an identification card signed by both Dornberger and von Braun. The size of a large airplane hangar, it performed much the same role . . . but what was inside was no ordinary aircraft.

Heinrich Himmler stopped and stared at what appeared to be a completed and flight-ready *Silbervogel*. Resting upon its tricycle landing gear, nose pointed toward the shed's double doors, the vehicle took up nearly half the enormous workspace. Fluorescent ceiling lights reflected off its burnished silver skin; rollaway ladders had been pushed up beside the fuselage, with one of them positioned next to the cockpit's open canopy. The entire vessel looked like it was ready to be towed out to a launch rail that hadn't yet been built.

"You've begun building it already?" Himmler asked, the eyes behind his glasses wide with awe.

"No, *Herr Reichsführer*." Dornberger was grinning from ear to ear, obviously pleased by Himmler's reaction. "This is a full-scale mock-up, used by our engineers to help them work out the design details. The airframe is made of white pine, with canvas stretched across it and painted to simulate the outer hull."

"I see." Himmler was obviously disappointed to find that this *Silbervogel* was nothing more than a model. Folding his hands together behind his back, he strolled toward the mock-up, giving it a cold and silent appraisal. "And the real craft, Colonel? Where is it?"

"On the other side of the mock-up," von Braun said. "If you'll follow me . . ."

Von Braun led him and his entourage around the mock-up; Himmler gave it little more than a passing look, no longer impressed now that he knew what it was. On the other side of the hangar, a skeletal frame lay half-finished upon a support cradle. Built of aluminum and stainless steel, it had a stubby bow but no nose, a pair of wings but no tail section. Bundles of multicolored wires were laced throughout the frame, held in place by black elastic tape. The cockpit lacked a canopy; in fact, it was nothing more than a small, empty tub, with neither instrument panel nor seat.

"This is it? This is all you've built so far?" Himmler's disappointment turned to anger. He waved a dismissive hand at the craft as if it were nothing more than a child's elaborate toy. "I've seen better work at the Junkers factory."

Again, von Braun had to keep his temper in check. The arrogance and ignorance of this . . . this former poulterer . . . was appalling. "*Herr Reichsführer,*" he said, somehow managing to maintain an even voice, "the Junkers factory builds airplanes on an assembly line. What we're doing here has never been attempted before . . . constructing a vehicle capable of penetrating Earth's atmosphere and flying all the way around the world on a single tank of fuel. It is more than merely revolutionary. It is the future."

Even as he said this, he knew that Himmler wasn't listening. This ignorant little man had no appreciation for the groundbreaking work that still needed to be done before Silver Bird would be ready to fly. Even the fuselage would be a new development. Experiments had shown that the only material capable of withstanding multiple atmospheric entries was titanium, perhaps with a graphite coating along the underbelly and leading edges. Germany's only source of titanium was in the Ukraine, though, where it would have to be mined even while the Army was struggling to hold the eastern front of the Russian invasion, and once that ore was extracted and shipped to Germany, it would still need to be subjected to the refinement process the Kroll laboratories had developed only a few years earlier.

If they were lucky, they'd have just enough titanium plating to cover the airframe, but the result would be an aeronautical advance generations ahead of anything done before. But try explaining any of that to a chicken farmer . . .

"Millions of Reichsmarks have been spent on this . . . !" Himmler snapped.

"And millions more will be spent before it's complete," von Braun said, and the *Reichsführer* glared at him, irritated by the interruption. "But when it's done, the Fatherland will have a craft beyond imagination . . ."

"And a weapon that cannot be defended against or defeated," Dornberger finished. "It will be worth the time and expense, sir. That I promise."

Himmler was quiet for a full minute. He looked first at the skeletal airframe, then turned around to gaze at the mock-up. Once again, he clasped his hands together behind his back, but now he rocked back and forth on his heels, the toes of his boots softly tapping against the concrete floor.

"Twelve months," he said at last, not looking at either Dornberger or von Braun. "You have twelve months to make this thing fly. Or the *Führer* and I will be . . . gravely disappointed."

Without another word, he marched toward the door, his officers trailing along behind him.

SKID

The rocket engine lay on its horizontal test bed, smoking in the desert sun. Sixty feet long, its components weren't covered by an outer skin but instead lay exposed; a liquid-oxygen tank, a kerosene tank, and a liquid-nitrogen tank, with complex turbopumps feeding their contents into a rear-combustion chamber. The maw of the exhaust bell pointed toward the distant horizon, giving the engine the appearance of an enormous gun.

Five hundred yards away, a dozen men huddled within a trench protected by a wall of sandbags. Tripod-mounted periscopes jutted above the barricade along with a motion-picture camera, but most of the onlookers simply peered over the sandbags, ready to duck if anything went wrong. Electrical cables snaked across the sand from the test bed to a nearby diesel generator, which in turn was controlled by wires leading to the trench. A couple of minutes earlier, the tanker trucks that fueled the engine had driven away from the test area. Now the prototype engine was on its own, wreathed in cold oxygen fumes and quietly groaning in the heat of a New Mexico afternoon.

The engineers who'd built the engine were clustered around an instrument box, carefully watching the dials and meters registering the status of the engine's fuel, pressure, and electrical systems. Finally satisfied, one of them looked over at the two Army officers standing nearby. "Ready when you are," he said.

Colonel Bliss turned to Lieutenant Jackson. "Jack?"

Jack Cube didn't lower his binoculars. "Tell 'em to go ahead, sir," he said quietly.

Bliss nodded to the engineers. One of them began a countdown, starting from ten. The movie camera purred as its operator began filming. Several people raised their hands to their ears.

At the count of zero, the chief engineer pressed a toggle switch in the center of the box. From the distance, the dull grumble of the primary ignition sequence sounded. A small reddish spark appeared deep within the engine bell, showing that the nitrogen had forced the kerosene and liquid oxygen together in the combustion chamber, where they'd been ignited by an electric heating element. A couple of seconds later, the grumble became a mighty roar that thundered across the plain. The small spark was suddenly replaced by a white-hot jet that flared from the engine like an enormous blowtorch, sending a dense black plume roiling up into the blue desert sky. The engine trembled and shook upon the test bed, straining against the iron straps and bolts that held it down. It no longer seemed to be a machine but instead a living creature, a metal tiger suddenly awakened and wanting to be freed.

A cheer rose from the engineers, almost loud enough to be heard over the engine. They clapped each other on the back and shook hands; a couple of them looked like they were on the verge of jumping out of the trench and running straight to the test bed. Even the guards were grinning, as were the three visitors nearby. Hands covering his ears, Bliss laughed out loud.

The only person who didn't share the enthusiasm was J. Jackson Jackson. He continued to watch the rocket engine through his binoculars, lips barely moving as he counted elapsed seconds beneath his breath: "Nine . . . ten . . . eleven . . ."

And then the engine exploded.

There was no warning at all. One moment, it was operating as it should. The next, it disappeared within the enormous fireball that erupted upon the test bed. It was as if the Army Air Force had chosen that moment to drop a one-ton bomb on the desert.

The blast made everyone duck behind the cover of the sandbags, which was just as well because the explosion sent twisted pieces of metal in all directions, with a copper pipe hitting the ground only a dozen feet from the trench. The movie camera almost toppled before someone grabbed its tripod and kept it upright, but one of the periscopes was blown over. A wave of intense heat rushed across the trench, hotter than the desert sun.

The explosion was still echoing off the distant mountains when Colonel Bliss slowly rose from his instinctive crouch to peer over the barricade at the smoking mess. "What happened?" he asked in dull astonishment, as if it weren't obvious.

"Who knows?" Jack Cube lowered his binoculars with a shrug that could have been mistaken for indifference. He was the only one who was unruffled by the catastrophe. "Bad welds causing a leak. Bad fuel-mixture ratio. Turbine failure. Any number of things. Maybe we'll figure it out when we pick up the pieces."

"You don't seem surprised."

Jackson gave him an incredulous look: *Are you kidding?* "I would've been surprised if it was a success. This is . . . this was . . . a prototype. They almost always fail even if they're built completely according to spec. And . . ."

He stopped himself, looked away from the colonel. "And what, Lieutenant?" Bliss asked. "Let's hear it."

Jack Cube hesitated, then slowly shook his head. "Sir, this is no way to run an R&D program. You can't expect our group to simply put stuff down on paper, then send it to someone else to build and test. You've got to let us get our hands on the hardware if we're going to . . ."

"Not a chance." The colonel grunted as he heaved himself out of the trench, disdaining the wooden steps that had been built into one end. He turned to offer Jack Cube a hand, only to find that the younger man had already climbed up and was standing beside him. "My orders are to keep the brain trust away from the rockets. What just happened here proves to me that it's a wise decision."

"Sir, I disagree. What it really proves is that you can't compartmentalize this project." Jack hesitated. "We have a solution. There's a manufacturer in Worcester, the Wyman-Gordon Company. A military contractor, making various components for aircraft companies. If we could arrange to have them build the main engine under the 390 Group's direct supervision . . ."

"And conduct tests where? Tell me a place in New England where you could fire an engine of this size and keep it a secret. That, plus the security risks of undertaking a secret military construction program in a major city . . ."

"It would be the last place the Nazis would look." Bliss gave him a skeptical look, but Jackson went on. "Think about it, sir. Who would expect anyone to build a rocket engine in Worcester? And in an aircraft factory, there would already be enough security in place to . . ."

"Out of the question." Shaking his head, Bliss walked away. "Enough, Lieutenant. This isn't why I asked you to come here."

"Yes, sir." Jackson knew better than to try to force the issue. Omar Bliss was stubborn by nature, and as Blue Horizon's project director, he had the last word. But as he fell into step with the colonel, he resolved to win the argument. Sooner or later, he'd make Bliss come around. He just had to come up with a better line of reasoning.

The three visitors who'd witnessed the test had climbed out of the trench. They'd lit cigarettes and were leaning against the sandbags, quietly chatting among themselves. At the colonel's approach, the two in uniform dropped their smokes and stood at attention, while the one in civilian clothes did not. All three had a self-confident, almost arrogant attitude that Jack Cube recognized from flight school. They were test pilots, and if Bliss was right, they were the best.

"Lieutenant Calhoun, Lieutenant Sloman, Mr. McPherson . . . if you'll come with us, please." The colonel walked by them without stopping, heading for a jeep parked beside the unfinished blockhouse, where construction had begun a few weeks ago.

The test pilots crowded into the backseat, and the colonel rode shotgun while Jack drove. A short ride over a bumpy, unpaved road brought them to a single-story prefab in the middle of the secret compound going up inside Alamogordo Army Air Field. Bliss and Jackson led the three men into the building and down a short corridor to the colonel's office. Just outside the door, a sign was on the corridor wall:

Whatever You See Here,
Whatever You Hear Here,
When You Leave Here,
It Stays Here.

Giving the sign a significant look, the colonel tapped it with his finger, then unlocked the door and opened it. His office was small, windowless, and lined with file cabinets, its government-issue desk covered with paperwork. Bliss beckoned to three folding chairs set up, then took a seat behind the desk. Jack closed the door and leaned against a file cabinet, arms crossed.

"Gentlemen, we've met already." Bliss nodded to Jackson. "Let me introduce Lieutenant J. Jackson Jackson. He belongs to a research-and-development team currently involved in the biggest military R&D program Uncle Sam has going. It's called Operation Blue Horizon, and what you just saw was the first major test."

"Looks like it was a success," Chuck Calhoun said drily. A short, beefy man with a red crew cut, he had a perpetual sneer that hinted at undying cynicism about everything.

"Yeah . . . a roaring success." This from Joe McPherson, a skinny, awkward-looking guy with jug ears and a pronounced Adam's apple.

The third man said nothing although a smile whispered at the corners of his mouth. Rudy Sloman was just a little taller than Calhoun, wiry and narrow-shouldered, with one of those homely-yet-handsome faces that either repels women or attracts them.

"Believe it or not, it was a success," Bliss said. "The engine ran for twelve seconds before it blew up . . ."

"Eleven seconds," Jackson said softly.

"Eleven seconds"—Bliss scowled at him—"which is pretty good considering that it's the most powerful liquid-fuel rocket engine yet built. The next one we build will last longer, and we'll keep working on it until we get something that can sustain 132,000 pounds of thrust for ninety seconds."

McPherson whistled. "That's a tall order. What are you planning to build here, some kind of rocket fighter?"

"Sort of like that . . . but not quite." Bliss looked at Jackson. "Lieutenant?"

"What we're building is a manned space vehicle that will operate above Earth's atmosphere," Jackson said. "The X-1 will be a fighter, yes, but . . ."

He didn't get to finish. Calhoun was already braying laughter, slapping his hands against his knees as he doubled over in his chair. McPherson tried not to laugh, but the smirk that appeared on his face betrayed his skepticism. Sloman shook his head disbelievingly but otherwise remained quiet.

"Man, oh man!" Calhoun was almost wheezing from the effort to speak. "You darkies sure are funny!"

"Knock it off!" Bliss snapped. "You'll address Lieutenant Jackson with the respect due to a fellow officer!"

Jack tried not to smile. Over the past couple of months, Bliss had gradually learned to regard him as being more than "a credit to his race," yet this was the first time he'd heard the colonel stand up for him. At least in one area, they were making progress . . .

"Yeah, yeah . . . sure, Colonel. Sorry." Calhoun snuffled back laughter, straightened up again. Then he looked at Jackson, and said, "So, Lieutenant . . . with all due respect, how many shoes did you have to shine to get those bars?"

Jack Cube's hands fell to his sides, reflexively curled into fists. He did nothing, though, except look at Bliss and quietly shake his head. "Okay,

Calhoun, get out of here," the colonel said, his voice tight with anger. "The program can't use someone like you."

"With pleasure." Calhoun shoved his hands in his pockets and strutted out of the shack. Just before he left, though, he began to whistle a tune. Jackson recognized it at once: "Suwannee River," an old minstrel-show song usually performed by white people in blackface.

Bliss waited until Calhoun slammed the door shut behind him, then let out his breath. "My apologies, Lieutenant. If you want, I can have him brought up on charges."

Jack shook his head. "That's all right, sir. I'm just glad we found a bad apple early." He looked at the other two men. "What about you? Any more humorous remarks?"

McPherson had already wiped the smile off his face. He shook his head. "Not at all, Lieutenant Jackson," Sloman said, speaking up for the first time. "Only too happy to be serving with you." He paused, then added, "A rocket ship? Did I understand you correctly?"

"Yes, you did. Blue Horizon is a crash program to build a fighter that will ascend to suborbital altitude of more than forty miles and return safely to Earth. We're doing this because the Germans are doing the same thing . . . and they intend to use it to bomb New York."

Sloman let out a low, soft whistle, but McPherson was unimpressed. Folding his arms across his chest, he raised an eyebrow. "Nazi spaceship. Uh-huh . . . now I've heard everything."

"Believe it, Mr. McPherson," Bliss said. "Army intelligence has received sufficient information to convince us that the threat is real. We wouldn't be going through all this if we didn't think otherwise."

"We can discuss details later," Jack Cube said. "For now, though, the reason why the three of you have been asked to come here . . . two, now that Mr. Calhoun has been dismissed . . . is because we need to find someone to fly this craft."

"I had a feeling you were going to say that." There was a sly grin on Sloman's face.

"I'd think that would have been obvious by now." Jackson gave him a brief smile in return. "Make no mistake . . . this will probably be the toughest mission you've undertaken. Training alone will be extremely difficult. As for the X-1 itself . . . it's still on the drawing boards, but have no doubts, gentlemen, it will be unlike anything you've ever flown before."

"Uh-huh. I see." McPherson rubbed his nose. "And what's in it for us?"

"That should be obvious," Jack said. "A chance to serve your country as no one else ever has, and a place in history if your mission succeeds." He didn't mention another obvious fact—the consequences of failure would be violent death and an early grave—because pilots seldom spoke of such things.

McPherson slowly nodded, then reached over to the colonel's desk and picked up a notepad and a pencil. He jotted something down, then tore off the page, folded it in half, and stood up to hand it to Bliss. "All that's well and good," he said, "but if you want the best, you're going to have to pay for it. That's my figure, Colonel. It's not negotiable."

Bliss opened the paper, glanced at the figure, then closed it again. "Thank you, Mr. McPherson. Would you please leave us alone for a few minutes? You can wait across the hall."

McPherson hesitated, uncertain how to interpret this. When the colonel didn't say anything further, he turned and left the office.

Bliss sighed, then passed the note to Jackson. "Who does he think he's kidding? That's more than my salary."

Jack Cube took a quick look at the paper, then folded it and put it in his pocket. "He'll negotiate if he wants the job. But we're going to need two guys, Colonel . . . one as the mission pilot, the other as the backup. And with Calhoun out . . ."

"I'm afraid you're right." Bliss shook his head and looked at the remaining pilot. "Okay, then, Lieutenant Sloman, that leaves you. Or are you going to give us trouble, too?"

"Who, me?" Sloman asked. "No, sir." Then a wry smile appeared. "But I don't think you understand where either of those other guys are coming from. Fact is, they're scared to death."

Jackson stared at him. "They didn't give me that impression."

"Of course not. They'd sooner die than admit it. Hell, they probably don't even realize it themselves. But do you think Chuck would've said those things to you if he didn't want to get the colonel to throw him out of here?" He looked at Bliss again. "And I don't know what Joe gave you as a figure, but I'd be willing to bet it was a way of making sure that you wouldn't call him back." He shrugged. "Truth is, they don't want to climb into something that might blow up eleven seconds after it took off. They just didn't want to say so out loud."

"And how do you feel about that, Lieutenant Sloman?" Bliss asked.

"Skid."

"Pardon me?"

"Everyone calls me Skid, sir. Or Rudy, if you'd like, but I think only my mother calls me that anymore."

"Where did you get that name, Rudy? Skid, I mean."

"Flight school in Pensacola, sir. I was bringing in a beat-up old Steerman when the landing-gear axle broke. Had to make a belly landing. Skidded all the way down the strip, but at least I didn't turn over." Another grin. "The name stuck, but I don't mind. Kinda like it."

"And you became a test pilot even after that?" Jackson asked.

"We weren't in a war yet, so there wasn't much call for fighter pilots. I wanted to fly warbirds, though, so I kinda just fell into it. Besides, I like the job. Taking up an experimental aircraft, seeing just how far I can push it . . . well, if there's anything more fun than that, I don't know what it is."

Jack Cube was beginning to like this guy. Bliss had brought Jack down from Worcester to help him select the pilot for the mission, figuring that someone with military flight training would know what to look for. Jack had already studied Lieutenant Sloman's record and was impressed even before he'd met him. All the same, though . . .

"This won't be an ordinary airplane," he said. "It's something entirely new."

"Is it going to have wings?" Skid asked, and Jack nodded. "Then I can fly it."

"We won't lie to you," Bliss said. "It's going to be dangerous as hell.

And we're not kidding about training. It'll be more rigorous than anything you've ever done before."

"Oh, now, Colonel, don't tell me that." The test pilot laughed. "Now I *really* want to fly that thing!"

Jackson looked at Bliss. "We've found our man."

"I think you're right." Bliss hesitated. "And McPherson? You want him as backup pilot?"

"Unless you've got someone else." Jack turned to Skid again. "We'll train him beside you, but he's just going to be there in case . . ."

He didn't finish, but Skid did. "In case something happens to me, and I buy the farm." He shrugged. "If you want that kind of insurance, go ahead and pay Joe what he wants. It'll be worth it. But to tell the truth, the idea of getting in the history books really appeals to me. I got a girl back home, see, who's kinda hard to please. Being the first guy in space might just do the trick."

Bliss smiled. "That's as good a reason as any, son."

Skid nodded. "Glad you see it my way, sir, because if I do this for you, I've got one condition to make." The colonel's smile became a scowl, and Skid laughed out loud. "Don't worry, I'm not going to ask for any more money. Far as I'm concerned, the Army pays me enough already just to have fun."

"Then what is it that you want?" Jack Cube asked.

The smile became a wide grin. "Just a little paint and someone who knows how to use it."

MORE THAN JUST THE ENGINE

═══════════

"You picked the pilot rather quickly, didn't you?" Walker asked.

Jackson shrugged. "I knew Skid was the right guy the moment I met him. Sure, we could have interviewed a dozen more flyboys, but we needed to start training our pilot immediately, and Skid . . . well, he was there and ready to go. Glad we found him, especially considering the way things came out with McPherson."

"Yeah, Skid was a pistol, all right," Henry added.

Walker nodded, then looked over at Lloyd to see if he had anything to add. Sometime in the last half hour or so, though, he'd dozed off in his wheelchair, head rocked forward and hands folded together in his lap. Without a word, his nephew reached forward and turned down the old man's hearing aid. Apparently, everyone was used to his doing this. Walker just hoped that Lloyd was awake again before the story was finished; he wanted to get as much input from all three 390 Group members as possible.

"That was the way we did things," Henry went on. "They spent months picking the crew for the first moon mission, but we couldn't afford to do that. Everything had to be as fast as possible because we didn't know how

far along the Germans were. Jack and Omar selected the pilot in one afternoon, and that was it."

"So you cut corners."

"No." Jack shook his head. "No, we did not cut corners. We just didn't
waste time, that's all."

"Look," Henry said, "we had a way of doing things back then that you
don't see too often these days. We didn't form committees or farm everything out to someone else. The 390 Group operated much the same way
Bob's original team did at Mescalero Ranch . . . everyone working together,
everyone pitching in to solve problems."

"It's the same sort of tiger-team approach Lockheed used when they
put together their Skunk Works," Jack said. "In fact, they copied it from
us. You get a whole lot of smart guys, put them in a room, give them a
problem that needs to be solved, then step out of the way and let them do
what needs to be done. Cut the bureaucracy, don't let the bean counters
and micromanagement types anywhere near the project . . . just give your
people whatever they need to do the job."

"That was Vannevar Bush's idea," Henry said. "Once he saw how Bob
had done things in New Mexico, he rightfully figured out that this was
the key to catching up with the Germans in a hurry. He put Omar in
charge because he believed that the colonel could manage this sort of
project, and he did pretty well . . . at least up to a certain point. Having
the engine built and tested in New Mexico was a real pain in the . . ."

Mindful of the women and children in the room, he quickly shut up.
"Ass?" Carl asked, grinning as he finished his great-grandfather's thought.

Several people chuckled as Henry glared at him. "Where did you learn
to talk like that?"

"Television," his mother said, trying not to laugh. "Go on, Grandpa."

"Hmm . . . well, that figures. Anyway, the propulsion system was just
one of many things we had to figure out. Getting into space isn't just about
engines, y'know."

"You wouldn't believe how much stuff we had to work out," Jack said.
"Take the space suit, for instance. One of the reasons why we were in a

hurry to select our pilot was that we needed his exact measurements so that we could custom-design pressure gear for him. That and the acceleration couch . . ."

"The whole cockpit," Henry added. "I mean, we even had to take into account whether he was right-handed or left-handed, because if he were a southpaw, we'd have to arrange the instrument panel to accommodate that. And that was just for starters. The gyroscope platform, the radar system, the landing gear, the reaction-control rockets . . ."

"We had a checklist as long as your arm," Jack said. "Now, some of this stuff we'd already figured out. The gyros, for instance, had already been developed at Mescalero . . . all we had to do was adapt them for our purposes. Caltech had done most of the research for our solid-rocket boosters, so that was another area where we had a head start." He smiled. "And then there were Bob's notebooks."

"Bob Goddard had been thinking about this stuff for almost thirty years," Henry said. "He was way ahead of everyone, even the Germans. And everything he thought about went into his notebooks. Whenever we hit a roadblock, Bob would remember something he'd jotted down ten, fifteen, twenty-five, or thirty years ago, and he'd rummage through all those binders he had stockpiled on the lab shelves, and more than half the time he'd find a design or a set of equations that, even if it didn't completely solve our problem, at least gave us a direction."

"Once the team got going, we moved pretty quickly," Jack said. "We'd report to the physics lab bright and early every morning and pick up where we'd left off the day before, and work straight through until lunchtime. An hour or so to get a bite to eat, usually at the school cafeteria or a lunchroom on Main Street . . . Bob always brown-bagged his . . . and then we'd come back to the lab and work until late afternoon or early evening. Esther would drive Bob in and pick him up again at the end of the day . . . Corporal Hillman was staying with them, and the colonel, too, when he was in town . . . the rest of us would all walk back to the boardinghouse. We'd have dinner, listen to the radio for a while, maybe play a few hands of poker and gin rummy, then it was off to bed. Next day, same thing again."

"Not always," Henry said. "I mean, maybe for you guys, sure but . . ."

"Oh, that's right. You had Doris."

"Uh-huh." Henry looked over at Walker. "I'm talking about my late wife . . . Carl's great-grandmother."

"Yes, you mentioned her earlier," Walker said.

"Oh, yes . . . yes, I did, didn't I?" Henry scowled and shook his head, a silent apology for an old man's forgetfulness. "Anyway, I was seeing her as often as I could without our babysitters catching on. I didn't want them to know that I'd met a girl because I was afraid they'd consider her a security risk and tell me to break it off. So I started brown-bagging, too, and at lunchtime I'd go over to the library and meet Doris there. There was a faculty lounge in the basement that wasn't much used, so we'd go down there and have lunch together."

"Did she know what you were doing?"

"No, of course not. So far as she was concerned, I was a graduate student in the physics department, that's all. She didn't learn the truth until later, when . . ." He suddenly shook his head again. "Sorry, getting ahead of myself there. Anyway, our routine might sound monotonous, but it really wasn't. I mean, we were designing a spaceship! Maybe even the world's first if we managed to beat the Germans . . ."

"Yeah, well, that was the plan," Jack said. "We didn't know it, though, but the Nazis had their own ideas about staying ahead."

ON ORDERS OF THE REICH MARSHAL

The bombs began falling shortly after 1 A.M.

Wernher von Braun awoke to the wail of air raid sirens. He'd barely opened his eyes when he heard what he first thought was a thunderstorm rolling in from the Baltic. Then he realized what was happening, and in moments he was out of bed. No time to get dressed; he found his robe and slippers in the abrupt, violent flashes of light coming through the bedroom windows, then he was racing down the stairs, taking the risers two or three at a time, even as he felt the house tremble from explosions coming closer with each passing second.

The streets of Peenemünde's residential area were filled with scientists, engineers, and military officers, all of them in their bedclothes as they scurried for the air raid bunker beneath the foreign workers' barracks. Von Braun found Lise Muller in the darkness; she was wearing only her nightgown, so he gallantly put his robe around her, then took her arm and led her through the yelling, shoving crowd. Frequent flashes and explosions from the northeast end of the island told him that the industrial center was being targeted, but the housing complex might be next. Above the rooftops, searchlights roamed across the black and pitiless sky, while the luminescent tracers of antiaircraft guns sought targets too high for them to reach. No sign of Luftwaffe fighters taking off to do battle with the invaders; the airfield had probably been the first thing destroyed. Von Braun could see nothing when he looked up, but a loud, rolling drone that sounded like a swarm of immense bees told him that that hundreds of British bombers were up there, bringing wave upon wave of destruction.

Walter Dornberger found him and Lise just as they reached the shelter; he looked odd without his uniform, and for once he wasn't smiling. They managed to make their way into the shelter just as the first bombs began falling on their houses. The concrete ceiling quaked, causing several women to scream in terror; Lise remained calm, but she clung tight to him. Taking her under his arm, von Braun shuffled through the crowded shelter, trying to find a place where, if the ceiling were to collapse, they might possibly escape being crushed to death beneath tons of rubble. It was a hopeless notion, of course—if a one-ton bomb made a direct hit, everyone down there would die—but it helped him feel just a little more in control.

For the next forty minutes, the people who'd taken refuge in the shelter listened as giants marched overhead, each footfall signaling another house, office, or workshop that had ceased to exist. The shelter was so tightly packed that no one could sit down; swaying lights revealed terrified faces and eyes that constantly peered upward as if expecting to see RAF Lancasters through the ceiling. Von Braun spotted Arthur Rudolph; he had his wife and children with him, and he was doing his best to comfort them. Looking around, he glimpsed various other members of his rocket team, peering out between the French and Polish workers who'd been the first to get belowground. He searched for Walter Thiel, his senior chemical engineer, but didn't see him; von Braun hoped he and his family were safe.

A little after 2 A.M., the bombs stopped falling. No one moved, though, until they heard the sirens sound the all clear. Someone went upstairs and threw open the steel double doors, and everyone began to leave, pushing against one another in their eagerness to get out of the cramped and airless bunker.

Yet the nightmare wasn't over. They emerged to find Peenemünde on fire, the flames spreading to even the places that the bombers had missed. Fire trucks raced through the streets, bells jangling as they headed from one blaze to another. Von Braun's house was intact, but the cottage *Fraü-lein Muller* shared with several other unmarried women was gone. A couple of blocks away, von Braun was horrified to discover that Thiel's house was nothing more than a burning heap of wood and brick. Soldiers were trying to put out the fire before it spread to other homes, but its occupants were nowhere to be seen. Staring at the Thiel home, von Braun realized that Walter and his family lay within the inferno.

The shock had barely settled in, though, when Colonel Dornberger found him and Lise again. There was no time to grieve; the colonel dragged them to the research-and-development district, which had been hit even harder than the residential area. There they found that the fire had reached *Haus 4*, and no firefighters had yet arrived to put out the blaze. As Dornberger ran down the street, yelling for everyone to drop what they were doing and save the headquarters building, von Braun and Lise took their chances and went inside. Keeping away from the part of the building that was on fire, they cupped their hands across their faces and made their way upstairs to von Braun's office, where they managed to break down the locked door. While von Braun gathered the most important papers and blueprints from his file cabinets, Lise opened the wall safe and took out the *Silbervogel* master study. They fled the building before the flames could reach them; Dornberger returned with a bucket brigade just as the roof fell in.

By daybreak, the fires had been put out, but as the sun came up, it became clear that the raid had been a success. Entire buildings had vanished into bomb craters, and blackened iron skeletons and smoking piles of debris lay where houses, laboratories, and offices had been only yesterday. Many streets were impassable; scores of parked cars and trucks had been crushed or burned. Hundreds of people were dead, ranging from foreign workers to top-level scientists. Walking through the ruins, von Braun saw so many bodies covered by sheets that he soon lost count.

Ironically, the nearby concentration camp was largely untouched. Only a handful of Russians died there when a stray bomb fell on their quarters. But the camp wasn't very large; because of the sensitive nature of the *Silbervogel Projekt*, it had been decided that prisoners would be used as forced labor as little as possible. Von Braun hadn't been involved in this decision, though, and he'd deliberately tried to ignore the camp's existence as much as he could, so the fate of its prisoners barely registered on his conscience.

Not all was lost. With the notable exception of Walter Thiel, most of the project's key scientists and engineers had survived. Like von Braun, they'd taken shelter as soon as they heard the sirens. Just as importantly—miraculously, in fact—the raid had missed *Wa Pruf 11*'s most valuable facilities, the construction and test complex at the northern tip of the island. Whether it was sheer luck or because the bombardiers couldn't see Peenemünde clearly from high altitude, von Braun didn't know. Nonetheless, the wind tunnel, the static test stand, the liquid-oxygen and gasoline storage tanks, and the control bunkers had all gone untouched.

Most crucial of all, the bombers hadn't hit *Silbervogel*. The spacecraft was in two adjacent work sheds: one containing the engine assembly, the other the unfinished fuselage. Neither was so much as scratched. When von Braun saw this, he felt his knees grow weak, and he had to grab Dornberger's shoulder for support. If Silver Bird had been destroyed, the entire project would have come to an end; there was not enough time or money to start over again. And he didn't want to even think about the *Führer*'s reaction. Hitler was notorious for not accepting failure even when it was for reasons beyond anyone's control.

All the same, it was obvious that *Silbervogel* had to be moved from Peenemünde. The RAF could return at any time, and the next raid might not miss the most important targets.

Only a few weeks ago, Himmler had come through on his promise to find a launch site. Von Braun hadn't yet taken a close look at the SS memo that had landed on his desk, but apparently it involved a couple of abandoned railway tunnels that had been carved into a mountainside somewhere in the Harz Mountains. There were also proposals to put the launch site in Poland or Austria, but both Dornberger and von Braun were opposed to this; it would be difficult enough to transport the spacecraft by rail across Germany, let alone to another country.

For now, though, the most immediate concern was cleaning up from the air raid. Von Braun set up a temporary headquarters office in his living room; Walter and Lise had found clothes by then, and both were working with him to organize the salvage operations. That would take a while, of course, but once that was done, the next step would be to work out a plan for relocating the entire project from the seacoast to the mountains.

Perhaps it was too soon to even begin thinking about such things, but von Braun needed the distraction. He felt numb, body and soul, from the violence of the night before; many people were dead, among them one of his oldest friends, and he was all too aware that the bombs had been meant for him, too. If he thought about it too much . . . No, it was better to work and exhibit the leadership the survivors needed just then.

He and Lise had only begun, though, when the rumble of motorcycles heralded the arrival of a motorcade. Von Braun had no sooner risen from his desk than the front door slammed open, and two soldiers stomped into the front hall. And right behind them, resplendent in a tailored white uniform, swaggered the bloated figure of Hermann Goering.

—————

"Wernher!" A broad grin stretched across the general's fleshy face. "So good to see that you're still alive!"

"*Da, Herr Reichsmarschall.*" Ignoring the friendship Goering pretended to share with him by using his first name, von Braun took a formal stance, back straight and arms at his sides. As usual, Dornberger came to attention, his right arm snapping forward in a brisk salute that Goering didn't seem to notice. From the corner of his eye, von Braun saw Lise stiffen. His secretary had once confessed to him, following one of the Luftwaffe leader's earlier visits, that she could practically feel Goering's eyes crawling over her. She'd begged von Braun never to leave her alone with him, and von Braun knew why. There were rumors about Goering's sexual appetite, and rape was not beneath him.

"And I'm pleased to see that your lovely secretary is safe as well." Goering hadn't forgotten her, and Lise blanched when he favored her with a smile. Removing his white kid gloves, Goering found an armchair big enough to support him and sat down heavily. "I don't suppose she could bring us coffee, could she?"

"*Fraülein, bitte?*" Von Braun dismissed Lise with a glance, and she disappeared through a swinging door into the kitchen. He hoped for her sake that she'd take her time. "So, *Herr Reichsmarschall* . . . what brings you here?"

Goering raised an eyebrow. "Come now, *Herr Doktor.* You don't think I'd abandon you in your moment of crisis, do you? As soon as I heard about the raid, I drove here straight from Berlin." Frowning, he shook his head in commiseration. "Horrifying. Utterly horrifying. England will pay dearly for its temerity."

"As you say." Von Braun had to work at keeping a straight face. It was well-known that Goering's stature within the High Command had taken a major blow when the Luftwaffe failed to bring about Great Britain's surrender. His planes could no longer cross the English Channel without being intercepted, and since he had forced Peenemünde to abandon the A-4 in favor of the far more ambitious *Silbervogel*, it was hard to see how he could make good on his threat.

Goering nodded. His pig eyes never left von Braun's face; Wernher knew that he was being studied, assessed for any sign of disloyalty or weakness. "Quite," Goering said drily. "I take it that you're following Herr Himmler's advice and preparing to move your operations to a less vulnerable location, yes?"

"As we speak, I'm preparing to determine how long it will take for us to relocate to . . ." Von Braun paused. "I'm sorry, but the name of this place escapes me."

"Nordhausen. That's the town nearby, but we will be calling the facility something else . . . *Mittelwerk*."

"Yes, thank you for reminding me. May I . . . ?" Goering gave him the slightest of nods, and von Braun resumed his seat behind the desk. "It may be some time before we can leave, though. Most of our casualties were among the labor force. Not just the foreign workers, but also the war prisoners we've been using lately. Without them . . ."

"I'll requisition more soldiers to assist you with the relocation effort. And you need not concern yourself with finding a source of labor at *Mittelwerk*. Herr Himmler has seen to this as well." Goering shrugged. "I'm sorry, though, but we'll no longer be employing any civilians who aren't German citizens. The security risk is too high . . . and I'm convinced that one of the reasons why the British were able to strike us with such accuracy is that they had spies among the foreign workers. We caught two already."

"That's entirely possible, *Herr Reichsmarschall*," Dornberger said, still standing at attention beside von Braun's desk. "However, I'd like to point out that, since late last year, we've been careful to keep foreign workers away from the vital facilities. I doubt very strongly that the British or their American allies have learned anything about *Silbervogel*."

Goering shook his head. "Perhaps so, Colonel, but we cannot take a chance based on that assumption. I've consulted Admiral Canaris, and on his advice, I've ordered the *Abwehr* to take active measures that will prevent the Americans from engaging in any countermeasures."

"Active measures, *Herr Reichsmarschall*?" Von Braun blinked. "My apologies, but I fail to understand what you're talking about."

"In the past, you've told us of the American scientist who's their key expert in rocketry . . . Dr. Robert H. Goddard, I believe?" Von Braun nodded, and the monster sitting across from him smiled. "You won't have to worry about him for very much longer. The *Abwehr* is taking care of that particular problem. *Herr Doktor* Goddard will be found and liquidated."

Von Braun felt a chill of horror. He suddenly wished that he'd never said anything about Goddard to Goering. He had nothing against Goddard; in fact, he greatly admired him even though Goddard had deliberately ignored Hermann Oberth's request to share technical information with the *VfR*.

"Do you really believe this is wise?" von Braun asked, choosing his words carefully. "If Goddard is . . . um, liquidated . . . wouldn't this alert the Americans that we're involved in a rocket program of our own?"

Goering gave him a condescending smirk. "Oh, Wernher . . . the Americans and the British must know what we're doing here. Why else would they have dropped bombs on you?"

"Da, Herr Reichsmarschall," Dornberger said, ever the fawning officer. "You are correct. Perhaps not the specific details of *Silbervogel*, but . . ."

"I wouldn't be surprised if they knew about that, too," Goering said, shaking his head. "And even if they don't, you yourself said that they are doubtless working to develop a transcontinental rocket . . . did you not?"

Once again, von Braun regretted Dornberger's exaggerations about the American rocket program. Had Goering figured out that it was all an elaborate lie to justify continued funding for Peenemünde and *Wa Pruf 11*? Yet even if he did, neither he nor Walter had any choice but to continue telling the lie. Goering had managed to get someone to drive him all the way from Berlin; he could easily return with von Braun and Dornberger as unwilling passengers, with the SS headquarters as their destination.

"You're right," he said. "I didn't realize that earlier. Eliminating Robert Goddard might be the most prudent thing to do."

"I thought you'd see things my way." Goering abruptly rose from his chair, wheezing quietly with the effort. "Well, then . . . if there is nothing else for us to discuss, I'd like to view the damage. Colonel, if you would . . . ?"

"It would be my privilege." Dornberger was already stepping to the door; von Braun wondered if he was going to remove his uniform jacket and lay it across the puddle of water that lay just outside. Goering walked past the colonel with only the barest acknowledgment of his presence, but then he paused to look back at von Braun.

"Good day, Wernher," he said. "May this be the end of your misfortunes."

"I certainly hope so, *Herr Reichsmarschall*." Von Braun watched him go but didn't let out his breath until he heard the rumble of motorcycles pulling away. Then he lowered his head into his hands and closed his eyes.

"He's gone, thank God." Unnoticed until she spoke to him, Lise had come back into the office. Then she lay a soft hand upon his shoulder. "Wernher, are you all right?"

"No . . . no, I'm not all right." Raising his head from his hands, von Braun looked up at her. "I'm afraid I've done a terrible thing. I've given permission for a good man's death."

THE PLOT AGAINST ROBERT H. GODDARD

SEPTEMBER 30, 1942

There was no moon in the predawn sky, no stars. Clouds lay thick above the eastern tip of Cape Cod. The only light penetrating the darkness of the Provincetown beach was the flashlight beam of a Coast Guard seaman.

Petty Officer Third Class Tom Hawkes let the light lazily swing back and forth. It was a cool night, the first taste of autumn mixing in with the salt air, but even in the wee hours of morning, there was always the chance of finding a couple of teenagers making out on the beach. Just last month, Hawkes had discovered some kids screwing in the dunes. His light had been on them for nearly a minute before they'd noticed, and ever since, he'd been hoping something like that would happen again.

No such luck. In fact, that had been the most exciting thing to happen to him since volunteering for Beach Patrol. Hawkes expected to be catching German saboteurs coming ashore, but after spending the last four months walking up and down the beach, just about all he'd found was driftwood, jellyfish, and pop bottles.

Tonight was different.

He was halfway to the breakwater when he spotted another flashlight beam. About sixty feet away, a spot of light appeared for a moment, shining, then vanished again. Shining at the water's edge, it came and went so quickly Hawkes couldn't tell which way it was aimed, down the beach or out across the water. Yet the radium dial of his wristwatch told him that it was nearly 4 A.M., not a likely hour for beachside lovers.

"Who goes there?" Hawkes called out, heading in the direction of the light. "Who is that?"

Silence, then a voice, male and with a thick Massachusetts accent, barely intelligible above the rumbling tide: "Who's that?"

"Beach Patrol . . . and I asked you first." The light came on again, its beam moving toward Hawkes; a second later, Hawkes located its source. A tall, slender man, just short of middle age, wearing oilskin waders, a denim trucker's jacket, and a long-billed cap. There was something in his other hand, but Hawkes couldn't tell what it was until he came closer: a long angler's rod, the kind used for pier fishing.

"Just out to catch 'em when they start biting." The fisherman bent over a tackle box that lay open on the beach beside him. "How's it going tonight? See anything interesting?"

"Only you, mister." Hawkes relaxed but didn't switch off his flashlight. "Don't think I've ever seen you out here before. You local?"

"Me? Naw. Just come down from Boston for a week." The older man pulled a reel from the box. "Couldn't catch anything from the pier except garbage fish, so I decided to come out here instead."

"Yeah, guess that makes sense." Hawkes glanced in the direction of town; its lights were over a mile away, with the municipal pier on the other side of the point. This part of the beach was uninhabited except for the one-room shacks rented to artists and summer vacationers; most of them were deserted now that the season was over, but it was possible that one or two might still be used by someone taking an autumn break from the city.

"Hope so." The Bostonian chuckled as he stood up to attach the reel to his rod, then he bent over again to pick up a roll of high-test line and a fishing knife. He fumbled a bit as he tried to hold them in his hands along with his flashlight. "Hey, since you're here, mind giving me a hand?"

"Sure." Hawkes came closer, within arm's reach. "What do you want me to do?"

"Hold your light on me while I put the line on." The older man switched off his flashlight, stuck it in his jacket pocket. "Shine it so I can see what I'm doing, okay?"

"No problem." Hawkes turned his flashlight downward, away from the fisherman's face. Its beam found the roll of fishing line in his left hand, but the hand holding the knife vanished the moment the light touched its serrated blade. Hawkes barely had time to wonder what the fisherman was doing when he felt a sudden, sharp pain at his neck just below his Adam's apple, and that was when he realized that his throat had been cut.

William Meriwell quickly stepped back, avoiding the blood that jetted from the seaman's severed jugular vein. The Coast Guard patrolman staggered forward a step or two, gagging, his hands desperately clutching his neck. Meriwell kicked away the flashlight he'd dropped, then silently watched as the young seaman collapsed face-first upon the wet sand, his white cap falling off his head to be immediately snatched away by the surf. He tried to crawl forward, but it wasn't long before he stopped moving and lay still.

Meriwell slowly let out his breath. His heart hammered at his chest, and he had an impulse to throw his fishing knife out into the water. He hadn't wanted to kill the other man, but the moment the sailor spotted him, he knew that he had no choice. The kid had been in the wrong place at the wrong time, simple as that. No one could be allowed to witness what was about to happen next.

Pulling out his flashlight again, Meriwell quickly checked his watch. Exactly 0400. He switched off the light, aimed it out into the water, then flashed it three times. He couldn't see anything in the moonless night, but if everything was going according to schedule, a U-boat had just surfaced about a mile offshore.

While he waited for a response, Meriwell picked up the dead sailor by his arms and, walking backward, dragged him across the beach into the dunes. He wished he had a shovel, but that couldn't be helped; he'd just have to hope that no one found the body for a while. He went back to the beach, found the sailor's flashlight, switched it off, and threw it into the water, then made himself busy by kicking sand over the trail he'd left. Meriwell had just finished his task when he heard a soft crunch behind him and turned around to see an inflatable dinghy coming ashore.

Its sole occupant was a man in a dark suit, overcoat, and fedora. He pulled in his paddle and waited for Meriwell to wade out into the shallow water and haul the dinghy the rest of the way in. *"Guten Morgen, Herr Schmidt,"* Meriwell said quietly as he took hold of the painter. *"Ich hoffe, Sie hatten eine guten . . ."*

"Shut up," Schmidt hissed. "You are never to speak to me in German. And my name is Smith, not Schmidt." His English was perfect, with no trace of a European accent.

"Sorry." Meriwell grunted as he hauled the dinghy the rest of the way to the beach. Once it was out of the surf, Schmidt—or Smith, as the *Abwehr* agent preferred to be known—stood up and stepped out, his trouser cuffs and dress shoes remaining dry. He turned around to retrieve a briefcase from the back of the boat, then looked around.

"Are we alone?" Schmidt asked. "Has there been any trouble?"

"Unfortunately, I was discovered by a Coast Guard sailor patrolling the beach." Meriwell produced his fishing knife again and thrust it into the dinghy's rubber side. With a soft pop and a quiet hiss, the boat began to deflate. "I killed him. His body is in the dunes over there."

"Damn it." Schmidt's voice was an angry growl. "And, of course, you neglected to bury him, didn't you?"

"I don't have a shovel, so . . ."

"Never mind. Where's your car?"

"Parked just off the beach road, about a hundred feet from here."

"Bring the boat and paddle. If we take them with us, maybe the police will figure that the sailor was killed for some other reason." Schmidt bent over to pick up the paddle, leaving the deflated dinghy for the American fifth columnist to carry. "Now hurry."

It took only a few minutes for the two men to reach the Chrysler sedan parked on the shoulder of a nearby dirt road. Meriwell shoved the boat and paddle into the backseat as Schmidt climbed into the front passenger seat; when he started the car, he was careful not to switch on the headlights, instead relying on memory and night vision to turn around and drive slowly away from the beach. The headlights didn't come on until the car was on the narrow blacktop that went out to the tip of the Cape. Only a few houses and a small inn lay at this end of Provincetown, and their windows were dark. No one saw the car as it left town.

"How far is Worcester from here?" Schmidt asked.

"About two hundred miles," Meriwell replied. "We can get you there in about five hours."

The German agent pulled back his shirtsleeve, checked the luminescent dial of his American-made watch—4:05 A.M. If his contact was right, they'd arrive in Worcester shortly after nine o'clock. "Very good. And you've located Dr. Goddard's home and studied his habits?"

"Oh, yes." A grim smile appeared on Meriwell's face. "I've been watching him for about two weeks now. The best place to find him won't be at his house, though. It'll probably be on campus, where he . . ."

"Let me make that determination." Schmidt's briefcase rested across his knees; he tapped his fingers against it as he gazed out the window. "Just get me there. I'll do the rest."

———

"Bob? Esther's got the car started. She's waiting for us."

"Oh, for God's sake . . ." Tugging on his raincoat, Robert Goddard hurried downstairs to his living room. He glared at Hillman, who stood patiently waiting for him at the front door. "Max, you're almost as bad as she is. Are you two working together to make my life miserable?"

"You got it, Doctor G." The young corporal grinned as he held out his hat and umbrella. "She's already taken your briefcase out to the car."

"Like I'd forget that," Goddard grumbled, and Hillman refrained from reminding him that he probably would. Over the past few months that Max had resided with the Goddards, living in their guest room and sharing most of his meals with them, he'd become less a military attaché and more like a family member, even a surrogate son. And if there was one thing Hillman had learned about Professor Goddard, it was that the old man was absentminded as hell.

A cold, slobbering rain was falling outside, bringing down a few more of the leaves turning color with the coming of autumn. Esther's car stood in the driveway, headlights on, windshield wiper clattering back and forth. Goddard didn't bother to open his umbrella, though, but instead pulled up his overcoat collar and put on his hat before he left the front porch and marched down the steps, Hillman behind him. Just as they were about to turn toward the car, though, Goddard noticed the neighborhood mailman coming up the front walk.

"Hold on a second," he said to Hillman, then walked over to the mailman. "Morning, Joe. Got anything for me?"

"Sure thing, Professor. Here ya go." The mailman reached into his shoulder bag, pulled out several letters, and handed them to Goddard. "Beautiful weather we're having, ain't it?"

"Lovely." Goddard tucked the mail into his inside coat pocket. "Think I'll go for a swim." Joe laughed and turned away, and Goddard hurried to the car, where Hillman was already holding the door open for him.

"One day," Esther said, as her husband climbed in beside her, "you're going to surprise everyone by getting to work on time. We'll have a parade and everything. Fireworks, balloons, circus clowns . . ."

"Oh, be quiet and drive. And for the record, I'm never late. Everyone else just gets there early, that's all."

Hillman laughed out loud from the backseat, and Esther gave him a wink in the rearview mirror as she backed out of the driveway. As she drove away from the house, she didn't notice the Chrysler sedan parked a short distance up Tallawanda Drive, or that it pulled away from the curb and began to follow them.

———

"Who is the man riding with them?" Schmidt asked.

"Some kind of assistant. Maybe a bodyguard." Meriwell drove

crouched over the steering wheel, peering through the heavy rain that the windshield wiper couldn't quite slap away. "He's living with them, that's all I know."

"Is he always with Dr. Goddard?" Schmidt asked, and Meriwell shook his head. "Then he's not a bodyguard. This is good."

Meriwell glanced at the gun in Schmidt's lap. The *Abwehr* agent had removed the Walther PPK from his briefcase en route from the Cape. It was now loaded, a black silencer fitted against its barrel, and Schmidt had pulled on a pair of thin leather gloves.

"I could pull up alongside them," Meriwell suggested. "From your side of the car, you could get all three."

Schmidt gave him a sharp look. "My orders don't include his wife or friends," he said, an angry edge in his voice. "If I don't need to eliminate them, then I won't. Is there ever a time when he's alone?"

Meriwell thought about it a moment. "He sometimes steps out for a smoke. I guess they won't let him do that in the lab, 'cause he comes out three or four times a day."

"Is he usually by himself when he steps out?" Schmidt asked. Meriwell nodded. "And is the lab near the street?" Meriwell nodded again. "Very good. Then we'll park nearby and wait for our chance."

———

Esther pulled over on Maywood Street. Goddard opened his door, stuck his umbrella outside and opened it, then reached down to pick up his briefcase. "So you're coming back after you're done with the shopping?" he asked Hillman, who made no move to get out of the car.

"Don't worry, sweetheart." Esther smiled at him. "I won't borrow Max for very long. I just want to have him carry the groceries to the car. You know how I hate doing that when it's coming down like this."

"My dear, you've become spoiled from all those years living in the desert. So much as a drizzle, and you think it's a downpour." Goddard gave his wife a mock scowl. "Just bring him back when you're done . . . and no fooling around!"

"Oh, no." Esther glanced back at Hillman. "We're in trouble now. He knows about our affair."

The corporal's face went red as the Goddards shared a laugh at his expense. Over the past few months, a running joke had developed among the three of them: Esther had taken Max as her secret lover, and Bob was blissfully ignorant of the whole thing. Nothing of the sort was going on, of course, but Bob and Esther had learned how to embarrass their house-guest with this little jest.

"See you later," Goddard said, then he climbed out, slamming the door shut behind him. The side door of the Science Building, which led straight to his lab, was only twenty feet from the street; he'd reached it even before Esther had driven out of sight. Pausing beneath the awning to shake out his umbrella and close it, Goddard paid no attention to the sedan that drove past the Science Building, turned around in a driveway across the street, then came back to park on the other side of Maywood.

As usual, the 390 Group was already there, but Goddard noticed at once that a few members were missing. Henry Morse wasn't in the room, and neither was Hamilton Ballou or Michael Ferris. Jack Cube and Colonel Bliss were absent, of course; they were still in New Mexico. Frank O'Connor was in his usual place, perched on a stool near the door and reading the morning paper.

"Where are the others?" Goddard asked as he added his umbrella to the collection propped against the wall beside the door.

"Mike and Ham went out to fetch coffee and doughnuts," Harry Chung said, barely looking up from the electrical wiring diagrams he and Taylor had laid out across the bench. "I don't know where Henry is."

"Library," Gerry Mander said. There was a sly smile on his face as he fixed his attention on the chemical reference he was studying. "Again."

"Hmm . . . well, yes, I suppose." Goddard had noticed that Henry was spending an unusual amount of time at the campus library. Most of his visits were necessary, of course—the team constantly needed to find some piece of information for their work—but lately it seemed that he was beginning his day there before coming to work at the lab. He caught the look that quickly passed between Gerry, Taylor, and Ham. If they were sharing a secret, they could have it. Probably none of his business anyway.

"Well, now that you're here . . ." O'Connor folded his newspaper, hopped off the stool. "'Cuse me, gents. Need to visit the little boys' room."

Goddard stepped aside to let the FBI agent pass; O'Connor left the lab, shutting the door behind him. Goddard was about to take off his overcoat when his hand brushed against the mail he'd brought with him from home. It was still in the coat's inside pocket. Esther usually took care of the bills, but there was no sense leaving the mail in his coat where it might fall out and get lost. Goddard removed the letters from his pocket and was about to transfer them to his briefcase when his eye fell on the top one. The return address was the City of Worcester, Office of Tax Assessment, and stamped in red ink across the bottom of the envelope was URGENT—OPEN IMMEDIATELY!

"Hello?" he murmured, then dropped the rest of the mail on a nearby table and tore open the envelope. No one paid any attention as he skimmed the letter inside, then . . .

"Oh, damn it to hell!"

Everyone jumped. "Bob?" Taylor asked. "What's going on?"

Goddard continued to stare at the letter even as he slammed a fist down on the table. "The damn city claims we haven't paid our property taxes for this year!" he snapped. "Now they're planning to fine us ten dollars a day until we cough up!"

Harry was baffled. "You haven't paid your taxes? But . . ."

"*Of course* I paid my taxes. I've been doing that every year since we moved to New Mexico. In fact, I made sure that . . ." Goddard stopped suddenly. He appeared to be lost in thought for a moment, then he closed his eyes. "I know what happened. I made arrangements with my bank here to pay my local taxes while I was gone, but when we moved back, I told them that was no longer necessary. And then . . ."

"You forgot to pay the taxes yourself?" Harry asked.

Goddard nodded. "The bank probably continued receiving my tax bills, but someone didn't forward them to Esther and me. And now . . ."

Not bothering to pick up his umbrella, Goddard turned to the door. "Look, I've got to take care of this right now. I'll be back soon."

Before anyone had a chance to say anything, he was gone.

———————

"Look!" Meriwell pointed through the windshield. "There he is!"

Just minutes after he'd entered the Science Building, Goddard came out again. Yet it was obvious that he wasn't stepping out for a smoke. Instead of lingering beneath the awning, he hurried to the sidewalk and began walking swiftly down Maywood, heading toward Main Street less than a block away.

Schmidt was out of the car in a second, but he took his time crossing the street. Nothing attracts attention more quickly than a running man, and Goddard was moving fast enough already. If anyone happened to look out a window of the Science Building or any other nearby university building, they couldn't help but spot one person chasing another. So Schmidt strolled after Goddard, keeping him in sight while gradually closing the distance between them, taking care not to make his presence obvious.

His overcoat was buttoned shut, but its right pocket had a hidden slit inside, big enough for him to put his hand and wrist through. In this way, he was able to carry his silenced Walther without its being seen. One he was close enough to Goddard and no one else was in sight, all he'd have to do was pull out the gun, take aim at the back of the scientist's head, and fire. The silencer wouldn't completely eliminate the sound of his gunshot, but it would muffle it enough that it wouldn't be heard by anyone nearby.

Then he'd simply drop the gun and walk away, again making sure that he didn't draw attention by running. He'd made sure never to handle the gun, its silencer, or bullets without wearing gloves. All the police would find would be a body, the murder weapon lying alongside it, with no fingerprints, witnesses, suspects, or apparent motives. A clean kill.

After that, Schmidt would have Meriwell drive him to the extraction point on the northern Maine coast, where the same U-boat that had brought him to America was scheduled to pick him up in two days. Unless someone connected Goddard's murder with the death of a Beach Patrol officer the same day, there would be nothing to indicate that it had been an *Abwehr* assassination . . . at least long enough for Schmidt to make good his escape.

As Schmidt approached Goddard, though, he realized that killing him wouldn't be quite so easy. He'd had already reached Main Street, where a streetcar was rapidly approaching. A couple of other people were already waiting at the corner trolley stop. Goddard joined them as the streetcar glided to a halt, and the three of them climbed aboard while Schmidt was still more than twenty feet away.

The assassin didn't try to board the streetcar as well. Running for it would have made him obvious. Instead, he turned and raised his hand to wave to the car. Meriwell had been watching the entire scene; seconds later, he pulled up alongside Schmidt.

"Follow the streetcar until he gets off," Schmidt said as he climbed in. "Don't let it out of your sight."

O'Connor returned to the lab. He was about to pick up his newspaper when he noticed that someone was missing. "Where's the professor?" he asked.

Harry glanced up from the blueprints. "Had to go out. Got a letter from the city, saying he hadn't paid his taxes. He . . ."

"Oh, for the love of . . . ! And you let him go?"

Gerry snorted. "Taxes, Frankie. You can't fight City Hall." He shook his head and grinned. "But you catch up with him, maybe you can help Bob try."

Muttering obscenities, O'Connor grabbed his raincoat and dashed out of the lab. Goddard was nowhere in sight, but the agent's car was parked in the lot across the street. He headed for it, still swearing at the irresponsible eggheads he'd been assigned to nursemaid.

———————

The clock tower upon Worcester City Hall's gabled rooftop was ringing the ten o'clock hour when the streetcar came to a halt out front. Goddard was among those who got off. Still angry at the letter he'd just received, he marched across the sidewalk to the ground-floor entrance, located beneath a circular stone staircase leading up to the second-floor main entrance. Finding that it was a locked fire door, the professor swore under his breath, then headed for the staircase.

It was a minor detour, but it gave Schmidt a chance to catch up. Meriwell had pulled over to the curb just as Goddard was about to walk the stairs. Climbing out of the car, Schmidt quickly strode across the sidewalk, yet Goddard had already opened the door by the time the *Abwehr* killer reached the stairs, forcing Schmidt to dash up the steps behind him. Goddard didn't notice Schmidt, though, as he walked into the building, letting the door slam shut behind him.

Schmidt might have lost another opportunity were it not for a stroke of luck. On the other side of the front door was a small entrance foyer, with a second door leading to the main lobby. The interior door was old, with a rusting iron knob that had a tendency to stick. As Schmidt came through the front door, he discovered that Goddard was still struggling to open the foyer door.

The foyer was dimly lit. Only Goddard and Schmidt were in there, and Goddard still hadn't noticed that he wasn't alone. Careful not to let the front door slam shut, Schmidt pulled the Walther from his overcoat. He'd only started to raise it, though, when Goddard finally managed to yank open the foyer door. Cursing beneath his breath, Goddard barged in, still unaware that he was being followed.

The main lobby was grandiose, designed in the overwrought style of the last century. Tall Corinthian columns supported a high ceiling above a black-and-white-tiled floor, and a broad marble staircase with an iron banister led upward to the mayor's office and the council chamber. The lobby was vacant except for the two men who'd just come in, and as Goddard paused to figure out where the tax assessor's office was located, Schmidt came in for the kill.

It was at this moment that Worcester police sergeant Clay Reilly came downstairs from the mayor's office, which he'd just visited to drop off some departmental paperwork. He'd just reached the landing and had turned to trot the rest of the way down when he spotted something incredible: in the lobby just below, a man with a long-barreled handgun was coming up behind another, older man.

It was obvious what was about to happen. Reilly's reflexes were quick. Snatching his service revolver from his holster, he took aim at the would-be killer.

"Stop!" he yelled. "Drop it!"

Goddard stopped, looked around in confusion, not knowing where Reilly's voice was coming from. Schmidt didn't share his bewilderment. Seeing the police officer on the stairs above him, he whipped around and started to raise his gun.

Sergeant Reilly was a crack shot, one of the WPD's best, and in that second the long hours he'd spent on the practice range paid off. Schmidt's finger hadn't even tightened on the Walther's trigger when Reilly fired his Smith & Wesson.

The first shot hit Schmidt in the stomach, the second in the chest. His gun fell to the marble floor a moment before he did.

Goddard was standing only a few feet away as the killer collapsed behind him. The professor was still staring at the blood seeping from beneath the stranger's body when the foyer door slammed open, then someone ran up behind him and grabbed his arm.

"Doc, are you all right?" O'Connor demanded.

Dazed, Goddard looked around to see the FBI agent. "Yes . . . yes, I'm . . . I'm fine, but . . ." He pointed to the body. "Who is this man? Why did . . . was he trying to . . . ?"

"I don't know. Damn it, Professor, why couldn't you have . . . ?" O'Connor shook his head as he tugged on Goddard's arm. "Never mind. Let's just get you out of here."

By then, Sergeant Reilly had come the rest of the way downstairs. Kicking the Walther PPK away, he knelt beside Schmidt and felt the side of his neck to make sure that he was dead. Drawn by the gunshots, office workers were emerging from nearby doorways. Cautiously entering the lobby, they stared in horror and curiosity at the dead man and the police officer who'd just shot him.

Someone stepped in front of Goddard just as O'Reilly, still crouched beside the body, was starting to look for him. O'Connor took the opportunity to turn Goddard around and propel him through the crowd to the foyer.

"Aren't we staying?" Goddard asked, as O'Connor pushed him through the front door and out into the rain.

"You can't get mixed up in this." Hand still wrapped around his arm, O'Connor led him down the wet granite steps. "The fewer questions you answer, the better. With any luck, no one back there recognized you."

O'Connor's car was still parked at the curb. The sedan that had followed Goddard downtown was already gone. When Meriwell had heard the dull gunshots from inside City Hall, he'd realized at once that they couldn't have come from Schmidt's silenced weapon. Meriwell knew instantly that something had gone wrong and that he'd better make himself scarce. As happenstance would have it, he'd driven away just as O'Connor showed up, giving the agent a convenient place to park.

"Yes, yes, I understand, but . . ." Goddard's eyes were wide behind his glasses, his face pale. "Why was that man trying to kill me?"

O'Connor said nothing, nor did he need to. As the G-man's car sped away from City Hall, Goddard arrived at the only possible answer.

"Oh, my," he murmured. "This changes everything, doesn't it?"

THE MONOMONAC GUN AND ROD CLUB

OCTOBER 2, 1942

A panel truck and three sedans drove down a wooded country lane near the town of Rindge, New Hampshire, until they reached an unmarked road. Turning right, the procession slowed to a crawl as it moved down the narrow, rutted trail. The man at the wheel of the truck was the only one who knew where they were going; he drove with a hand-drawn map open in his lap, occasionally glancing down to check their route. He was sure that he'd understood the directions he'd been given, but it wasn't until he caught a glimpse of blue water that he knew for sure he wasn't leading everyone the wrong way.

Passing a rusted PRIVATE PROPERTY NO TRESPASSING sign nailed to a tree, the vehicles arrived at their destination, a two-story hunting lodge on the shore of the nearby lake. The truck brakes squealed; one by one, the sedans following the van came to a halt. Doors swung open, and passengers climbed out.

"Okay, I'll bite," Ham said. "Where the hell are we?"

"From the looks of it," Taylor murmured, "I'd say we're a long way from anywhere else."

"I get it." Gerry lit a cigarette and carelessly dropped the spent match on a clump of pine needles. "We've been taken on a picnic." He pointed to the small dock floating beside the beach. "See? We can go swimming and everything. Water might be a little cold, but . . ."

"Knock it off." Henry stamped out the smoldering match before it could start a fire, then turned to Omar Bliss. "Are you serious, Colonel? This is where you're moving us?"

"That's right." Bliss had just climbed down from the truck cab. The driver walked up beside him, hands in the pockets of his leather jacket. "From here on out, this is the place you're calling home."

"Uh-huh . . . yeah." Mike gave the lodge the once-over and shook his head. "Colonel, I know you mean well, but . . . I dunno, couldn't you have done better?"

"Not on short notice, no . . . and we had to get you out of Worcester as fast as we could. The guys who tried to take a shot at Bob . . . and I think we know who that was . . . may try again. Next time, they might not be so subtle and do something like plant a bomb in the lab."

"Where are we?" By then, Goddard had emerged from the last car in the procession, the one driven by Lloyd. Esther at his side, he sauntered forward to join the rest of the group. "I recognize Lake Monomonac all right, but I don't think I've ever seen this place before."

"It belongs to the Monomonac Gun and Rod Club," the truck driver said. "Sort of a weekend retreat for rich Boston businessmen, or at least it was before the war. Most of its members have gone off to fight, so it's been closed for a while. Someone in my office knew about it, so . . ."

"And who are you again?" Henry regarded him as if he was a stranger who'd joined their group uninvited. Which was exactly what he was.

"David Coolidge, from the FBI's Boston field office." He walked over to the back of the truck, unfastened its doors, and swung them open. Two more men were seated on benches inside, next to the file cabinets and crates that had been transported from Clark University. "And these are Joe Sabatini and Pete Arnold from the same place. We're your new security detail."

"We prefer Max," Esther said quietly.

"Frank, too," Ham added.

"They fucked up," Sabatini muttered. He caught a withering look from Goddard as Esther's face turned red. "Pardon my French, ma'am, but that's why we've replaced them. If they hadn't been careless . . ."

"I understand." Goddard slowly let out his breath, then looked at Bliss and nodded. "This is fine, Colonel. I'm sure we'll be able to work here."

"Sure." Gerry exhaled smoke, rolled his eyes. "Just let me get my moose gun, and I'll hunt down some dinner."

"I said, I'm sure we'll be able to work here!" Goddard snapped.

Gerry turned pale. No one spoke for a couple of moments. In the past, Goddard would have immediately apologized after snapping at someone. He might have even added a quip of his own. But over the last few days, it had become increasingly obvious that his brush with death had robbed him of his sense of humor. No one had seen him so much as smile since then, and, even with Esther, he'd become short-tempered.

The uncomfortable silence lingered until Bliss coughed into his hand. "Yes, well . . . anyway, Bob, you and Esther won't be staying here. You've got a place of your own just down the road." He pointed to a cedar-sided cabin about fifty yards away, just visible through the trees. "We'll have an agent with you at all times, and the two other men will be bunking with the team here at the lodge."

"Bunking?" Mike asked. "Did you say bunking?"

"Umm . . . and another thing, Colonel." Henry half raised a hand. "You still haven't told us why Lloyd and Harry aren't here. Will they be joining us soon, or . . . ?"

"Kapman and Chung have been reassigned," Bliss said. "They're still working on Blue Horizon, but they won't be working here with the rest of you." He raised a hand before anyone could ask any further questions. "I'll explain everything once you've all unpacked and settled in. We'll meet in the living room in . . . say, an hour?"

"That would be fine, Colonel." Goddard looked at his wife. "Come along, dear . . . let's go see our new house."

Esther nodded unhappily. She was clearly not pleased about having to leave Worcester and relocate to a summer cabin out in the middle of nowhere. But she clung to her husband as they walked down the dirt road. Watching them go, Henry reflected that Goddard suddenly looked his age. He'd never thought of him as being an old man, but now . . .

"I'm not liking this." Ham Ballou had moved up beside him; his voice was little more than a whisper. "I'm not liking this at all."

"You and me both." Henry was thinking about the fact that the 390 Group been spirited away so quickly that he hadn't gotten a chance to find Doris and let her know that he wasn't going to be seeing her for a while. "And even less than you do."

Wielding a broom like a baseball bat, Henry crept toward the wasp nest dangling from the loft's bare rafters. Several wasps clung to the plate-sized honeycomb, mindless of the human a few feet away. "Ready back there?" Henry asked, not taking his eyes off the nest.

"Ready when you are," Mike replied. For some reason, he spoke in a near whisper.

"Okay, then, on the count of three." Another couple of steps, and Henry was almost directly beneath the nest. "One . . . two . . . three!"

He swung the broom in a clean, swift arc. It hit the wasp nest and knocked it from the rafter beam; as it fell to the floor, Henry leaped away, nearly falling over one of the steel-frame camp beds lined up on both sides of the narrow room. Wasps were already swarming from the fallen nest as Ham darted forward, spray gun in his hands.

"Die, you bastards! Die!" he yelled, pumping the gun as fast as he could to drench the nest with insecticide. At once, the loft was filled with an alcohol stench. The wasps caught in the spray fell to the floor and flopped about in dying spasms, but a handful were still airborne and angry. With high-pitched whines, they began to dart toward the giant who'd dared attack their colony.

"Retreat! Retreat!" Ham lunged for the door behind him, but one of the steamer trunks at the foot of each bed got in his way. He yelped as he tripped over it and fell face-first to the bare wooden floor, the sprayer gun skittering out of his reach. "Damn it!" he yelled, swatting at a wasp that flitted past his face. "Hey, someone help me!"

As Henry reached down to pull Ham to his feet, Mike snatched up the sprayer. Careful not to use it until the other two were clear, he hastily pumped more insecticide at the wasps, then followed Ham and Henry through the door. They slammed it shut, then stood for a minute on the small landing at the top of the stairs, trying to get their wind as they shared a laugh at their own silliness.

"I hope . . . we got 'em all," Henry gasped.

"Hope so too." Ham was half–bent over, hands on his knees. "Some-one's got to . . . go back in there and open a window . . . air the place out." Catching the look on Henry's face, he shook his head. "Not me. I'm on their . . . most wanted list."

"Yeah, they've got it in for you," Mike said, then he saw how the other two were eying him. "Whoa, Nellie. Not me . . ."

"I can't believe that's where we're all going to sleep," Henry said, shaking his head in disgust. "Six beds in one room. Feels like I'm in the Boy Scouts again."

"Yeah? If you like that, you're gonna love this." Ham pushed open the door across the hall, revealing a bathroom not much larger than a closet. Inside were an old-fashioned claw-foot tub and a sink with exposed pipes. "Notice anything missing?"

"Yeah. Where's the . . . ?" Mike stopped. "Oh, no. Don't tell me it's outside."

"Yup. The outhouse is in the backyard, about ten feet from the kitchen door." Ham shrugged. "At least it's got its own woodstove."

"Wow. The lap of luxury."

"Leave it to Uncle Sam to spare no expense." Ham shook his head. "And leave it to our nursemaids to claim the downstairs bedroom. 'Secu-rity reasons,' my ass."

"Yeah, well . . ." Henry checked his watch. "'Bout time for everyone to meet up in the living room. Maybe we can persuade Igor to spring for a couple of prefab houses."

The other two chuckled at the mention of the nickname the 390 Group had recently bestowed on Omar Bliss. "Ignorance is Bliss" became a whispered catchphrase when the colonel stubbornly resisted the group's more radical proposals, and this led to some team members referring to him as Ignorance for a while until they realized that this wasn't entirely true: Bliss wasn't ignorant, really, just a bit behind the times. So Ignorance was shortened to Igor, which suited him even better: If you squinted a bit, the colonel did look a little like Dr. Frankenstein's henchman. No one called him that to his face, though.

The colonel was already in the living room when Henry, Mike, and Ham came down from the loft and trooped in through the porch door. FBI agents Sabatini and Arnold were leaning against the fieldstone fireplace; they might have been a couple of weekend hunters were it not for the shoulder holsters visible beneath their unbuttoned jackets. The three team members had just taken seats when Gerry and Taylor came in. They'd spent the last hour unloading everyone's belongings from the cars and were looking forward to taking a break before starting on the truck.

"Where's Bob?" Taylor asked, looking around the room as he sat down on the couch next to Henry. "Aren't we waiting for him?"

Bliss shook his head. "No, we're going to have this meeting without him. I told him and Esther they're excused so that they could make themselves at home, but the fact is there's some things I want to talk about without his being around."

The team members glanced at one another. "It's about what happened the other day, isn't it?" Ham said quietly.

"What else?" Taylor also kept his voice down. "I've worked with Bob for years, and I've never seen him like this. I mean, I don't think he's said ten words to me in the last couple of days . . ."

"Someone tried to kill him, and they damn near succeeded." Mike scowled at him. "That would give anyone the heebie-jeebies." He turned to Bliss. "Colonel, none of us are crazy about moving up here, but you probably did the right thing. If that guy was a German spy . . ."

"Was he a kraut?" Ham looked over at the two G-men. "Has anyone learned anything about him yet?"

"Nothing conclusive," Sabatini admitted. "He wasn't carrying any identification, and if there was someone working with him, he made a clean getaway. But his gun was German-made, and my office thinks he may also be responsible for the murder of a Beach Patrol watchman on Cape Cod earlier that morning." The FBI agent shrugged. "So, yeah, it's a safe bet the guy who tried to shoot Dr. Goddard was a Nazi."

"Which means two things," Bliss said. "One, the Germans consider Bob to be enough of a threat that they went to the trouble of sending someone over here to knock him off. And if that's the case . . . two, the British air raid wasn't entirely successful, and Silver Bird hasn't been destroyed."

Grim nods from around the room. The group had been informed of the RAF air raid on Peenemünde the day after it happened, and they'd hoped that it would have knocked *Silbervogel* down enough that the Germans might simply give up and cancel the project entirely. Indeed, there had been less urgency about Blue Horizon in recent weeks. Although work in Worcester continued, there was no longer a feeling that 390 Group was in a race against time. They were designing an experimental spacecraft that might still be used, but probably not before the war was over.

Their attitude changed as soon as they heard about what happened at City Hall. The colonel's observation reinforced what they'd come to suspect: Goddard wouldn't have been targeted if the Nazis didn't think he might develop a deterrent to their antipodal bomber, and therefore Silver Bird was still under way.

"We've relocated you here in case he had accomplices," Bliss continued, "but that's not the only reason. Bob's shook up by this, and so is Esther. We can't have him trying to work on this project while worrying if he's going to catch a bullet whenever he walks outside, and we risk having anyone going after you guys, too. I'm sorry the accommodations are a bit rough, but . . . well, we'll try to make you as comfortable as possible, so long as you're here."

"And how long will that be?" Henry asked.

"Until your work is finished," Bliss replied. Groans and irate murmurs greeted this remark, and he quickly held up his hand. "I know that's a long time to keep you sequestered, but . . ."

"Sequestered?" Gerry stared at him. "What do you mean by that?"

Bliss hesitated, and Sabatini stepped in. "What this means is that new security protocols are now in effect. No one is to leave this camp without an FBI escort. We'll drive someone into town to buy groceries, cigarettes, newspapers, or whatever else you need, but otherwise, you're to remain here."

"What about mail?" Mike asked.

"It'll still come to Worcester. So far as anyone you know is concerned, you're still at Clark University. And if you send anything out, it'll be mailed from Worcester, too, so it'll have that postmark." Sabatini paused. "Naturally, you'll refrain from saying anything about this place. Don't give us reason to start reading your letters to make sure that you're in compliance."

"And the phone?" Henry asked. "I haven't found one yet."

"That's because there isn't one here and never has been. The guys who started this club were serious about getting away from it all." Sabatini shrugged. "No loss. I've seen the local switchboard. It's in the back of the general store, same place you'll be buying food. The operator is an old biddy who looks like the type who'd be an eavesdropper, and the last thing we want is to have her hearing anything about Blue Horizon. That's why we'll be installing a radiotelephone next week. It'll only be used for official communications, so don't even think about using it to call your girlfriend."

Henry stared at him, and Sabatini grinned. "Yeah, we know all about her," he went on. "Frank figured out you were seeing someone on the sly and had us check her out, just to make sure she wasn't a spy. She's a peach, all right . . . but I hope she's the patient type, because it's going to be a while before you'll see her again."

Henry said nothing but instead fixed his gaze upon the floor. "Sorry, man," Taylor said to him quietly, then he looked at Bliss again. "You still haven't told us why Lloyd and Harry aren't here. Couldn't you fit more beds in the loft?"

Gerry shook his head. "Like there's any more room up there."

"Available space was one consideration, yes," the colonel said, "but there's another reason. Now that we're getting close to actually bending metal, I've decided to send them down to Alamogordo, where they'll join Lieutenant Jackson."

"Lucky," Taylor muttered.

If Bliss heard what he said, he chose to ignore him. "The Goodrich company will soon be delivering the pressure suit you've designed, and I want Lloyd there to make sure the breathing mixture is correct when our pilot tries it on for the first time. He'll also be working with Harry on further tests of the main engine once it's built and been sent to New Mexico."

Mike was in the midst of pulling out his briar pipe when the colonel said this. He stopped tamping tobacco in the bowl and peered at Bliss. "Come again? I thought the engine was going to be built down there."

"Yes, well"—Bliss hid his apparent discomfiture by coughing in his fist—"there's been a change of plans. The engine's going to be built and static-tested here in New England."

This caught the team flat-footed. The five remaining members of the 390 Group stared at Bliss in shock, their mouths falling open. For months, Goddard had been campaigning to have the main engine assembled somewhere close enough for them to have firsthand participation in its construction and testing, only to hear the same arguments against it repeated again and again. Now, all of a sudden, the colonel had apparently changed his mind.

"Why are you . . . ?" Henry began.

"Dr. Goddard wouldn't let us relocate the project unless we were willing to make certain concessions. He pointed out that, if we came all the way up here, we'd be even more isolated than we were before, and that could cause significant delays. He and Lieutenant Jackson had been pushing for the Wyman-Gordon Company to be hired as prime contractor since that would put the engine R&D phase in Worcester, and the Pentagon has been considering this for a while. Recent events just . . . um, speeded up the decision-making process a bit, that's all."

"I don't care if they made it by flipping a coin," Taylor said, a grin stretching across his face. "That's great news!"

"Does Bob know yet?" Ham asked, and Bliss shook his head. "Well, this ought to cheer him up."

"Yeah, but now we've got another problem," Henry said. "Where are we gonna test the damn thing once it's built? I mean, you can't just light up an engine that size anywhere near a city and not have someone notice."

"Yes, well . . . that's one more thing for you characters to figure out." Bliss frowned. "Speaking of which, how are you coming with the missiles?"

Henry, Taylor, and Gerry shared a look; developing the X-1's armament was their job. "Not so good," Henry admitted. "The missiles themselves are no problem . . . a couple of solid-fuel rockets launched from under the wings, that's all . . . but we're still trying to figure out how our pilot's going to get a dead bead on Silver Bird when both ships are traveling at different relative velocities."

"It's like trying to hit a bullet with another bullet," Mike added. "Or like trying to shoot a car from another car that's moving at a different speed." He shrugged. "Give us five or ten years, and we might be able to give you some kinda guided missile, but we just don't know how to do that yet."

"I understand," Bliss said, "but we don't have five or ten years. I'm not sure we even have five or ten months. British intelligence has reason to believe that the Germans have moved Silver Bird from Peenemünde . . ."

"Hey, when did that happen?" Ham was as surprised everyone else. "How did the Brits figure out . . . ?"

"I can't tell you because I don't know either. All I know is that MI-6 has some way of knowing what the Germans are doing. According to them, the Nazis have transferred Silver Bird from the Baltic coast to an inland location." Bliss looked at Henry. "Appears that one of your guesses might be correct. MI-6 thinks the new site is somewhere in the mountains, possibly near a town called Nordhausen."

"Ah, so . . ." Ham gave Henry a wink. "All that time you've spent in the library has paid off. Besides sparking with a certain librarian, I mean."

Henry cast him a foul look as the others chuckled. All except Bliss. "If I'd known about that . . ." the colonel began, then he sighed and shook his head. "Never mind. That's something I don't have to worry about anymore . . . is it, Henry?"

"No, sir," he said quietly. "It isn't."

"Good." Bliss stood up and stretched his back. "Very well, then. If no one has any other immediate business, I suggest we get back to work."

"Anyone want to help with the file cabinets?" Taylor asked as he got up from the couch. "They're pretty heavy, and Gerry and I could use a hand."

"Sure, I'll pitch in," Ham said, and Mike nodded as well. "Henry, you want to . . . ?"

"No, I don't." Without another word, Henry stood up and marched out of the living room. The porch screen door squeaked on its hinges as he opened it and banged into its frame when he let it slam shut behind him.

No one spoke; everyone looked a little embarrassed. But as they filed out of the living room, Taylor came up beside Ham. "I think you might've rubbed him the wrong way," he said quietly. "He's pretty serious about Doris."

"Sorry. Didn't know." Through the front porch's screen windows, they could see Henry walking down to the beach. "I'll go apologize to him."

"Give him a chance to cool down first," Taylor suggested, then he slapped Ham on the shoulder. "C'mon. Let's get those file cabinets inside."

Henry was still down on the beach when Ham came to see him. He'd found a couple of weather-beaten Adirondack chairs near the water and was watching the sun as it began to touch the trees on the other side of the lake. He looked around at Ham as he sauntered over to him, but he didn't say anything.

"Hey, I'm really sorry about that crack I made back there." Ham sat down beside him. "I mean, what goes on between you and Doris is your business, and I was way out to line to . . ."

"Forget it. I know it was a joke. Just a bad one, that's all." Henry reached into his shirt pocket, pulled out his cigarettes, shook one out, and offered the pack to Ham. "What bugs me is Igor and those FBI goons telling me I can't see her anymore. I mean, it's bad enough that I didn't even get a chance to say good-bye before we were hustled up here . . ."

"You didn't?" Ham asked, taking a cigarette from him, and Henry shook his head. "Oh, man . . . are you in the doghouse!"

"Maybe. I sure hope not." Henry lit his cigarette. "Doris is pretty smart. I didn't tell her what we're doing, but she figured out on her own that it's some sort of hush-hush government project. She . . ."

He was interrupted by a raucous honking sound from above. Both men looked up to see a flock of Canadian geese above the lake, forming a ragged double-V formation as they flew toward the south.

"That's pretty," Ham murmured.

"Yeah, it is," Henry said. "Anyway, the grad-student bit didn't fool her for a minute. So suddenly disappearing like this . . . well, I don't think she's gonna think I dumped her. But she's going to be worried, and that's what . . ."

All of a sudden, they heard sharp, distant bangs from the opposite shore. The geese honked louder as the shotgun blasts echoed across the lake, then a goose near the front of the formation abruptly fell downward, its wings flapping uselessly as it plummeted toward the water.

"Hunter got one, looks like," Henry murmured. "He must be hiding over there in the trees."

"Wherever he is, he's a good shot." Ham searched for his matches, and Henry handed him a box. "Thanks. I tried it once but gave up. There's a trick to bringing down geese that I never got the hang of."

"Oh, yeah? What's that?"

"Well, you don't aim for the birds themselves. They're too high up, and you'll miss 'em if you fire at them while they're above you. What you need to do is figure out where they're going to be a second or two later and shoot at that instead."

"I see," Henry said. "So you don't aim for the geese, but where they're going . . ."

All of a sudden, his voice trailed off, and his eyes widened as if something had just occurred to him. "I'll be damned," he said softly. "It can't be that simple."

"What? What's not that simple?"

Henry got up from the chair and began to quickly walk back to the lodge. "C'mon . . . I think I just figured out how to take down Silver Bird."

SIMULATION OF THE VOID

Skid Sloman sat in the cramped cockpit and gazed out at space that wasn't space, Earth that wasn't Earth.

The stars were realistic enough as they slowly rotated above him, until they passed across one of the welded seams in the hemispherical sky. When that happened, the slight yet discernible way the ceiling warped them revealed that they were nothing more than pinpricks of light cast by a planetarium projector. When he looked down, he could see Earth beneath him, as seen from a suborbital altitude of about forty miles. It was a clever replica, too, but this illusion had its limits as well. Not only did it not move, but because no man-made object had ever gone this high, the artists who'd painted the simulator floor had only maps to guide them. So the lakes and rivers were just a bit too well-defined, and there was never a cloud anywhere above North America.

Skid didn't care. This was his nineteenth simulated journey into space, and it wasn't going much better than the eighteen he'd made before.

"Desert Bravo to X-1, do you copy?" Jack Cube's voice crackled in his headphones. It, too, was probably more clear than it ought to be. In fact,

it would be a miracle if the ship's wireless system worked well enough for him to maintain ground communications.

"Roger, Desert Bravo." As he spoke, Skid was careful not to snap his gum. Everyone had been on his back lately about his chewing Juicy Fruit while in the simulator. He couldn't smoke here, though, and considering how many times he'd flown this stupid thing already, he needed something to help his nerves.

"Report position."

Skid glanced down at the radium dials of his compass and gyroscopic altimeter. "Azimuth 88 degrees northeast, altitude 40.2 miles." This was nonsense, of course; his instruments were displaying only what the controllers were feeding the simulator. But Jack was doing this to get Skid into the habit of radioing his bearings to home base, something military pilots didn't often do.

"Roger that, X-1. Prepare for your target run, over."

"Wilco, Desert Bravo. Hit me with your best shot."

False bravado, which Skid soon paid for. Right hand on the stick, Skid craned his neck as much as the high seatback would allow and searched the fake sky. He'd just lost the flavor of the gum he was chewing when a familiar shape appeared almost directly above him: a luminescent silhouette of the Silver Bird, much the way he was supposed to see it if everything went well.

"Silver Bird sighted," Skid said. "Vectoring for attack run."

As gently as he could, he pulled back on the stick, squeezing the red trigger within its pistol grip. The cockpit shuddered slightly as the simulator faked his reaction-control rockets firing, then it tilted back on its rotary gimbals. Below him, the painted terrain fell away, disappearing from sight as the simulator "climbed." The change in attitude was easy enough to perform, but the stick was incredibly sensitive. It was designed to emulate the lack of atmospheric resistance his craft would experience, and Skid had learned that any careless movement could send the ship wildly off course. Once again, he clenched his teeth as he tried to line up the crosshatch painted inside the canopy with the Silver Bird silhouette.

For a brief instant, he almost had it, but he was a half second too slow firing the RCRs again to stop the upward pitch. Skid watched helplessly as Silver Bird started sliding downward until it vanished beneath the prow, meaning that his craft was now on a trajectory which, if uncorrected, would cause it to fly over the enemy vessel.

"Hell's bells!" Skid pushed the stick forward, and an instant later the silhouette reappeared. But it was larger now, and off-center as well. Skid pushed the stick to the left, and the starboard RCRs fired—Newton's third law was something he always had to keep in mind—but even though the turn was successful, he was now in danger of going into a barrel roll.

"Well, okay then," he muttered, "let it roll." Skid had been thinking about this since the last time he'd climbed into the simulator and had come up to a tentative hypothesis: a sustained roll along the craft's long axis might actually stabilize him, just the way a bullet is spun when fired from a gun. Sure enough, even though the eight-ball attitude gauge was spinning like a top, and the cockpit was cartwheeling, the prow had neatly lined up on the silhouette.

"Gotcha." Skid reached for a pair of toggle switches on the instrument panel. If he could keep this up just long enough to get within range and send the rockets on their way . . .

Suddenly, the cockpit seized up on its gimbals. Before Skid could react, his seat was yanked upright as the simulator returned to its starting position. From the other side of the canopy, he could hear servomotors whining as they lost power. Someone had thrown the switch on him.

"Aw, c'mon!" he yelled. "What was wrong with that?"

"Nothing, except that maneuver would've killed you," Jack Cube replied.

"Like hell! The roll wasn't nothing I couldn't handle . . ."

"Except the way you were going, you would've slammed into the upper atmosphere and burned up like a torch. Maybe you didn't notice, but Silver Bird was beginning its next skip when you started your run. That's why you overshot it. By the time you reacquired the target, you wouldn't have been able to pull out in time."

"At least I would've shot it down," Skid grumbled.

"*If you were lucky, maybe . . . but I'm not training you for a suicide mission. Now, c'mon, climb down from there. I've got a couple of people I want you to meet.*"

Ceiling lights flashed on, wiping away the starscape and revealing the dull grey interior of the metal sphere surrounding him. The simulator cockpit was held in the sphere's center by two horizontal spars jutting out from either side of the dome; a motorized yoke held the cockpit in place, its gimbals allowing the pilot to practice maneuvers with a nearly full degree of motion. The whole thing was an ingenious—and expensive— means of training a spacecraft pilot, but Skid had lately come to regard it as his own personal torture chamber.

As he unbuckled his seat harness, a technician walked across the narrow catwalk on top of the starboard spar. He unlocked the canopy and slid it open, then reached down to help Skid out of the cockpit. The test pilot followed him back across the catwalk, taking a moment to spit his gum over the side. It landed somewhere in Ohio; the technician glared at him, and Skid grinned. The simulator team really hated it when he did that.

The technician unlatched the egress hatch and pushed it open, then led Skid down a rollaway service tower. The thirty-foot-diameter sphere stood upon a concrete pedestal within an enormous hangarlike building. The control station stood to one side; scientists and engineers in white lab coats were huddled over its consoles, examining the results of the last test. They barely looked up at Skid as he walked down the ladder, and once again the pilot wondered if they considered him to be a slightly more intelligent version of the chimpanzees they'd used in the first phases of ground tests.

Hearing voices suddenly raised from nearby, Skid paused on the ladder to gaze at the other end of the building. Several men stood before an open door leading through the thick concrete wall that divided the building in half. On the other side of the wall was another machine that had been making his life so interesting lately: a rotary centrifuge, with another mock-up of the X-1 cockpit at the end of its twenty-foot boom.

The centrifuge was a bit more fun—Skid enjoyed riding the thing even when it was squashing him back in his seat at seven g's—but not everyone shared his opinion. Joe McPherson stood in front of the door, arguing with the scientists who operated the machine. Skid couldn't hear what they were saying, but he knew what it was about: money. Joe had reached a compromise agreement with Colonel Bliss when he was hired to be the backup pilot: a flat fee, plus hazard pay for any training beyond what professional test pilots usually had to endure, the rate dependent upon the amount of time and the risk factor. None of this was graven in stone, though, so every time Joe climbed into the simulator, the centrifuge, the rocket sled, or any of the other devices being used to train him and Skid, there was always another argument about how much more he'd get on his next paycheck.

Skid shook his head in disgust as he continued down the tower. Like everyone else involved in the project, he was sick and tired of McPherson's attitude. He needed a backup pilot, though, and there was no time to find and train someone else. Joe knew this, so he was milking it for all it was worth. *Grab the dough while you can,* he'd privately told Skid over drinks in the officers' club. *That crazy thing will never get off the ground, so you might as well make some bucks off it while you can.*

Skid had said nothing. He was doing this for reasons that Joe would never understand, and money was the least of his concerns.

Jack Cube was waiting at the bottom of the tower. Over the past few months, Skid had gradually gotten used to the fact that, regardless of whatever mood he was in—pleased, angry, confused, irritated, anxious— Jack's expression rarely changed. Skid had known that Lieutenant Jackson was a cool customer the very first day they met, but Jack Cube raised stoicism to a kind of art. You had to look at his eyes to figure out where he was coming from . . . and just then, he wasn't happy at all.

"You want to tell me what you were trying to pull in there?" the chief trainer asked.

"Umm . . . coming up with a way to kill Silver Bird?" Skid unzipped a breast pocket of his flight suit and pulled out a pack of Camels. "That's what I'm supposed to do, ain't it?"

"You're supposed to be learning how to fly something no one else has ever flown before." Jack impatiently shook his head when Skid offered him a smoke. "It's not helping that you won't get over the idea that this isn't an airplane, and all those slick dogfight maneuvers you know won't work here."

"Jack, it's got wings . . ."

"How many times do I have to tell you? You're not going to use 'em until you're on your way home. Which will be as a meteor if you don't listen to what I . . ."

"Yeah, yeah, yeah." Skid lit his cigarette with a Zippo lighter.

Jack sighed, then stepped closer. "Rudy, look," he went on, a little more quietly now, "this is serious business. See Mutt and Jeff over there?"

Skid looked past him. The two military physicians who'd been assigned to Blue Horizon as his medical team were standing near the control station at the base of the platform. They had proper names, of course, but Skid, Joe, and Jack had started calling them Mutt and Jeff because of their resemblance to the comic-strip characters. But the nicknames were a private joke and nothing more: The doctors outranked both Jack and Skid, and they didn't appear to have a sense of humor.

"How could I miss 'em?" Jack muttered. "They've used so much Vaseline on me, I could use it to lubricate the centrifuge."

Jack Cube showed no outward sign of amusement, but the twinkle in his dark eyes told Skid that, deep down inside, he was cracking up. "Yeah, well . . . look, they were behind me during that last run, and I could hear them talking, and apparently Mutt's got some harebrained idea that zero gravity may cause you to lose your mind . . ."

"What?"

"Shh . . . keep it down." Jack made a shushing motion with his hands. "He has a theory that someone who experiences extended periods of free fall might lose his equilibrium because he won't be able to tell left from right or up from down, and that could lead to a mental breakdown."

"Oh, for the love of . . ." Smoke jetted from Skid's nostrils. "Please take this guy up in a plane and do a few power dives. He'll blow his lunch, but he won't go crazy."

"Well, he's got Jeff half-convinced that his theory might be correct, and Jeff even thinks it might be possible that you'll have a cardiac arrest because your heart won't function in . . ." Jack stopped himself. "Never mind. The point is, when you pull stunts like that in there, that makes them wonder if you could go nuts up there and put the whole mission at risk." He paused. "I'm almost liable to agree although for different reasons."

Skid glared at him. "You think I'm crazy?"

"No . . . just reckless. And if you keep screwing around like this, they'll pull you from the number one slot and put McPherson in there instead."

"Aw, c'mon, Jack . . . Joe doesn't even believe X-1 can fly!"

"I know he doesn't. But he's managed to impress Mutt and Jeff, and they've got a vote over who gets certified. So a word to the wise . . . cut the crap and get serious."

Skid didn't respond at once. As he dropped his cigarette and ground it out beneath his bootheel, his gaze wandered to the centrifuge entrance. Apparently, Joe McPherson had reached some sort of agreement with the operators because they were no longer standing there. But the centrifuge chamber door was still open, and Mutt and Jeff were strolling in that direction, with Jeff writing something on his clipboard. Probably another evaluation to be added to Skid's medical folder. What was it going to say this time?

"Okay, all right," he said quietly. "No more monkey business . . . I promise."

"Good. I'm going to hold you to that." A momentary smile that vanished almost as quickly as it appeared. "C'mon . . . we've got a couple of new members on our team, guys I knew in Worcester. I want you to meet them."

Skid let Jack lead him over to the control station, where two men in civilian clothes were studying the simulator's pen-scroll from the most recent session. One was a wiry little dude with a Groucho Marx mustache, the other a Chinese guy. Both turned to him and Jack as they walked up to the station.

"This is Lloyd Kapman," Jack said, "and this is Harry Chung. I worked with them in the 390 Group before I was sent down here . . . and now they've been assigned here, too." He laid a hand on Skid's shoulder. "This is Lieutenant Rudy Sloman, also known as Skid. If he'll grow up and stop horsing around, he might become the first man in space."

"The first American, at least," Skid added as he shook hands with first Lloyd, then Harry.

"Either way, we'll make sure you'll come back alive." Lloyd gestured to the giant sphere looming above them. "We watched that last test. Very impressive, Lieutenant . . . a good performance, if I may say so."

Jack coughed in his fist, and Skid had to fight to keep from grinning. "Thanks, but . . . um, I think I can do better."

"We can talk about this over lunch," Jack said. "Once Lieutenant Sloman changes out of his flight suit, I'm sure he'd be only too happy to buy you some."

"Hey, now wait a minute." Skid glared at him. "You didn't tell me you were gonna stick me with . . ."

Lloyd was already laughing, and Harry was grinning as well. "Jack, you haven't changed," Lloyd said. "Same warm, friendly guy."

"Was he this way in Worcester?" Skid asked. "I thought it was just me."

"Naw, Jack's got a chip on his shoulder for everyone. I mean, the night he showed up . . ."

"Look, you can tell all the lies you want about me once we get some chow." Jack Cube headed for the door that would take them outside. "Or maybe you'd rather have the nickel tour, first."

"No," Harry said. "First food, then tour. We haven't had a decent meal since we left New England, and I'm definitely not counting the ham and cheese sandwiches they gave us on the plane."

"Trust me," Jack said, "the food's not any better here."

―――――――――

In only a few months, the Blue Horizon compound at Alamogordo Army Air Field had grown from a small collection of Quonset huts and prefab buildings to a full-fledged military research installation where more than fifteen hundred people lived and worked. Machine shops, assembly sheds, laboratories, test facilities, and warehouses shared room on narrow dirt streets with barracks, cottages, PXs and commissaries, mess halls, clubs for both enlisted men and officers, even a bowling alley. And on the outskirts of the compound, a launchpad was being built. The blockhouse was complete, and now the pad itself and its rollaway gantry tower were under construction.

As they walked to the officers' club, stepping aside every now and then to let a jeep or truck rumble by, Lloyd and Harry brought Jack and Skid up to speed on recent events in New England. The two lieutenants had already heard about the attempt on Dr. Goddard's life, but not in any great detail; however, they weren't surprised by the revelation that the Nazis were probably behind it.

"No one else would have wanted Bob dead," Jack said.

"Except maybe one of us," Lloyd added.

What was more unexpected was the news that the rest of the 390 Group—with the exception of Harry and Lloyd themselves—had been relocated to a hunting lodge just across the Massachusetts state line in New Hampshire. Jack Cube had believed that the entire team, Bob and Esther Goddard included, would have been packed aboard a military transport plane and sent to New Mexico, so he was stunned to learn that they were being kept in New England.

"It's this whole compartmental . . . y'know, whatever . . . the War Department has got us locked into." Lloyd threw up his hands in frustration. "It's never made any sense to me, putting the R&D team on the other side of the country from the rest of the project, but you'd think they would've learned their lesson by now."

He glanced at Jack Cube, as if silently begging for an explanation. Jack acknowledged his friend's bewilderment with a commiserating nod and shrug, but otherwise remained quiet. Criticizing decisions made by the brass wasn't his style, especially not when it was possible that anything he said might be overheard and make its way up the chain of command.

"It's not all bad news," Harry added. "From what I heard, Bliss finally knuckled under and agreed to relocate main-engine assembly and testing to Massachusetts, where the team can get their hands on it."

"He did?" Jack gave him a sharp look. "Where in Mass?"

"A defense factory just outside Worcester . . . Wyman-Gordon, I think it's called."

Jack smiled. It was the same place he'd been begging the colonel to consider since last winter. "That's good," he said, quietly deciding not to claim credit for helping change Bliss's mind. "I'm sure it'll work out."

"Yeah, well, it better," Skid murmured. He still hadn't changed out of his flight suit, but it didn't matter. Jack would probably march him straight back to the simulator after lunch. "Hate to say it, but unless someone gives us a rocket that won't blow up as soon as we light the candle, this whole thing's gonna be a waste of time . . . and me," he quietly added.

Everyone knew what he meant. So far, three prototype engines had exploded during static tests. The fact that each engine had run a few seconds longer than the last one was of little comfort to the pilot being trained to ride it in space.

"We'll get it built." Harry was confident, as if they were discussing nothing more than a university research project that had developed a few kinks. "Don't sweat it."

"Really? Don't sweat it, huh?" Skid suddenly came to a halt, causing everyone else to stop as well. He raised a hand, crooked a beckoning finger. "C'mere . . . I want to show you something."

Lloyd stared at the test pilot as he turned to walk away. "I thought we were going to get lunch."

"We're still going to eat," Skid said over his shoulder. "C'mon . . . this will take just a second." Lloyd and Harry gave Jack Cube a questioning look, but he only shrugged and gestured for them to follow him.

Skid led the other three men back toward a massive hangar they'd just passed. The largest building in the compound, it was built of steel-reinforced concrete and had no windows. Instead, it was cooled by a huge air-conditioning unit in its flat roof. The double doors at the end facing them were closed, but an MP stood guard in front of a smaller side door.

Recognizing Skid and Jack Cube, he stepped aside to let them pass, but Skid stopped just before he opened the door.

"You guys have been stuck in a lab all this time, playing with slide rules," he said to Lloyd and Harry, "so maybe this whole thing has become just a little abstract. Kind of a thought experiment, if you know what I mean."

"We haven't forgotten . . ." Lloyd began.

"Yeah, well"—Skid opened the door, walked inside—"lemme show you something anyway."

The hangar was a cool, well-lit cavern, its concrete floor illuminated by rows of fluorescent fixtures suspended from the steel rafters high above. In the center of the hangar, resting within a mobile cradle and surrounded by scaffolds and catwalks, was what appeared to be an unfinished aircraft, yet one that had never been seen before. Long, swept-back wings, already covered by unpainted steel plates, jutted out from a skeletal frame that would eventually become a fuselage, while at the far end of the room, workmen in welders masks used acetylene torches to assemble a long, sleek nose.

As Lloyd gawked in amazement, Harry whistled just under his breath. "Damn," he said quietly. "So this is the X-1."

"That's what you guys call it, sure." Hands on his hips, Skid regarded the spacecraft proudly. "Me, I call it the *Lucky Linda*. The day Jack and Colonel Bliss asked me to fly her, I told them I would, so long as I got to name her after my sweetheart. She's kind of hard to please, so . . . well, never mind."

He turned to Harry and Lloyd again. "She's a beauty, my *Lucky Linda*, and I've got to hand it to you guys . . . you're giving me a real sweet flying machine. There's only one problem . . ."

"No engine," Lloyd said quietly.

"That's right . . . she ain't got no engine. And if *Lucky Linda* ain't got no engine, she ain't going nowhere except the junkyard. And worse than that, if she doesn't fly but the Silver Bird does, there won't be nothing to stop the Nazis from dropping bombs on New York. Which would really break my heart, because I'm from Brooklyn, and my baby lives there, too."

As he spoke, Rudy Sloman slowly walked toward them, never raising his voice but not looking away either. Neither Harry nor Lloyd said anything, even as the test pilot stopped just a foot away from Harry and stared him straight in the eye, his gaze cold and unwavering.

"So, yeah, I am going to sweat it," he said. "And I'd appreciate it if, the next time you talk to your friends in New Hampshire, you'd tell them to sweat it, too, and gimme an engine that won't blow up under my ass. Okay?"

"Okay," Harry croaked, his voice barely audible.

"Well, all right then." A big grin spread across Skid's face, then he swatted Harry's arm and Lloyd's as well. "Let's go get some chow."

The two men bobbed their heads nervously, then watched with wide and fearful eyes as Skid turned and walked away. "Oh, man," Lloyd said softly when he thought Skid was out of earshot, "he's crazy."

"Yeah," Jack muttered as he walked past. "Tell me about it."

AUTUMN IN NEW ENGLAND

Shadows were beginning to lengthen ever so slightly across the living room floor, but the three old men continued to speak. Lloyd had awakened from his nap, and once he'd turned up his hearing aid again, he rejoined the conversation.

"I was glad to . . . go down there," he said haltingly, pausing to take a glass of water his nephew brought him from the kitchen. "It was a lot warmer in . . . New Mexico than it was here."

"Yeah, we were pretty envious of you and Jack . . . Harry, too." Henry had just come back from the bathroom; he lowered himself into his chair, carefully placing his cane where he could reach it. "This place is pretty nice in the fall, but once November rolls around, and it starts getting cold at night . . . well, we had to start taking turns for who would go out to the woodpile and fetch some more firewood."

"Weren't you using the porch for most of your work?" Jack asked.

"Uh-huh. The porch table was the only place big enough for us to spread out all our blueprints and notes. It wasn't so bad during the day, but once the sun went down, and we still had work to do . . ." Henry shivered at the thought. "Yeah, it could get kind of brisk. Especially when the wind was up."

"But didn't you have Dr. Goddard's house to go to?" Douglas Walker asked.

"Sometimes we did, when it got too cold. But their living room was too small for us to all get together at the same time and still lay out our notes, and besides, Esther was . . ." Henry hesitated. "Esther was becoming very protective of Bob."

"How come?"

"She'd never wanted him to come back from . . . Roswell in the first place," Lloyd said.

"The weather in this part of the country was bad for him, especially in the fall and winter," Henry said. "He was a tuberculosis survivor, but he'd never shaken it completely. And the smoking didn't help. He'd managed to get through that first winter back in Worcester without any serious issues because Esther would drive him straight from home to the lab and back again, but once we moved up here, he'd have to walk from his cabin to the lodge several times a day, then work outside on the porch for hours at a time. All of us came down with colds at one point or another, so you can only imagine what it was like for him."

"I understand that's when his health began to decline," Walker said.

"Yes, it was. We all noticed that he was coughing much more frequently and that he was becoming a little more pale, but . . ." Henry sighed. "It didn't really seem important to anyone but Esther, but even she couldn't do much about it. Bob was completely dedicated to this project. Once we got the missile problem licked . . . after I saw those geese, the solution was so obvious we couldn't believe that we hadn't figured it out earlier . . . the last big hurdle was devising a main engine big enough to give us the thrust we needed without blowing up."

"Yeah, I remember that," Jack said. "We had a spaceship in a hangar that we couldn't finish building until we had the engine, and when Colonel Bliss moved that part of the program to New England, that put pressure on you guys."

"We were here for months, all the way to the end of the year." Henry shook his head at the memory. "Working day in and day out, getting up at the crack of dawn and working straight through the day and into the night. The engine was still just one part of it, you understand. There were about a hundred . . . a thousand . . . other details that needed to be worked out. The stress was unbelievable."

"How were you communicating with Alamogordo?" Walker asked.

"Every day or so, an Army motorcycle courier would come up from Massachusetts. We'd collect written memos from him and send back memos and reports and blueprint corrections, and he'd put them on a plane and send them to New Mexico. For short queries that had to be answered immediately, we had the radiophone, with one of the FBI guys acting as our communications man. Otherwise, though, we were pretty isolated out here."

"It wasn't much fun . . . for us either," Lloyd said softly.

"Oh, no." Jack shook his head. "We'd get your material a day or two after you sent it, and sometimes we'd just have to hope that you guys knew what you were doing. Toward the end, there wasn't enough time to run everything through the wringer. It was build it, test it once or twice to make sure it worked, then stick it in and hope for the best. But the engine was the hard part."

"Wyman-Gordon started building it in mid-November," Henry said, "working from specs the courier brought down from New Hampshire. The company was putting it together in an unused warehouse in the back of their yard, and the Army posted a twenty-four-hour watch on the site. Every couple of days or so, someone from our group . . . usually Bob, Taylor, or me . . . would be driven down there by one of the G-men, getting there sometime after dark. We'd supervise the construction and answer any questions the engineers and craftsmen might have, then we'd be driven back to the lodge."

"We were putting in a lot of hours," Jack said, "but it never seemed to help. We were in a race against time, and we knew we were losing."

Hearing this, Walker's eyes widened. Before he could ask the obvious question, though, Jack went on. "How did we know? Oh, we weren't completely in the dark about what the Nazis were doing. MI-6's signal intelligence operation in Bletchley Park was a big help. The breakthrough came in late September, when they used their Enigma machine to crack the message code used by the Luftwaffe rocket-research teams. When that happened, we suddenly had an ear to the ground as to what they were doing . . ."

"And, most importantly, where," Henry said. "I'd sort of figured out that they'd move Silver Bird's launch operations to somewhere deep in Germany, but it wasn't until Bletchley Park was able to read Luftwaffe dispatches that we knew exactly where . . . the *Mittelwerk* facility near Nordhausen. Once that was accomplished, though, we had a window on their operations."

"More like . . . a peephole." Lloyd shook his head. "We didn't know . . . everything that was going on there. The horrible parts . . ."

"No, we didn't." Jack's face was grim. "And if we had . . . I don't know what difference it would have made, really, except make us even more determined to ensure that we didn't fail."

"Didn't you try to see Grandma then?" Eileen asked.

"The feds still wouldn't let me get in touch with her," Henry said. "I tried to hope that Doris loved me enough to believe that I hadn't dumped her, and was smart enough to figure out that there was a good reason for me leaving without telling her where I was going." He shrugged. "And then I just got tired of hoping and decided to do something about it."

DAME TROUBLE

NOVEMBER 17, 1942

Henry had plotted his escape well.

His first thought was to stay up late, waiting until everyone else went to bed before slipping out the door. He realized, though, that deviating from his usual behavior might make Sabatini and Arnold, the two FBI agents living in the lodge, suspicious; it was also possible that one of the other guys might decide to stay up with him. So he kept to the pattern the group had established over the past six weeks; shortly after ten o'clock, he put down his work, stood up and stretched, said good night to everyone, and shuffled upstairs to the bunk room.

He undressed, taking care to leave his clothes where he could easily find them in the dark, then read in bed while he waited for Gerry, Mike, Ham, and Taylor to come up as well. It wasn't long before they did, and the five men made small talk until, one by one, their bedside lights went out, and the loft became dark and silent.

Henry lay quietly in bed, pretending to sleep but instead closely listening to everything around him. Sharing quarters with the other guys had always been a little hard—Mike and Ham snored, and Gerry was a restless sleeper—but just this once he was thankful for their habits; when the snoring began and Gerry finally stopped tossing and turning, he knew that they were fast asleep. And he'd never had to worry about Taylor; he was dead to the world as soon as he closed his eyes. From downstairs, he heard the faint sounds of Sabatini and Arnold moving around for a little while. He was afraid that they might leave their bedroom door open, and breathed a quiet sigh of relief when he heard it swing shut. And then the lodge became quiet.

Henry lay in the darkened loft for another hour and seven minutes—he knew how long because he was still wearing his watch with its luminous dial—and kept himself awake by listening to a barred owl hooting somewhere along the lakeshore—*who cooks for you, who cooks for yoooou?*—and trying to figure out how far away it was. At exactly midnight, he pushed aside the covers, sat up, and reached for his clothes. He was prepared to tell anyone who woke up that he was just going down to the kitchen for a glass of milk, but none of the other guys woke up as he passed their beds on the way out of the loft.

The hardest part was making his way downstairs. The steps tended to creak, so he had to go down slowly and carefully, putting as much weight as he could on the banister. But the rubber soles of his outdoor boots muffled his footsteps as he crept past the downstairs bedroom to the porch, and he managed to open the inside screen door without waking the FBI bodyguards.

Henry had left his jacket and hat on a porch chair. He put them on, then opened the outside screen door and, one cautious step at a time, walked down the back steps. He lingered for another moment outside the lodge, watching the windows to see if any lights came on. When they didn't, he headed for the beach.

The lodge was furnished with a rowboat and a couple of wooden canoes. They lay overturned on the beach just a few feet from the water's edge. The men had used them a few times until it became too cold to go out on the lake; yesterday, when he was sure no one was watching, Henry had taken a paddle from the basement and hidden it beneath the smaller of the two canoes. Still working as quietly as he could, he turned it right-side up, placed the paddle in the stern where he could get to it, and slid the canoe most of the way into the water.

Henry was about to climb in when he thought he saw something from the corner of his eye: a tiny spark of light, like a firefly that hadn't yet noticed that summer was over. It seemed to come not from the lodge, though, but a little farther down the lakeshore, where the Goddards' cabin was located.

He froze, peering into the darkness for any other movement. But the night remained dark and quiet, and after a while he decided his eyes were playing tricks on him. He climbed into the canoe, careful not to rock it enough to make any noise, and once he'd settled into the wicker seat in the stern, he picked up the paddle and used it to shove off.

It was a cold night but not windy; the air lay still upon Lake Monomonac, and he gradually warmed up once he started paddling. The half-moon shrouded by high clouds cast little light upon the waters, but nonetheless Henry stayed in the shadows of the lakeside trees until he was out of sight from the lodge. He paused for another moment or two, making sure that no lights had come on behind him; when he saw nothing and heard only his friend the owl, he decided once and for all that he'd made a clean getaway.

As the crow flies, Lake Monomonac's western end was only a mile and half from the lodge, just around a bend on the northern side. The lake straddled the Massachusetts and New Hampshire borders; Route 202 crossed the state line at the tip of the lake, and it was there that a small tackle shop and marina were located. Henry had noticed the shop during one of his infrequent trips into town, and this was the place he picked for the rendezvous.

The arrangements had been tricky. He couldn't send Doris a letter, and calling her from the lodge had been impossible. His break had come a couple of weeks ago, when he joined Esther and Agent Coolidge on a Saturday shopping trip. They usually bought groceries at the little general store in Rindge, but this time they needed to restock the pantry with more than what the Rindge store offered, so instead they drove to Jaffrey, the next-nearest town, where a large grocery store was located. As luck would have it, there was a telephone booth just outside. While Coolidge helped Esther pick fresh vegetables, Henry excused himself to find a restroom and instead made a quick trip to the phone booth.

A handful of dimes and five minutes was all he needed. Doris's number was something he'd memorized a long time ago.

He thought that he'd have to wait for her, but when he finally reached the marina and tied up the canoe on the floating dock, a figure stepped out of the shadows behind the tackle shop. For a second, he thought that it might be a caretaker or even a town cop, but then he heard a soft voice call his name, and he realized that it was her.

The very fact that she'd even showed up meant that Doris still cared for him. Or at least so he hoped.

A quick hug and a kiss, then they went to her car, a six-year-old Ford coupe that she'd parked beneath the lonely streetlight in front of the tackle shop. "You'd better be grateful," Doris said as she slid in behind the wheel. "This trip is going to use up the rest of my gas ration for the month." She tapped a finger against the windshield sticker. "I'm probably going to have to take the trolley till after Thanksgiving because . . ."

"Thank you," Henry said, then kissed her again.

She had many questions, of course, but Henry asked her to hold off until they found someplace where they could have a comfortable conversation. She reluctantly agreed, so they made small talk as she continued up Route 202, heading farther north into New Hampshire. There was almost no traffic on the highway that time of night; a pair of headlights appeared behind them as they drove through Rindge, but they paid no more attention to them than they did to the cars and trucks that periodically went by the other way.

There was nothing open in Jaffrey, so they went on to Peterborough, where they found a railcar diner in the center of town. The restaurant was an all-nighter catering to long-haul truck drivers; it was almost empty except for a couple of men hunched over the lunch counter and a middle-aged waitress who cheerfully greeted Henry and Doris as they came in and asked if they wanted coffee. They took a booth at the far end of the diner and waited until the waitress brought them two mugs of black coffee, but as soon as she was gone, Doris put down the paper menu she'd been pretending to study and stared across the table at Henry.

"Okay, out with it," she said. "Where have you been the last seven weeks?"

Henry had tried to prepare himself for this very question. He'd rehearsed his answer countless times in his mind, seeking an answer that would be honest yet elusive. Now that the moment was here, though, he found himself tongue-tied. It was impossible to lie to those sharp green eyes.

"I've been working on something," he said, which was all that he could manage. An irritated look crossed Doris's face, and he quickly held up a hand. "I'm sorry. You're right, that's a lame excuse." He took a deep breath, tried again. "I've been involved in an Army research project that Dr. Goddard had been running at the university. Very secret, stuff no one's supposed to know about . . ."

"I know that already, remember?" Doris reached for the sugar dispenser, sifted a little into her coffee. "You said it was something you couldn't talk about, so I let it go at that . . ."

"And I appreciate it. I really do." Henry sipped his coffee. After the long, cold trip he'd made in the canoe, it was exactly what he needed to warm himself. He probably could have used a sandwich, too, but his stomach was full of butterflies. "You let me get away with . . . y'know, not telling you everything, so . . ."

"So now I need to know." Doris didn't look up as she added a dollop of milk to her cup. "I'm sorry, Henry, but you're going to have to be a little more candid."

"Doris . . ."

"No. Listen to me." She slowly stirred the coffee, turning it light brown. "The last time we saw each other . . . last day of September, remember? . . . you said you were tired of sneaking around behind everyone's backs and that it was time we had a real date together. You wanted to take me out to dinner, then go dancing or to a show, then"—a reddish glow appeared on her cheeks, but she still didn't look at him—"well, whatever. And I said, yeah, sure, let's pencil it in for next Saturday night. You said fine, we'll do that . . ."

"And I meant it, too. Doris . . ."

"And then you kissed me good-bye right outside the library and went off to the Science Building, and that's the last I saw of you. Not even a note or a phone call, just . . . nothing, no explanation. You vanished."

Henry started to speak again, but she held up a hand. "Let me finish," she said, and although her voice was still soft, it now had an unmistakable quaver. "You disappeared without a trace. When I didn't hear from you for a few days, I went over to the Science Building and asked around, and people told me that Dr. Goddard had taken a leave of absence . . . health problems, they said . . . and that the advanced-level course he'd been teaching had been canceled. Then I went over to the place on Birch Street where you were staying, but the FOR RENT sign was up, and the landlord told me that everyone who'd been living there had just moved out."

She started to pick up the coffee, but her hand shook so much that she had to put it down again. She took a deep breath, nervously adjusted her glasses, and went on. "Do you know what that did to me, Henry? Finding someone who I really like . . . and I got to tell you, I've always had a hard time trusting men, but you . . . and then you just dropped me like . . . like . . ."

"Doris, I'm sorry." Henry reached across the table and tried to take her hand, but she jerked it away. Behind him, the cowbell dangling from the door jangled and he felt a cool breeze against the back of his neck. "Really, I didn't mean to hurt you. I didn't want to go away, but . . . look, something came up, and I didn't have a . . ."

"Hello, Henry," a familiar voice said. "Fancy meeting you here."

Henry felt the blood rush from his face. Doris's eyes widened as she stared past him at the woman who'd just come in. Henry looked around and found Esther Goddard standing next to the table.

"Esther," he murmured, not quite believing she was there. "What are you . . . ?"

"This isn't a coincidence." She smiled, hands in the pockets of the plaid wool hunting jacket her husband had bought for her shortly after they'd relocated to the hunting lodge. "I followed you. In fact, I've been trailing you since the minute you got in that canoe."

The tiny spark he'd spotted from the direction of the Goddards' cabin, like someone's lighting a cigarette. The headlights behind Doris's car all the way from Rindge. No other explanations were needed, except . . .

"Who else is here?" Henry turned his head to peer out the window. "Is Bob . . . ?"

"No. He was asleep when I stepped out for a smoke, and I don't think he woke up when I took the car. Insomnia sometimes has its advantages, don't you think?"

"Who are you?" Doris was glaring at her, confusion wrestling with anger. Her gaze shifted to Henry. "Is this why you . . . ?"

"I'm sorry, I don't think I've introduced myself." Esther offered a hand. "I'm Mrs. Robert Goddard. I'm a friend of Henry's . . . an old friend."

"Yes, I'm sure you are." Doris didn't take her hand, and there was no mistaking the suspicion in her voice.

Coarse laughter from the two drivers seated nearby. They'd turned their heads a little, indiscreetly observing the confrontation. "Guy's got dame trouble," one of them muttered. The waitress kept her back to them, chatting quietly with the cook through the kitchen window. Esther glared at the drivers until they looked away, then she returned her attention to Doris.

"A friend and nothing more," Esther said, "so whatever you're think-ing, it can't be further from the truth. May I sit down, please?"

Doris didn't budge, so it was up to Henry to slide to one side and give Esther a place at the table. "You must be Doris, right?" she said once she'd sat down. "I've heard about you . . . not from Henry, I might add, but from the . . . well, the people who've been assigned to protect us."

"Protect you?" Doris stared at her. Her anger was dissipating, but she was still confused.

"Uh-huh. Him, me, my husband, and everyone else who came up here from Worcester." The waitress started to approach the table, but Esther shook her head and waved her off, and she retreated to the other side of the counter. "When they found out about you and Henry," she went on, leaning forward a little and lowering her voice, "they checked up on you, just to make sure that . . . well, you're what you appear to be and nothing else." A quiet smile. "I'm glad you are. Henry's needed to find someone like you for quite some time now. I just wish we could have met under different circumstances."

Doris said nothing for a few moments. "And what are our circumstances now?" she asked at last. "Why is Henry here? Why does he or anyone else need protection?"

"Please listen to me and try to believe that what I say is true." Esther slowly let out her breath, then dropped her voice even more. "There's very little either he or I can tell you, except that Henry is working with my husband on a high-priority military project. A project so secret that, if anyone finds out that you know anything about it . . . even that it exists . . . then you could probably find yourself sitting out the rest of the war in a prison cell. Do you understand?"

"Yes." Doris's face had become pale. "I think so."

"Good." Esther nodded. "Then I'll let you know a couple of more things. First, the reason why they're up here is so that they can be kept safe while they continue their work in privacy. That's why Henry had to leave so suddenly. Worcester wasn't safe for them anymore, so they had to go. I'm very sorry he couldn't let you know, but . . ."

Esther stopped herself, then went on. "Second, when this is all over, you'll know the whole truth." A smile appeared. "And believe me, if this works out the way we hope it will, you'll be so proud of Henry, you'll forget you were ever mad at him."

"I kinda doubt that," Henry murmured.

"No." Doris shook her head. "You're wrong. If what she says is true, then . . . well, I suppose I'll get over it." A tentative smile. "If it's really that important, then yes, I'll be proud of you for being part of it."

Henry looked at her, and in her eyes found something that hadn't been there a minute ago: acceptance, forgiveness, even love. All at once, he was ashamed of himself. He wasn't worthy of this woman. She was more than he deserved.

"Doris, I . . . I don't know what to say. I mean, I . . ."

"Don't say anything you shouldn't. Just don't say anything you don't mean, either."

He was still fumbling for words when Esther nudged him with her elbow. "Look, I hate to break this up, but . . . I'm sorry, Henry, but you can't stay here. We've got to get back before anyone discovers you're gone. If they find out you ran off to meet her . . ."

"Yeah, okay." For an instant, Henry had an impulse to walk away from the project. Give up his role in Blue Horizon, go back to Worcester with Doris, and the hell with the consequences. Like it or not, though, he didn't have that option. "Just give me a minute, will you?"

"I'll give you two minutes." Esther slid out of the booth. "Meet you at the car."

———

The drive back to the lodge was mostly in silence. Esther didn't say anything after Henry kissed Doris good-bye but simply waited in her car until he left the diner. Neither of them said anything until they'd nearly reached Rindge, when Henry happened to check his watch.

"Nearly 3 A.M.," he said, then fought back a yawn. "Don't think either of us are getting much sleep tonight."

"Yes, well . . . insomnia's always been my problem." Esther smiled. "At least this is more interesting than the book I'm reading."

Henry gazed out the window. The night seemed darker now. The moon had disappeared behind the clouds, and very few lights could be seen from the farms they passed. It seemed as if the whole world were sleeping. "What if someone wakes up when we come in? What are we going to tell them?"

Esther thought about it for a moment. "How 'bout we tell them I couldn't sleep and neither could you, so we decided to go for a little drive?"

"You think they'll believe that?"

She looked at him askance. "Would they have a reason not to? So long as Doris keeps her mouth shut . . ."

"She will. I got that across to her before we left. She promised . . . not a word to anyone, ever."

"Good." Again, Esther smiled. "But 'ever' is a long time, Henry. You're going to have to stick with her for quite a while to make sure she keeps her promise."

He gave her a sharp look. "What's that supposed to mean?"

"Oh, nothing. Just thinking out loud."

HORROR AND MISTLETOE

DECEMBER 12, 1942

God forgive me, Wernher von Braun thought, *what have I done?*

A vast canopy of camouflage netting concealed the construction site in the river valley that ran through the Kohnstein range of the Harz Mountains. Made of parachute silk, opaque triangular segments interspaced with transparent segments, the nets were suspended eight meters above the ground from long poles, effectively hiding the construction site from any enemy reconnaissance aircraft that might happen to fly overhead. Indeed, when von Braun had flown in from Peenemünde, he had had trouble spotting the site from his Storch; everything below looked like a forested mountain ridge. Yet even the most clever camouflage couldn't hide what lay below from anyone who walked beneath the nets.

A long monorail, shaped in cross section like an isosceles triangle with its broad side against the ground, was being built beneath the net. Five meters in height and already one and a half kilometers long, it stretched out along the dry valley like a white ribbon made of steel-reinforced concrete. Perfectly horizontal and painstakingly flawless in every detail, the half-finished monorail would have been an engineering marvel worthy of admiration were it not for the reason it was being built.

Although von Braun tried to focus his attention on the *Silbervogel* launch rail, his gaze kept returning—reluctantly, despite his best efforts—to the men laboring in its shadows. Dressed in tattered and grimy prison stripes, their feet often bare despite the fresh snow that lay thick upon the ground, the men were so emaciated that they resembled walking corpses; shaved heads and missing teeth only added to their ghastly appearance. Hundreds of men, perhaps as many as a thousand, struggled to build the rail: pouring concrete, mixing cement, pushing wheelbarrows, using pick-axes to dig a path across the frozen ground and break down rocks and boulders in their way, laying down steel rebar and hammering it into place . . . all beneath the watchful and merciless eyes of soldiers who strode up and down the site. The sounds of men at work were punctuated with the crack of leather whips, the occasional agonized cry.

And those were the lucky ones, the prisoners who got to work outside. Behind him, the rail made a long, gradual turn that went up a slope to a large, n-shaped iron tower still under construction. On the other side of the tower, the monorail merged with a railroad track; from there, the monorail and the rail track split apart and, running in parallel, continued uphill to the nearby mountainside, where they disappeared into giant tunnels that had been excavated in the steep granite bluff.

Von Braun knew what was going on in the tunnels. And although it was his duty to visit them, it was the last thing he wanted to do.

"It's coming along well, don't you think?" A short, barrel-chested man with dark brush-cut hair and a thick mustache walked alongside von Braun, gloved hands thrust in the pockets of his wool overcoat. It was a cold morning, and everyone except the prisoners was bundled up against the brisk wind that moved through the mountains. "One and a half kilometers of launch track already laid, ahead of schedule."

"Yes . . . ahead of schedule." Von Braun was distracted. Not far away, an old man—probably really only in his early fifties yet withered by starvation and cruelty—dropped a sledgehammer and sagged against the rail, his head dropping to his chest.

"Not progressing fast enough for you, Wernher?" Eugen Sanger peered at him, thick brows furrowing. "I assure you, the track will be finished by summer even though we've had some problems we're still trying to overcome."

"What sorts of problems?" Von Braun watched as one of the guards angrily stormed over to the prisoner. Two other laborers had stopped what they were doing to try getting their companion back on his feet, but the soldier yanked them away as if they were nothing more than mannequins. He grabbed the old man's shoulder and shook him roughly, yelling something von Braun couldn't quite hear.

"Well, as you know, this track has to be perfectly straight and level for its entire length from the point of engine ignition." *Silbervogel*'s designer and the Luftwaffe's chief engineer at *Mittelwerk* pointed toward the eastern end of the valley, the direction in which the monorail was being built. "So much as the slightest bend or dip and"—he threw up his hands—"*poof!* the sled goes off the track, and Silver Bird is destroyed."

"Yes, of course," von Braun said. "I can see how that might be . . ."

His voice trailed off. Instead of standing up, the old man fell forward, collapsing on his hands and knees at the soldier's feet. The soldier was still shouting at him, but the prisoner was exhausted past the point of being able to get up on his own power. Another prisoner started to come forward to help him, but two other men held him back.

The soldier said something more. Von Braun couldn't be sure, but it sounded like, "Go to hell." Then he pulled his Luger from his belt holster, planted its muzzle against the back of the old man's head, and squeezed the trigger.

Von Braun quickly looked away. The gunshot was still echoing off the valley walls when he felt Sanger touch his arm. "Don't show your feelings," he said softly. "There's nothing you can do, and someone might see you."

Von Braun darted a glance at Sanger, was surprised to see sympathy in his eyes. Until then, he'd always considered the Austrian engineer to be something of a cold fish, obsessed with making his creation a reality at the expense of all else. It was a small relief to discover otherwise.

Von Braun had been secretly pleased when Goering finally ceded to

Sanger's repeated demands that he be allowed to supervise the final steps of Silver Bird's construction. That gave von Braun an excuse to remain in Peenemünde, which continued to be *Wa Pruff 11*'s headquarters and research facility, while the final vehicle fabrication moved south to *Mittelwerk*, the underground rocket base built within unfinished railroad tunnels in the Harz Mountains. He'd never liked Eugen Sanger very much, but there was also another reason why he was reluctant to move to *Mittelwerk*.

Like many other German citizens, von Braun had tried hard to ignore the concentration camps that had sprung up around the country. At first he'd pretended that they didn't exist, or that the only people there were criminals who deserved to be incarcerated. And even after it became obvious that the Gestapo and SS were cleaning out the cities and towns and sending anyone they considered to be less than a perfect German—Jews, gypsies, Catholics, homosexuals, dissidents, or anyone else they determined to be detrimental to the Third Reich—he'd preferred to believe the newsreel footage of the camps: clean and uncrowded dwellings with comfortable beds, good food served in dining halls, contented "detainees" tending vegetable gardens and sewing Army uniforms in workshops. Anything else was nothing more than ugly rumors that had no basis in truth.

Concentration camp prisoners had done hard labor at Peenemünde, but they were mainly foreigners, Russian and Polish soldiers who'd been sent to Germany. None of them seemed to be mistreated, at least not so much to draw von Braun's notice. So when he was presented a form requisitioning prisoners from the nearby Dora camp to *Mittelwerk*, he signed it without a second thought. Himmler's demand that *Silbervogel* be ready to fly by late next spring was his top priority; the project was already behind schedule, and it needed a new source of raw labor if it was going to be completed by its deadline.

It wasn't until lately that he'd discovered the horror that he had helped create.

And there wasn't anything he could do about it.

Sanger took him by the arm and gently turned him away from the monorail. "The main engine has been installed within the fuselage," he said, deliberately changing the subject, "but I'd like to test it again, just to be sure."

"It was given a final static test before it was shipped down here," von Braun said.

"Yes, it was . . . but still, I'd like to make sure." Sanger motioned to the iron tower that straddled the launch rail. "Once the mating tower is complete, I think we can use it to brace Silver Bird for a short ignition test . . . say, ten to fifteen seconds. We can do the same for the launch sled. In fact, I'd recommend it."

Von Braun nodded, barely noticing that Sanger was leading him uphill toward the tunnels. "That would be a good idea, yes. And it will give us a chance to practice the procedures for mating the vehicle with the sled . . . but only if we can do so without damaging either of them," he added.

Sanger chuckled. "Wernher, the very last thing I'd ever do is damage my Silver Bird. You know that."

My Silver Bird. This wasn't the first time von Braun had heard Eugen Sanger refer to the spacecraft as if it were his personal possession. On the other hand, he couldn't be blamed for doing so. As much as von Braun hated to admit it, the fact of the matter was that Silver Bird was a more ambitious—indeed, more imaginative—design for spaceflight than the multistage rockets von Braun and the other former *VfR* scientists had been pursuing. It would never reach the Moon, of course, but later versions might be able to lift into orbit the components of a lunar spacecraft, perhaps even ships for a Mars expedition. Sanger himself saw Silver Bird as the prototype of an intercontinental transport, one capable of carrying passengers from one side of the world to the other in only a couple of hours. Although von Braun was still irate that the A-4 had been canceled just as it was on the eve of success, he was forced to acknowledge that *Silbervogel* was superior technology . . .

If it worked. And if its maiden flight was a success, its birth would be marked by the violent deaths of thousands of American civilians.

Not for the first time, von Braun wondered if Sanger had forgotten this or even cared. But then, hadn't he himself chosen to accept the same willful ignorance?

By then, they'd reached the top of the slope. The tunnels lay ahead, giant stone-lined shafts cut straight into the living rock. They slowly approached the tunnel on the left, following the railroad tracks that prisoners were hammering into place. From the tunnel came the echoing sounds of the work going on within: sledgehammers pounding away at granite, the hissing roar of acetylene torches, the occasional clang of iron beams being dropped.

Von Braun was just about to follow Sanger into the tunnel when something caught his eye: a raised wooden platform erected just outside, with three tall posts shaped like upside-down L's rising behind them. It wasn't until he saw a coarse hemp rope tied into a noose dangling from one of the posts that he realized what they were.

From the corner of his eye, he saw that Sanger was watching him. "How often has that been used?" he whispered.

"Four times," Sanger whispered back, his face carefully neutral. And then he added, "That is, four times yesterday."

Nausea swept through his stomach. Von Braun hastily looked away. A soldier stood nearby, submachine gun cradled in his arms. The guard seemed to be closely observing him, watchful for any sign of emotions that, in turn, might betray disloyalty to the Fatherland. Von Braun pretended not to notice as he let Sanger lead him into the tunnel.

Before the war, the two tunnels had been intended to allow passenger and freight trains to pass beneath the Kohnstein range. Work had stopped on them a couple of years ago; now they were being enlarged to serve as an underground hangar for Silver Bird and its launch sled. The pounding noise came from the far end of the tunnel, where slaves broke granite beneath the flickering light of oil lamps. The air they breathed was heavy with rock dust, their hands were swollen and bloody, and they sweated like animals. Not far away, their companions slept uneasily upon four-tier bunk beds that were little more than storage shelves for human beings; anyone who had a blanket was fortunate. No one dared speak in the pres-

ence of the guards or even try to rest. There was only one form of punish-
ment; if you were lucky, it came swiftly as a bullet to the brain, and if you
weren't so lucky, you slowly choked to death at the end of a rope.

Silver Bird lay within a cradle that rested upon the flatbed train car
that had carried it down from Peenemünde. It took up most of this end
of the tunnel, with each wingtip just a couple of meters short of touching
the walls. The craft was clearly complete; workmen on scaffolds were weld-
ing the last titanium plates to its fuselage, while technicians standing
beside open service panels beneath the wings were rigging the control
surfaces. As von Braun strolled past the spacecraft, he noticed his reflec-
tion, distorted yet distinct, upon the sleek surface of the lower hull.

At least Silver Bird was living up to its description. What remained
to be seen was whether it would actually fly. It bothered him to no end
that there would be no test flights before it was sent on its mission, but
the High Command was adamantly opposed to anything that might
prematurely reveal the existence of Germany's secret weapon. So all
tests were being done on the ground, under conditions of maximum secrecy.

"We're still awaiting delivery of the acceleration couch," Sanger said,
pointing to the open cockpit hatch. "I trust that the pilot's dimensions
haven't changed, yes?"

"Not unless someone decided to change the pilot." Von Braun hesitated, then quietly added, "If that happens, you'll be the first to know . . .
after me, that is."

A knowing smile played beneath Sanger's mustache. Although he,
Arthur Rudolph, and von Braun had coauthored a long memo to Goering
carefully specifying the requirements for the Silver Bird pilot, the final
selection hadn't been up to them. Goering had interviewed a dozen Luftwaffe pilots before settling upon four final candidates, then a committee
comprised of him, Himmler, and Propaganda Minister Joseph Goebbels
had picked the one who'd have the honor of being the first man in space.
Von Braun had met him when Goebbels escorted him to Peenemünde:
Lieutenant Horst Reinhardt, twenty-seven years old, a Messerschmidt

Bf-109E fighter ace with seven confirmed kills over Britain, and more recently a test pilot for the Luftwaffe's experimental jet-aircraft program. Upon talking with him in his office, it didn't take von Braun long to determine that Lieutenant Reinhardt was an unimaginative drone who barely comprehended the nature of his mission. However, intelligence probably wasn't the reason why he'd been chosen; blue-eyed and blond-haired, he was just the sort of Aryan superman the propaganda minister adored. He'd look great in newsreels once his mission was complete.

"Yes, well . . ." Sanger coughed in his hand. "If it does, please tell me at once. We'll need not only to alter the dimensions of the couch, but we'll also have to adjust the cockpit's oxygen-pressure variables to suit him."

Von Braun nodded, his face grim. That was something else he didn't like to think about, the high-altitude research done by a physician Sigmund Raschler, for the Luftwaffe Institute. When Dr. Raschler had expressed reluctance to use Luftwaffe pilots for his experiments, Himmler had given him a solution: concentration camp prisoners. One by one, detainees had been marched into decompression chambers or submerged in tubs of ice water, their reactions closely studied until they died. The results had been volumes of medical data invaluable for the development of manned spaceflight, but at a hideous and inhuman cost.

Von Braun looked away from Silver Bird, toward the interior end of the tunnel. The tunnels were being expanded for reasons beyond the current mission. If it was a success, the plan was for more Silver Birds to be built until there were enough for the Third Reich to impose its military might across the entire globe. No place on Earth would be beyond their range. The spacecraft could dive from space and drop their bombs on an enemy nation's cities, killing civilians by the thousands, until their governments surrendered.

Or at least that was the idea. Privately, von Braun doubted it would happen. The *Silbervogel Projekt* was far more expensive than anyone had anticipated, draining human and material resources from the war effort. The cost of the titanium alone was so high that he doubted that they'd be able to construct even a second spacecraft, let alone a fleet. If so much time and energy hadn't already been committed to building Silver Bird, von Braun had little doubt that the High Command would have already pulled the plug.

Yet Goering was convinced that Silver Bird would change the course of the war. Hitler might not conquer the world, but if the Americans invaded Europe—which was inevitable, and everyone knew it—at least he'd be able to dictate terms for their withdrawal. Once that happened, the Reich would be able to solidify its control of western Europe, and a new German empire would be born.

Many years ago, as a teenager entranced by Hermann Oberth's visions, von Braun had decided to devote his life to the exploration of space. This was not where he'd ever expected to find himself, and he doubted that Sanger had either, despite his unswerving dedication to *Silbervogel*. One day, perhaps soon, a spacecraft would carry men to the Moon, maybe even to Mars. But the idea that it might bear the red swastika flag . . .

We will pay a terrible price for this, he thought. *If we are successful, history will never forgive us for the way our victory was achieved.*

———

In the nearby village of Nordhausen, a sedan driven by a young woman named Greta Carlsberg came to a halt in front of the small Bavarian-style cottage on the outskirts of town. Climbing out of the car, Frau Carlsberg took a moment to look around, as if to admire the remote and wooded place where she'd chosen to live. Then she opened the trunk, pulled out a couple of suitcases, and lugged them beneath the garden trellis and up the flagstone walk to the front door. Putting down her luggage, she retrieved a brass key from a pocket of her shapeless overcoat and used it to let herself in.

Greta Carlsberg was a sort of woman who'd become sadly familiar in Germany: a war widow, her husband recently killed in service to the Reich. Until then, she'd lived in Berlin, where she'd made a living as a commercial artist. Her husband's death in Russia had shattered her—she didn't even have his body to bury since it had been left on a battlefield outside

Leningrad—and she'd soon discovered that she could no longer bear to remain in the apartment they had shared until he'd joined the Army. So she'd decided to sell the apartment, pack up her belongings, and move away from the city to a place in the country where she could quietly paint and be alone with her grief.

This was what she'd told the real estate agent who'd searched for a furnished house that she could rent for a year or two. At her request, he'd looked for something in Nordhausen, a town Greta fondly remembered from family vacations when she was a little girl. She was lucky; just such a place was available. So here she was, taking occupancy of the place where she could retreat from the world while she recovered from her loss.

All of this was, in the parlance of the espionage profession, a "legend" created to conceal the truth. Frieda Koenig was her true name; although she had indeed been born and raised in Germany, her family had moved to England when she was a child, and most of her adult life had been spent working as a deep-cover field agent for MI-6. Operating under the code name Mistletoe, she'd visited Germany twice already during the war, using her carefully constructed background for short-term intelligence-gathering missions. A couple of months earlier, the newly formed Office of Strategic Services had borrowed Frieda from MI-6 for another assignment, perhaps a little more sedate than the ones she'd done before but also more important.

She paused to shut the door behind her and take off her coat, then carried her bags through the cozy sitting room to the bedroom in the back of the house. The rest of her belongings were still out in the car, including the easel and paints she'd use to establish the appearance of a reasonably talented painter—which in fact she was—but just then her first priority was the concealment of the most important thing she had brought with her from England.

Placing the smaller of the two suitcases on the bed, she opened it to reveal what lay inside: a Type A Mk III wireless radio, specially designed by the British Army for covert operations. Built into the suitcase itself, it was completely self-contained except for the power supply, which could run on either alternating or direct current. The radio didn't have a microphone but instead relied on a Morse telegraph key, yet it had a range of eight hundred kilometers, sufficient to reach MI-6 headquarters in London.

Frieda closed the bedroom door and took a moment to check the window before running the power cord to a wall socket and plugging it in. She examined the crystal to make sure that it hadn't been damaged, then turned on the radio and, once it was warmed up, fitted the headphones over her ears. The telegraph key was located on its wood plaque; she rested it on her leg, turned the frequency knob to the proper setting, then tapped out a quick, coded message—**Mistletoe arrived and in position**—before switching off again. Repeating the message or waiting for confirmation was an unnecessary risk; if the Gestapo picked up the transmissions, they might be able to trace them to their point of origin. As it was, she was on and off the air so fast, it was doubtful that she'd even been noticed.

Frieda switched off the Mk III and unplugged it, then put everything back into the suitcase, closed it, and found an innocuous place for it on a closet shelf. Now she could begin the more routine business of making herself at home. But first, she wanted to get a look at the scenery. After all, it was the principal reason why she was here.

A back door from the sitting-room door let her out into a small garden, its flower beds and rosebushes colorless with the coming of winter but no doubt quite pleasant the rest of the year. The cottage was surrounded by woods, with no other houses in sight; her privacy was assured, but it still made sense for her to set up her easel here and get started on a painting, to provide an explanation to anyone who might happen to drop by as to why Frau Carlsberg spent so much time in the backyard.

Standing with her arms folded across her chest, Frieda gazed into the distance. Beyond the trees, she could see the Harz Mountains just a few kilometers away to the north. Approaching the rocket base MI-6 knew to be hidden somewhere within them would be risky, even if she pretended to be lost, but those weren't her orders. Her job was to simply maintain an observation post: watch, listen, and immediately report any unusual activity.

Frieda smiled to herself as she turned to go back inside. An important assignment, yes, but probably rather tedious as well, at least on a day-to-day basis. At least she'd get a chance to broaden her skills with a few landscapes. Being a spy was only her wartime occupation; once this was all over, she intended to become an artist for real.

THE CHRISTMAS TEST

DECEMBER 25, 1942

The first snow of winter fell on Worcester the night of Christmas Eve, a tender and sparkling powder reminiscent of childhood, lifting spirits depressed by a war that was only a year old but had already cost thousands of American lives. It put a sugarcoating across rooftops and sidewalks and cars and glittered as it drifted through streetlights. The snow softened the footsteps of families who went door to door, singing yuletide carols while collecting pennies and nickels for the Red Cross. It quietly hissed as it fell, and when the midnight hour came, it whispered secrets.

The City Hall bell tower had just tolled twelve when a pair of double doors parted at a massive warehouse deep inside the Wyman-Gordon Company's sprawling factory complex on the outskirts of town. The factory was silent this evening; all three shifts had the day off, so the only people present were night watchmen and custodians. Or at least this was the appearance that had been deliberately created. Yet, although the doors were being opened by workmen, no lights shone from within the warehouse. The ceiling fixtures had been turned off; the only illumination permitted were handheld flashlights, and even those were shielded with cardboard strips to narrow their beams, making them hard to spot from a distance.

Once the doors were open, one of the workmen stepped onto the railroad tracks leading into the warehouse. Facing away from the building, he raised his light above his head and flashed it three times. From another side of the factory grounds, three more flashes answered him. He stepped off the tracks and waited, and a few minutes later a diesel locomotive slowly rumbled from the darkness.

The locomotive approached the warehouse backward, the engineer and brakeman leaning from the cab windows to watch the flashlight signals of the man beside the tracks. The big machine backed into the darkened warehouse and slowly came to a halt, brakes making a shrill shriek that nearby residents had become so used to that they barely noticed it, until there was the loud bang of railcar couplings coming together. Long minutes passed. Then, slowly and still with the minimal amount of light, the train emerged from the warehouse.

The locomotive now had six cars: three tankers, two of them refrigerated; a flatbed carrying a diesel electric generator and other pieces of equipment; a passenger car whose windows had been blacked out by heavy curtains; at the end, another flatbed, this one holding an enormous, vaguely cylindrical object concealed by heavy canvas. U.S. Army infantrymen in winter gear and bearing submachine guns rode on each corner of the flatbed; others were in the locomotive and the passenger car.

Slowly and quietly, the train followed the tracks until it left the factory through the north rail gate. There it switched to the siding, which, in turn, led it to a freight line just outside town. The train had no trouble going on the line; there was no schedule for it to keep save its own. In cooperation with the War Department, the company that owned this particular railroad had cleared the tracks so that, for a six-hour period in the wee hours of Christmas morning, only one train would be able to use them between Worcester and Greenfield, about a hundred miles to the west.

The train picked up speed once it left Worcester; it moved quickly into the rural countryside of western Massachusetts. The engineer didn't once blow the air horn when the train approached a crossing, nor did he need to; at each crossing, the soldiers on the rear flatbed caught glimpses of others maintaining a series of roadblocks along the route, not letting anyone get near the tracks. Some might hear the train as it went by, but few would actually see it.

An hour and a half after the train left the Wyman-Gordon yard, it entered the Pioneer Valley of western Massachusetts, where the Connecticut River forms a lowland east of the Berkshires. At the valley's north end lies a small range of low mountains. Bordered by the villages of Sunderland, Montague, and Leveritt, with Greenfield the nearest large town, these Berkshire foothills were largely uninhabited. Farms had come and gone from here since the 1600s, leaving behind exhausted fields the forests had reclaimed; only loggers, hunters, and hikers ventured into the mountains, save for the occasional hermit who'd inhabit a lonely shack in solitude.

The train slowed as it came into the hill country, and the last house lights had already vanished when it entered a narrow ravine between Mount Toby and its smaller neighbor, Roaring Mountain. Once again, brakes squealed as the train came to a halt. A brakeman jumped down from the engine and, lantern in hand, ran forward to a siding running parallel to the tracks. Four concrete pillars, each five feet tall with deep grooves running through their flat tops, had been recently built on the siding by the Army Corps of Engineers, two on either side of the tracks. The brakeman pulled down the switch beside the tracks, then raised the lantern and swung it back and forth. Once again, the locomotive huffed and slowly moved forward, pulling the cars onto the siding. The brakeman carefully guided him until the rear flatbed was exactly between the four pillars, then he swung the lantern again. The train stopped, and several things happened at once.

The soldiers who'd been riding the rear flatbed jumped off and trotted down the track in both directions, taking up positions fifty yards east and west of the siding. As they did this, other soldiers climbed onto the first flatbed and unloaded four portable spotlights. Once they'd set them up in a ring around the siding, they ran insulated cables from them to the generator. It growled to life; a second later, the tripod-mounted lights flared on, wiping away the darkness with a bright oval flecked by falling snow.

The lights had barely come on when more men emerged from the passenger car. Three figures dressed in hooded aluminum suits trudged forward to the tanker cars. As they checked the gauges and began uncoiling the thick fuel hoses, soldiers trotted back to the last flatbed, climbed up on its platform, and began untying the ropes that held down the canvas tarps hiding its cargo.

By then, several civilians had disembarked from the passenger car. They spent a few moments stamping their shoes against the ground and blowing into their gloved hands, then the oldest turned to the man standing beside him.

"You'd better take care of that, Henry," Robert Goddard said quietly, nodding toward the soldiers on the rear flatbed. "See that they don't hurt our girl."

"Sure thing." Henry Morse pulled down the earflaps of his hunter's cap, then trotted forward. "Hey, there . . . mind what you're doing with those ropes!"

Gerry Mander looked around uncertainly, shoulders hunched against the cold. "You sure no one's gonna hear this? I can't see any house lights, but even out here . . ."

"Oh, we might wake up someone." Ham Ballou pulled his muffler more tightly around the neck of the fisherman's sweater he was wearing. "There's towns on the other side of these mountains. But this time of night on Christmas, y'know who's going to be up? Kids waiting for Santa Claus, and who's gonna believe anything they have to say?"

"Yeah, that'd be good." Taylor Brickell grinned from the depths of his parka hood. "Daddy, I heard Santa fly over last night, and he was *really loud*!"

"Okay, wise guys, knock it off." Omar Bliss came up behind them, boots crunching against snow-covered cinders. "We don't have much time, so let's get to work."

The remaining members of the 390 Group moved away to perform the few tasks they still needed to do. Only Goddard stayed where he was. Battered fedora pulled down low against his head, coat lapels pulled up against the chill wind that spit snow against his face, he stood with his hands in his pockets, quietly observing everything. Bliss watched him for a moment, then stepped closer.

"How are you doing there, Professor?"

Goddard nodded.

"Sure you wouldn't be more comfortable in the passenger car?"

Goddard shook his head.

"Well . . . all right, then. Let me know if I can help you."

Goddard didn't reply. Bliss lingered another moment, then walked away.

A couple of minutes later, the last tarps were removed from the rear flatbed, and the rocket engine lay revealed in the bright glare of the spotlights. Sixty feet long, the stainless-steel temporary skin that protected the liquid oxygen, nitrogen, and kerosene tanks, along with the turbopump, coolant, and ignition complex gave it the appearance of an oversized septic tank with a conical nozzle at one end.

The entire assembly was securely bolted to a concrete pedestal custom-built into the flatbed platform. Soldiers unloaded two short I-beams from the diesel flatbed and carried them back to the engine flatbed; they laid the beams atop the pedestals across the tracks, then secured them with heavy chains. Other soldiers hammered iron chocks into place between the car wheels and the rails. Braced by the beams and the chocks, the car was transformed into a static test platform, which—hopefully—would remain immobile for the duration.

This was the solution the 390 Group had devised for the problem of how to test a large rocket engine built in a major New England city. Its outcome was more than a matter of pride. If the engine failed to ignite or sustain thrust, then it was back to scratch paper, notebooks, and slide rules . . . and if it blew up, then clearing the debris from the tracks would be the least of their worries. Either way, Blue Horizon would probably be taken away from them entirely and given to someone else. Bliss had already warned Goddard and his people that the Secretary of War was nudging the president to turn the project over to Howard Hughes. If that happened, then the 390 Group would become little more than civilian advisors, and the entire operation would be thrown months, if not years, behind.

The test had to succeed. That was all there was to it.

The fuel men finished loading LOX, kerosene, and liquid nitrogen into the engine. Carefully disconnecting the hoses, they pulled them away from the flatbed. The soldiers helped them carry the lines back to the tankers, then one of the railroad men used a sledgehammer to uncouple the rear car from the rest of the train. The engineer released the brake and throttled up the diesel, and the train slowly pulled away, moving back onto the main line. The flatbed with the engine remained on the siding, captured within a ring of spotlights.

Still standing beside the rocket engine, Henry watched as the train went about a hundred yards farther down the ravine, then came to a halt. He looked down at Taylor and said, "Bring on the juice."

Taylor nodded, then jogged up the tracks to the train. Two soldiers riding the flatbed with the diesel generator began unreeling a large spool of insulated electrical line. Taylor picked up its end and carried it back to the siding, where Henry knelt to pull it up on the engine flatbed. Once Taylor climbed aboard, the two of them opened a panel in the engine cowling, located the main electrical bus, and attached the cable to it.

The two of them spent the next few minutes connecting other electrical lines within the engine's control systems, consulting a hand-drawn wiring diagram Henry carried in his pocket. They checked to make sure everything was the way it should be, then Taylor straightened up from his crouch. "Think that's got it?"

"We'll soon find out, won't we?" Henry kissed the tips of his gloved right hand and patted the engine. "Make us proud, sweetheart." Then he turned to hop down from the car. "Okay, let's get out of here."

The soldiers who'd been guarding the eastern end of the tracks joined the two scientists as they ran back to the train. They were the last to leave the siding. Everyone else was already crouched behind the rail embankment beside the train except for the 390 Group, who'd returned to the passenger car.

Henry and Taylor jogged up the steps into the car, passing Colonel Bliss along the way. "We're ready, Bob," Henry said.

The car had been turned into a mobile launch control center. The seats at one end had been removed to make room for Bakelite instrument panels and patchboard circuitry systems. A tripod-mounted 35 mm camera stood nearby, its lens pointing through a window, even though no one believed that any useful photos would come out of this nighttime test. Goddard sat at the master control panel, Mike Ferris beside him, both eying the gauges and meters arranged before them.

"Very well," Goddard said quietly, "I think we're just about ready here, too." He looked at Bliss. "Give your men the two-minute warning, Colonel. We're counting down from 120 seconds, starting"—he flipped open his pocket watch, studied it for a couple of moments, then raised a finger—"now."

As Bliss leaned from the car door to blow a shrill blast from a whistle, Goddard turned to his team. "Mike and I will monitor the test. The rest of you don't need to be here. If you'd like to watch outside, feel free to do so." The briefest of smiles appeared beneath his mustache. "Unless, of course, you feel safer in here . . ."

"Are you kidding?" Gerry asked, then he was out the door, rudely shoving past Colonel Bliss. The others grinned. They knew what he meant. If the engine blew up, they wouldn't be much safer inside the train than they'd be outside.

Taylor shrugged, then he moved to follow the kid from the train. Ham did so as well. Henry started to do the same, then he paused to look back at Goddard. "Professor . . ."

"Good luck to you, too," Goddard said quietly.

Climbing down from the train, Henry saw that everyone had taken cover behind the track embankment. He crouched on hands and knees between Ham and Gerry and peered over the rail. Illuminated by the spotlights, the flatbed looked like a toy left beneath a Christmas tree. Its nozzle was pointing toward them, for good reasons: not just so that they could watch the ignition, but also for range safety should the engine happen to break loose from its moorings.

"How much time left?" Ham asked.

"I don't know," Henry replied. "I wasn't counting either." It was just then that he noticed that snow was no longer falling. The wind had died down, too. Glancing up, he was surprised to see a few stars glimmering above the ravine. "Hey, what do you know?" he said aloud. "It's starting to clear up."

Ham followed his gaze. "Well, I guess that's good news. I . . ."

The engine ignited.

First, there was a deep rumble, like some steel behemoth clearing its throat. As that happened, an orange glow appeared deep within the nozzle as turbopumps forced volatiles together in the combustion chamber, where they met a tiny yet significant electrical spark. Within an instant, the orange glow became yellow, then white . . .

And then, all at once, a violent jet of flame shot forth from the engine with a roar that thundered through the ravine like a sonic flood, vanquishing the shadows and forcing the men to slap their hands over their ears. A spotlight was snatched up and hurtled away, smashing to bits against a nearby tree, while another one simply fell over. A half second later, a hot torrent of air rushed down upon the men, and winter vanished for a few moments to be replaced by a brief and tempestuous summer.

Henry had seen liquid-fuel rocket engines fired before, but never like this. This was as different from the ones they'd tested at Mescalero Ranch as . . . there was no comparison, really. Watching this massive thing howling and blazing in the night, he suddenly realized that something new had just been born. Something that would take men to other worlds or destroy the one they already had.

The infernal roar seemed to go on and on and on, drowning out the shouts and cheering of the men around him. The engine visibly shook on

its platform; it stayed anchored, but for several seconds, Henry was afraid
that the chocks and I-beams would fail, and the carriage would be hurled
down the siding, to be derailed and explode across the main line. But then,
as suddenly as it had begun, the engine abruptly died. Just as if a switch
had been thrown, the flame and noise abruptly went away, leaving behind
only an ionized stench and diminishing echoes from the ravine's rock
walls.

"Was that it?" Gerry asked. "Is it . . . ?"

"Yeah." Henry slowly let out his breath. His ears were ringing; he could
barely hear the kid. He couldn't take his eyes off the engine. "Yeah,
that's . . ."

"A hundred seconds!"

Mike Ferris leaped down from the passenger car. Dancing from foot
to foot, he threw both fists in the air. "A hundred seconds!" he yelled again,
as flashlight beams caught his manic dance. "Ten seconds longer than the
minimum performance standard!"

The other members of the group stared at him for a second, then they
scrambled to their feet and ran to him. "Impulse-per-second ratio?" Henry
snapped, grabbing Mike's shoulders.

"Three hundred ten, with a propellant mass flow rate of 425.7 pounds
per second." Mike grinned back at him. "Right on spec."

"So where did the extra ten seconds come from?" Gerry asked. There
had been just enough fuel in the tanks for a ninety-second test, which was
the length of time it would take for the ship to reach its operational altitude.

"Doc throttled the engine down 75 percent for the last fifteen seconds.
When we saw it wasn't going to blow up, he wanted to see just how much
longer a lower thrust ratio would extend the flying time . . ."

"Which means the pilot can reserve fuel if necessary," Henry finished,
and Mike nodded happily. "Wow. Nice to know."

"'Nice to know'?" Ham snorted. "Morse, sometimes I swear . . ."

Henry ignored him. Pushing past Mike, he trotted down the tracks
to the passenger car. Goddard was where he'd left him, seated at the con-

trol panel. A spiral notebook lay open before him, and the pencil in his hand indicated that he'd just finished jotting down some figures, yet that wasn't what he was doing just then. Instead, he was slumped in his chair, staring straight ahead as if exhausted by a physical task.

"Bob . . . ?"

"Worked out rather well, didn't it?" A weak smile; Bob barely looked at him. "We ran it until the fuel was all used up," he added, then looked around at Colonel Bliss, who was standing behind him. "I rather believe we could've run it even longer, if we'd had a larger fuel capacity."

"Next time, Professor." With uncommon warmth, Bliss patted Goddard's shoulder, then he looked up at the members of the team. "Good work, gentlemen. Outstanding. Now, if you'll assist the soldiers and the train crew, I think we can get out of here and go home."

"Yeah, great." Ham slowly let out his breath. "Back to Worcester for the engine and the lodge for us . . ."

"No, not quite." Bliss shook his head. "We're sending the engine straight to New Mexico aboard this same train. You're going back to the lodge just long enough to pack your bags, then you'll fly down to Alamogordo."

The men said nothing for a moment or two, then Gerry suddenly cut loose a rebel yell that caused everyone to break down in relieved laughter. Twelve weeks of enforced isolation were finally coming to an end. The hunting lodge in New Hampshire had lost whatever rustic charm it once had; they were ready to spend the rest of the winter in a warmer climate.

Surprisingly, though, Goddard shook his head. "If it's all the same to you . . ."

All of a sudden, he doubled over and, holding his hand against his mouth, erupted in a spasmodic fit of coughing that came from deep within his chest. Henry started forward, but Goddard held up a hand, warding him off. Henry stopped in midstep, but only because he knew that Bob wanted no one's help. Nonetheless, these fits had become more frequent lately; the year he'd spent in New England had taken its toll.

"If it's all the same with you," Goddard went on, once he'd recovered himself, "I'd just as soon ride down with the engine. I'm afraid I'm not much for air travel."

Bliss hesitated. "It's not going to be very comfortable."

"I'll make do." Goddard looked at Henry and the others. "Tell Esther I won't be long. Just taking Nell off to school, that's all. Don't want her to get lost along the way."

"Yeah, all right . . . sure thing, Bob." Henry turned to his colleagues. "Okay, boys, you heard the boss. Let's get our baby ready for a little road trip."

ROLLOUT

The hangar doors parted to allow the big Ford tractor-trailer rig to growl forward into the desert morning, and the hundreds of men and women standing outside broke into applause as the *Lucky Linda* saw the light of day.

The spaceship lay horizontal upon its carriage, its burnished steel hull reflecting the sunlight so brightly that it dazzled the eye. The solid-fuel boosters hadn't yet been attached, and its missiles were still being tested, but otherwise the ship was finished. The rocket engine brought down from Massachusetts five months ago had been fully integrated within the hull and ground-tested again, and all the other major components were flight-ready, from its radar array to its landing chute.

At long last, the time had come to move the ship from its assembly hangar to its just-completed launchpad, where it would undergo final tests before being placed on standby. It was a day for celebration. For the past fifteen months, *Lucky Linda* had been the object of devotion for all these people who were standing outside its hangar; they clapped and cheered and whistled, making the most of the moment. More than a year of constant effort had led up to this, and everyone wanted to savor it.

"There she is," Henry said to Goddard. Along with the rest of the 390 Group, they had an honored position in the crowd, right next to the place where the truck would carry the spacecraft. "Our little *Linda*, having her coming-out party."

"Our little Nell, you mean." As the truck approached them, Goddard regarded the nude girl painted on the ship's nose with tight-faced Yankee disapproval. "If I'd known our pilot was going to do that to her . . ."

"Say what?" Skid Sloman was standing just behind Goddard. He bent closer and mockingly cupped an ear. "Sorry, Doc, didn't quite hear you . . . everyone's making too much noise!"

Goddard scowled but said nothing. Henry traded a look with Jack Cube, who stood on the other side of the professor. Jack remained stoical as always, his eyes hidden behind his aviator shades, but he shook his head ever so slightly. Skid had rubbed Bob the wrong way the moment they met, when he spit out a wad of chewing gum just as he was stepping forward to shake Goddard's hand. The gum hit Bob's shoe, and Skid hadn't noticed, let alone apologized, and that was it; from that moment on, it was Goddard's opinion that Lieutenant Rudy Sloman was the wrong man for the job, and never mind the fact that he'd mastered the training exercises so well that he could probably fly *Lucky Linda* in his sleep.

From the corner of his eye, Henry caught a glimpse of Joe McPherson. The backup pilot stood next to Skid, and there was no mistaking the look of contemptuous envy on his face. From what Jack had told him, it wasn't until *Lucky Linda* was nearly completed that McPherson began to really take the mission seriously. Up to that point, the X-1 was just some silly experimental aircraft that would probably never get off the ground. When it became clear that *Lucky Linda* would indeed fly, though, and the man who piloted it into space would earn far more than just a paycheck, McPherson suddenly became intent on bumping Skid from his place at the front of the line.

Fat chance of that. Over the past eleven months, Jack and Skid had become close friends. Were it not for the fact that Jack was too tall for the cockpit, he would have been Skid's backup pilot, not Joe. But this hadn't stopped McPherson from kissing up to Bob Goddard . . . and when that failed, because Bob liked brown-nosers even less than smart-asses, he'd become obsessive about logging more hours in the simulator and centrifuge than Skid, a vain effort to prove that he was better qualified to be the primary pilot.

Henry looked at the spacecraft again. It had pulled abreast of them by then, its port wing passing over their heads. On impulse, he reached up, standing on tiptoes as he stretched out his hand as far as he could. He was rewarded by feeling the wing's underside lightly brush his fingertips; it was already warm in the desert sun, and he knew that the ship would be covered by canvas shrouds once its carriage raised it erect within the launchpad's gantry tower.

"Hey, what're you trying to prove?" Ham Ballou snapped, pretending to be annoyed. "Get your mitts off my nice clean spaceship!"

"It's mine, too." Henry felt a touch of embarrassment as he fell back on his heels. "Keep your shirt on."

Ham shared a laugh with Taylor and Gerry, and Henry decided to let it pass. Truth was, he didn't know what had come over him just then. He and the others had spent the last five months crawling all over the *Lucky Linda*, and he'd never been sentimental about touching the ship before. But then he glanced at Goddard, and to his surprise he saw that Bob had lowered his head just a bit so that he could run his fingers under the rims of his glasses and wipe tears from the corners of his eyes. Apparently, Bob noticed Henry watching him, because he quickly dropped his hand. Yet there was no doubt that the professor had felt the same thing he had. They'd come a long way in such a short time, and it was nothing less than astonishing to see the results of their efforts made real, a dream come true.

The truck moved on, towing *Lucky Linda* behind it as it headed for the pad. The applause gradually faded as the crowd broke up. No ceremonies, no speeches, no brass bands; everyone still had jobs to do, and the day wasn't getting any younger. Henry watched as Goddard turned to walk back to the administration building. He thought about joining him, but he had his work cut out for him at the blockhouse, which was still being fitted for the coming mission . . . whenever that would be.

Henry found a couple of Corps of Engineers electricians who happened to be going the same way and hopped into the back of their jeep. He spent the rest of the morning on the floor of the concrete igloo, crawling around on hands and knees to make sure all the multicolored wires went to the places they were supposed to go, and when he was done, he had the inevitable paperwork that needed to be signed by someone with scrambled eggs on his hat.

So he hiked back to the administration building and paid a visit to Bliss's office. As usual, the colonel wasn't around. His secretary informed Henry that the colonel was in a meeting on the other side of the base and probably wouldn't be back until after lunch, so Henry added the form to the stack already on the colonel's desk and left. Lunch sounded like a good idea, and Henry had learned to take advantage of the days when he actually had a chance to enjoy one.

On the way out, though, his steps took him past Goddard's office. The door was ajar, and he heard music—Mozart's Symphony No. 39, if he wasn't mistaken—coming from inside. Henry stopped and, gently tapping his knuckles against the door, peered into the office.

"Bob?" he asked.

Goddard was sitting at the utilitarian wooden desk he'd been issued, a clothbound book open in his hands. Even after five months, he hadn't yet finished unpacking all the boxes that had been shipped down from the New Hampshire hunting lodge; his feet were propped up on a crate marked TECH. JOURNALS, a black cigar smoldering in a brass ashtray at his elbow. The music was coming from the portable phonograph that seemed to follow him wherever he went, and it was just loud enough that he didn't hear Henry until he said his name. But when Henry looked in, he noticed that Goddard's attention wasn't on the book but instead was on the distant launchpad, visible through the window above his desk.

"What . . . ? Oh, yes, hello . . . come in." Marking his place with a finger, Goddard half closed the book and sat up a little straighter. "Just reading an old favorite and . . . well, ruminating a bit."

"Which book?" Henry asked as he stepped into the office.

Goddard held up the book so that he could see the frayed red dust-cover: *The War of the Worlds* by H. G. Wells. "I've been carrying this around with me ever since I was a boy," he said, a sly smile beneath his mustache. "Pages are beginning to fall out, print's barely readable, but . . . I don't know, I just can't bear to toss it away and buy a new copy."

"That's the one you read when . . . ?"

"Uh-huh. The day I climbed up that apple tree and decided what I wanted to do with my life."

Henry knew the story well; all of Bob's close friends did. This was the first time, though, that he'd ever seen the actual book that had sent Robert H. Goddard down his life's path. "You'd never want to throw out something like that," he said, taking a seat in the office's only other chair. "It means too much to you."

"I agree." Looking at the book fondly, Goddard chuckled. "Not long after we met, Esther tried to replace it by giving me a nice new copy for my birthday. She meant well, of course, but . . . well, she was rather upset when she caught me reading this copy instead, with the one she'd given me still untouched on the shelf. I thought I'd given her a reason to divorce me that day."

Henry grinned. Bob was exaggerating, of course; Esther wouldn't leave her husband if a gun were pointed to her head. "How's she doing?" he asked. "Heard from her lately?"

"Talked to her on the phone just the other day. I told her I'd try to get out to the ranch sometime soon." Although Esther had followed Bob from New Hampshire, the Army hadn't permitted her to join him on the base, or even enter Alamogordo as a visitor; so far as the military was concerned, she was a civilian with no security clearance at all. So she'd moved back to Mescalero Ranch, where her husband visited her on weekends. When he had time, that is . . . which wasn't very often.

Again, Goddard's gaze drifted toward the window. "I hope they're being careful with that thing," he said quietly. "It's not like we've got a spaceship assembly line."

Henry leaned forward to peer past him. The truck had parked alongside the gantry tower, and servomotors were slowly tilting its carriage upward, raising the *Lucky Linda* to a vertical position upon the launch ring. Ham and Taylor were overseeing this part of the operation. Deciding that three chiefs were too many, Henry had deliberately stayed away, but there was no reason why Bob had to do the same.

"I'm sure no one would mind if you went out to . . ." he began.

"No. I'd rather not, thank you." Catching a querying look from the younger man, Goddard let out his breath. "Y'know, there are times when I don't know whether I love that thing or hate it." Henry raised an eyebrow, and Goddard shook his head. "No, no . . . don't misunderstand me. I'm proud of what we've done, really. We've done something here no one else . . . well, maybe the Germans . . . has ever done, and built the first manned space vehicle. We're far ahead of everything anyone thought might be possible, even your science fiction magazines. But . . ."

His voice trailed off. "But what?" Henry asked.

Goddard hesitated. "This wasn't what I intended," he said after a moment. "When I set out to build a spacecraft, it wasn't to make a military vehicle . . . it was to go to Mars. Making something that we'd use to wage war was the last thing on my mind."

"Yes, well . . . unfortunately, the Germans had different ideas."

"Really? I wouldn't be so sure of that. I heard from the German Rocket Society before the war, when they tried to get technical information from me about my first engines. Whatever else he might have become since then, I know for a fact that Wernher von Braun's main interest was going to the Moon, not dropping bombs on New York. I wouldn't be surprised if he didn't get pushed into this by the Nazis."

Henry glanced over his shoulder. The hallway outside was vacant, but nonetheless he leaned back in his chair to push the door shut. No sense in getting unwanted attention. Secrecy at Alamogordo was such that even an offhand remark like that could be misconstrued as a possible security breach, even if it came from Blue Horizon's technical director.

Goddard didn't notice; his eyes were still turned toward the window, his thoughts even further than that. "When this is over, I hope the X-1 goes into a museum somewhere and never flies again. I want the next spaceship we build to be for peaceful purposes only, that it won't have any missiles or guns. That's the future I want, Henry. The exploration of space, not . . ."

From somewhere outside, an interruption: the earsplitting jangle of an ambulance siren, getting louder and closer by the moment.

The two men had barely glanced at one another when a van with a red cross on its side raced past the window, raising a cloud of sand that obscured the distant rocket. Henry stood up from his chair and craned his neck to see which direction it was going, and just then the phone on Goddard's desk rang.

The professor snatched up the receiver. "Yes? What did . . . ? Who? Oh, my God . . . yes, we'll be there right away!" He dropped the receiver and jumped up from his chair. "C'mon, Henry," he snapped as he headed for the door, "there's been an accident!"

"Where?" he asked.

Goddard didn't seem to hear him. He was already trotting down the hall. Following him out the side door, Henry let the professor lead him across the compound. Another emergency vehicle, a fire truck, roared by, but Henry didn't see any signs of smoke. So why was . . . ?

Then he saw a small crowd gathered in front of the training facility, and suddenly he understood. There had been an accident inside, possibly in the simulator or . . .

The centrifuge.

He and Goddard had just reached the building when its door swung open and the two ambulance medics emerged, carrying a stretcher between them. One of the flight doctors—the tall one, Dr. Wysocki, whom the pilots had nicknamed Jeff—strode alongside them, holding the wrist of the man on the stretcher. A couple of MPs were doing their best to hold back the crowd, but Goddard managed to push through, with Henry right behind him. Henry gazed over Goddard's shoulder and saw who was being carried out:

Joe McPherson, the backup pilot.

The medics reached the ambulance and loaded the stretcher aboard, but then Dr. Wysocki scrambled into the back before they could get going. He clamped his stethoscope against his chest, listened for a moment, then he and one of the medics turned McPherson over on his stomach and elevated the test pilot's elbows while the doctor gently, repetitively pushed down on the upper part of his back. The other medic stood on the other side of the stretcher, holding his fingers against McPherson's neck while keeping an intent eye on his wristwatch.

Standing outside the ambulance's open rear gate, everyone watched quietly as the doctor struggled to save McPherson's life with the Holger-Nielsen cardiac-resuscitation technique. From deep within the crowd of scientists, soldiers, and technicians, Henry heard a woman praying in a low and solemn voice.

A couple of minutes went by, then Dr. Wysocki straightened up and let out his breath. He looked at the medics and shook his head. The one across from him didn't reply but instead reached down to pull the stretcher's top sheet over McPherson. The other medic closed the tailgate, then went around to the cab, climbed in, and started the engine.

The ambulance had just driven away when Henry heard Goddard ask someone what had happened, and he looked around to Jack Cube and the other flight surgeon—Dr. Sinclair, aka Mutt—standing behind them. Both were in shock, and it was obvious that neither of them wanted to be there just then, yet they couldn't refuse a question from Blue Horizon's technical director. Not when a fatal accident had just occurred.

"He shouldn't have gotten in that thing." Jack kept swinging his head back and forth, as if denying what he'd just seen. "He shouldn't have . . . I mean, I shouldn't have let him, but . . ."

"Nonsense, Lieutenant. It's not your fault." Sinclair stared at him. "McPherson was reckless. He told the operator to keep him at seven g's for as long as he could take it, and there was no reason for that except that he was trying to prove something . . . and you and I both know what that was."

Goddard shot a look at Jack. "Oh, for God's sake, are you telling me he was . . . ?"

"Trying to top Skid's time in the centrifuge, yes, sir." Jack Cube looked even more miserable than before. "Skid set the record at three minutes, thirty-four seconds at seven g's, and Joe somehow figured that . . ." Again, he shook his head. "I don't know what he was thinking, really. Maybe he thought that if he could stand launch acceleration for a longer period of time, we'd bump Skid and move him into the pilot's seat."

"Idiot," Henry muttered.

Goddard cast him a cold glare, but Dr. Sinclair slowly nodded. "I hate to say it, but I agree," he said softly. "This sort of prolonged stress on the coronary arteries can cause even a healthy man to have a heart attack, especially if it happens over and over again. He may have even been born with some sort of anomalous condition that I wouldn't have been able to detect." He paused to give Goddard a meaningful look. "The fact that he was a pack-a-day smoker couldn't have helped."

"Yes, well . . ." Goddard brushed off the pointed reminder about his own health risks. "Whatever the reason, I'm afraid that puts us in a tenuous situation now, doesn't it?"

As if on cue, someone else came out of the training facility. Skid Sloman also wore a jumpsuit, its helmet dangling from his left hand. His face was ashen, his eyes wide; for the first time since they'd met, the pilot didn't have the cocky, go-to-hell expression Henry had come to expect.

Goddard, Jack Cube, Dr. Sinclair, and Henry turned to him as he shuffled through the door. "I was in the control room, waiting my turn," he mumbled. "I didn't know . . . I mean, no one knew what was going on till he stopped talking to us, then . . ."

"It's okay, Skid." Jack placed a hand on his shoulder. "No one knew, and it was no one's fault. It just happened, that's all . . ."

"How is your training coming along?" Goddard asked abruptly.

Startled, Skid blinked several times before answering. "Ummm . . . it's going well, Doctor G. At least it was until . . ."

"You know how to handle the X-1?" Goddard stared at him, his face devoid of sympathy. "You have confidence in your ability to perform your mission?"

"Well, yeah, I think so . . ."

"You'd better do more than just think so," Goddard said. "As of now, you're the only man qualified to fly this spacecraft. So no more slipups, no more mistakes." His eyes were cold and grey as he turned to the others. "That goes for you, too, and everyone else."

And then he shoved his hands in his pockets and stormed away. Jack Cube started to follow him, but Henry grabbed his arm and shook his head.

"Let him go," he said quietly. "Just . . . give him some room, okay?"

Jack's mouth tightened, but he nodded without saying a word. On the other hand, Skid was visibly angry. "Who the hell does he think he is?" he demanded, watching Goddard as he walked off. "A man just got killed here!"

"Oh, he knows that, all right." Henry's voice was very low. "Believe me, that's all he's thinking about."

HAMMER OF THE GODS

JUNE 1, 1943

A sergeant raised a whistle to his mouth and blew a sharp note, and the squad of soldiers standing on either side of the launch ramp pulled the ropes dangling above their heads. The camouflage netting fell away, revealing what lay beneath it.

Silbervogel rested upon its launch sled, the massive horizontal-thrust engine at its rear resembling the thorax of some immense wasp. Even in the dull light of a cloudy sky, the spacecraft gleamed in the late-morning sun, making the black crosses painted on its wings and stubby tail fins stand out. The launch rail stretched away into the distance; during the night, its own camouflage had been removed, the poles that had once supported the nets cut down by Dora prisoners and hauled away.

The moment Silver Bird's camouflage was pulled away, a military marching band struck up the German National Anthem, almost drowning out the applause of the senior officers and party officials gathered nearby. Assembled on the wooden viewing stand one kilometer from the launch site, they'd come at the special invitation of Goering himself to witness the historic event. Some had had no idea that the *Silbervogel Projekt* even existed until they'd arrived; the operation had remained classified all the way to the end, in hopes that the Allies would remain ignorant of its existence until the moment the bombs dropped on America. Others knew about Silver Bird yet had not yet been apprised of its objective. Very few knew all the essential details, and they had been sworn to secrecy.

Standing in the front row, Heinrich Himmler turned to Eugen Sanger and, still clapping his hands, smiled at the Austrian engineer. "A magnificent creation, *Herr Doktor*," he said, raising his voice to be heard over the noise. "This must be a great day for you."

Sanger didn't say anything for a moment. Noticing the silence, Wernher von Braun glanced at Sanger. There were tears in the corners of his eyes, and his chin trembled a little beneath his heavy mustache.

"Like a father seeing his child for the first time," Sanger said quietly, his words nearly lost beneath the orchestra.

His child, von Braun thought. *How pathetic*. Sanger had apparently forgotten Himmler's threats about what Hitler might do if he was informed that Silver Bird wasn't completed by the deadline Himmler had imposed on the project. That deadline had come and gone nearly two months ago, and it was only Dornberger's fast-talking that had saved all of them from Himmler's petulant wrath.

Now the strutting little chicken farmer was behaving as if everything had been forgiven and forgotten. And it probably was . . . so long as they were successful today.

Von Braun had to make a conscious effort not to grimace. It wasn't just Himmler he had to worry about. Goering was there, too, as were Goebbels, Speer, Keitel . . . everyone except the *Führer* himself. Hitler had given no reason for not attending; through an aide, he'd simply sent word that he would not be there, and that was it. When he'd heard this, von Braun had been secretly relieved. He'd been forced to wear the loathed SS uniform again, but at least he wouldn't have to play host to the *Führer* as well as the rest of the High Command.

"Of course it is," von Braun said to Himmler as he gently tapped Sanger on the arm, drawing his attention. "Now, if you'll excuse us . . ."

"Yes, of course. You have your duties." A dismissive flip of the hand, as if von Braun were nothing more than a minor technocrat rather than the project's scientific director. "Go."

"Thank you, *Herr Reichsführer* . . ."

"Wait," Goebbels snapped. A wiry and glowering little man, the propaganda minister reminded von Braun of a carrion bird. "Couldn't we meet Lieutenant Reinhardt one last time, to give him our best wishes for his mission?"

Again, von Braun had to work to keep a neutral expression. He was perfectly aware of the official photographers lurking at the edge of the platform, ready to dart forward at Goebbels's slightest gesture. The propaganda minister didn't want to give Reinhardt his blessings; all he wanted was to have his picture taken, shaking hands with Silver Bird's pilot. Von Braun had come to realize that everyone in Hitler's inner circle had his own personal agenda; dealing with such colossal egos was a job of its own.

"I'm very sorry, but that's impossible. Lieutenant Reinhardt is on his way to the Silver Bird even as we speak." Turning around, he peered at the distant spacecraft and managed to spot a large truck pulling up beneath the bottom of the launch sled. "There, see?" he asked, pointing in that direction. "There is his support vehicle now."

"Yes, I see." Goebbels's face darkened. "And why weren't we given an opportunity to meet him earlier, as I requested?"

Before von Braun could answer, Walter Dornberger came to the rescue. "I'm sorry, *Herr Reichsminister*, but we were unable to comply with your request. We deliberately kept Lieutenant Reinhardt in medical quarantine for the last forty-eight hours, to make sure that no one carrying any germs or viruses would inadvertently make him sick just as he was about to carry out his mission. I'm sure you understand."

Goebbels said nothing although his expression became even more vulpine than ever. If he was about to respond, though, he was cut off by a voice booming from a loudspeaker mounted on a nearby post: *"Launch in sixty minutes! Repeat, launch in sixty minutes! All technical personnel, please report immediately to control bunker!"*

"We must go," von Braun murmured to Sanger and Dornberger, then he turned to the dignitaries in the front row of the viewing stand. "Thank you for your best wishes," he said, giving them a hasty bow. "We'll brief you following the conclusion of this mission."

Without another word, he went as fast as he could to an open-top sedan parked nearby, Sanger and Dornberger trotting along beside him. He was relieved that none of the High Command insisted upon joining them; they weren't so arrogant not to realize that their place was here, not in the bunker. Making a brief appearance at the viewing stand was something he and the others were obliged to do. Now that it was over, their real task lay before them: getting Silver Bird safely off the ground, into space, and on its way to its target.

The day had come. By the time it was over, New York would be in ruins.

———

Frieda Koenig was about to bicycle into town to go shopping when, from somewhere in the far distance, she heard something odd. Halfway to the front gate, she stopped, put down her market basket, and listened intently. No, there was no mistake. It was the *Deutschlandlied* that she heard echoing off the granite bluffs of the nearby mountains: *"Deutschland, Deutschland über alles, Über alles in der Welt . . ."*

In the months she'd been living in Nordhausen, carrying on the impersonation of a recently widowed artist, she'd seen and heard enough to confirm OSS suspicions that the Nazis had a secret missile base located in the mountains not far from town. All these things she'd dutifully reported to London during her radio transmissions, which she was careful to keep brief and at irregular intervals. Yet this was the first time she'd heard martial music coming from the vicinity of *Mittelwerk*.

Listening, Frieda frowned. The only reason the Nazis would break out a brass band was if they had something to celebrate. On the other hand, it was only a few hours ago, just as she was getting out of bed, that she'd heard a couple of twin-engine Junkers transports passing low overhead, as if coming in for a landing. Party officials paying a visit? Very possibly, yes, but why . . . ?

Suddenly, a bike ride to the village grocer was no longer important. Picking up her basket, Frieda hurried back into the cottage. She'd learned to leave a ladder propped up against the back wall of the house; the rooftop made a good observation post, with the chimney hiding her from the road. Once she climbed up there with her binoculars, she might have a chance to see what was going on.

First, though, she went into the bedroom. Frieda pulled the suitcase radio down from the closet shelf, placed it on the floor beside the bed, and plugged it in. Better get the wireless warmed up, just in case . . .

Stiffly and slowly, the rubber-insulated leather of his flight suit resisting his every move, Horst Reinhardt climbed down into *Silbervogel*'s cockpit. Once again, he was astonished by just how small it was. Not even the experimental Messerschmidt jet fighters he'd been flying before being recruited for this program were as cramped as this. He gritted his teeth as the two technicians standing on either side of the cockpit eased him into the heavily padded seat, one holding his arms at shoulder height while the other fitted his legs into the horizontal well beneath the instrument panel. The parachute he wore pushed against his lower back, making him even more uncomfortable. He muttered an obscenity, knowing that no one would hear him; his throat mike wasn't yet plugged in, and the airtight goggles and full-face breathing mask that made him resemble a bug muffled his voice.

Once he was seated, though, he was able to move a little more freely. As one of the technicians reached down to move the air mask's oxygen hose from its portable unit to the valve located beneath the dashboard, Reinhardt ran a line from his throat mike to the wireless system. "Radio check, radio check," he said, clamping the throat mike between his thumb and forefingers. "Do you hear me, Control? Over."

"*We understand you,* Silbervogel." The voice in his headphones was unfamiliar. Apparently Dr. von Braun wasn't in the control bunker. Probably still shaking hands with the brass.

"Thank you," Reinhardt said. "Time to launch?"

"Launch in fifty-one minutes, thirty-one seconds."

"Very good. Proceeding with preflight checklist." A small notebook was attached to the upper-right corner of the instrument panel. While the technicians leaned in to wrap his seat and shoulder straps in place around him and clamp them shut, Reinhardt looked at the first item on the list. "Primary electrical system, on . . ."

———

The control bunker was a steel-reinforced concrete pillbox built into the mountainside not far from the tunnels, on the other side of the launch rail from the viewing stand. Resembling an oversized gunner's nest, its slot windows were fitted with quartz glass five centimeters thick. The precautions were necessary, for the bunker was located only a hundred meters from the launch rail.

Within the bunker, nearly a dozen men were seated at workstations divided into two rows, each facing the windows and the large wall map between them. Pneumatic tubes were suspended vertically from the ceiling to each desk. Von Braun discarded the uniform jacket as soon as he came through the vault door that was the bunker's sole entrance. Ignoring the brisk salute given him by the soldier standing guard, he pulled on his white lab coat as he headed straight for his station, the center desk in the third row back. Walter Dornberger sat down beside him, while Sanger went to a desk in the second row, the logistics section.

Von Braun sat down at the desk and pulled on a pair of headphones. He took a moment to light a cigarette, then opened the loose-leaf binder on the desk. Through the headphones, he heard both Lieutenant Reinhardt's voice and those of the flight controllers as they made their way through the prelaunch checklist:

"Oxygen-fuel pressurization, complete."

"Confirm oxygen-fuel pressurization completion."

"Initiate gasoline-fuel pressurization."

"Initiating gasoline pressurization."

"Gyro platform check."

"Gyro operational."

They'd rehearsed the launch procedure countless times over the past four months, in practice sessions that lasted hours on end. This time, though, there was a tension that had been lacking before. Everyone knew that this was the real thing, not just another exercise. Scanning the room, von Braun saw that everyone was focused entirely upon the dials and meters before them. Now and then, there was a short, sharp hiss, then the hollow clunk of a message capsule dropping into a cup beneath the pneumatic tubes that carried handwritten data from one workstation to another, removing the need for the controllers to stand up and walk across the room. Otherwise, the bunker was quiet, disciplined.

Von Braun glanced to one side of the room, where three clocks hung against the wall. The first was the mission clock; it stood at L minus twenty-nine minutes and counting. The second clock was Berlin time: 11:31 A.M. The third clock was the most critical one: 5:31 A.M. New York Time. Once Silver Bird left the atmosphere, it would take one hour and thirty-seven minutes to reach its target. Because there was a six-hour difference in time zones, the plan called for the attack to occur at approximately 7:40 A.M. New Yorkers would be on their way to work by then, so it had been calculated that a strategic bombing at that time would increase the fatalities among commuters, with more deaths caused by the firestorm that would rage across Manhattan and the greater metropolitan area in the aftermath.

Von Braun forced this thought from his mind as he lit another cigarette from the first one. He wasn't the only person chain-smoking. The glass ashtrays on the desks were already beginning to fill up, and the ceiling fans labored to remove smoke from the room. He flipped another page of his notebook and tried to concentrate on the checklist.

"Launch minus twenty-two minutes and counting."

"Fuel pressurization complete."

"Confirm completion of fuel-pressurization cycle."

"Pilot ready for takeoff. Seal cockpit."

"Confirm cockpit seal."

"Check landing-gear servomotors."

"Landing-gear servos operational, check . . ."

Hearing this, von Braun shut his eyes for a moment. According to the flight plan, once its mission was complete, *Silbervogel* would begin a long supersonic glide from an altitude of seventy kilometers, crossing the Atlantic until it reached Germany, where it would land on the *Mittelwerk* landing strip just a few kilometers away. Yet everyone who'd closely studied this part of the plan knew that it was optimistic at best. The spacecraft would be out of fuel by then, its pilot capable of making only dead-stick maneuvers. The math might support the notion of a glide return all the way to base, but common sense did not. It was more likely that Reinhardt would be forced to ditch in the ocean, and although he'd been given a parachute and a life preserver, the chances of his surviving a supersonic bailout, then spending countless hours in the high seas before being located by the U-boat that had been dispatched to the North Atlantic as an emergency recovery vessel, were not good.

This was to be a suicide mission. Everyone knew it, even if no one said so aloud. If Horst Reinhardt weren't aware of this, then he was either a fool or a madman. But everything von Braun had observed about the young Luftwaffe lieutenant suggested that he was nothing more or less than what he appeared to be: a dedicated young pilot whose devotion to National Socialism and Adolf Hitler was so complete that martyrdom would be a death he'd welcome.

"Launch minus ten minutes and counting."

"All personnel, clear launch area."

"Switch to internal electrical systems."

"Internal electric system on standby, check."

Suddenly restless, von Braun stood up from his seat. He felt Dornberger's eyes upon him as he walked past the rows of controllers to the window. *Silbervogel* lay upon its sled, fully revealed now that its gantry scaffold had been pulled away. The cockpit was closed, its windows barely visible. The ground crew was hurrying away, and even the soldiers were deserting the launch site. Reinhardt was alone in his ship, waiting for the countdown to end and the order to launch.

"Good luck," von Braun whispered. Not for the mission, but for the man.

———

"L minus sixty seconds and counting."

"All systems prepared for launch." Horst Reinhardt turned the last page of the checklist, then curled his fingers within his thick gloves one last time before resting his hands on the control yoke. He took several slow, deep breaths to calm himself; nonetheless, he could feel his heart thudding deep within his chest. In all the thousands of hours he'd spent in cockpits, never before had he been so anxious about a takeoff.

With the canopy shut, the cockpit was oppressively close, made worse by the fact that, aside from the retractable bombsight periscope in the belly, he had no direct forward view, only two narrow windows on either side of his seat. The engineers who'd designed Silver Bird had never been able to completely solve the problem of maintaining cabin integrity while also making the hull capable of withstanding the stress caused by repeated skips across the upper atmosphere. The weak point was always the forward cockpit window, which was located in the very place where atmospheric friction would cause a plasma cone to form. The periscope and the side windows were a necessary compromise; for most of the flight, Reinhardt would be relying on his instruments for navigation.

It could be done, of course, and the pilot had spent countless hours in the Peenemünde simulator learning how. All the same, though, it was hardly comforting to know that he would be flying blind. So Reinhardt barely glanced at the windows before returning his gaze to his instruments.

"L minus forty seconds and counting." Suddenly, the voice he heard was familiar. Dr. von Braun had taken over the microphone. *"Ready, Lieutenant?"*

"Yes, *Herr Doktor*," Reinhardt replied. "For the glory of the Fatherland and Adolf Hitler."

Von Braun's response was dry, unemotional: *"Sled ignition in nineteen seconds."*

"Understood." Reinhardt gave his straps a final hitch, then fastened his hands around the yoke. "Main engines pressurized and ready for primary ignition sequence."

"Sled ignition in ten . . . nine . . . eight . . . seven . . ."

Reinhardt instinctively braced himself, then remembered his trainer's advice: stay loose, relax your body, let the seat absorb the shock. He had just done so when the countdown reached zero.

"Five . . . four . . . three . . . two . . . one . . ."

From outside, he heard the muffled roar of the sled's giant solid-rocket engine firing. This was controlled by the launch bunker. Yet the sled didn't move at once; for the next eleven seconds its brakes remained engaged, allowing the engine to build up thrust. The spacecraft shook like an overeager racehorse pushing against its stall.

"Launch in five . . . four . . . three . . ."

From the corner of his eye, Reinhardt saw oily black smoke billowing up around his canopy windows. Licking his lips, he raised his left hand to the instrument panel and gently placed his fingers on the main-engine ignition switch. In his headphones, he heard von Braun's calm, detached voice:

"Two . . . one . . . launch!"

The sled brakes were released, and the massive machine bolted forward. Reinhardt was immediately thrown back against his seat. For an instant, he nearly lost contact with the all-important toggle switch for the main engine, yet he managed to shove his arm forward again and get his hand back where it belonged.

The sled hurtled down the long concrete track, its speed doubling, then doubling again, with each passing second. On the viewing stand, the officers and party officials had seen the sled engine ignite but had heard nothing. It had taken nearly three seconds for the sound to reach them, and by then the sled was already in motion. They were still puzzled by this when thunder, louder and more prolonged than any created by a natural storm, hit them like a tangible object, a blast that shook the viewing stand and blew hats off their heads and caused them to step back in fear.

"Stop it!" Himmler screamed, hands clamped over his ears, eyes wide with terror. "Stop it! It's going to blow up!" Goering howled with laughter, while Goebbels cackled and clapped his hands like a child amused by a trick pony at a circus.

In the control bunker, cement dust was falling from cracks that had suddenly appeared in the ceiling. The windows shook in their frames, distorting the view of the sled as it rocketed away from the bunker.

Von Braun was on his feet, watching it go, microphone clutched in his right hand. "Steady . . . steady . . ." he said, fighting to remain calm. "Stand by to release . . ."

Flattened against his seat, pushed back by mounting acceleration, Horst Reinhardt watched his instruments through eyes threatening to squeeze shut, his hands locked on the yoke. The sled was traveling at five hundred meters per second when he yelled "Main-engine ignition!" and snapped the toggle switch.

The engine roared to life, and as an invisible hand shoved him even farther into his seat, he heard von Braun shout, *"Release!"*

Knowing that this meant that the sled's cradle was no longer holding him, Reinhardt pulled back on the yoke with all his might.

Like a hawk taking flight, Silver Bird rose from the sled. It shot upward at a steep angle, stub wings clawing at the sky, main engine pounding across the valley and echoing off the mountainside. Far below, the launch sled reached the end of the track. Traveling too fast for the hydraulic brakes to slow it down, it ripped through the track, smashed into the ground, and exploded, an inferno giving birth to a phoenix.

In the control bunker, Eugen Sanger leaped to his feet. "My Silver Bird flies!" he shouted, fists raised above his head. "My dream is alive!"

Letting go of his breath, von Braun slumped in his chair. Through the windows, he could see *Silbervogel* rising upon a fiery pillar, thundering like a hammer of the gods.

"It's done," he muttered under his breath. *And may God help us,* he silently added.

———

Standing on the cottage roof, hugging the brick chimney as if it were a lover, Frieda Koenig felt the house beneath her tremble as the shock wave rumbled across the valley. Treetops swayed in the supernatural wind, pine needles and leaves ripped from their branches, and somewhere below her a window shattered, but she barely noticed these things. All she saw was the silver dart streaking up from the other side of the valley, faster than any aircraft she'd ever seen, leaving behind it a thick vapor trail that formed an arch across the sky.

"No," she whispered. "No, no, no . . ."

Suddenly, she remembered where she was, what she was supposed to do. Letting go of the chimney, she squatted on her hips and skidded down the roof, heedless of the shingles tearing at the back of her skirt and legs. Somehow, the ladder had stayed where it was. Turning herself around and planting her feet against the rungs, she climbed down as fast as she could, dropping the last few feet to the ground.

From somewhere far above, a loud boom. She turned and looked up, half-expecting to see that the craft had blown up. Yet it was nowhere in sight; she saw only the vapor trail, its base already beginning to dissipate.

No time to wonder about that now. London had to be alerted.

Frieda was in the house in seconds, grateful that she'd had the foresight to plug in the radio and let it warm up. She'd already opened her codebook and turned it to the correct page for the day; she checked to make sure she was using the correct encryption key, then lay a finger against the telegraph key. Taking a deep breath to calm herself, she began to send her message:

Mistletoe to Big Ben. Black Umbrella is open. Repeat, Black Umbrella is open. Mistletoe out.

There. It was done. And so was she. Her mission was complete, and there was no point in remaining here any longer. In fact, it was dangerous to stay in Nordhausen. If her signal had been intercepted, then the Nazis might trace it back to her.

Frieda took a few moments to discard her frayed dress and put on a fresh one, then she gathered the documents she'd need, made sure she had enough money in her purse, and left the cottage. Within minutes, she was in her car and driving away, her life as a war widow already a thing of the past.

———

Horst Reinhardt didn't hear the sonic boom caused by his craft breaking the sound barrier, nor was he aware of the chaos he'd left in his wake. He heard only the roar of Silver Bird's main engine, felt only the pressure against his body.

As the spacecraft continued its climb, his vision began to blur, forming a tunnel through which he fought to see clearly. Fortunately, the instruments were directly in front of him, and he'd memorized his flight plan so well that it was thoroughly ingrained in his memory.

He continued to climb, watching his altimeter carefully the entire time. When he saw that Silver Bird was 5.4 kilometers above the ground, he reached down and pushed forward the throttles for the two auxiliary engines. Silver Bird surged upward even more; he concentrated on breathing, making sure that the acceleration didn't force the air from his lungs and cause him to black out. He couldn't scc his instruments well, but he knew that he must be pulling nearly ten g's. But only for a few seconds, just a few more seconds . . .

Gradually, the roaring of the engines diminished, slowly becoming a muted grumble. Reinhardt's gaze swept across the instrument panel, then he throttled down the main and auxiliary engines and pulled back the yoke. An eerie silence descended upon the cabin; the pressure completely left him, and it suddenly seemed as if his body was lighter, without any weight at all.

Something drifted past his goggles, a tiny metal ring. A washer dropped by a careless workman. Fascinated, Reinhardt raised a hand and gently tapped it with a fingertip. At his touch, the washer tumbled away, turning end over end, until it reached the starboard side window and bounced off.

That was when Reinhardt saw where he was. Earth stretched out below him as a vast green shield, flecked with filmy white clouds, veined by blue rivers and lakes. He was somewhere over Poland, or perhaps even the Soviet Union; there was no easy way to tell, without any obvious borders to distinguish political boundaries. And above it all, a sky so black, it seemed like an abyss he could fall into forever.

Lieutenant Horst Reinhardt was the first man to see Earth from space.

He didn't give himself an opportunity to reflect on this. No time to admire the view; he had a mission to accomplish. His altimeter was useless, now that it no longer had atmospheric pressure to register, but his gyroscope told him that he was climbing toward his maximum altitude of 130 kilometers. That was when he'd fire the auxiliary engines again, vector them so that his nose was pitched downward, and commence the series of atmospheric skips that would carry him around the world.

Reinhardt clasped his throat mike. "Control, Control, this is Silver Bird. Launch successful, orbital altitude achieved. Preparing to commence antipodal trajectory."

He listened carefully, and for a moment he thought he heard voices through the static. Hopefully his message had been received, but it was possible that he was already out of radio range. This had already been taken into consideration, though. He would remain incommunicado for the duration of his mission; it was not until after he'd completed his objectives that he'd try to contact the U-boat that would act as his recovery vessel should he need it. Otherwise, the next time he spoke to anyone in the Fatherland, it would be when he stepped down from his cockpit and offered a salute to his beloved *Führer*.

That was a pleasant thought. Reinhardt kept it in mind as Silver Bird soared above Earth, on its way to New York and victory.

THE FLIGHT OF THE *LUCKY LINDA*

JUNE 1, 1943 (CONTINUED)

Within minutes, Frieda Koenig's radio message made its way around the world.

First it reached MI-6 headquarters in London, where a duty officer decoded the signal and, realizing its importance, alerted his superior. The Naval Intelligence officer instructed the duty officer to relay the signal to Washington, D.C., as a priority flash message.

In a Pentagon basement, a radio operator alerted a U.S. Army intelligence officer. This captain had been briefed on Silver Bird; he ordered alert messages sent to both McChord Field in Washington State and Alamogordo Army Air Field in New Mexico.

Silver Bird had just completed its first atmospheric skip when the *Hollywood Babe* took off from McChord. From his seat in the back of the B-29's cockpit, Lloyd Kapman spotted the German spacecraft as it approached the American coast. The bomber's radio operator sent a confirmation message to Alamogordo, which was already scrambling to prepare *Lucky Linda* for immediate launch.

And then . . .

"Six . . . five . . ."

Henry Morse's voice reverberated through loudspeakers as Robert Goddard, standing at the periscope, watched the distant launchpad with the growing realization that he was too far away. He shouldn't be in this concrete igloo, protected from the noise and the blast, but outside, where he could see the rocket lift off with his naked eyes.

"Four . . . three . . ."

"Primary ignition!" Goddard shouted. He didn't stick around to see Harry Chung push a large red button on his console. Instead, he bolted away from the periscope and rushed toward the door. Startled, Omar Bliss tried to stop him, but Goddard impatiently shoved him out of the way.

"Two . . . one . . ."

"Coming through!" he snapped at the MP guarding the door. The sergeant shoved it open, and Goddard charged outside just in time to see a distant flash across the desert sands.

"Zero . . . launch!"

Brighter than the rising sun, white-hot flame poured from *Lucky Linda*'s main engine, followed an instant later by the simultaneous ignition of its six solid-fuel boosters. Dense grey smoke billowed out of the blast pit beneath the launch ring, a massive rooster tail of spent rocket fuel. For a moment, it seemed as if the spacecraft weren't going anywhere, and Goddard felt his heart stop.

Please, no, he thought, unable to breathe. *Please, God, no, not after all this . . .*

Then, slowly at first, the spaceship rose from its pad, perched atop a blazing shaft that looked like nothing less than a column of hellfire.

"Go!" someone in the nearby trench shouted, and his cry was picked up by others around him. "Go! Go! *Go* . . . !" Goddard found himself joining the chant. *"Go! Go! Go . . . !"*

As *Lucky Linda* cleared the tower, a thunderball rolled across the desert, shaking the TV platform and causing the onlookers to clamp their hands over their ears, followed a moment later by a hot wind against their faces.

Goddard watched the craft as it hurtled upward. The thunder became a steady, crackling roar, louder than anything he'd ever heard before; it sounded as if the sky itself were being torn open. Shielding his eyes with an upraised hand, he suddenly found himself speechless. Here was his life's ambition, born in a childhood moment of epiphany, made real; he was no longer looking at a weapon of war but the opening of the road to the Moon, Mars, and beyond. He was seeing the future.

Within seconds, the rocket became a brilliant circlet of lights moving swiftly away, leaving behind it a dense white trail as it veered to the northeast. The noise was just beginning to subside when Goddard remembered where he needed to be. Ears ringing, he turned and rushed back to the blockhouse.

Inside, he found his team no less excited than anyone who'd watched the launch from the trenches. They were all was on their feet, yelling at the images on the television screens, clapping each other on the back, tears streaming from their eyes. Only Jack Cube remained calm. Bent over his microphone, hands clasped against his headphones, he sought to hear something from the man in the spacecraft's cockpit:

"*Lucky Linda*, this is Desert Bravo, do you copy?"

From the speakers, a voice filtered through the crackling static: "*Desert* . . . Lucky Linda. *All systems* . . ."

"*Lucky Linda*, can you repeat . . . ?"

"Everyone, be quiet!" Goddard shouted. "Back to your stations!"

Silence fell across the blockhouse as everyone remembered what he was supposed to be doing. They sat down at once, returning their attention to their consoles. "Trajectory nominal," Gerry Mander reported from the radar screen. "Range thirty-two miles, altitude forty-five thousand feet, velocity five thousand feet per second and rising. She's . . ."

"*Wa-hooo!*"

Skid Sloman's yell burst from the ceiling speakers, startling everyone in the room. Goddard jerked, his eyes widening behind his glasses. "Oh my God, is he . . . ?"

"This thing's climbing like a bat out of hell!" Sloman shouted. *"Oh, yeah*, Linda . . . *bring it to me, baby!"*

"He's fine, Bob." Jack smiled. "Just having the ride of his life." He touched his mike again. "We copy loud and clear, *Lucky Linda*. Keep talking to us, Skid."

"Perhaps he shouldn't." Bliss moved up beside Goddard. "May I remind you that he's broadcasting in the clear?"

The colonel had a point. *Lucky Linda* was transmitting on a shortwave frequency of thirty thousand kilohertz, with sufficient power and range for Sloman's voice to be picked up by ham operators from Southern California to the Maine coast.

"Little late to think of that now, isn't it?" Henry asked.

Goddard simply smiled and shook his head. "Colonel, whatever happens next, if you think you're going to be able to keep this secret any longer . . ."

He didn't finish the thought. Now wasn't the time to argue about military secrecy. *Lucky Linda* had gotten off the pad, but their work was only beginning.

———

Never letting his gaze leave the instrument panel, Skid Sloman clutched the attitude controller within his left hand and the main engine throttle with his right. Acceleration shoved him back in his couch; vibration constantly shook his body, rocking him back and forth. Skid hung on, though, consciously taking deep breaths as he peered through eyelids being squeezed shut by mounting g-force.

"*Lucky Linda* . . . still go," he managed to gasp. "Altitude . . . ninety thousand feet. Velocity . . . seven thousand feet per second." He checked the chronometer and fuel-pressure gauge. Yes, everything was going according to the mission flight plan. "Time to booster jettison . . . five . . . four . . . three . . ." He reached between his legs, found the yellow ring next to the attitude-control stick. "Two . . . one . . ."

He yanked the bar upward and heard a series of sharp, muffled bangs as explosive bolts fired along *Lucky Linda*'s stern. He couldn't look back, but the sudden kick he got in the back told him that the six strap-on boosters had been successfully jettisoned. They would be falling away behind him now, leaving the spacecraft to continue its ascent on main-engine thrust alone.

The boosters were no longer needed. *Lucky Linda* was at the edge of space. Looking up from the instrument panel, Skid saw that the sky was rapidly changing from dark blue to black, the sun a merciless spotlight that threatened to blind him the instant he looked in that direction. The vibration was easing off, the ride becoming smoother. He could barely hear the engine.

"*Bravo to* Linda." Jack Cube's voice was thin and distorted by static, yet still discernible. "*Coming up on main engine cutoff.*"

"Roger that, Bravo." Skid checked his instruments. Yes, his altitude was nearly thirty miles. Time to cut the main engine. He raised his right hand, found the engine's toggle switch. "Cutoff in five . . . four . . . three . . . two . . . one . . ."

He snapped the switch, and instantly everything became still and silent. The vibration ceased entirely, and there was no more noise; the g-force pressure left his body at once, leaving behind a strange and ethe-real sensation of lightness. It was free fall, of course; he'd felt this before, in fighter planes he'd put into power dives, but never quite like this.

No doubt about it. He was in space.

Skid laughed out loud. "Zero g and I feel fine. Tell Mutt and Jeff they've nothing to worry about."

A moment passed, then he heard Jack's voice again. "*I'll let 'em know. They'll be happy to hear that. We got a lot of people down here gnawing their fingernails. Want to tell us your position, just so we know you're not really in Texas?*"

Skid looked at his instruments again. Without a functional pitot, his air altimeter and airspeed indicators were useless; the gyroscope, compass, and theodolite were his primary navigation instruments. But there was an easier way of figuring out where he was.

He toggled another switch to activate the orbital maneuvering system, then grasped the stick and—ever so carefully, the way he'd spent countless hours learning in the simulator—moved it to the left. *Lucky Linda* made a slow roll to starboard, maneuvering thrusters along its midsection silently firing to change its attitude. As Skid looked up through the canopy, his breath caught in his throat as Earth rolled into sight, a vast panorama of green, brown, and tan, traced by rivers and spotted with lakes that reflected the early-morning sun. The horizon was curved slightly at the ends; it stretched away for miles and miles and miles, farther than he'd ever seen before. There was a thin blue haze above the limb of the Earth, and it took him a moment to realize that it was the atmosphere.

"Oh, wow," he murmured. "Jack, you gotta see this."

"If you're trying to make me jealous, you're doing a good job. What's your position?"

Checking the compass, Skid confirmed that he was on a fifty-seven-degree north-by-northeast bearing, then he peered more closely at the ground below. No oceans in sight; he must be somewhere over the American heartland. Yet there was a long, twisty river just ahead, with another river converging upon it from the west. He grinned with recognition: the confluence of the Mississippi and Missouri Rivers.

"I'm above Missouri," he said, "just about to fly over St. Louis." The city was too far below for him to see; he was relying on his memory for geographic location. Something he'd read in the paper came back to him and he grinned. "Hey, I think the Yankees are playing the Cardinals today. Maybe I'll drop in for the game."

"Roger that." Jack's voice was terse. *"Doctor G says to stop kidding around."*

Skid rolled his eyes. Goddard had no sense of humor. "Understood, Bravo," he said. They were right, though. He had work to do.

Skid moved the stick to the right again, and once more *Lucky Linda* rolled around. Earth disappeared from sight; Silver Bird wouldn't be coming from that direction but instead from somewhere above. That was where he needed to look for it.

He reached to his left side, unfolded the collapsible handle of a small, vertically mounted wheel, and began to slowly turn it. From just behind his head there came a small thump as a hatch in the cowling was opened; Skid twisted his head around as much as his helmet would let him and saw that the periscope had been successfully deployed. He had to strain against his pressure suit to reach the horizontally mounted eyepiece and telescope it over his right shoulder, but once the L-shaped reflector was in place, he had an adjustable rearview mirror to show him what was going on above and behind the ship.

The helmet had to go. He wouldn't be able to use the periscope well while he was still wearing it. A quick glance at the interior pressure gauge to make sure that the cockpit hadn't sprung a leak, then he reached up and twisted the helmet away from the suit-collar ring. A slight hiss, then his ears popped; he took a deep breath, then shoved the helmet between his legs and shut off the suit air. He adjusted the eyepiece and nodded to himself. Yeah, that was better.

Skid snapped another toggle switch, and the small radar screen in the center of the instrument panel glowed to life, tiny concentric circles pulsing outward every fifteen seconds. Nothing yet, but he knew Silver Bird was out there.

"*Lucky Linda* to Desert Bravo," Skid said. "Time to go hunting."

Silbervogel fell toward Earth.

Horst Reinhardt's suit was plastered with sweat, so much that he'd decided to trust the cockpit's integrity and remove his mask and goggles. The sweat didn't only come from the heat generated by the seven atmospheric skips his craft had made in the past hour and twenty-two minutes. It came from the effort it took for him to keep the ship on course as it circled the globe.

Reinhardt had been warned that Silver Bird would be difficult to fly, so he'd prepared for that. During the months spent training for this mission, he'd had countless sessions in a cockpit simulator, learning how to navigate with only a few instruments and celestial bearings to rely upon; he wouldn't be able to use the bombsight periscope until he opened the bomb bay doors, and he couldn't do that until he completed his final atmospheric entry. He'd become adept at instrument flying during the simulator sessions, yet even so, actual practice was proving to be more difficult.

Silver Bird had no maneuvering thrusters other than its auxiliary engines, and he'd used up the rest of his fuel in the first minutes of his flight. Inertia, gravity, and the aerodynamic properties of his craft were the factors keeping it airborne. Each time gravity pulled *Silbervogel* back into the upper atmosphere, the ship would lose a little more momentum and altitude. Each of those dives tested Reinhardt's abilities to their limits; he had to carefully watch the angle of pitch and yaw, since too steep an attitude would cause him to burn up during reentry, while at the same time making the minute course corrections that would keep him on a precise east-by-southeast heading. And it didn't help that the damn ship handled more like a brick than a bird; Reinhardt was glad that he'd committed a couple of hours each day to weight lifting and running track because he needed all his strength to control the yoke during the skips.

Somehow, he'd managed to maintain a suborbital trajectory that had carried him across the southern Soviet Union, Mongolia, northern China, and the Pacific Ocean to the shores of hated America. His last skip had been just east of the Rocky Mountains, somewhere above the Black Hills of South Dakota; he was beginning to make his final descent, the one that would take him into the atmosphere one last time, on his way to New York and victory.

According to his instruments, his altitude was approximately eighty kilometers, his velocity nearly 2,700 km per hour. *Silbervogel*'s prow was pitched downward, and although he couldn't see straight ahead, his view through the side windows showed him the sunlit curve of the horizon slanting toward him at the desired angle. Through most of the flight, the stars had been his best means of checking his position. This close to Earth, though, at this time of day, he discovered to his dismay that the morning sun all but obliterated the stars, making all but the brightest difficult to see.

Leaning closer to his port-side window, Reinhardt peered outside, trying to get his bearings. Although he could barely make out Draco or Ursa Minor, far below was an enormous, finger-shaped swatch of blue, like an inland sea. Lake Erie, if he correctly remembered the geography of North America. He was over Cleveland, with Pennsylvania just ahead. And after Pennsylvania . . .

Something lanced the window's thick glass, a bright glimmer of light that stabbed the corner of his eye and made him wince. Startled, Reinhardt cursed beneath his breath and reflexively looked away. Then the intuition of a Luftwaffe fighter pilot kicked in. The sun was above him, yet the gleam had come below. A sundevil. A stray beam of light, reflecting off . . .

Another spacecraft?

"Impossible," he muttered. All the same, he peered through the window again. For a couple of seconds he saw nothing except Earth far below. And then, far away yet nonetheless distinct, a tiny silver shape moved into sight, catching the light.

As incredible as it might be, he was not alone.

―――――――

Radar picked up Silver Bird before Skid's eyes did, just as he'd expected. Nonetheless, he was startled when it made a sharp *ping!* indicating that its waves had connected with a solid object. There had been a couple of those already, yet when they didn't repeat, he knew that they'd been nothing more than small meteors passing through his range on their way to disintegration in the upper atmosphere. This time, he waited thirty seconds . . . and *ping!* there it was again.

Lucky Linda was above the Midwest by then, still climbing at a shallow angle as it soared over the southern Great Lakes region. For the last fifteen minutes, Skid Sloman had searched the black and nearly starless sky, praying that Goddard's bright boys hadn't been wrong when they'd estimated *Silbervogel*'s likely flight path. He'd seen nothing, though, and was beginning to wonder if everyone was wrong and the damn Nazis had sent the thing over the Atlantic . . .

Then he looked up, and there it was, slightly to his right and almost directly overhead, a tiny winged shape that caught the sun as it coasted across the black sky.

"Hello, sweetheart," he said, a predatory grin spreading across his face.

"Lucky Linda, *this is Desert Bravo.*" Jack Cube's voice sounded as if it were coming from Mars. *"Please repeat."*

"Desert Bravo, I've acquired Silver Bird." Skid was surprised by how calm he was. "He's at eleven o'clock, range"—he glanced at the radar again—"approximately seven miles."

He heard a commotion somewhere in the background. Although he couldn't make out what anyone was saying, it wasn't hard to imagine what was going on in the blockhouse. Then Goddard's voice came over the wireless. *"You're still out of range,"* he said, his voice clear and sharp. *"Don't fire until you've got a dead bead on him."*

"Affirmative, Bravo." Like it or not, Doctor G was right. The missiles didn't require a precise targeting, but nonetheless he had to time their release just right; once they were fired, there was no way to guide them. And he'd learned in the simulator that he needed to get within four miles of Silbervogel to have a chance of hitting it.

Even before he looked at his radar, he knew from the increasing repetition of each ping that he was getting closer. The scope told him that he was nearly five miles from target and closing. When he glanced up again, though, he saw that Silver Bird was no longer in sight. A second later, the pings abruptly ceased, and when he looked down again, he saw that the radar screen was suddenly empty.

Silver Bird had vanished.

Startled, he anxiously swung his head back and forth, trying to spot the German spacecraft, before he realized what was going on and checked his periscope. Yes, there it was, above and behind him at one o'clock. *Lucky Linda* must be traveling faster than *Silbervogel*; within seconds, it had passed the other spacecraft from underneath.

Yet his trajectory was still angled upward as opposed to Silver Bird's descent angle. If he wasn't careful, he'd overshoot the other craft entirely and lose the chance to target it.

"Now or never," he muttered.

"*Lucky Linda, please repeat.*" Jack Cube had taken the mike back from Goddard.

Skid ignored his friend. Keeping a close eye on his periscope, he carefully nudged his stick to the left. The starboard RCRs fired, and in the eyepiece he watched Silver Bird move toward the center of the eyepiece. When it was where he wanted it to be, he braked his sidewise momentum by moving the stick back to the right, firing the thrusters on his port side.

Silver Bird was directly above and behind him. He could see the Nazi spacecraft clearly now; it looked like a little metal toy he might find in a Woolworth's back home. He couldn't tell for sure, but he was almost certain that it was just within four miles of his own ship.

He had two missiles, but he realized that there was no point in keeping one in reserve. If he missed the first time, there was no way he'd be able to perform the complex maneuver he'd need to retarget Silver Bird before it left his range and entered the atmosphere. Both missiles had to be fired at once.

"Target acquired," Skid said as he reached forward to two bright red toggle switches positioned just above the radar screen. "Firing missiles."

And then he snapped the two switches.

———

Horst Reinhardt watched helplessly as the other spacecraft—it had to be American; there was no other explanation for its existence—approached *Silbervogel* from below, coming closer with each passing second.

Frustrated, he slammed his hands against the yoke. With no fuel for his engines, he was unable to maneuver; with no guns, he was unable to fight. The Americans would have no ability to strike at him before he completed his mission, so weapons and countermeasures were unnecessary—that was what he'd been told all along. Well, someone was wrong, wasn't he?

Reinhardt wasn't even able to tell that particular someone how badly he'd underestimated the enemy. He was out of radio range of the U-boat standing by in the North Atlantic. If he died today, no one would know how . . . except the pilot who killed him.

The American spacecraft disappeared as it passed beneath him. A few seconds later, *Silbervogel*'s forward radar array began to echo. Looking down Reinhardt saw a small blot appear on his scope. The American was closer now, yes, but it also appeared to be moving ahead of him.

A smile slowly crept to his lips. Was it possible that the American pilot had made a mistake? Reinhardt couldn't tell what sort of armaments the other ship might have, but he sincerely doubted that they could be fired backward. And if the enemy craft continued to fly upward as he continued to descend, *Silbervogel* would pass behind the American and begin its final atmospheric entry untouched.

Reinhardt intently watched the scope. The American was still below him, just a little more than six kilometers away. He couldn't see it through either of his side windows, but it appeared to be . . .

Suddenly, the radar pinged three times in rapid succession, and Reinhardt looked down to see two more blotches on the scope, smaller than the first one and quickly moving away.

Damn it! Missiles!

But then he saw that the blotches were moving away from him, and laughed out loud. "You idiot!" he shouted at the unseen American pilot. "There's nothing in front of you! You missed me!"

Still laughing, he watched as the two small blotches continued to move away from him, angling upward so that they would cut across his angle of descent . . . and then they suddenly blossomed, becoming a pair of large, irregular patches directly in front of him.

The missiles had detonated less than two kilometers from his ship, and they'd left something behind.

Looking up, Reinhardt turned his head to peer through the left-side window. His breath caught in his lungs as he saw what appeared to be a translucent black mist spreading before him, one that sparkled in the sunlight as it came closer.

He was still wondering what it was when he heard a dull tap against the prow. Then there was another, louder this time, against the hull just in front of his window, and he caught a glimpse of a small object as it bounced away.

A nail, a few centimeters long. Reinhardt chuckled. Just a common nail . . .

And then *Silbervogel* flew into a cloud of thousands of them, and he barely had a chance to scream before they ripped his ship apart.

—————

Through the periscope, Skid watched as Silver Bird disintegrated.

The German spacecraft never had a chance. It was probably traveling several thousand feet per second when it entered the swarm of roofing nails the missiles had carried as their payloads. At that speed, the result couldn't be anything except lethal. The German spacecraft came apart as if it had been thrown into a shredder, pieces of it flying away in all directions, oxygen spewing from what was left of its cockpit. Skid hoped that the guy flying the thing was dead by then; he almost felt sorry for him.

And then something must have short-circuited the electrical system controlling the bombs in the payload bay, for what remained of the ship was lost in a massive yet completely silent explosion. Skid winced as he saw this, but it was too far away for it to pose any threat to him. He'd veered away just after firing the missiles, to avoid running into the nail cloud himself.

That was it. Silver Bird was gone.

"*Desert Bravo to* Lucky Linda. *Do you read? Please respond.*"

Skid let out his breath. It had probably been only a few seconds since he'd fired his missiles, but he had no doubt that Jack Cube, Doctor G, and everyone else in Alamogordo were ready to faint. Time to let them know how things stood.

"*Lucky Linda* to Desert Bravo." Skid grinned; he'd been waiting to say this for months. "Silver Bird is nailed. Repeat, Silver Bird is nailed. And I'm coming home."

INTO THE FUTURE

"The news broke even before *Lucky Linda* got home," Henry said. "The colonel was right about Skid's transmitting in the clear. Every ham operator in the country picked up his ground communications, and it didn't take long for some of them to figure out what was going on."

"A lot of people saw Skid when he . . . came in for reentry." Lloyd accepted another glass of water his nephew had fetched from the kitchen; Henry and Jack waited patiently while he took a drink. "No one had ever heard a sonic boom before, so . . . when he flew in over New Jersey . . . it was hardly a secret."

"Uh-huh." Jack Cube nodded. "Rudy told me that the last thing he expected was to find a crowd waiting for him. But there were probably a couple of thousand folks on hand when he touched down at Lakehurst Naval Air Station."

"Wasn't Linda there?" Doug Walker asked. "His girlfriend, I mean."

"No, that's just a legend . . . one of many, I'm sure you know. That shot of him kissing his girl at Lakehurst wasn't taken until a couple of days later, when a *Life* photographer asked him to restage his climbing down from the cockpit." Jack shrugged. "Like the raising of the flag at Iwo Jima, it's a picture everyone remembers even though it's not as spontaneous as it seems."

He stood up to stretch his legs. It was late in the afternoon. Although sunset was still several hours away, the shadows on the den floor had become long. "All the same, Skid was proud of that picture. He autographed copies of it for the rest of his life, and long after he retired from the Air Force and took a job as a civilian consultant, he made a sideline telling his story on the lecture circuit." He shook his head sadly. "Rudy passed away about fifteen years ago, and I still miss him. He was a great friend."

"And everyone else?" Doug asked. "I know what happened to the three of you and Dr. Goddard, but the rest of the 390 Group . . . ?"

"Scattered hither and yon." Jack walked across the den. "Like leaves on the wind." He found a framed photo on the wall and took it down. "We came back out here again after the war for a little get-together," he said as he carried the photo to the journalist. "That's from the reunion."

Walker studied the black-and-white photo. Everyone who'd belonged to the rocket team was standing at the lodge's side door, with the notable exception of Goddard and Bliss. "This was the first time I saw this place," Jack said. "I know the others weren't crazy about it, but I kinda liked it . . ."

"Oh, so did we," Henry said. "Just not after it got cold, that's all."

"The government bought the lodge and . . . gave it to us," Lloyd said. "Sort of a . . . goodwill gesture. We've kept it . . . in our families ever since . . ."

"And held reunions out here every few years or so," Jack finished. "After a while, it was just about the only time any of us saw each other again." He shrugged. "And no one knew about what we did, really, except our families."

"Once Silver Bird was shot down," Henry said, "there really wasn't much point in the 390 Group's staying together. *Lucky Linda* went into a hangar until it finally got put in the National Air and Space Museum, and Skid became as famous as Lindbergh, but as for the people who designed and built it . . . ?"

"Classified," Lloyd rasped. "Top secret. Couldn't talk about . . . what we did."

"Except for Bob," Henry said, nodding. "When the press came searching for answers about who built *Lucky Linda*, the Army pushed Colonel Bliss and Bob forward as being the masterminds. I don't think Omar minded very much . . . especially not after he was promoted to general and, after the war, put in charge of the new U.S. Space Force . . . but Bob wasn't crazy about the attention. However . . ."

His voice trailed off, and he looked down at the floor. "He died only a couple of years later," Walker said quietly, finishing what he might have said.

"Yes," Lloyd said. "At the ranch . . . with Esther by his side."

"Returning to New England wasn't good for his health," Henry said, "and all those cigars didn't help either. That and the stress he went through did a number on him. He came down with throat cancer. A few months before he passed away, he lost the ability to speak. I went to see him, and all he could do was write notes to me."

"So he never met Wernher von Braun, did he?" Walker asked.

"No, they never met," Jack said. "Bob was already on his deathbed by the time von Braun was brought to the United States along with the rest of the German rocket team." He shook his head in dismay. "I'm not sure the two of them would've gotten along, anyway."

"I wouldn't say that." Henry looked at him sharply. "I was there when von Braun delivered the dedication speech at the Goddard Space Flight Center. He said that Bob was a lifelong inspiration for him, and that manned space exploration wouldn't have progressed as quickly as it did if it hadn't been for him."

"Don't forget that he . . . was arrested and . . . put in prison," Lloyd added.

"Yes, that's right," Walker said. "As soon as the High Command heard that the *Silbervogel* had been destroyed, Himmler ordered the S.S. to arrest von Braun on suspicion of sabotage. He spent several weeks in prison and just barely escaped being executed before Speer talked Hitler into releasing him."

"They let him go only because the Nazis still needed him," Jack said. "They tried to get the A-4 program going again, but by then it was too late. They'd spent too much time and resources on Silver Bird, and so their long-range-ballistic-missile research suffered as a result. The only thing they ever got off the ground were the buzz bombs, and the Brits soon learned how to shoot them down."

"Von Braun surrendered to the Allies as soon as he heard that the Third Reich had fallen," Henry said. "He and Dornberger managed to talk Army intelligence into bringing him and the rest of the Peenemünde scientists to the U.S., where Bliss put them to work for the U.S. Space Force."

"But you didn't join them?"

"No." Henry sighed, shook his head. "By then, I'd gone back to Worcester and found Doris . . ."

"That's a great story," Ellen interrupted, looking over at Walker. "Family legend has it that when Grandpa tracked down Grandma and started to explain what he'd been doing, she just said, 'Oh, I know. You were building a spaceship.'"

"She wasn't surprised a bit." Henry was smiling at the memory. "In fact, I was the one who got taken by surprise when she said she'd be happy to marry me even before I asked." The smile faded, and his expression darkened. "Anyway, I was like Bob . . . I didn't decide to devote my life to space travel just to find new ways of killing people. When it became clear that the Space Force's priorities were almost entirely military, I dropped out and became a science fiction writer instead."

"Hey, don't knock the Space Force." Jack glared at him. "They got us to the Moon, didn't they?" He turned to Walker again. "Anyway, everyone in the 390 Group pretty much went his own way after the war. After I went back to school and earned my doctorate, I joined up with the Space Force and was with them all the way through the Ares program, then retired after we got someone on Mars. Taylor went to work for Lockheed and became a systems engineer for their Skunk Works operation. Ham moved to St. Louis and went to work for Monsanto. Harry returned to Caltech. Mike landed a desk job at NASA after it got started and eventually became its Chief Administrator during Bobby Kennedy's administration . . ."

"Gerry was the one who went the furthest," Henry said. "He joined the Space Force, too, but only because that was the quickest way to get into space. Somewhere along the line, he decided that he wasn't content just to be an engineer . . . he actually wanted to go out there. So he entered astronaut training, got picked for the space station project, and after that made his way into the lunar exploration program." He grinned. "I've still got a moon rock on my desk that he sent me as a souvenir."

"We saw each other . . . from time to time . . . over the years," Lloyd said. "Sometimes here, and also at . . . space conferences and places like that."

"But no one except our immediate families knew about our involvement in Blue Horizon." Henry sighed. "It wasn't fun, knowing that we had a place in history that we couldn't claim. But the Pentagon wanted to make sure that the Soviets wouldn't get to us and . . . I dunno, kidnap us to Russia and force us to build a moonship for them . . . so the 390 Group wasn't publicly identified until just a few years ago. By then, no one cared anymore."

"Well . . . maybe my book will change all that." Walker glanced at his watch. He didn't need to make mention of the time. It was getting late, and the story had come to a close. He let out his breath, then picked up his recorder and switched it off. "Gentlemen, thank you for . . ."

"There's one thing you haven't asked us," Jack Cube said.

"I'm sorry?" Walker looked up at him again. "What did I forget?"

"Was it worth it?" Jack asked.

Walker blinked. "Umm . . . well, of course it was. If you hadn't built *Lucky Linda*, Silver Bird would've bombed New York, and that could have changed the course of the war."

"Oh, that's obvious." J. Jackson Jackson brushed it off. "I mean everything that happened since then . . . people going into space, landing on the Moon, heading on to Mars, all that. Did Blue Horizon push us into doing all that, or . . . ?"

"Don't listen to him." Henry picked up his cane, slowly pushed himself to his feet. "Jack's been carrying on like that for years, trying to take credit for something he didn't do. It was inevitable, and he knows it . . . we would've made it to Mars eventually, Blue Horizon or not."

"Old business," Lloyd wheezed as his nephew began to push his wheelchair from the room. "Save it for . . . another time."

Jack started to object, but Henry ignored him. Instead, he beckoned for his great-grandson. "C'mon, Carl. Let's take another look at your rocket, see if we can figure out what went wrong."

"Sure." As Ellen came forward to help Henry shuffle out of the den, Carl bent over to pick up his iPad. Waking it up, he noticed that the message light was blinking. "Hold on," he said to his mother. "I think I got something from Dad."

"All right, go ahead and check it. We'll be out on the porch."

Carl nodded, then sat down again. As the adults around him continued to follow one another from the den, he ran his finger across the screen to open the video app. As he'd expected, the menu told him that his father had called just a couple of hours earlier and left a message.

Carl touched the menu again, and his father appeared on the screen. He was seated in what appeared to be a departure lounge; behind him was a ticket counter and a gate, with several other travelers visible in the background. As usual, his father was using a public phone, and there was a rueful look on his face as he addressed the camera.

"Carl, hi, it's me. Hey, I'm sorry, but it looks like I'm not going to make it to the reunion. My connecting flight from the Moon got delayed and . . . well, I'm stuck in orbit again. Tell your mother I'm sorry, and give Grandpa Henry my best. Hope you enjoy the weekend. Love you, son . . . see you later."

The image froze, the replay arrow transposed over his father's face. Carl was about to close the app when he noticed something else in the background: the flight schedule on the wallscreen behind the ticket counter. Curious, he used his fingertips to expand the image, and now he was able to read the board clearly:

TWA Translunar Service
Tranquility Station to New York LaGuardia Flight 902
DELAYED New Departure Time 1230 GMT
Shuttle: Robert H. Goddard

Smiling to himself, Carl closed his iPad. He had an answer to Jack Cube's question.

AFTERWORD

V-S Day is a novel that goes back to the beginning of my career as a science fiction author and is preceded by several different versions.

I came up with the story over twenty-five years ago while I was researching and writing my first novel, *Orbital Decay*. During that time, I'd moved to Worcester, and it wasn't long before I discovered that it was the hometown of Robert H. Goddard. That led me to examine Goddard's life and work—including visiting the site of Goddard's first rocket launch in nearby Auburn—but it was when I stumbled upon a mention of Eugen Sanger's antipodal space bomber in an appendix of Willy Ley's *Rockets, Missiles, & Space Travel* that I realized all this could be the basis for an alternate-history story. I originally conceived it to be a novel, but once I sold *Orbital Decay* to Ace, my editor, Ginjer Buchanan, encouraged me to write and publish some short fiction to introduce myself to readers before the book came out. I therefore decided to reduce the novel to a short story, which could be written and sold more quickly.

The first version, "Operation Blue Horizon," was published in the September 1988 issue of *Worcester Monthly*, a city magazine to which I was a regular contributor. Its publication preceded both "Live from the Mars Hotel," my official literary debut in the mid-December 1988 issue of *Asimov's Science Fiction*, and *Orbital Decay*, which came out a year later. That's because *Worcester Monthly*'s editor, my good friend Michael Warshaw, wanted to scoop both *Asimov's* and Ace by pushing the story into print. I didn't mind. Like this novel, "Operation Blue Horizon" had its roots in Worcester, so it was only appropriate that the story be published there.

I wasn't completely satisfied with the way "Operation Blue Horizon" turned out, though, so when Gregory Benford approached me a couple of years later to contribute a story for the What Might Have Been series of alternative-history anthologies he was coediting with the late Martin H. Greenberg, I rewrote and revised it as "Goddard's People." Gardner Dozois bought the same piece for *Asimov's*, where it was published in the July 1991 issue, and I later included it in my first collection, *Rude Astronauts*, first published by Old Earth Books in 1992.

I suppose I should have let it go at that, but deep down inside, I considered it to be an unfinished work. In 1995, I published *The Tranquillity Alternative*, an alternate-history novel that used "Goddard's People" and its companion story, "John Harper Wilson" (*Asimov's*, June 1989, and also *Rude Astronauts*), as pseudohistorical background. By then I'd realized that the original story was flawed by historical errors: some my fault, others the inevitable result of later research by historians uncovering facts that contradicted what had been accepted truth at the time I wrote the first two versions. However, there wasn't much I could do about it; "Goddard's People" had been reprinted several times by then, and in that pre-ebook era, I couldn't easily revise that which was already in cold print.

In 1997, though, I got a chance to set things right when an independent filmmaker, John Ellis—with whom I'd previously worked in an effort to turn *Orbital Decay* into a movie—optioned the film rights to "Goddard's People." John was working on the HBO miniseries *From the Earth to the Moon* at the time, and it was his intent to pitch "Goddard's People" to them as a made-for-cable movie. I wrote the screenplay adaptation, during which I added, expanded, and revised many scenes. John also brought aboard illustrators and spaceflight historians Scott Lowther and my friend Ron Miller to act as technical advisors and concept artists, and they contributed their knowledge and insights to the multiple drafts the screenplay went through over the next couple of years.

Unfortunately, HBO took a pass on "Goddard's People," and John was unable to find another studio that was interested in the project, so my screenplay went into a file cabinet. In 2005, a young Worcester impresario and Goddard buff, Robert Newton, bought the film rights and wrote a screenplay of his own, with the intent of pitching it to The History Channel, but nothing came of that, either. My involvement in the latter effort was minimal, and after it failed, I became convinced that a movie would never be made of this story.

A couple of years ago, while fishing through my file cabinet in search of something else, I found the screenplay I'd written a dozen years earlier. Out of curiosity and perhaps nostalgia, I pulled it out and reread it, and realized that my original idea had been the right one: The story really should have been a novel all along.

That screenplay gave me a rough outline for a much longer story. However, there are several places where the novel departs from the original story and my screenplay (Rob Newton's script was not used as a source). A close reader may also find a couple of instances where *V-S Day* is inconsistent with *The Tranquillity Alternative* or "John Harper Wilson." This is because I tried to stick as close to historical fact as I could, taking advantage of information I didn't have in the eighties and nineties, and therefore decided that this was more important than trying to maintain consistency with material I wrote decades ago.

As before, I had considerable help from my friends. Both Ron Miller and Scott Lowther returned as advisors, letting me bounce ideas off them and also contributing new illustrations of *Silbervogel* and *Lucky Linda*. Larry Manofsky, fellow high-school alumnus and former member of NASA's astronaut training staff, reviewed the original Sanger-Bredt study and gave me a technical analysis that answered many questions I still had. Dr. Christopher Kovacs, MD, came to the rescue when I needed to find a way to kill someone in a training centrifuge. Rob Caswell acted as first reader, often making suggestions that resulted in even more rewrites but also helped the novel become stronger. If there are any mistakes this time around, it's not because we didn't try.

For their encouragement many years ago, I'd like to thank Mike

Warshaw, Greg Benford, the late Marty Greenberg, Gardner Dozois, John Ellis, and Rob Newton, all of whom were the original story's godfathers at one point or another.

Finally, special thanks to my editor, Ginjer Buchanan, and my agent, Martha Millard, for making it possible for me to take care of unfinished business, and my copy editors, Sara and Bob Schwager. As always, my greatest appreciation goes to my wife, Linda, who served at different times as muse, research assistant, travel agent, and ambulance driver.

—WHATELY, MASSACHUSETTS
JUNE 2012–APRIL 2013

SOURCES

Clary, David A.; *Rocket Man: Robert H. Goddard and the Birth of the Space Age*. Theia Books, 2003.

Collins, Larry, and LaPierre, Dominic; *Is Paris Burning?* Simon and Schuster, 1965.

Goddard, Robert H.; "Autobiography"; *The Coming of the Space Age* (Arthur C. Clarke, editor). Meredith Press, 1967.

Goddard, Robert H.; *The Papers of Robert H. Goddard* (Esther C. Goddard and G. Edward Pendray, editors). McGraw-Hill, 1970.

Hagerty, Jack, and Rogers, Jon C.; *Spaceship Handbook*. ARA Press, 2001.

Herzman, Robert Edwin; *The Nazis*. Time-Life Books, 1980.

Joubert, Sir Philip; *Rocket*. New York Philosophical Library, 1957.

Keegan, John; *Intelligence in War: Knowledge of the Enemy from Napoleon to Al-Qaeda*. Knopf, 2003.

Ley, Willy; *Rockets, Missiles, & Space Travel* (revised edition). Viking Press, 1957.

Melton, H. Keith; *The Ultimate Spy Book*. DK Publishing, 1996.

Neufeld, Michael J.; *The Rocket and the Reich: Peenemünde and the Coming of the Ballistic Missile Era*. The Free Press, 1995.

Neufeld, Michael J.; *Von Braun: Dreamer of Space, Engineer of War*. Vintage Books, 2007.

Pendle, George; *Strange Angel: The Otherworldly Life of Rocket Scientist John Whiteside Parsons*. Harcourt, 2005.

Polmar, Norman, and Allen, Thomas B.; *Spy Book: The Encyclopedia of Espionage*. Random House, 1998.

Ryan, Cornelius; "Man's Survival in Space: Testing the Men." *Collier's*, March 7, 1953.

Sanger, Eugen, and Bredt, Irene; "A Rocket Drive for Long Range Bombers." Deutsche Luftfahrtforschung, 1944 (English translation, U.S. Department of Navy, 1952).

Sanger, Hartmut E., and Szames, Alexandre D.; "From the 'Silver Birds' to Interstellar Voyages"; *History of Rocketry and Astronautics* (Otfrid G. Liepack, Volume Editor). American Astronautical Society, 2011.

Taylor, James, and Shaw, Warren; *Dictionary of the Third Reich* (revised edition). Penguin, 1997.

Von Braun, Wernher; "German Rocketry"; *The Coming of the Space Age* (Arthur C. Clarke, editor). Meredith Press, 1967.

Wistrich, Robert; *Who's Who in Nazi Germany*. Bonanza Books, 1982.